By Tehlor Kay Mejia

Sammy Espinoza's Last Review

Sammy Espinoza's Last Review

A Novel

TEHLOR KAY MEJIA

Dell | New York

A Dell Trade Paperback Original

Copyright © 2023 by Tehlor Kay Mejia

Published in the United States by Dell, an imprint of Random House, a division of Penguin Random House LLC, New York.

DELL and the D colophon are registered trademarks of Penguin Random House LLC.

LIBRARY OF CONGRESS CATALOGING-IN-PUBLICATION DATA
Names: Mejia, Tehlor Kay, author.
Title: Sammy Espinoza's last review: a novel / Tehlor Kay Mejia.
Description: New York: Dell, [2023]
Identifiers: LCCN 2022057993 (print) | LCCN 2022057994 (ebook) |
ISBN9780593598771 (trade paperback) |
ISBN 9780593598788 (ebook)
Subjects: LCGFT: Romance fiction. | Novels.
Classification: LCC PS3613.E44434 S36 2023 (print) |
LCC PS3613.E44434
(ebook) | DDC 813/.6—dc23/eng/20221209
LC record available at https://lccn.loc.gov/2022057993
LC ebook record available at https://lccn.loc.gov/2022057994

Printed in the United States of America on acid-free paper

randomhousebooks.com

2 4 6 8 9 7 5 3 1

Book design by Virginia Norey

For the girl I used to be—with love, at last

Sammy Espinoza's Last Review

1.

People like to say you can't go home again, but for me that's more a literal statement than a figurative one. Because I never had a home to come back to.

When you spend your childhood following your mother in her search for a great love—or at least for an apartment you won't get evicted from—you end up a bit of a wanderer.

It never bothered me much until recently, when life decided to sucker punch me and then keep on wailing.

For starters, I broke my rule about dating musicians again. Karma really hates it when I do that. A fact she proved categorically when my indie-rock goddess girlfriend Juniper Street delivered the killing blow to our seventeen-month relationship *onstage* in a song *literally titled* "Goodbye, Sammy."

Of course, the emotional damage wasn't the extent of it. Because I had to go and break another one of my rules. This time it was the one about not using my well-respected music column (written under the pen name Verity Page) or its thousands of subscribers to lie about said musician's mediocre band in print. In *many* pieces spanning the entire last month of our doomed relationship.

I thought it might save me and Juniper, but instead it lost me my job. (Well, nearly anyway. More on that later.)

For anyone counting, that's two major life pillars down in the space of a weekend—and I'm not even done.

I started thinking about what people do when their twenties

are not what they dreamed them to be. About sleeping in a bed you've outgrown. Letting your parents cook for you when everything is falling down around you.

That's when I first had the bright idea to travel to Ridley Falls, Washington. Population seventeen, or something. The closest place to home I've ever really had. The place I lived with a family friend for a year when I was nine because my mom's boyfriend of the moment didn't like kids.

The place where my parents grew up, and at least one set of my estranged grandparents still lived.

Only when I called Dina Rae, my flighty mother, to run this plan past her did she "accidentally" let slip that my father's father had *died* the year before and no one bothered to tell me. And she only mentioned it after she had tried to talk me out of visiting "that hellhole" in three other ways.

Knowing my mom, she had been hoping this news would activate my *too-complicated* bail-out chute. The one I inherited from her. Instead, it led to the biggest fight we've ever had. One where I told her she had a lot of nerve trying to control my perception of the world when it had taken me four days to even get her on the phone.

Worst of all, it only strengthened my resolve to do the opposite of what she wanted. And in that moment, the opposite of what she wanted was me in Ridley Falls, as soon as possible.

What better place to heal, right? I asked myself during an admittedly wine-soaked pity party a few days later. To nurse my wounds and stick it to my flaky mom and remember the joy that can be found in the simple act of living small—or whatever the big-city rom-com heroines say.

In my defense, I came up with a lot of awful plans to heal and/or reinvent myself in my post-breakup wallowing period. This one might have stayed at the bottom of the empty bottle with the rest if it hadn't been for the article I read that night—less than five hundred words on a site without a stellar reputation for journalistic integrity.

I personally hold that article responsible for the email I sent my boss (a woman whose approval I have been desperately chasing for nearly a decade) at 12:14 in the morning. In said email, I promised I could fix everything. My column. My disastrous love life. The relationship with my mother I was starting to fear I'd outgrown.

I wish I hadn't included *all* of that in the email, but more than that I wish Esme hadn't agreed. Hadn't let me charge a Greyhound ticket to my company card and sent me off on a no-other-expenses-paid odyssey to the absolute middle of nowhere.

You have two weeks, she'd written. **This is your last chance, Sammy.**

Like I said, it's been a ride.

I step off the Greyhound in Ridley Falls with a kink in my neck and a storm cloud over my head. The guy next to me on the way here from Seattle was a talker. And not just the polite conversation type, but the here's-the-tortured-story-of-my-failed-marriage-do-you-have-any-advice? type.

Unfortunately, this isn't the first time I've spent a bus ride with someone's tragic life story. I attract oversharers like a front man attracts girls with daddy issues. I used to think it was what made me a good journalist—this ability to draw deeply personal information out of the most reluctant stone. But I'm not even sure I'm a journalist anymore.

I'm not sure of much of anything, really.

Which, of course, is why I'm here. In a town deep in the boonies of Washington State where I spent what could be defined as the most normal year of my childhood. The place I always picture when someone says the word *hometown*, even though I didn't live here long enough to claim it.

I imagined I could sense the shift the moment the bus passed the sign: THERE'S SOMETHING ABOUT . . . RIDLEY FALLS! Like maybe this was the very moment my life would start to change for the better.

But it's been twenty minutes since then. I'm surrounded by shuffling, zombie-like Greyhound ticket holders in the closet-sized station. I try to remember the feeling of watching that sign pass. The feeling that there's something big at stake here.

But it's hard not to focus on the negative. And boy, is there a lot of that. Starting with the general approach to sanitation in this building.

My phone buzzes in my back pocket, and I lean my massive leopard-print suitcase against my thigh, shifting aside the matching duffel and backpack to retrieve it. I wish for the millionth time I was the kind of person who traveled in sweats, or leggings. Something more comfortable than the tight, expensive jeans and satin bomber jacket I chose for myself this morning.

I can hear my mom's voice in my head, chastising me for even daring to think it. *How do you know you won't be seated next to a movie star, huh? You know I met Denzel once on a flight to Vegas . . .*

Even though I'm currently very annoyed with her, there's something about advice your mom gives you. Especially when she's not really the advice-giving type. So here I am, actually dressed even though there's literally no chance a movie star would have taken a Greyhound bus from Seattle to Ridley Falls. I know this, because I sort of already know the most famous person who would ever set foot here.

I shudder again, thinking of my oversharing email to Esme. But I shake it off as I extract my phone at last. There will be plenty of time for self-loathing when I'm in a place that doesn't look like it could give me tetanus.

As my phone rings, the caller's contact photo takes up the whole screen. Willa's face, squished next to mine on a wine-tasting trip to the Willamette Valley before her wedding, cheeks flushed and eyes a little squinty. Simpler times.

"Please tell me you're here somewhere," I answer without preamble. "I'm afraid the guy from the bus is going to follow me to the bathroom for more free therapy."

"Boundaries, babe," she says breezily. "And seriously? You need to read that article I sent you about the capsule wardrobe, your luggage is large enough to replace Pluto as the smallest planet."

"Pluto isn't even technically . . ." I begin, then trail off, looking around frantically.

The line goes dead, and I finally spot Willa in the flesh—all gawky six scarecrow feet of her. Her auburn hair is in a messy bun, her overalls cuffed a solid four inches above her Birkenstocks.

There's an even bigger smile on her face than the one in the picture. For a split second, it's enough to make the weight of my luggage (and all my problems) disappear.

It was Willa's family who took me in when my mom was on her journey of self-discovery with Robb the childless wonder. I had never met the Crosses before, but Willa's mom was my mom's teenage babysitter when she was a kid, and she promised me they'd stayed great friends. That I'd be in good hands.

Even so, the thought of living with strangers had been terrifying.

As the grown-up Willa approaches me from across the bus station, I can still see the toothless little girl she was on the porch that day. Her smile hasn't changed at all—except to grow a few important teeth back—and it has the same effect on me today as it did then.

I feel instantly at home. Like as long as I have her by my side, I can handle whatever comes. Back then it was a two-week stay with a strange family that turned into a year. Today, it's a breakup, a near-firing, and the growing sense that my entire life is totally out of control.

A few seconds later we're face-to-face for the first time in way too long, hugging and laughing and, okay, crying a little, too.

"How long has it been, six months?" I say, sniffling into her hair, which smells like rosemary and apples from the soap she makes herself. We might text daily and FaceTime once a week, but there's no substitute for the real thing.

"It would be less if you'd visit *me* more, you know?" she says teasingly, stepping out of the hug to examine me from her significant height advantage.

During our year as pseudo-siblings, Willa's mom called us the Opposite Twins, and as goofy as it was, it makes sense. Where Willa is lanky as a baby giraffe, I'm all circles and curves. She's pale as weak winter sunshine while I've got a perpetual sepia filter thanks to the dad I never knew. Willa's hair is auburn and wispy, mine is jet black, thick as a horsetail, and currently escaping the sleek, low-maintenance ponytail I put it in before the four-and-a-half hour trip.

The one thing we share is a dusting of freckles across our noses and cheeks. As kids we said it was how the fairies had marked us sisters.

Her eyes twinkle when she finishes her assessment—it's how I can tell she's glad to see me, and that she isn't really mad about me making her do all the traveling during the bulk of our two-decade long-distance friendship.

I hug her again, I can't help it.

"What are we gonna do with you, huh?" she asks into my hair, squeezing me back, tight.

My life crashes back into me with all the weight of the bus that brought me here. "Help me," I groan. "Please."

"I'll help you," she says, pulling away with a somber expression. "With everything but those bags." She smirks and gestures toward the parking lot, keys to her little Toyota pickup in her hand.

With my thousand tons of luggage secure in the back of the truck, we trundle down Main Street in comfortable silence.

During the drive, I try to refamiliarize myself with Ridley

Falls—which for me has existed only in memories for twenty years. It looks different through adult eyes. I remember it being quaint, like a postcard. But now I can see the dingy little stores. The restaurants that have changed owners a dozen times trying to stay afloat in a failing tourist economy.

I wanted to come back and prove my mom wrong about this place—to discover that this could have been the home we deserved. But looking at the reality out the window, I'm suddenly afraid she was more right than I gave her credit for when she called it "trashy" and "backwoods."

Willa seems to sense my deflation. Her cheeks are a little flushed when I glance over at her. "I know it's not much," she says. "Especially when you're used to Seattle."

"It's great," I say with all the enthusiasm I can muster. "Seriously, I'm just . . ."

I gesture at myself as if it's all visible. Juniper leaving. My mom keeping secrets. My job. My whole life.

"Hey, no brooding allowed," Willa says. "You're here to heal, not dwell. Especially not about *Juniper.*" She applies just the right amount of ex-girlfriend disdain to the name.

"What kind of a name is that, anyway?" I grumble. "*Juniper.*"

Willa snorts. "The exact name you would expect from—" She cuts herself off, glancing at me as she changes lanes. On the left is downtown Ridley Falls, which does little to counteract my earlier feelings of disappointment.

I try to tap into the nostalgia I wanted to experience. To remember my nine-year-old self staring up in wonder at the looming Ponderosa pines. Following behind Willa's parents with a dripping ice cream cone in one hand and my best friend's sticky fingers in the other.

"Sorry," grown-up Willa says. "Are we in make-Juniper-the-villain mode or mope-about-how-good-she-was mode?"

I pull my attention from the ominous clouds, currently casting everything in a sort of romantic pre-storm light. I don't answer the question, though, because I don't know how. "You're the best friend," I say instead.

"I know," she replies, a little smug but in such an endearing way you can't even be bothered by it. "And in that spirit, I will simply say: Juniper's name is fitting."

"Her name is stupid," I say, suddenly sure I'm in make-her-the-villain mode after all. "Do you think it's even her real name? I have my doubts. She never let me look at her driver's license."

"*Juniper Street?*" Willa asks with a snort. "Please. I bet her name is something like Sarah Thompson."

"But you can hardly call your band Sarah Thompson," I say, easing back into our best friend banter like no time has passed.

"'Anyone who names their band after themselves is desperate for personal and professional validation and doomed to live a life devoid of either,'" she says. "'Juniper Street is no exception.'"

"Did you just quote one of my reviews off the top of your head?"

"Well, I replaced The Dave Jones Experience with Juniper Street but otherwise your tough-but-fair critique has been fully preserved."

I sigh, looking out the window as we make our way into the residential streets. Nothing is familiar. I'm not sure why I thought it would be. Just because you remember a place doesn't mean it's home.

"I used to be good," I say, my breath fogging the window. "And now I don't know what I am."

"You are Sammy Espinoza, and you deserve the best." Willa reaches over to squeeze my hand. "Juniper might not get that, and your boss might not get it. Even your mom might not get it sometimes. But I always will."

My eyes well up for what is probably not the last time today. I squeeze Willa's hand, but I can't speak. Not yet. *This* is why I really came back, I think to myself. Even if all else fails, Willa still feels like home.

"Oh, damn," she says, interrupting my emotional moment as Ridley Falls Senior High School looms ahead of us. I never went here, of course. I was too busy attending five different schools in the years between ninth and twelfth grade. But Willa's letters from that time were descriptive enough to paint a picture remarkably similar to the scene now visible through the windshield.

The school is a ramshackle two-story building with a disproportionately large gym and a regulation-sized football field, brightly lit even now. Nothing immediately jumps out as distressing.

"What? Low on gas?" I ask.

"No," Willa says guiltily, opening her mouth to explain when I see it. My heart jumps into my throat, hammering painfully.

Lit from beneath is a massive sign at the football field's entrance. One that definitely wasn't there twenty years ago. I might not have remembered Ridley Falls accurately, but I would have remembered this.

Dark blue letters on a bright white background.

ESPINOZA MEMORIAL FIELD.

"I'm so sorry, Sammy," Willa is saying, hitting the gas to speed past like it isn't already burned into my retinas. "They dedicated it for the thirtieth anniversary last year. I should have taken another route, I was just on autopilot."

"It's okay," I say, shaking myself. "It's not like I didn't know he was from here."

"If you want to talk about it . . ." Willa begins, her eyes cutting over to me at the next stop sign.

"Thanks," I say, but I don't. Not now. Maybe not ever.

As we drive the rest of the way without talking, I realize this might have been too much to take on. The family I never knew. The home I wasn't allowed to have. A broken heart. A career in shambles. A plan that feels more impossible every second . . .

My stomach growls, breaking the silence.

"Don't worry," Willa says with a smile. "Brook is cooking."

Those words, at least, will always get a smile out of me.

2.

In my yoga pants, my hair held in its bun by some fancy metal chopstick things Willa keeps in a jar on the bathroom counter, a *large* glass of red wine in my hand, I feel a little less like I've made a horrible mistake coming here.

Willa and Brook's house is so cute it belongs on someone's Pinterest board. I've seen it, of course. Every Sunday morning on FaceTime. I know the arrangement of the rooms, and the way the sunlight halos Willa as she sits at her kitchen table, talking to me, sipping her coffee.

It's so strange, feeling at home in a place you've never been. But I do. It's almost enough to smooth the edges of my imperfect arrival.

What FaceTime couldn't show me is the vibrancy of each room's wall color. How well the art and the shelves of books and fresh flowers complement one another. The way every piece of furniture is comfy without being shabby.

Out back are two adorable acres where Willa runs a minifarm and Brook sells its bounty to local restaurants. They do the farmers' market circuit to make ends meet, but their dream is to own their very own farm-to-table restaurant someday.

In short, they have a beautiful home. A beautiful marriage. And after my most recent series of life-disrupting disasters, it all kind of makes my heart ache for what I don't have. What I never had.

My mom gave birth to me when she should have been a senior in high school. She did her best, but I think she was always hoping for a different kind of life. One she was sure she'd find in the next town, or at the next job, or with the next guy.

As far as I know she's still looking.

Some people might blame Dina Rae for being a bit of a flake in the parent department, and after what we've been through the past few weeks I couldn't really fault them for it. But those people don't know what I know, deep down. How much it messed her up to get pregnant at sixteen. To lose her own single mother when I was barely three and be unmoored for good.

Dina Rae raised me on her own with no family, no support, and no money, and it's because of that sacrifice that I can never stay mad at her for long. She gave up her chance at a normal life, for me. That's not the kind of thing you can ever repay someone for.

I settle onto a bar stool at the kitchen counter as Brook (Willa's wife, and the only person on this earth I'd trust with her heart) creates what is undoubtedly culinary genius in the bright yellow kitchen. Her platinum hair hangs boy-band-like into her electric blue eyes. Her cheeks are rosy from the steam.

She looks like every cliché lesbian fuckboy from an *L Word: Gen Q* casting call, but secretly her heart is the size of Robert Plant's ego, and she's utterly smitten with Willa in that forever way you can see written all over her face. Willa, for her part, is chopping scallions at the kitchen island. She keeps sneaking glances at Brook. A contented, secret smile curls her lips at the corners.

My newly broken heart trembles along its fault lines.

No one deserves happiness more than Willa. I'd never be-grudge her a soul mate. But it wasn't so long ago I thought I'd found my own . . .

Or maybe I just wanted to believe I had.

"So, you're here for some R and R," Brook says, tossing something delicious-smelling into a frying pan as flames dance dra-matically beneath it. "How long until you have to get back to Seattle?"

I freeze, my glass midway to my mouth. I *might* have left out the job-saving plan when I asked for last-minute lodging. I figured it was the kind of thing better explained in person. When it was too late to talk me out of it.

"So . . . about that," I hedge, setting my glass back down. "It turns out I may be here for slightly more than healing after all."

Willa's and Brook's heads both swivel toward me.

I sigh dramatically. "Okay, listen," I begin, twisting my fingers in my lap. "I swear I meant to just come back for a visit. But then I saw this article, and I realized I might have a chance to save my job."

"What article?" Willa asks sharply. I try to remember if I've ever kept a secret from her, even for the length of a bus ride.

"An article about Max Ryan?"

"Oh my god, *Max Ryan*?" Willa and Brook reply in unison. They look at each other in surprise, then at me, then back at each other.

"Max Ryan, the lead singer of Seven Shades of Monday?" Brook clarifies, just as Willa says:

"Max Ryan, the degenerate I haven't forgiven myself for introducing you to when we were eighteen?"

I push my wineglass away. There's no point. It won't be strong enough to get me through this.

"Yes," I say glumly, to both of them.

Brook turns her back on the stove and gives me her full attention for the first time since I walked into the house. "Wait, you *dated* Max Ryan?"

I groan. "I can't believe you know who he is. That makes this all so much more humiliating. And no, I didn't *date* him, as Willa's pitying expression proves. I spent one magical night with him, hinged my entire adult fantasy-future on the promises he made, and was ghosted without so much as a goodbye."

"Listen," Brook says, hopping over the counter to sit beside me. "You might have been the first to build a fantasy future around Max Ryan, but you were *not* the only, okay? People used to bring

MARRY ME, MAX signs to Seven Shades of Monday shows. One girl showed up in a full gown and veil, I swear there are still pictures on their old website."

"Not helping," I mumble into the hands still covering my face.

"Like, he touched my hand at Warped Tour once?" Brook goes on, oblivious to my anguish. "And you know I'm not into the dangly bits, but even I couldn't help but get a little twitterpated, okay?"

"Brook was a Hot Topic queer," Willa says to me by way of apology.

"I'll deal with you later," Brook says with a faux glare at Willa. "I knew Max was from Ridley Falls but you never told me you *knew* him, and you know our therapist says an omission is still a lie."

"I will spend the rest of my life making it up to you," Willa promises solemnly, though her eyes sparkle with amusement.

"Wait, sorry, sidetracked!" Brook says, returning her attention to me and my misery. "How does a former screamo god play into your secret work plan? Seven Shades hasn't toured in years."

"I know," I say.

"Since Max threatened to go solo after two platinum albums and the band broke up—"

"That's just a rumor," I reply weakly.

"Is it a *rumor* that he walked offstage at the Staples Center in the middle of a world tour?"

I just shake my head. There's no stopping her now.

"Or that he disappeared from the spotlight, never to be heard from again?"

I sigh. This plan seems even more ridiculous and impossible in the face of Brook's prescient reminder: Max Ryan is a god. And I am no one.

"Wow, the fan forum is still bizarrely active." Brook is on her phone now, scrolling with a feverish gleam in her eye. "There's a 'Where's Max' conspiracy channel where people post blurry photos of people with similar hair in lines in airports and restaurants and stuff . . ."

I don't uncover my face, but I'm listening intently, of course I am.

"Ooh, in this one they hunt for clues in old liner notes and Seven Shades music videos to try to pinpoint the date of Max's solo album release." A pause while she catches up. "Okay, like twelve of these have already passed, but there's another one next year people seem really excited about."

This makes me snap my head up at last. "They're talking about a solo album?" I ask.

"Endlessly," Brook confirms. "Why? Do you know something?"

The answer to that question is complicated at best.

I flash back to my Capitol Hill apartment circa three days ago. The cereal bowl full of ice cream balanced on my laptop as I scroll the music news sites, my plan of visiting Ridley Falls barely percolating in the back of my mind.

Before my bleary breakup eyes, a familiar name in a headline makes my bloodied heart leap:

Max Ryan's Return: Former Seven Shades of Monday Front Man Teases Solo Album

After swapping the ice cream for pinot grigio, I made myself read it. Sure, it was little better than a fan theory, but it got the point across.

According to "an anonymous source close to Mr. Ryan" he was hard at work on solo material once more. "Raw and honest" material, according to the article. *Acoustic* material.

I relay all of this to my now-rapt audience, with a dramatic pause before revealing the key piece of information that had finally crystallized my plan to return to Ridley Falls.

"'Our source tells us'," I read from a screenshot on my phone. "'That there was no better place to take this leap back into the world of music than a private studio Mr. Ryan built *in his hometown.*'"

Willa gasps dramatically. Brook drops the jar of white pepper she's holding. It spills all over the kitchen floor.

"Max is *here*?" Willa asks in a small voice.

"There's really gonna be a solo album?" Brook asks in a much louder one.

"I mean, I certainly thought so when I read it," I say. "Which is why, in a wine-soaked stupor, I told my editor I have an 'inside source' to hear it early. I promised Esme I could interview Max in depth, listen to the album, and review it for *Scavenger* before its release. Which is the *only* reason she didn't fire me on the spot."

The silence that greets this statement is absolute until Willa says:

"But . . . why would you tell her that? How are you even going to find Max? Just hang around town until you run into him and pretend it's all a big coincidence? And then what, *hope* he decides to play the album for you? It's not like you can tell him you're a columnist semi-famous for making musicians cry."

"Obviously I didn't know there was an *active Max Ryan conspiracy theories forum* when I bought my bus ticket." I moan, slumping down on the counter again. "And I never said it was a great plan to begin with."

"Yeah, but there's *not great* and then there's . . . impossible," Willa says gently. "Isn't there some better way to get your confidence back, sweetie?"

"No, wait, I think it's awesome!" Brook scoops the last of the white pepper off the floor with the dustpan and dumps it in the trash. "Many birds, one stone right? You get revenge on a guy who ghosted you in your formative years to heal your current broken heart. You spend a week with people who love you. In the meantime, you write a huge story to get your column back." She snaps her fingers. "Simple as that."

"You sound like Drunk Sammy," I grumble.

"Don't listen to Brook," Willa says. "*She* just wants you to succeed so she can hear the new Max Ryan album."

"Excuse me," Brook retorts, pointing a vivid teal spatula at her wife. "Being a fan does not preclude me from being a good friend, and for your information . . ."

I try to keep listening to Brook and Willa's wifely banter, but suddenly this adorable, cozy kitchen is too bright. The neck of my self-cropped T-shirt is too tight. I'm pulling in the deepest breath I can, but my lungs won't fill.

"I'm gonna go . . . get some more pepper," I say, not knowing if I'm interrupting, just that I have to get out of here, get some air, think about what the hell I'm doing. "It's my fault it spilled," I continue when no one replies. "So I'll just go get some more and I'll be right back, okay?"

Anyone else might ask questions, try to talk me out of it, but Willa just glances at my still-full wineglass, then at me, and says: "Take the truck." She's scribbling something on a pad of succulent-themed sticky notes and she hands it to me with the keys. "Our address." She smiles. "I know how you are at memorizing anything that isn't song lyrics."

"Thanks," I say. The tightness in my chest eases the tiniest bit as I stick the note in my wallet and head for the door.

She's saying something else behind me, but my pulse is too loud again, a pounding drumbeat ready for the soaring, spiraling solo of my panic to kick in for real. Luckily, I get my feet into a pair of someone's hiking boots and make it out the door before I can become the nervous system version of a hair metal song.

By the time I'm in the truck (which starts with a little cajoling) I feel silly for bailing. But the source of my anxiety hasn't faded. I've been riding some kind of my-heart-is-broken-so-nothing-worse-can-happen-to-me high for the past week, but Brook's nostalgic ramblings about the persistent cult of Max Ryan has cleared the fog to expose the horror of my situation in full.

Every feeble part of this plan I glossed over in my drunken, desperate state is so obvious that it's ridiculous I even got on the bus. How *did* I think I was going to find Max? I remember a hazy vision of confronting him about the ghosting, demanding that he allow me to review the album as penance for the past, but nothing about actually *locating* him, which now seems like a key point . . .

"What was I thinking?" I ask myself aloud. As I turn in to the Safeway parking lot, the rain that's been threatening since the moment I got off the bus lets loose at last. Not just a sprinkle, but a bonafide deluge. Perfect.

For some reason, in my memories of Ridley Falls, it's always a blustery fall day. I'd forgotten it rains ten months out of the year. Another addition for the cons column.

I didn't grab a jacket from the house, so it's just me and the 2010 Sasquatch! Music Festival shirt I bought the one and only time I attended. It didn't protect me from the downpour that weekend either—and it was a whole shirt back then.

Inside the store, I catch a glimpse of my bedraggled, washed-out reflection in the window.

This doesn't even count, I tell myself. The store is deserted, and the sign out front says they close at six. I'll get in and out, no one will see me, and I'll have my *real* first day in town tomorrow. In a much cuter outfit. Wearing my own shoes.

Armed with a plan (for the next twenty-four hours, if not my life) I grab the pepper and two bottles of pinot (grigio for me, noir for Willa and Brook) before slinking anonymously up to the register. I can feel my hair falling out of its chopstick bun, and I avoid my reflection this time, repeating my mantra: *Tomorrow will be better, cuter, and will happen in my own shoes.*

The cashier is a tall, gangly kid barely old enough for a driver's license. I'm really about to pull this off without being seen by anyone else, and on impulse I grab a bag of Flamin' Hot Cheetos from the rack beside the conveyor belt to celebrate.

"ID, please?" the kid asks, and I let myself be flattered. "Sorry, it's company policy to ask anyone who looks under forty."

"Well," I say, "if I can't look twenty-one anymore at least I don't look forty, right?"

The cashier just looks at me with an uncertain half-smile.

"Oh hey!" he says, clearly trying to turn this interaction around as he examines my license. "Espinoza! Like the football field! Any relation?"

He has to blink like three times before I say anything back, and I can tell he's wondering if I overdid it on my meds or something. The truth is I'm trying to remember how to breathe around the boulder suddenly sitting on my chest.

"N-no," I manage at last. I snatch my ID back with a little more force than I intend. "No relation."

The kid gives up on talking to me altogether at that point, which is just as well. I'm barely aware he's there. *Breathe in, breathe out,* I tell myself. Sure, I didn't anticipate the football field sign, but it's fine. Everything is fine.

"Here's your receipt," the cashier kid says.

"Thanks." I shove my wallet awkwardly into my armpit. "Have a good night."

"You, too," he replies, a little warily.

And despite the events of this bizarre interaction I'm almost thinking I might. I run out to the truck in the rain, wine bottles clanking, knowing there's dinner and friends awaiting me back at Willa's . . .

But the truck's battery—its very *dead* battery—has other plans for me.

3.

In a way, this is a fitting end for the kind of day this has been, I think as I rub my hands together in the freezing cab of this useless hunk of truck-shaped metal.

My phone is dead, I discover when I try to call Willa for a rescue. The oversharer on the bus was an outlet hog, too.

The Safeway parking lot is empty. In a matter of minutes, the store will close, assuring that no one else has any reason to drive through here, and I absolutely refuse to go back in there to ask the cashier kid for help. Even if that's not his *bicycle* chained to the front of the store.

The only places open this late are probably downtown—which is a ten-minute drive down the road, and the rain is pounding so hard on the roof of the truck I'm afraid it might be leaving dents.

I'm completely, totally stuck, and it's already been such an overwhelming day that all I can do is shove handfuls of Flamin' Hot Cheetos into my mouth and laugh.

Laugh about Espinoza Memorial Field, and the fact that this isn't even my real hometown, and Max Ryan and his stupid screamo god status that hasn't even *faded* in the past seven years he's been off the map, and the fact that absolutely none of these things would matter if I hadn't been stupid enough to think I could fix everything by coming here.

Maybe my mom was right. Maybe this *is* the place dreams go to die.

That thought is the most depressing one of all. I'm laughing so hysterically that I don't notice when a single headlamp lights a path of raindrops through the dark parking lot leading right to my little Toyota island.

I don't stop until someone taps on my window.

And then I scream.

I can't see through the glass, fogged by my own hysterical breathing and slicked with the rain outside. There's just a silhouette, one with broadish shoulders and shortish hair I assume belong to a man—or at least a masculine-presenting individual—and it's all just the cherry on top of my shit sundae so I laugh some more.

"If you're here to murder me don't bother!" I call through the obscured window. "I'm doing a pretty good job of dying on the inside, which, I assure you, is worse!"

"I just wanted to see if you needed a jump," calls a deep voice from the other side. "I promise I'm not a murderer."

"That's exactly what a murderer would say!"

I empty the rest of the Cheeto crumbs into my mouth. Most of them end up on my shirt and in my hair. I pretended to be a vegan the whole time I was dating Juniper, so I kind of forgot how hot these things really are. Maybe they'll deter the mystery dude if he tries to get too close to . . . any part of my face. Or chest.

"Far be it from me to rescue you against your will," said mystery dude shouts, his silhouette turning away. "Hope the next guy who comes along isn't a *real* murderer!"

"Oh see, that's where you lose me, Creepy Parking Lot Guy." I toss the Cheeto bag into the passenger seat and roll down the window. "I *hate* it when men casually use the prevalence of violence against women as some kind of contrast to make themselves look less complicit in this misogynist hellscape."

He turns back slightly. Rain plasters his long-sleeved shirt to his chest and shoulders. His slightly too-long hair drops into the one eye I can sort of see in the harsh glare of his motorcycle headlight.

Hot? Maybe. But only someone horribly try-hard would ride a

motorcycle in the rainiest state in the continental United States in late September.

"It's this *nice guy* facade," I continue, spurred on by irritation and the beginnings of definite Cheeto heartburn. "You don't get a gold star for not murdering women in parking lots. And if you use the fact that some men *do* murder women to scare me into accepting you as a safer, nicer option against my will? That still makes you a jerk."

I can barely see the guy, but it's obvious when he starts laughing because his illuminated, sopping shoulders shake.

"Wow, yeah, I'm so glad you think this is funny." I start to roll the window back up. My rage is breaking down, leaving something feeble and sad in its wake. "Now, if you don't mind," I call as I struggle with the hand crank. "I'm gonna get back to thinking about my dead dad and worrying about my flighty mom and obsessing about my ex-girlfriend traveling around Europe with her entourage of Free People catalogue girls. Have fun swimming your *super cool* motorcycle back to shore."

It would be the perfect parting line if the window had the decency not to get stuck.

But of course, it doesn't.

The man is still maintaining a careful distance from the truck—probably in case *I'm* actually the murderer in this situation—but even from the cut of his silhouette in the headlights it's clear he's gorgeous as he laughs some more.

Laughs at your misfortune! cries the reasonable part of me.

Semantics, says the part that's swooning a little.

That's when I remember the Cheeto crumbs, and the Sasquatch! shirt fraying on its DIY kitchen scissor line, and the general drowned-rat-in-yoga-pants vibe I've been cooking up in here.

"So, a jump then?" he calls.

"Can you even jump a truck with a motorcycle battery?" I ask, squinting my puffy, makeup-less eyes in an attempt to look disdainful instead of desperate.

"Only one way to find out."

Unfortunately, I don't have a better offer. So I open the door. Step out of the truck. Revealing my whole mess of a Cheeto-covered self and setting myself up for a moment of pure, concentrated regret unmatched by anything my life has served up so far.

Because out here, I can see what I couldn't from inside the truck. The identifying features of the statuesque, backlit shape I was shamelessly admiring mere seconds ago.

And it's so absurd it can't be true. But it's also so absurd it has to be.

Max Ryan, soaking wet T-shirt clinging to every one of his lean muscles, is smiling at me like we're even on the same *plane of reality* we were ten seconds ago. Like he's still an anonymous potential murderer, and I'm just a snarky stranger in reluctant need of a jump.

In this moment, I know something a million hours of cyber-stalking and down-to-the-tiniest-detail planning never could have told me. A pathetic truth I have never admitted to myself until this moment of forced-by-shock honesty:

After eleven years, two major relationships, and countless hookups and flings, this boy (this *man,* I correct myself after giving him another surreptitious once-over) still turns my insides to absolute Jell-O in the least productive way.

More lights flood the parking lot, and I nearly faint in relief. It's Brook, at the wheel of a little blue Subaru that Willa is already jumping out of. She puts up the hood of her rain jacket and runs over to where I'm still standing, dumbfounded, just a few feet from him.

"You didn't hear me say the thing about giving it some gas when you turn the key, did you?" Willa asks, her back to Max, not even noticing the worst part of all this in her haste to get us home.

"Not so much," I say with a borderline-tearful chuckle.

"Did your phone die?"

I just nod.

"Scoot over," Willa says with an affectionate eye roll, waving to Brook who takes off back toward home.

I look over her shoulder to where Max, apparently reassured that I'm no longer in need of a white knight, has turned back to his motorcycle. If he recognized me, he certainly isn't going to say anything, and that's fine with me after the way I've behaved during this interaction. All I want is to get away from here as fast as possible and forget any of this ever happened.

Willa starts the truck up.

Max, at the sound of the engine, turns and waves.

And that's it. We're gone.

"You okay?" Willa asks after a few minutes of navigating through the storm.

I watch the rain streak the windows. I can't even look at her. "I . . . don't know."

"It's okay not to have it all figured out," Willa says, trying to be consoling even without the context I can't bear to give her yet. Even if I knew how to explain the way it felt to see Max after all this time, the version of me that was completely defeated by five seconds of his silhouette in a rainstorm isn't one I'm overeager to share.

"Thank you," I say, sniffling a little, still staring out the window. Willa doesn't speak again until we get back to the house, where Brook is waiting with the door open. I grab the wine and the pepper and the empty Cheeto bag and make a dash for the door.

Inside, the table is set for a truly delicious-looking meal, and I feel worse than ever for holding it up. There's nothing like friends who have their shit together to remind you of all the ways you deeply do not.

Willa shakes off her raincoat. "Okay, here's the deal," she announces as Brook tosses me a towel from the kitchen for my hair. "No more Max Ryan talk tonight. Sammy, you came back for good reasons. Reasons that are totally valid even if you can't track down that talentless has-been. So let's focus on those, and—"

"Um," I interrupt. "Turns out it wasn't as hard to track him down as we anticipated."

Willa stops her inspiring speech in its tracks, her mouth still slightly open.

Even Brook appears speechless, her arm extended as she hands me a glass.

I take it, sitting at the table without even bothering to change. Before I explain, I drain the wine in three gulps.

"What do you mean?" Willa asks finally, sitting cross-legged in the chair next to me. "You were just at Safeway, how could . . ." An expression of gradually dawning horror eclipses her confusion. "That wasn't!"

"It was."

"The guy on the—"

"Yup," I say grimly.

"What are the odds!" Willa says, smacking her forehead.

Brook, no stranger to my and Willa's half-sentences, waits patiently to be filled in. In the meantime she fills my wineglass again and heaps pasta with bacon and blackened zucchini in cream sauce on my plate.

"When I couldn't start the truck," I begin, the wine armoring me against the memory. "I ate a whole bag of Flamin' Hot Cheetos in the cab, looking like this." I gesture, wineglass in hand, at my bedraggled state. "Then, a strange man on a motorcycle arrived asking if I needed a jump."

Brook's eyes get wide.

"I proceeded to insult him through the foggy window for several minutes, refused his help, and rounded the experience out by confessing some things even my therapist might have been surprised by."

"No!" Brook says, covering her mouth.

"Only to open the door and discover . . ." I gesture widely, my wine sloshing in its glass.

"No way," Brook says, her eyes big enough to reflect me twice.

"Yes way. Our favorite musician turned celebrity mark turned witness to my utter humiliation." I don't find it necessary to disclose the whole insides-turning-to-Jell-O thing. This is already embarrassing enough.

"Oh, honey," Brook says, trying to stifle her laughter.

It doesn't last long. Soon we're all laughing. And the wine and the friends and the food help, but they do not change the fact that my life is now even more of a disaster than it was when I arrived.

4.

I'm sitting in the detritus of my exploded suitcase, examining last night's text from my mom when Willa taps on the door to the botanical-themed guest room the next morning.

"Check it out," I say, flashing her the photo Dina Rae sent. "Three days ago we got into a massive fight because she didn't think to tell me my only grandfather was dead. Today she's texting me from a singles' cruise, finding L-O-V-E with a man in a Hawaiian shirt."

"Yikes," Willa says. "How do you feel about that?"

I roll my eyes, half-exasperated, half-affectionate. "This is how it always goes. I hit my boiling point, we cool off, she texts me something ridiculous and we go back to normal. She has the attention span of a goldfish."

"Or she doesn't respect your totally valid anger, and is trying to avoid accountability by changing the subject."

Even though I've spent the last few days being absolutely furious with my mother, I prickle a little at the tone in Willa's voice. Maybe it's being here, in the town Dina Rae was basically shamed out of for getting pregnant. Being confronted with the sacrifices she made for me.

Either way, I paste on a smile and say: "It's actually kind of a relief to let it go. Two fundamental life crises is plenty for the moment. And look at this. The text literally says 'L-O-V-E could always be just around the corner!! Say YES to LIFE, girlie!' How can someone who texts like this be related to me?"

Willa purses her lips, clearly clocking the subject change. "She's really something," she says after a moment, letting it go.

I can't really blame her for not being my mom's biggest fan. Willa was the one who dealt with me crying myself to sleep in her bottom bunk every night after Dina Rae dropped me off. She's the one who had to share her parents and her hometown with me because I never had my own.

I've tried to explain that my mom sacrificed her whole adolescence to raise me alone, and that part of our relationship is me cutting her the necessary slack because of it. It's something a person with two loving, goofball parents who would never deny them anything just can't understand. Being overprotective of my heart is one of Willa's few shortcomings as a friend. We work around it.

"I love what you've done with the place," Willa says, her way of transitioning out of the Dina Rae minefield. "It's like . . . Goth bass player's dressing room meets Anne of Green Gables."

A normal person probably would have had less to shove back into their suitcase after eighteen hours, but I have this obnoxious habit of exploding the contents of mine all over regardless of the length of my stay.

"Bass player, ouch."

"Sorry! I like bass players!"

Okay, maybe she has two flaws.

"Anyway, I came to check on you. How are you feeling after the run-in last night?"

"Honestly, I'm doing my best not to think about it." Of course, I've been horribly unsuccessful. But she doesn't need to know that.

"That's good," Willa says. "I just wanted to remind you that this plan was an afterthought. There are plenty of good reasons you came back to Ridley Falls. I don't want you to let one jerk from a lifetime ago stop you from finding what you came here for."

I nod. "I was just thinking about that, actually. I think I'll stay the two weeks anyway."

Willa beams.

"Maybe this place is cursed for me like it was for my parents, but I'm already here," I continue. "I might as well rest, heal my broken heart with Brook's pasta, hang out with you." I pause here, gearing myself up. "I want to try to find out more about my grandma, too. And if Max's album falls into my lap or I happen to think of a more realistic job-saving idea along the way? All the better."

The pursed lips are back at the mention of Max. "I like all of it, except the part where you count on anything to do with *him*."

"Not counting *on*," I clarify. "Just not counting out. Yet."

She's clearly gearing up for another ten rounds on Max's character, so I dodge to a subject I know will be more enticing before she can.

"Actually," I say, looking down into my half-empty cup. "I was thinking I might visit my dad's grave today."

As predicted, Willa's eyes go round as quarters. The truth is, I've never actually been to the place where my father was buried. In fact, I can count the number of times I've even *mentioned* him to Willa (or anyone) on one hand..

My mom never talked about him, and she regarded Ridley Falls much like a cat does a swimming pool—so of course she never offered to take me. By the time I was old enough to be curious, I already knew bringing him up to Dina Rae would hurt her more than it helped me.

But my mom isn't here now. And even though I've mostly forgiven her for the lie by omission about my grandpa, the whole debacle did bring something into focus for me. I'm not a child anymore. I deserve to learn my own truths about the Espinoza family, about Ridley Falls, rather than relying on hers.

Only how can I confront the living woman who never wanted to know me if I don't face the boy who made us family in the first place?

"I'm proud of you," Willa says into my thoughtful silence. "I know we don't really talk about it. Talk about *him*. But I think it's really brave of you."

"Thanks," I say, not trusting myself to say more. Trusting that Willa knows how much it means to me.

"Do you want me to go with you?" she asks.

For a moment, I consider it. How much easier it would be with her there. But in the end I shake my head. "I think I need to do this on my own," I say. "But I appreciate you."

"Understood, but at least let me give you a ride," she says as I finish my coffee and get to my feet.

"Already called a Lyft," I say guiltily, holding up my phone.

Willa blanches, and at first I think I've mortally offended her by seeking alternative transportation. "A Lyft?" she says. "Uh, there might be something I should have mentioned . . ."

"CITY SLICKER!" is the only thing I hear before the door of Ridley Falls's only Lyft bursts open and a whirl of tie-dye and gray ponytail overtake me.

The hug knocks the wind out of me, but in a good way. One more thing in the feels-like-home column.

"Dad, please release my friend," Willa says calmly from the porch, looking down on the pocket-sized front yard where I'm currently gasping for breath.

"Hey, Mr. Cross," I wheeze as he steps back to take a better look.

"*Mr. Cross,*" he says, waving me off. "You know it's Larry."

"When did you start driving a Lyft?" I ask, brushing off the front of my black sweater dress and attempting to salvage the giant sunflowers that have just been crushed between our bodies.

"When Maeve told me my retirement was the most irritating thing since remotes with too many buttons," Willa's dad says, almost proudly. "I was driving her bananas at the store, and at the house, she said I needed to find a hobby, and Ridley Falls doesn't have an official tour guide, so here we are!"

He gestures at the banged-up blue Astro van like he's presenting an award. Painted on the side in slightly listing letters are the words LARRY'S CAR. I stifle a giggle.

"Maeve wouldn't let me call it the Batmobile," he says. "But this gets the point across, doesn't it?"

"It definitely does," I agree.

"Okay, Dad," Willa calls. "You know your only bad reviews are from people who are late to stuff because you're such a *great conversationalist.*"

Larry looks up at his daughter in mock horror. "Sammy would never leave me a bad review? Would you, Sam?"

"Five stars, guaranteed," I assure him.

"In that case, I'm running every red light."

"Good thing this place only has one."

Larry Cross guffaws, then loops his arm around my shoulder and steers me toward the van.

I settle into the front seat with the sunflowers on my lap. Larry hops in and starts up the engine, honking twice at Willa, who waves from the porch, looking a little concerned. I wave back with all the confidence I can muster—confidence that isn't bolstered by Larry nearly hitting Willa and Brook's mailbox as he fiddles with the radio.

An oldies station comes in clear, midway through "Riders on the Storm" by The Doors.

"I love this song," Larry and I say at the exact same time. He laughs, reaching across to pat my hand.

"I remember you going through my old forty-fives like you were at a museum," he says in that nostalgic-parent voice that's so rarely been directed at me. "You thought they were just pictures. The look on your face when you found out they played songs, too . . ."

He laughs again, that timeworn chuckle. Jim Morrison growls over the discordant instrumental.

"I remember," I say, feeling the Crosses' orange shag carpeting under my bare knees as I chose record after record. After a while, Larry even let me put them on the turntable myself, plug in the big plushy headphones.

Listening to his collection, the little skips and scratches of the vinyl, I could close my eyes and pretend to be anywhere. On a ship at sea. In outer space.

Even with my mom, in the kind of home I'd always imagined for us.

Larry and I are silent until the song ends, the comfortable quiet of two people whose hearts beat in 4/4 time.

"Great tune," he says, obeying the GPS when it prompts him to turn left.

"Mhm," I agree, the final chords still echoing in my ears.

"So," Larry says as an ad for a winery concert tour begins to play. "The cemetery, huh?"

This is the first time I almost wish my Lyft driver were a stranger. Larry's eyes are pitying when he glances at me, the very expression I avoid at all costs—usually by never mentioning my father to anyone.

Of course, that's not an option in a town where our shared last name is emblazoned on a football field. In a town where the people who know me don't know me by my pen name first.

"Yeah," I say. "My grandpa died last year I guess, and it just sort of made me think about everything that happened between my mom and them. How you don't have forever to make things right."

Larry nods, uncharacteristically quiet for a moment. The next stop sign is obeyed without any lurching.

"Well, I'm glad you're back, sweetheart," he says at last. "Whatever the reason. Don't like waiting for a big event just to pinch those cheeks of yours."

It hits me when he says it. Willa's wedding was the last time I saw them. Five years ago. And only a handful of times in the years before. They came to my high school graduation, I remember. And visited the city with Willa to celebrate when I landed my job at *Scavenger*.

Like everything else, it's different seeing him here. It feels like I've been missing out.

"Sorry it's been so long."

"No need to apologize," he says, waving a hand. "Willa tells us all about your writing, honey. We know you're busy, and we're so proud of you. Making a name for yourself in the big city. Make sure you go see Maeve while you're in town, hm? She's always loved you like her own."

"I will. I promise," I say around an embarrassing lump in my throat.

As we drive the last two minutes to the Ridley Falls cemetery in silence, I try to think of the last time my mom told me she was proud of me. I'm still sifting through memories of giving her relationship pep talks, or pretending to believe the man she met online is really *the one* this time when I give it up, feeling guilty again.

It's not Dina Rae's fault she isn't like Willa's parents. Larry and Maeve Cross have support. They have each other, and a whole extended family, and educations and careers.

My mom had a baby at seventeen. It's hardly fair to compare them.

"Here you go, sugar," Larry says, shaking me from my guilty thoughts as he eases up to the cemetery gate. "You want some company over there?"

I shake my head, smiling at how much he sounds like Willa. "Thanks, but I think I have to fly this mission solo."

"Roger that," Larry says. "I can wait? Take you back after?"

"Not sure how long I'll be," I say, already opening the door. "I'm sure you have people waiting on you. But thanks, Larry. It was really good to see you."

He kills the engine, gets out, and hugs me again. "You be good now, Sammy," he says. "And remember Maeve and I are always here if you need us."

This time, I really can't answer, so I just nod. Luckily, Larry seems to understand.

When the van is gone, I turn toward the gate. Behind me is the closest thing to a father figure I ever knew. In front of me, somewhere, is the one I never got to.

5.

The thing about me that people don't understand is that I've never really been sad about my dad dying. It's probably the reason I hate that pitying expression so much. It doesn't feel honest to let people feel sorry for me.

I mean, don't get me wrong, it's a tragic story and I get sad when I think about it. I'm not a monster. But my sadness feels like the vicarious emotion you get when you read about other people's parents dying. It doesn't feel personal.

In any case, it's all part of the reason why I avoid talking about him at all costs. The few people who do know he's gone probably assume it's because I'm too overcome with grief to discuss it. The truth is more complicated. See, I'm not afraid I'll break down if I talk about him, or discover some secret well of grief I've been hiding from myself for twenty-nine years . . .

I'm afraid I won't.

Because what kind of person would that make me?

I assume it'll take a long time to find the right grave among all the others—I'm kind of counting on it, actually. But it only takes a few minutes. It's right at the center of the field, marked by a massive headstone, fresh flowers laid before it like someone's been here recently.

White lilies, to be more specific. The flower of mourning—a fact that I only know because Juniper Street handed me one after she broke up with me onstage and said, "Let the flower mourn for you, and remember me happy, Samantha."

Pretentious drama queen.

Anyway, there's no one here now, and I approach slowly with my own flowers. I'm waiting for a moment of catharsis. Some emotional lightning bolt. Maybe dread, sudden and overwhelming, will make it impossible to approach his grave. Or huge sobs will take me to the ground, ruining the knees of my semi-sheer tights, purging me of the last of my unacknowledged pain.

But none of that happens, and the anticlimax is proof of everything I've been afraid of. That my heart is made of the same stone as this grave marker bearing my dad's name.

JUAN "JOHNNY" ESPINOZA, it reads. BELOVED SON. QUE EN PAZ DESCANSE.

It doesn't say BELOVED FATHER, I notice, which makes it all the more bizarre that I'm standing here in this dress trying to figure out how to be sad correctly.

The dates are below, his death year the same as my birth year. He was eighteen years old. Quarterback of the state champion football team. Recipient of an athletic scholarship to the University of Washington. He was also a guy who got his girlfriend pregnant, jeopardizing his entire future and royally pissing off his Mexican Catholic parents.

But the thing he mostly is now, almost thirty years later, is a kid who was killed by a drunk driver the night of his high school graduation. An act that would devastate the town who loved him, irreparably mess up the sixteen-year-old girl pregnant with his baby, and, apparently, turn said baby into an emotionally hollow husk who doesn't get sad at cemeteries.

I lay the flowers at the foot of the grave to have something to do with my hands. It only takes a second. It seems absurd to leave so soon, I think, so I stand there, shivering a little in the weak morning sunlight.

I try to settle into the moment. But all I can feel is the awkwardness of it all. The fear that someone's going to see me, and guess who I am, and judge me for not grieving right.

In movies, everyone's always talking to their dead parents. Somehow I can't imagine being the kind of person who does that. Besides, what would I say? And am I talking to my father as he would be now if he'd lived? Or the boy he was when he died?

Five more minutes, I tell myself. Five more minutes and I can tell myself I did it.

I shift from foot to foot. I wish I'd given myself three minutes instead of five. Five minutes is a long time, apparently. Especially when all you have to look at is a headstone with nine words on it.

Half of which are in a language you don't speak.

My eyes start wandering almost immediately, restless, taking in the treetops and the gentle slope of the hill. A robin looking curiously at me from a branch. I don't see anything worth stopping the clock for until I realize there are more lilies at the foot of the grave beside this one. An identical bundle to the one currently competing with my sunflowers.

ROBERTO JOSÉ MOLLINA ESPINOZA, reads this headstone. A birth date in the 1950s, a death date last year.

I should have known they'd be next to each other, I guess. But somehow I wasn't expecting it. It was one thing to hear about this man's death as my mom's flippant afterthought, but it's another to be standing here in front of his grave. In front of *their* graves.

The amount I know about the two men buried before me seems laughably inadequate. My mom rarely spoke of my dad, and even less of his father. It was his mother I heard most about. And then only in disparaging or colorful language.

I never blamed my mom for hating my grandmother—at least, not after she told me the story. How Paloma Espinoza threatened to disown Johnny if he stayed with my pregnant, teenaged mother. How she told him to choose between us and his family's money.

She snubbed my mom at the funeral. Four months pregnant in her prom dress. They never returned her calls. Just isolated themselves with their grief in their big house on the hill and never spared a thought for the granddaughter they'd never know, or the girl who would be irrevocably messed up by their son's untimely death.

I used to wonder about my grandparents, sometimes. I even imagined they might show up in their fancy car and whisk us away on vacation to Europe or an island with white sand. That they'd have dark hair and eyes like mine, and they'd teach me Spanish. Tell me everything I ever wanted to know about my dad.

Eventually, I grew up. The fantasy evaporated. After that, my awareness of them shrank to occupy a back burner in my mind. Like the existence of taxes before April, or the fact that you're probably overdue for a teeth cleaning.

I knew I'd probably never meet my grandparents—the only earthly connection I ever had to my father—but I didn't realize until I found out one of them was gone how much space that back burner was taking up. That night, I did the math as best I could. Paloma would be in her late seventies by now. Even though I didn't know her, I could lose her. Like I already lost my father, and my grandfather.

I think of her now, alone in the big house my mom described. My grandmother lost both these men, too. She might be the only one who can tell me how it felt to love them.

I meant to call Willa when I was done at the cemetery. She was going to pick me up and take me to brunch at Sassy's—a diner we always went to after her soccer games when I lived here.

Instead, I find myself heading through the cemetery gate without even pulling out my phone. Walking up the tree-lined road it sits at the end of. Regretting the choice of not-quite-broken-in velvet Doc Martens with every blister-making step, but too lost in thought to change course.

As I make my way toward Willa and Brook's, I wonder what my grandmother is like. All I know of her is the sneer my mother's mouth curls into when she says her name. Maybe she's as bad as

Dina Rae says—her depiction of Ridley Falls is proving to be pretty spot on, after all.

But after all these years, maybe Johnny's mother regrets the choice she made back then. Maybe it's not too late.

Even if she's as awful as my mom makes her sound, I reason, I'm old enough to find out for myself. I tell myself I'll look her up, wondering if I'll be brave enough.

After almost an hour of traipsing through the streets, Willa and Brook's yellow house finally comes into view. I push the door open hoping for a good old-fashioned pep talk from my best friend. Except she's nowhere to be seen.

"Hello?" I call into the empty living room. "Willa, I know this is weird, but I actually need advice about stuff so could you—?"

I expect Willa to bound out with her I-know-exactly-what-to-do face on. What I do not expect is to be caught in a whirlwind of flapping hands and near-unintelligible gay screeching as Brook and Willa both come careening out of their bedroom.

"Sammy, where have you been!"

"Your wallet—"

"It was in the parking lot—"

"And he came and—"

"Willa was in the shower, he wouldn't—"

"I don't know if it's a good idea—"

"SLOW DOWN!" I yell, altogether too overwhelmed, exhausted, and in my own head to deal with all of . . . whatever this is. "One at a time, please," I say when they finally calm themselves.

Willa and Brook start at the same time, stop, look at each other, and wait.

I sigh. "You," I say, pointing at Brook. "Talk."

"Max Ryan has your wallet!" Brook blurts before I even fully form my last word.

Max. In all the examining of my childhood issues I almost let myself forget last night's humiliation, but as I swing my purse

around and start digging through it frantically (and unsuccess-
fully) it replays in high definition.

The awkward wedging of my wallet in my armpit as I dashed
through the monsoon.

The Post-it note with this address on it stuck inside.

Max Ryan has my wallet.

"Of course he does," I groan, slumping into a dining room
chair in utter defeat. "What did he say?"

"He showed up about ten minutes after you left for the cemetery," Brook says when my hysterics have died down. Her voice is
oddly high and breathless, and her cheeks are flushed like she's
reliving the whole thing in detail. "Willa was in the shower, and
he said he didn't want to give it to a stranger. He left this . . ." She
shoves a botanical Post-it note into my hand.

Scribbled on it in adorably untidy handwriting is an address
and a phone number.

At this point, I'm too empty to laugh. I can't even feel the blister
on my heel anymore. I'm at a total loss.

"I have to go," I say as I'm realizing it. "I have to go to Max
Ryan's house and get my wallet. And while I'm there I have to
confront him about the ghosting and guilt him into letting me
review his album to save my job."

"No," Willa says, at the same time Brook says, "YES."

I sigh again.

"Sammy, you're here to *heal*," Willa says, leaning forward. "I
don't know if diving headfirst into your most formative heartbreak is the best way to do that."

"If I don't do this, I will be unemployed when I get back to
Seattle," I say, trying to make her understand. "I agree hunting
him down was a long shot, but this . . . feels like a sign. That
maybe I can still fix at least one part of my life."

"There are lots of jobs," Willa says, but it's feeble and she
knows it.

"I don't have a degree," I say. "I write under a pen name. I worked my way up from the mail room at *Scavenger*. Without a reference from Esme, I'll never write for a major publication again." I don't remind her I don't have the same familial safety net she does. Or Brook's family money. But I think they hear it in my silence, because Willa doesn't argue again.

"Putting aside the yoga pants, and the chopsticks bun, and the Cheeto dust, and the babbling about all my sad problems, I think I owe it to myself to take this one last shot."

"You *totally* do," Brook agrees.

"As long as you promise not to let him get in your head," Willa warns, but I can tell this is her way of surrendering.

"And . . . if it's not too much trouble while you're there," Brook hedges, "*maybe* you could get me an autog—"

Willa elbows her into silence before she can finish.

Having the support of my two favorite people (even if one of them offers it grudgingly) helps, of course it does, but neither of them can go with me to confront Max. To leverage the most embarrassing experience of my adolescent life to save my column.

You made your bed, I remind myself, thinking back to the first saccharine review I wrote of Juniper Street's deeply derivative EP. The way I turned it into a series of raves for every show of her opening act tour. One case of bad judgment, my readers might have forgiven me for. But I rode that train for weeks, and the comments left me no place to hide.

I used to trust Verity Page, but these recent reviews read like a paid ad for a terrible band. Canceling my subscription.

I hope Juniper Street bought Verity a car for this one.

Getting my reviews from Rolling Stone *from now on.*

Esme read them all to me in her office as I hung my head. Most of them are still burned into my brain as a reminder of how easy it is to lose trust.

But I have a chance to redeem myself. One last chance.

I pick my head up off the table. "I'm going," I say, in my please-don't-talk-me-out-of-it voice. "But when I get back I want one of those fancy cocktails with weird herbs or sticks or whatever in it, okay? And if this goes even a *little* bit badly"—I point at Willa—"you are forbidden to say you told me so."

"Deal," Willa says, her face still creased with worry.

Brook is trying to be cool, but she's practically vibrating with excitement.

"*You* need to get out more," I say to her, then flounce off to the guest room for a costume change.

6.

Forty-five minutes, one shower, and about six outfits later, Willa's botanical guest room is a disaster again and I am in Brook's Subaru on my way to Max Ryan's house.

In the end, I went with an old standby. Black jeans with an artful hole in one knee, a forest-green T-shirt, and my favorite leather jacket. There are two obvious choices when it comes to soundtrack—something mellow to give me perspective and chill me out, or something to arm me against what's coming.

I choose the latter, of course. This isn't a nostalgic reunion, this is an exchange of prisoners. Absolution for his cliché front-man behavior in exchange for my career. Seems like a fair trade.

At least that's what I tell myself when the drive doesn't take long enough and I'm forced to give myself a pep talk in the parked car across the street.

I'll be honest: Ever since I read about Max Ryan's "hometown studio" I've been picturing one of those hipster monstrosities you see on every other corner in Capitol Hill. A three-level box with huge windows and some eco-friendly-looking wood paneling. Chrome light fixtures. An electric car in the driveway. One of the four horsemen of the gentrification apocalypse.

Only Max's Ridley Falls home is, at first glance, just a regular house. A smallish blue house with a slightly overgrown front lawn. It looks charming and cozy and nothing at all like I expected. There's not even a car, for fuck's sake, just the motorcycle from last night parked in the driveway. A vintage-looking one with a faded black tank that looks like it's traveled actual miles on the actual road.

This is just the outside, my inner voice assures me. I make a bet with myself that the inside is a shrine to the Max Ryan glory days, and that's the only thing that convinces me to get out of the car. In fact, I even start composing my column in my head as I walk up the path to the front door.

While on the outside, this former heartthrob attempts to fit the neighborhood aesthetic, inside his true nature rears its ugly head. Crippling nostalgia categorizes the décor, the mark of a man who's spent ten years trying to maintain his cultural relevance—if only in his own mind.

"I've still got it," I say under my breath as I take the three porch stairs in one step and knock on the door.

As I wait for someone to answer, I realize I'm hoping for a trophy wife, or a sulky eight-year-old here for an awkward weekend with dad. Even a few of Juniper's Free People girls would do the trick, actually. Anything to ground me back in the expected before I can be further thrown off by this humble, comfy vibe.

Once again, my expectations are dashed. Max opens the door in low-slung faded Levis and an impossibly soft-looking blue T-shirt. His slightly curly brown hair hangs into his hazel eyes. Eyes that seem to legitimately light up when he sees me standing there.

"Ah! I wondered if I'd see you again."

I ignore the warmth beginning to kindle in my battle-scarred heart region. Later, I tell myself, when he's not *right there* looking like *that,* I'll find a way to spin this into something pathetic. The kitschy backdrop of his fall from grace . . .

"Yeah," I say now. "Kind of hard to avoid when you make off with my legal proof of identification and all my credit cards."

He smiles, and suddenly I'm wrestling for control of my mind with the eighteen-year-old version of me. The one who used baggy band tees and men's Dickies to pretend she didn't have a body and thought lime-green eyeshadow and Sharpie eyeliner constituted a makeup look. The one who thought the sun rose and set with this smile . . .

"Yes, I'm a very accomplished pickpocket," Max says, breaking into my reminiscence. "Stole it right out of the parking lot puddle where you obviously left it for safekeeping. Insidious, I know."

I shake myself. I am not eighteen anymore. The sun only appears to rise and set because of the Earth's rotation. And I have to look out for myself. Which means getting my life back, by whatever means necessary.

"Well, if you don't mind, I need it back, now."

"It's inside," he says. "Come on in."

This is what I was hoping for, of course. An invitation into the den of Narcissus. But it's with considerable trepidation that I actually step over the threshold.

My first impression is that it's larger than it looked from outside. The front door opens up right into the living room, which is painted bright white and glowing with early afternoon sunlight. The wood floors look original, warped and discolored with age in a few places, but a beautiful deep brown. The main room is sparsely furnished to show off the house's incredible bones, but what's there is tasteful. A large white sheepskin rug. A low-backed burnt-orange sofa. A mid-century modern coffee table with three brass-tipped legs.

Open on the table is a leather notebook with a few scribbles. The walls are bare save for one massive, minimalist painting that's mostly squiggles and triangles, and three gleaming guitars on wall hangers.

A fourth is leaning against the sofa as if he just put it down, glossy black. A Taylor. I can practically hear the warm tones filling the room—which I'm sure has unbelievable acoustics. A room that's actually kind of perfect . . . you know, if you didn't walk into it looking for evidence that the man now walking through it in wool socks once made his living screaming to thousands of rabid fans wearing checkered wristbands and eyeliner.

But there's nothing. No self-indulgent promo photos, or walls of magazine covers, or even a nostalgic tour poster. It's like Max Ryan was born this modest, small-town man with impeccable taste in accent tables.

In my mind's eye, the first paragraph of my column catches on fire.

"Nice accent tables," I say, feeling suddenly awkward now that it's clear there's no fodder for my article here.

Max chuckles, a deep rumbling thing that makes me shiver a little.

"Thanks," he says, pulling out a small drawer from a bookshelf near the kitchen and producing my wallet at last. "I'm never sure anything really matches, but I'm the only one who has to look at it, so I guess it's good as long as I like it, right?"

"Right," I say, my mind already skipping ahead. He's the *only* one who has to look at it? That means my trophy wife theory is out.

I try to convince myself I'm disappointed by this from a teen-screamo-sensation-turns-cringeworthy-self-absorbed-dick angle, but eighteen-year-old Sammy refuses to be banished, and right now she's louder than I am.

He's single! she crows.

I tape her mouth shut in my mind. That's *not* why we're here. These cursed butterflies are just aftershocks from the devastation earthquake Max caused. We know better now.

"Here you go," he says, handing me the cheetah-print wallet that has never looked as dingy as it does in his hand.

I open it, mostly just to have something to do. "Hey, there was forty bucks in here!"

Max's smile fades, his eyebrows shooting up. "I swear I didn't take it! I didn't even look through it after I saw the Post-it note and checked the ID to make sure it was yours, seriously." He runs a hand through his hair. "Look, here, I'll just give you forty, okay? No hard feelings."

I start laughing, I can't help it. "I'm just fucking with you, man, calm down. Who even carries cash anymore?"

He exhales all the air in his lungs in one loud puff, reaching back up in an unsuccessful attempt to rearrange the hair he messed up in his agitation. "Wow," he says. "Wow."

"Come on, that was funny." I'm still laughing in a way I know makes my chin do a weird thing, but I can't help it. He looks legitimately horrified. "You should see your face."

Finally, a smile breaks through, a wry, self-deprecating one I've never seen before. "No, you definitely got me," he says. "After the tongue-lashing you gave me in the parking lot last night, I was sure I was about to hear exactly how men profit off their attempts to help women by stealing their last forty dollars or something."

I try not to focus on the way he says the word *tongue*.

"I could still tell you about that," I offer.

"That's okay," he says, holding his hands up as if to protect himself.

I'm wasting time and I know it. It's time to go into attack mode. Address the eleven-year-old elephant in the room and watch him squirm until the exact moment when he's repentant enough to make up for it. But just as I'm steeling myself, he clears his throat. Like he has something important to say. It's cute, and I'm curious, so I wait. The tape begins to peel off Teen Sammy's mouth with the effort she's making to be heard.

"Listen," he says. "I probably should have just left the wallet with your friends. But I wanted a chance to say something, and I hope you'll forgive me for luring you here under mostly false pretenses."

All I can manage to do is raise an eyebrow, which I hope looks cool and aloof. Because on the inside? Teen Sammy and I are perfectly in tandem for once. *Is this it?* I wonder. Is he going to say he made a huge mistake back then?

He takes a deep breath.

I can't breathe at all.

"I just wanted to say . . ."

What? Say what?! Teen Sammy and I scream internally.

"That I'm genuinely sorry if I scared you last night," he says, now twisting the hem of his T-shirt in his beautiful, long-fingered hands. "And about your dad," he goes on. "And your mom, and your ex-girlfriend and the . . . was it Free People catalogue models? I'm sure they aren't as cool as they seem on social media."

"Oh," I say, cringing at the reminder that I *really did say all of that*. "It's okay. I probably overreacted. I was having a bad night."

"I gathered that much." His adorable nervous expression is giving way to an even more adorable smirk, and I know it's now or never. I have to skewer him with the past before he can charm me any further.

But he's not finished. "I saw the Seattle address on your ID," he continues. "And I'd just hate to think I gave you the wrong impression of Ridley Falls. It's actually a pretty great place if you get to know it, and I . . ." Another throat-clearing sound, as my heart sinks to my stomach and doesn't bother to stop there. "I was kind of hoping you'd be sticking around to find that out for yourself."

In the silence that follows this statement, my heart wedges itself beneath the soles of my checkered Vans and sets up shop like it might stay there awhile. For the second time in twenty-four hours, Max Ryan has managed to send every bullet point of my careful plan spinning out of my head.

. . . By having absolutely no idea who I am.

7

It was muggy the night I met him, I remember. The first week of July. My first summer in Seattle.

After my year as Willa's bunkmate, my mom and Willa's mom lost touch. But Willa and I did not. We wrote letters and postcards until we were allowed email and MySpace. I wrote Willa from new schools, new apartments, sometimes a couch or a basement. Once from the room of an incredibly fancy hotel where my mother had conveniently slipped in the lobby.

Dina Rae's Next Best Thing tour never slowed down, fueled by her near-supernatural ability to attract a new man or fall into a new lifestyle. Willa was the only constant in my life—her and the Walkman Larry had given me as a parting gift when Dina Rae returned for me a year after leaving me on the Crosses' doorstep.

Willa and I planned to move to Seattle together the moment we graduated high school—she was ready to escape Ridley Falls after a lifetime of small-town claustrophobia. I wanted to be at the epicenter of live music in the Northwest.

The plan itself had felt like a pipe dream until suddenly it was real. Willa and I rented a room in Capitol Hill. She was doing an internship at a socialist agriculture collective while I worked at a café, but I spent most days applying for entry-level jobs at every record label in the city.

I had a plan. I was going to do A&R at a label, even if I had to start as the lowliest assistant. I was going to discover bands and make their dreams come true. To that end, I went to shows almost every night, at every grimy club that would let me in.

Live music fed the fire sparked by Larry's old vinyls until it blistered anything that came close. I was no longer alone in the world of my headphones, I was a part of something. The energy exchange between the stage and the bodies in the crowd, our hearts all beating to the same drumbeat.

For me, it was paradise. Dina Rae was living in a room in Bellingham at the time, studying for her real estate licensing exam, and I was happy to have some distance from her constant reinventions. But Willa got homesick quickly. She'd been hypothetically excited about shedding her small-town skin, but she'd never been away from Ridley Falls or her family for so long.

I was terrified she would leave me alone, so when she bounced into our room one day with a flyer, flushed with excitement, I was ready to agree to anything that made her happy. "A band from home is playing at The Crocodile this weekend!" she said, thrusting the little paper rectangle at me. "I saw them a few times senior year, I think you'd love them. They're not much older than us, one of the guys graduated when I was a sophomore."

They were the bottommost band on the flyer, their name in the tiniest font. The opener for the opener. Guaranteed their set wouldn't be more than four songs. But I lived for the chance to discover a new band. A new sound. I agreed without hesitation.

The night of the show, that muggy July night, didn't seem to be anything out of the ordinary at first. Just Willa and me, out on the town in black clothing and too much eyeliner like every other Friday. I wasn't expecting anything life-changing.

It only took Seven Shades of Monday half a song to change my mind.

Sure, they were rough around the edges. A Washington State garage band playing yet another van tour. But they had something, you could tell right away. Or, at least, *he* did.

Max Ryan was a clumsy guitarist. His lyrics were derivative. He growled too much and didn't seem to know what a gift his voice was.

But his stage presence was electric.

He barely looked human as the emotions of the set ran through his body. A live wire. He guided every one of those feelings straight into the hole in my heart. The one I'd always filled with music. In just a few songs he reminded me I wasn't alone. Even if Dina Rae was a hundred miles away. Even if Willa went back to Ridley Falls.

I felt like I had in Larry Cross's den, with those big squishy headphones covering my ears. Plenty of people, before and since, have described music as an escape. But for me, it was the opposite. For me it always felt like coming home.

When they were done, Willa made her way to the side of the stage. The guys remembered her, happy to see a hometown face in an unfamiliar venue. They swept us up in the current of post-show energy and we went along more than willingly.

That was the first time I felt what it was like to bask in the glow of being "with the band." We took over a booth at the back of the venue once their gear was loaded, and the bartender ignored the black X's on our hands that said we were too young to drink.

We shared pitchers with the guys, growing louder and more raucous as we watched the rest of the show. I was at the end of the crowded booth, Willa on my left, until Max slid out to check on the van—which they'd left in a loading zone.

When he returned, he sat right next to me, our arms pressed together. He didn't seem so otherworldly close up, just a guy in ripped jeans and a flannel, his damp hair hanging into his eyes. But in his smile was something of that onstage persona. That sparkle that would one day capture the hearts of millions of fans . . .

"I'm Max!" he called over the blast beats of the second band's set.

"Sammy!" I called back.

He smiled again. "Feel like going up there?"

I would have gone anywhere with him.

We moshed in the sparse crowd, clinging to each other's arms and screaming along to words we didn't know. I stopped drinking after a while, wanting to keep my cool, but he downed cheap beers like water. Until he was loose and heavy and his smile seemed permanent.

The show let out well after two, but I wasn't nearly ready to go home. We piled into the van with the guys and headed for an after-party at the second opener's house. A sprawling single-story where it seemed like half of Seattle's post-hardcore scene was currently crashing.

I don't know what magic bound Max to me that night, but he stayed close. Even when the house filled with people. With girls covered in tattoos who weren't marked with the underage Sharpie brand.

Instead of staying where the action was, Max grabbed a bottle of whiskey and a pack of cigarettes and led me onto the house's sloping porch. We sat together on a lumpy couch, passing a smoke back and forth. That's when we started talking.

At first, he asked me questions about myself. Talking to him was so easy that I found myself confessing more than I had in a long time. I talked about my dream of working at a label, maybe someday opening my own. A small one that nurtured and protected new bands. Let them make the music they loved, not just the music the suits thought would sell.

But that wasn't all. I told him about my mom. How I worried about her now that we weren't living together anymore. About how hard it had been moving around all the time as a kid, and how much I relied on music to help make sense of my world.

Before we got to my dad, I turned the tables. Asked about him, surprised to find him just as open as I had been. None of that sly band-guy banter.

He told me about how scared he always got before going up onstage. About how he started playing music just to help his little sister sleep. About how he wanted to make her proud, help his family with their bills, but he was worried he would never make it big enough.

There had been A&R reps at their last few shows, he confessed, after we'd been talking for hours. The band had been sending demos everywhere for over a year. No one had called. Max was starting to give up hope. Then he asked me what I *really* thought about their performance.

I wanted to lie. To say it had been perfect just so he'd stop looking so desperate. But I couldn't let myself down—not even with a beautiful, talented boy sitting so close to me, his eyes saying he'd believe whatever I told him.

So I told the truth. That the lyrics could go deeper. That he should sing more, let one of the other guys take the screaming. That his real gift was how he channeled the emotion in his songs, and the guitar was only getting in the way. He connected to everyone in the room. That was what made him special.

That's why I was sure he would get that call.

He was quiet for a long time, and then he turned to face me. I could feel his breath on my face. "Thank you," he said, and then he kissed me.

Despite my claim that I was a fan of *music* not just musicians, I had spent countless hours imagining what it would feel like to kiss a rock star. In my mind it had been fierce, passionate, all tongue and teeth. A kiss that felt like a mosh pit.

Kissing Max Ryan was nothing like that. It felt like listening to his music had. Like I wasn't alone. Like I finally belonged somewhere.

The kiss deepened as the sky lightened. "I've never clicked with a girl like this before," he whispered, raising goosebumps on my neck before he moved to kiss it. "You make me feel like I can do anything."

"You can," I whispered back as his hand drifted down to my waist, pulling me closer. I meant it.

The whole house was sleeping it off. It was probably almost six in the morning. I had kissed a few people before in my life, but had never wanted it to go further. I'd seen what falling in love twice a month did to my mom and I wasn't ready . . .

Only now I didn't just feel ready, I felt eager.

When Max pulled me onto his lap, I let him. I wanted him. To be worthy of him. There was some animal in my body just coming to life, living beneath my skin. Wearing it better than I ever had.

"Is this okay?" he asked before sliding a hand up my shirt.

"Yes," I breathed, not overthinking for once. Just letting this fated moment unravel, leading me to the rest of my life.

"We should go inside," he said sometime later, his voice ragged and breathless.

I did that to him, I remember thinking. *I made him sound like that.*

"Yes," I said again, getting to my feet, seeing it all. The way we'd go upstairs, find somewhere quiet. The way he'd be my first, and after there'd be breakfast, and after that . . .

The phone in his pocket rang before we could get back through the front door. The sound was foreign, an intrusion.

"Do you have to?" I asked, standing behind him, my hands in his hoodie pocket.

"No," he said automatically, but he glanced at it anyway. "It's an out-of-state number."

The gravel was gone from his voice. There was something else there now. This cautiousness that said he'd been let down so many times he was afraid to hope this call might be the one.

"I shouldn't answer," he said. His eyes asked me for permission.

"Of course you should."

He smiled. My heart did a somersault. The phone kept ringing.

"Will you do it?" he asked after a beat, handing his phone to me with a shaking hand. "I don't know if I can."

The vulnerability in his expression was so poignant in that moment. The live wire again. I wouldn't have denied him anything.

"Max Ryan's phone," I said when I picked it up. He pushed his hair off his face, his eyes intent on mine.

"Hi there, little lady, is Mr. Ryan around?"

"Who's calling?" I asked.

"Brian from Victory Records. Tell him he'll want to wake up for this one."

Max was so close to me he heard every word. His face was pale, his eyes too large. He reached for the forgotten whiskey bottle before the phone, taking a deep swig, steeling himself.

"This is Max," he said when he was finally ready.

I watched him transform in front of me as the smooth-talking Brian launched into his I'm-about-to-make-your-dreams-come-true speech. I watched his nervous disbelief fade as the mantle of future fame began to settle around his shoulders.

When Max hung up, his hands weren't shaking anymore.

"They're flying us out on Tuesday," he said, pulling from the bottle again. "We're getting a deal. A record deal. It's . . . happening. It's really happening."

I tried to be happy for him. I really did. After the past few hours together I knew what this meant to him. But all I could think was that we definitely weren't going upstairs to a quiet room now. There wouldn't be breakfast, or after . . .

"It was you," he said, snapping me out of my melancholy. "You're, like, my good luck charm."

"No way," I said, blushing. "You guys worked your asses off for this."

"I know," he said, eyes sparkling, taking my shoulders in his hands. "But you said it would happen, and just like that it did."

"Well then, you're welcome," I said, trying to smirk through my disappointment.

"Look," Max said, running a hand through his hair in what I was recognizing as a quirk of his. "I have to go in and tell the guys, but first . . . this is going to sound absolutely insane. But I really felt something tonight. Something I've never felt before. And you were so right, about everything you said. The lyrics. The scream-ing. The guitar getting in the way of connecting. All of it."

I wasn't even breathing, I remember that clearly. Nothing felt real except his hand on my shoulder. His eyes boring into mine.

"I want you to come with me," he said. "To Chicago. I want to know there's one person there who'll always be honest with me. And I definitely want to pick up where we left off with *this* . . ."

He leaned forward and kissed me again. Short and sweet. The kind of kiss that promises not to be the last.

Standing there, I was aware that this exact impulse was what had dragged me back and forth across the state of Washington for my entire childhood. This belief of my mom's that the next guy was the one. The next city. The next life.

But I didn't have a kid in tow. For once, there was only me. And I wasn't going to miss this chance.

"Yes," I said for the third time that night. "Yes. I'll go with you. I'll tell you the truth." I heard myself giggle. A sound I was sure I'd never made before. "Yes."

"Yes!" Max said, picking me up and spinning me around. "It's gonna be crazy for a couple of days, we have to go home and get ready, tell everyone, I can't even think straight. But here—" He handed me his phone again and I put in my number. I was the one shaking now. "I'll call you tomorrow. We're flying out of Seattle so we'll be back on Tuesday and you'll meet us at the airport and we'll . . . we'll go. Okay? Really?"

"Really," I said, saving myself as a contact, feeling like there was a little sun shining out of my chest, warming my whole body. "Really."

"Okay," Max said. "Oh my god. Okay. Here we go."

Together, we walked into the house. Max shouted the news. Everyone lost it. Within the hour, they were gone, back to Ridley Falls to pack for the rest of their lives. And I was going with them. Me. Sammy Espinoza. Off on tour with America's next great rock band . . .

* * *

I don't think it really sank in that he wasn't going to call until Tuesday night.

Willa had been happy for me, and relieved that she could go back home without disappointing me. We packed together, found subletters for our room, planned our phone call schedule for as long as I was in Chicago.

When the phone didn't ring the next day, I didn't worry too much. It was a wild time for Max, he had told me it would be busy. He would call the next day, for sure, and we'd plan everything out. I knew it.

And then the weekend passed without a word. Willa's eyes turned pitying every time I mentioned Max, so I stopped. But I left everything packed. On Monday I literally stared at my phone all day.

Had I entered my number wrong? Had he been trying to get ahold of me this whole time?

But I hadn't entered it wrong. I knew I hadn't. I'd triple-checked it.

He just hadn't called.

On Tuesday, I still hoped that maybe a last-second whirlwind plan would fall into place. That Max would call all full of apologies, show up in a limo rented by the label. That it would all be a great story we could tell our grandchildren someday.

The story of how for a day or two, I'd really believed he wasn't coming.

Willa let the subletters down easy. She unpacked all of our stuff and promised to stay the rest of the summer. She'd be starting in September as an intern on a massive organic farm only twenty minutes from her parents' house.

I tried to be happy for her, but I was spiraling. I spent a week drifting around like a ghost, giving customers the wrong orders at the café, letting application deadlines for temp jobs at labels pass.

I asked myself over and over why this had happened. I mourned a fantasy that had never really been mine, and the boy who had taken it from me just days after he created it.

When Seven Shades of Monday's highly anticipated album dropped nine months later, I was no closer to achieving my dreams. I had promised myself I would never listen to it, but one of my co-workers put it on at the café, and in the next forty-nine minutes, my life was changed forever.

Max no longer played guitar. He was a true front man, more electric than ever. The lyrics were deeper, and the rhythm guitarist handled all the growling and screaming. They had taken my advice. All of it. And they were better for it.

I'd expected the album to break my heart all over again, but instead it gave me a renewed sense of purpose. A whole new path. I had been right. I had told the truth, and it had made a band I loved even better.

Maybe I could do it again.

That night, I decided to become a music writer. A few weeks later, I landed my job in the *Scavenger* mail room, and decided when I finally got to write my first article it would be under the pen name Verity. An homage to the boy that had made me believe I could tell the truth, and it would matter.

It was the beginning of everything. And I never saw Max Ryan again.

8.

Now, at twenty-nine, I'm standing in Max's tastefully
decorated living room. I'm aware that I've been quiet for too long.
Every single gear in my brain has seized up as I decide what the
hell I'm supposed to do next.

The commonsense answer is to stick to the plan. To tell this
man who I am, make him feel like a complete jerk, and use those
guilty feelings to leverage the review I came here to get.

There's just one problem. For the past eleven years, I've relied
on this wistful, romantic narrative that I crafted around Max's disappearance. One where his bandmates or some label suits talked
him out of bringing a girl on the road. One where it had been a
tough decision for him—one that still plucked at his heartstrings
when a review praised his deep, emotional lyrics, or he reached
his arms out to a sold-out crowd with nothing in the way.

I even imagined that sometimes, between highly publicized
dates with B-list actresses and recording sessions in wildly expensive studios, Max had looked out a rain-streaked tour bus window, and thought of me, and regretted it all.

It was the fantasy that had helped me move on back then, casting Max and myself as equals who had simply met at the wrong
time. Who had changed each other's stories for the better. My
honest feedback had helped Max and Seven Shades find their
most authentic sound. The confidence that came from that experience had started my career as Verity Page.

But the jarring idea that, in reality, I didn't even warrant a footnote in Max's memory? It's much more than just a thorn in my present-day plan to save my job. It threatens the very mythology I've built my life on. And in that moment, as his expression goes from expectant to puzzled, I know something about myself for sure. Even after all these years, I would rather be nobody to Max Ryan than some humiliated girl who clung to a fantasy alone for eleven years. Even if that means dooming my column.

Max is definitely nervous now, or he thinks I'm legit losing my marbles in his living room. Either way, I smile like it isn't costing me something precious and say: "I was actually just visiting some friends. I won't be around long. But it was nice meeting you." I hold up my wallet and turn toward the door.

"You didn't," he says, doing a kind of half-jog around me before I get to the door.

"Excuse me?"

"You didn't meet me. Not yet anyway." The smile is back, and so are the stupid butterflies. He sticks out his hand for me to shake. "I'm Max."

"Sammy," I say, and when his palm meets mine, our fingers clasping, I'm suddenly back at The Crocodile on that July night. He's sliding into the booth beside me. My life is about to change.

"Well, at least tell me you got to see the falls," he says, gaze still holding mine.

"The what?"

"The falls—you know, they're in the town name."

I feel ridiculous admitting it, but I actually had no idea Ridley Falls was named for actual waterfalls. Maeve and Larry aren't really the hiking type, and I was too young to do much exploring on my own back then.

"Right," I say, suddenly desperate to get out of here. To process the deeply buried skeletons that have been disturbed today. "Maybe next time."

I make for the door again, and this time he lets me pass. My hand is on the doorknob before I hesitate. Or maybe Teen Sammy does. Somehow, we both know that walking out this door will be like leaving a no-reentry venue. We'll never get back inside.

"So . . . these falls," I say without even deciding to. "Are they worth naming a whole town after?"

He's beside me again in a heartbeat, his smile crooked, his hair falling into his eyes. "Can I take your change in tone to mean you might be willing to find out firsthand?"

I know I should say no. Take what's left of my dignity and go home before this gets any worse. But beneath the incorrigible butterflies, a new plan is just beginning its instrumental intro. A plan where I go hiking with Max Ryan, and we get to talking about our jobs, and he's so charmed by me that I end up with the review I need *minus* the admission that he once shattered my barely formed heart.

If it goes badly, I justify, I can let it go knowing I did everything I could.

It's for these reasons (and these reasons *only,* I insist to Teen Sammy) that I agree to meet Max at the Ridley Falls trailhead tomorrow at 9 A.M.

Instead of going straight back to Willa and Brook's, I make a pit stop downtown.

It's been long enough that I have to google the exact address of Willa's mom's shop, but when I pull up out front, Mystical Moments Emporium looks just like I remember it.

This place, with its faint patchouli smell and glittering fantasy figurines, seemed so magical to me as a kid. Willa was good-naturedly skeptical about her mom's crystals and tarot cards and candles even back then, but I always secretly loved it here. Almost as much as I loved the magical woman who's now throwing open its doors to me.

"Oh, honey," Maeve Cross says, tears already glittering in her eyes. "You came home."

"Sorry it took me so long."

She ushers me inside, letting the door close behind us and folding me into a hug that lasts a long time. One that feels like she's reading something in my bones—which, I remind myself, she actually might be.

When we pull apart to examine each other, I see the extra lines and the grays that mean it's been too long. Avoiding this place always felt like a law of nature. Something intrinsic to my genetic makeup. But being here, I realize how much of that was just Dina Rae making her problems mine.

Maeve is probably in her early sixties now. She was Dina Rae's teenage babysitter when she was in middle school, so she was a slightly more appropriate age to become a mother. She has the stern yet kindly face of a woman who has given punishments and bandaged knees. Someone who's been both the soul of a family and the authority figure who keeps it honest.

I've always felt a little guilty for how much I adore her. Especially since she and my mom had their falling out. Dina Rae would never talk about the reason for it, so all I know is that after she picked me up at the end of the school year we never visited again.

"You look beautiful," Maeve says now, lifting a lock of my hair and letting it fall. "But a little sad. Want to tell me about it?"

"Yes," I sniffle. There are so few people in my life who make me feel safe enough to fall apart.

"Come on back, I'll make tea."

Mystical Moments survives on the curiosity of tourists and the selection of glass pipes for sale in the front display case, but its real draw is the back room. A room that's only open to friends, family, and Maeve's trusted clients.

And me, I guess.

Tapestries cover the walls, a little round table sits in the middle with a smooth black mirror in the center. A weathered wooden bookshelf holds a few volumes, as well as about fifty decks of cards in boxes.

There's incense burning, and candles, but the smell isn't over-powering. Walking in here, I feel more relaxed than I have since I got off the bus. Or on it. Or maybe since way before that.

"Have a seat, sugar," she says, bustling over to her hot plate as I take the place in.

It's so comfortingly the same. I bask in it until Maeve takes her seat across from me at the table with two mugs of tea and a well-worn tarot deck.

"Tell me what's going on, hm?" she says, and I want to tell her *everything,* everything. I expected to. I open my mouth thinking it'll all just fall out. The cemetery, my dad and grandpa. Max then and Max now . . .

Instead, I'm too aware that my problems are much deeper now than the last time I sat across from Maeve. That I don't know how to articulate how I feel about the Espinozas, or tomorrow's plans with Max, or anything at all . . .

Maeve smiles sympathetically, though I'm still sitting here like someone pressed Pause on me mid-chorus. "Sometimes words aren't the thing, are they?" she says.

I shake my head, helpless. "It's just . . . a lot right now."

"That's why I grabbed these." She smiles, holding up the deck. "How about a little guidance? No talking required."

"That might work," I say, already anticipating Willa's teasing.

Maeve shuffles the cards methodically, then asks me to cut the deck in two. After that, she begins laying them out between us. I sip my tea, looking at the images even though they don't mean much to me. Cups, swords. A naked man and woman beside each other under a vibrant sun.

"Hm," she says when she's finished.

"What?" I ask, already flinching.

She doesn't answer immediately, just studies the cards in front of her like the secrets to the universe are written there. I'm sud-denly worried she's seeing more than I want her to. That maybe this was a mistake . . .

"You weren't kidding when you said it was a lot." She's X-raying me now, and I'd almost forgotten what an unnerving feeling it is. Maeve always knew when kids were being mean at school, or when I was missing my mom, or when I was feeling guilty for not missing her.

I'm not sure what to say, so I just wait. I picture Max as a card, and my grandparents, and Esme, and even Teen Sammy.

"What I'll tell you is that your issues aren't as separate as you think," Maeve says, looking at the cards now. "You came here as a response to what seems like several different problems, but they're all entangled. They're fed by the same source."

"So what do I do?" I ask, wondering if it can really be this easy. If Maeve will just tell me what to do and I'll get my interview and heal my broken heart and know exactly what to do about the grandmother I never knew and—

"Stay," Maeve says finally.

"Stay? Like, in this chair?"

"Whatever it means to you; although someone else is scheduled to sit in that chair in half an hour so probably not that." She cracks a smile.

"Stay," I repeat. "In Ridley Falls, I guess . . ."

"Wherever the cards are asking you to stay, or whatever emotion they want you to stay with, it won't always be easy," Maeve cautions. "You'll want to run. You'll even be able to justify it. But your higher self knows that all these seemingly separate parts have to be resolved together. You can't address one without the other, and if you run they'll only follow."

I picture the tarot-card versions of Max and Teen Sammy and Grandma Espinoza chasing me down Main Street and shudder.

"The good news is," Maeve says, smiling at me reassuringly. "You're in the exact right place to begin this work. All you need to do is be honest with yourself. And selfishly, I'm hoping you heed the guidance here and stick around awhile. We've missed you, and I know Willa needs you right now."

I barely resist the urge to scoff. Willa has never really needed me. At least not as much as I've always needed her.

"And what do I do about this one?" I ask to change the subject, pointing to the naked man and woman. *The Lovers,* it says at the bottom.

"I'm glad you asked," Maeve says with a smirk.

9.

I'm almost back to Willa and Brook's twenty minutes later, thinking about Maeve and her reading.

Stay, even if it's not easy. A simple enough instruction, but one that goes against my very nature. I learned picking up and starting over from the best, and it's always been my go-to when things got to be too much. Even the events of the last few hours have been plenty to send me running for the hills . . .

Beside me on the front seat of the car is a brown paper bag, folded at the top. Maeve let me have it on the house and told me not to open it until I was ready for its medicine.

"Maybe it's a time travel potion," I mutter into the uncharacteristic silence. I didn't even put on an album for the drive—which is usually the first sign I'm unraveling a little. Even my first post-Juniper days had a soundtrack. A very depressing one, but still.

As the little yellow house comes into view, I remind myself Maeve's reading was just advice. If things go well tomorrow, it's what I was planning to do anyway. If they go badly, I only promised Willa eight more days . . .

"Okay, tell me again," Brook is saying, her eyes nearly bugged out of their sockets, her platinum boy-band hair pushed back off her face for once, like she doesn't want to miss a single moment. "He *doesn't remember who you are.* You're devastated. Ready to leave empty-handed, and then . . ."

"And then he asks me to go hiking." I'm trying to be as matter-of-fact as I can. To not alert my captive audience to the pesky winged insects I have not quite exorcised from my stomach region.

"*Hiking*," Brook repeats, cackling. "Do you even *know* what twenty of my closest friends from college would pay to be in your shoes right now?"

"Honestly, hitting them up for rent money might be a better plan than the one I came here with." I'm being outwardly self-deprecating, but her enthusiasm is a little contagious. What felt like a last-ditch, doomed-to-fail consolation plan is now starting to feel almost . . . possible.

"Okay, but what if he googles you?" Brook asks, her eyes shining. "I mean, he could find all your reviews and that would totally blow your cover."

"I've only ever published under Verity Page," I say, almost surprised to have such a commonsense contingency in place. "And Esme is intense about privacy after a musician stalked one of her writers, so there's no way to trace the Samantha Espinoza of my driver's license to my online persona."

"Smart," Brook says, giving me finger guns.

"So, what's in the bag?" asks Willa. Though she reacted in the right places during the story, she's been a little quiet since. I know she's worried about this. The date-like feel of my plans with Max. The potential for further heartbreak. Usually I'd ask her about it, but the shimmering soap bubble of hope in my chest feels so fragile I actually prefer Brook's unqualified cheerleading at this moment.

There'll be time, I tell myself as I pick up the bag.

"I went into Mystical Moments on the way back, to see your mom," I say.

"I'm sure she was very helpful," Willa says with an affectionate eye roll. "Let me guess, the cards gave you some advice that sounds suspiciously like what she would have told you to do anyway?"

I give Willa my best "play nice" expression, and move on at Brook's insistence. "Maeve says my issues are all interconnected, and I'm in the right place to heal from them," I say. "That even if it feels hard, I should stay."

Willa's laugh says I've just proved her right. "And the last one was somehow an invitation to Sunday dinner. The supernatural is truly a mystery."

I laugh along, feeling some of the burden of Maeve's reading lightening now that I'm back on solid ground. "There was a card with naked people on it that she didn't elaborate on," I continue, getting into the spirit of things. "She said whatever message it had would be solved by this."

Brook leans forward eagerly to examine the contents of the bag, but Willa's eyes are still steady on my face in a manner not at all unlike her mom's—for all their supposed differences.

"A Ritual for Attracting Abundance in Matters of the Heart," Brook is now reading aloud from a handwritten instruction sheet. She's surrounded by the other contents of the bag. Shiny pink stones, a bottle of what looks like oil with leaves floating in it, a baggie of rose petals and lavender, and a tall pink candle.

"Arrange the crystals in a circle, preferably outside, and sit in the center," Brook reads aloud. "Seems pretty straightforward so far."

Willa is holding one of the crystals now, examining it. Brook's enthusiasm must be infectious because she's smiling, that worried line disappearing from between her brows.

"Anoint yourself and the candle with the attraction oil, then light it and close your eyes." Brook sets the paper down, her blue eyes sparkling.

"I don't think we should be messing around with witchcraft as powerful as my mother's," Willa says wryly. "We don't want all the eligible bachelors and bachelorettes of Ridley Falls knocking down our door."

"Willa, please," Brook says, brandishing the instruction sheet. "It says right here on the top it's not *just* for romantic or sexual love. It can be for self-love, creative drive. Um . . . establishing a more loving connection with pets?" She chokes a little. "We have to do this, you guys, come on."

From the look on Willa's face, it's clear to me that she wants to put the shenanigans aside. But something of the reading is still lingering. My love life, connected to my career, to my relationship with my mom, and my dad's family. If they all need to be healed together, is this the worst place to start?

"Why not?" I say, trying not to let on how much I want it to be real. "There's nowhere to go but up at this point."

Ten minutes later, I'm sitting on a paving stone in Willa's garden as Brook arranges candles and crystals and dried rose petals around me. I'm trying to picture the source Maeve mentioned. Like a tree, but every branch is one of my personal catastrophes.

"Come on, Willa!" Brook is saying as her wife stands to the side, observing. "Loosen up a little!"

"One of us has to stay tethered to the earthly plane," she deadpans, but she can't resist Brook, so she disappears into a clump of flowering bushes and returns with an armful of pink begonias, placing them on the ground between the crystals.

Soon, we're all giggling. Stars begin to appear one by one in the darkening sky. The clouds have taken a break today. The extra vitamin D must have made us all loopy.

"Anointing time!" Brook calls, holding out the bottle of oil.

I hold out my arms imperiously and let them dab the oil on my wrists, on the sides of my neck.

"Hey, this is the rose oil I made!" Willa exclaims. "I didn't say she could use this for *love spell* kits." Still, she puts some on her pulse points.

"Stop, you're already *too* irresistible," Brook says, snatching the bottle away and putting some on herself, too.

I groan. "GET A ROOM!"

"We used to have two," Brook purrs, still looking at Willa with lidded eyes.

Willa swats her away playfully, the moment dissipating, but my heart is aching again. Juniper and I never had this. We never would have. But is it too much to hope that someday I'll have it with someone?

Is that what this ritual can give me? An open line to the kind of love I've secretly been hoping for beneath my feigned indifference? And what will it look like when it arrives?

"What's next?" Willa asks when we're all greased with rose oil. I'm totally surrounded by pink blossoms and crystals. A tiny moth is flying dangerously close to the candle's flame.

"The most important part of all," Brook replies. "Close your eyes, Sammy."

I do as I'm told. I try to calm my jangling nerves and return to the image of the tree. Willing it to be healthy enough to nourish all the branches that are currently drooping under the weight of my issues.

I see my dad's grave. My grandfather beside him.

Max's cozy house. His hand, electric in mine.

The past I've worked so hard to keep buried returning for a final encore.

"Okay, it says to take a moment to fully visualize your desired outcome," Brook reads out, "with special attention paid to sensory details. What does it feel like, what does it smell like, taste like . . ."

Visualization has never been my strong suit, but I'm surprised by how quickly an imagined future makes itself clear. In it, I'm standing in a recording studio, a young band playing their hearts out on the other side of the glass. I lean down to whisper something to the engineer, satisfied with the progress they've made.

Behind me, the door to the studio opens and a fuzzy figure walks in. They walk up close to me, reaching out for my hand, kissing me on the temple in a casual way that only happens when you're in love.

I'm proud of you, says a voice I can't quite make out. I'm almost afraid to look at their face. To put a face to the warmth I feel in my chest when they're near me.

The door opens again, and more people file in. Willa and Brook, Maeve and Larry. My mom. An old woman I somehow know is Paloma Espinoza.

Look up, they tell me, and with their support I finally can. I turn, angling my head up, taking in the mystery face in full.

It's Max. Not the cocky twenty-year-old I fell for when I didn't know better, but the man I saw today. Somehow more handsome for time's effect on his face. There's genuine affection in his eyes as he looks down at me. The feeling is indescribable.

I push up onto my tiptoes. His lips move closer to mine.

In the split second before they meet, I force my eyes open, returning to the garden.

"Well—?" Brook begins, but I stand up before she can finish the question. Stones and flower petals go flying. The candle in its glass wobbles alarmingly.

"That's enough witchcraft for one day." I must look like I mean it, too, because no one asks any more questions.

I wake up at 4:30 A.M. from a dream even more unnerving than my visualization.

There are still a few hours until I'm supposed to meet Max at the Ridley Falls trailhead, but there's no way I'm getting any more sleep. Not with my jangling nerves, and the scent of rose oil still on my skin, reminding me of all the things I didn't even know I wanted.

I take out my phone, thinking of my mom and her last text. L-O-V-E. Say YES to LIFE. We haven't spoken since our argument about my grandfather last week. But what I said to Willa is true. This is just the way we relate to each other. Push and pull. A roller coaster.

I rarely ask Dina Rae for advice, but she always takes far more of an interest in me when I'm pursuing a man. Maybe reaching out about Max will work as an olive branch.

Before I can overthink it too much, I press her contact, holding the phone up to my ear. Maybe she'll even remember Max from my early Seattle days. The reason I started writing reviews . . .

The call goes straight to voicemail after two rings. "You've reached Dina Rae!" she says in a voice that makes it clear this number is mostly used for screening potential dates. "Please leave your name, phone number, height, and net worth at the tone."

It's supposed to be a joke—a nod to her perpetual falling in and out of love. So what if I think it's a little ridiculous. Aren't we supposed to cringe at our parents?

"Hey, Mom," I say. "It's me. Just wondered if you had a minute for some boy talk. Call me back when you're on dry land."

I wait a few minutes just in case she calls right back, but the phone stays quiet.

I've showered off most of the rose scent and tried on every one of my outfits three times. I'm looking for anything remotely appropriate for *hiking,* a thing I haven't done since my mom dated an outdoorsy guy when I was thirteen.

Brook and Willa are up. The former is cooking breakfast while the latter sorts through a basket of carrots freshly pulled up from the garden.

"Good morning, sunshine," Willa says with a beatific smile. "How'd you sleep?"

"Don't ask," I grumble. "Can you hike in Doc Martens?"

Brook slides me a cup of coffee across the counter. "No," she says. "And also this is decaf. Can't have you overcaffeinated and jittery for your *daaaate.*" She pantomimes a middle school make-out session with her spatula. I throw a carrot at her—dirt still clinging to it.

She laughs and tosses it back into the basket, but the wrinkle is back between Willa's eyebrows.

"I know it's all fun and games," she says carefully. "But let's not get too carried away with the date stuff. Sammy is going out for a reason, and it's not to start up some second-chance romance with a degenerate who didn't even remember her name."

This speech is ostensibly intended to rein Brook in, but I can't help but feeling like the words are actually a dig at me.

"Don't worry," I say. "My priorities are ironclad. No amount of ritual or rose-scented oil is gonna change that."

"Good," she says, turning back to the carrots. "You can borrow my hiking boots. They're by the door. And Sammy?"

I glance at her on my way to retrieve the boots.

"You can do a lot better than Max Ryan."

Brook is laughing again before I can fully process the way these words make me feel. She's saying something about how the *Shadies* would respond to a proclamation like that on the fan forum—even though she totally agrees with Willa, of course—but my attention is divided.

"I'm gonna head out a little early," I say. "Get the lay of the land. Thanks for the boots."

"Sure," Willa says, and I'm hoping it's just my pre-hike, pre-Max jitters that lead me to wonder if something is off between us.

10.

The least rock and roll thing about me is my compulsive need to arrive to social engagements twenty minutes early. I like to get the lay of the land, pick a table, have the high ground when everyone else arrives.

My therapist has her own theories about this—mostly stemming from her Willa-esque failure to understand my relationship with my mother—but old habits die hard. Which is why I pull into the dirt parking lot of the Ridley Falls trailhead at exactly eight forty.

The lot is empty, thankfully, and I kill the engine along with the very loud black metal I used to torture Willa's ancient speakers on the way here.

My music nerd card would probably get revoked for saying so, but I don't really have a favorite genre. I'm always looking for pure emotion. Music that—regardless of genre or era or even skill level—makes my whole body respond.

Today it was black metal. Tomorrow, it might be Britney Spears. It all depends on the circumstances. The feeling.

I step out into the parking lot in Willa's slightly-too-large boots. It rained last night, of course, but the sky is mostly clear this morning. I try to run through the New Plan again before Max arrives—a plan that's long on the career talk and short on the butterflies—but I'm distracted by the quiet, which feels almost smothering after the volume of my music. The trees moving slightly in the morning breeze. The individual droplets of water clinging to their needles.

Once I get used to it, I notice that the forest has its own kind of rhythm. Nothing compared to the damage guitar, bass, and drums can do, of course. But evocative in its own way.

When Max arrives—five minutes early, I might add—I'm surprised at how much time has passed. Maybe being alone with your thoughts isn't as hard when you're not being overwhelmed by everyone else's.

I lean against my car, scoping him out as he swings a leg over his motorcycle, stashing his helmet in a saddlebag. He's wearing some dark gray outdoorsy-looking pants, a long-sleeved black T-shirt, one of those little hiking day-packs, and boots that clearly fit a lot better than mine.

Annoyingly, he's even better looking than the fantasy version of him my mind conjured last night. His hair is pushed back today, a few relaxed curls escaping. His stubble defines his jawline and dark brows make the green in his eyes pop in a way I'm sure a hundred fans have called *mesmerizing* on those forums Brook is so obsessed with.

Cool it, I warn Teen Sammy, who's already swooning again. *This isn't a date.*

"Morning!" Max calls. He's holding two travel thermoses, I notice as he makes his way over to me. "I honestly wasn't sure you'd show up."

I meet him halfway across the parking lot, taking the matte-green thermos he hands me. It's one of those fancy ones from REI, with a carabiner attached. It's warm in my chilly hands.

"My location is on, and people know where I am," I warn, half-jokingly. "Plus I googled you to check for past misdeeds."

He winces a little. "Wow, you googled me and you're still here. I guess that's a good sign, right?"

I smirk. "How do you know I don't have a thing for wristbands and guyliner?"

Max rolls his eyes. "It was a cultural moment, okay?" he teases. "One that is thankfully over now."

"So the decision to leave my hot-pink studded belt at home was a good one. Noted."

I twist the top on the travel mug to hide my genuine grin. This would be a lot easier if he didn't come across so . . . normal. Nice. Charming.

"So, this better be some kind of potion that makes you good at hiking, because I haven't exactly been a regular in the great out-doors."

"It's tea," Max says as I sniff it.

Jasmine, if I'm not mistaken. With honey. Kind of an adorable choice. I'm usually a rocket fuel kind of girl, but the tea is really good. Better than I'm willing to admit. Kind of like the whole vibe of this totally-not-date . . .

"Thanks," I say. "For the tea."

"You're welcome."

There's a beat of silence that might have turned uncomfortable, except he's definitely using it to covertly check me out. Suddenly I don't mind that the only remotely hiking-appropriate attire I packed are leggings that make my ass look great.

Not part of the plan, I chastise myself. But I let him look.

"Um," he says after a beat too long, his expression a little sheep-ish. "Should we get going?"

"Sure."

I let him lead the way past the trail marker. Two massive pon-derosas seem to welcome us onto the well-worn path into the forest, just wide enough for a couple people who don't mind a little elbow bumping.

We walk in companionable silence for the first few minutes, settling into a rhythm. The forest feels so alive in here, ferns sprouting up between the massive trees, moss dripping from everything. After the rain the air feels clean, and I think it might be actively healing my lungs after years of smoky clubs.

"So, can I address the obvious?" I ask after a few minutes of nature gawking.

"Be my guest."

"What's a former rock sensation doing in the literal middle of nowhere?"

He chuckles a little. "*Sensation,* wow. Why does that sound like an insult coming from you?"

I smirk, but I don't let him change the subject.

"Um," he says, lifting a low branch and letting me pass under it. "The simple answer is I grew up here. My parents are gone now, split up and both remarried. My little sister is in college down in Oregon. But Ridley Falls just . . . feels like home."

"And the complicated answer?" I ask, glancing his way, feeling my stomach swoop at the sight of his profile.

"I usually save the complicated stuff until at least the second-mile marker," he smiles at me and I sip my tea, resolving to keep my eyes on the trail from now on.

"Second-mile marker, huh?" I ask when my cheeks have cooled. "How far away are these falls, anyway?"

"A mile and a half," Max answers.

I laugh, a genuine sound that surprises even me.

"So what about you?" he asks. "What brings a Seattleite to Ridley Falls if it's not the great outdoors?"

I step over a branch laying across the trail, feeling my feet slide a little in Willa's boots and wishing I'd worn an extra pair of socks. "The simple answer is that my parents are from here," I say, aware of how many potential landmines this conversation has just sprouted. "My mom left when she got pregnant with me, and we moved around the state a lot, but this place always had a pull for me."

"And the complicated answer?" Max asks, holding a sagging branch to one side to let me pass.

"I'll save mine for that second-mile marker, too."

He smiles again. Keeping my eyes on the trail doesn't block it from my peripheral vision, and unfortunately it's just as butterfly-worthy. "Guess I sort of set myself up for that one."

"Guess you did."

"Okay, so you have a head start because of your Google search," Max says as we stroll along the path at a leisurely pace. "What do you do?"

I know this is the perfect moment to make my confession. That I'm a journalist and I've heard of his new album and I'd love the chance to review it early. But at the last second I chicken out. I need more time to gain his trust, I reason. I'll know when it feels right.

"Any and all information about me will be communicated on a need-to-know basis." I hope I'm coming across cute and not shady.

He quirks an eyebrow, but doesn't push.

"Look, my job is kind of a disaster right now and I'd rather talk about literally anything else if that's okay," I say, setting myself up. He'll feel sorry for me, and then later when I confess he's the one person who can help it'll trigger some intrinsic white knight complex and boom. Problem solved.

"Totally okay," he says. "I like a girl who doesn't define herself by her job, anyway."

I almost laugh at the irony, but I decide not to. That, too, can be saved for later.

The incline of the path increases then, and I barely have enough lung capacity to breathe, let alone speak. Between the ill-fitting boots and the fact that this is my first hike in at least a decade (the last one was to impress a cute musician, too) I'm regretting all my life choices within ten minutes.

The trees press in close, a tunnel of greenery that only magnifies my misery by adding claustrophobia to the mix.

"Do you torture all your victims like this?" I gasp when the trail finally levels. "Or is this a punishment because you didn't get to keep my wallet?"

Max—who is annoyingly sweat-free and doesn't even seem winded—hands me a water bottle, which I exchange for the empty thermos. "Don't worry, it'll be worth it."

"I find that very hard to belie—"

I'm interrupted by the dense greenery parting, the claustrophobic tree tunnel opening up to what is truly one of the most spectacular views I've ever seen. The Ridley Falls are at least a hundred feet high, careening joyfully down a maze of mossy boulders into a pool below.

The torturous climb has left us about halfway between the peak and the pool. A little wooden bridge stretches across for maximum visibility. There's no one else here, which only adds to the magic of it all.

"You were saying?" Max inquires as he gestures for me to step onto the bridge first.

After the last ten minutes of climbing, the cool mist feels blissfully good on my face. I stop in the middle to look down at the pool below, where the morning sunlight is making rainbows of the droplets.

Max joins me on the bridge, which is narrow enough that I can feel him just behind me. The solid warmth of his body.

For a long moment, we're silent, and I sort of understand why people go to nature together. There's something about taking in this miracle, knowing he's seeing it too, that makes me feel close to him.

"So," I say to break the spell. "Second-mile marker or not, I think I've earned the complicated answer. Don't you?"

There's this interviewer's trick I learned my first year working for Esme. People are much more apt to be confessional when you're both looking the same direction. It takes away the pressure that a face-to-face conversation can create.

"I suppose that's fair," Max says to the waterfall, still leaning on the railing behind me.

He's quiet for a long minute, and I let it stretch. Rookie journalists will sometimes feel the pressure of a silence. Fill it with chatter and softball yes or no questions. But in my experience, patience is usually rewarded. Today is no exception.

"When the first Seven Shades album dropped, that was the best time of my whole career." He's so close I can almost feel the words rumbling in his chest. "There was all this possibility, all this magic building, but no one knew us yet. It was like this awesome secret we had."

My eyes are trained on the water as I wait for more. I tell myself my interest is strictly professional, but in this moment my life in Seattle, at *Scavenger,* feels troublingly far away.

"The record took off after that, and I'm grateful, don't get me wrong. But everything changed." Max is quiet for a minute. "People knew all the lyrics to my songs. They decided I was like them, or I wasn't. They felt like I belonged to them. Like I owed them something. Writing the second record was harder because I was so afraid to let them down. I was so afraid I wasn't going to live up to whatever they wanted from me."

His words don't sound interview-practiced or first-date-with-a-stranger smooth. He sounds confessional. Vulnerable.

Just the way you want a source *to sound,* I remind myself with a little effort.

"After it all ended, I felt so burdened by those thousands of expectations. I knew I had let everyone down by leaving, and I couldn't really face that. So I came back here."

His tone lightens then. There's relief in it.

"Here it's different. No one expects me to narrate their life, or to save it. To introduce them to my manager or get them an early copy of something new. Some of them remember me from fourth grade, but no one is going to get angry if I change, or grow."

It's this part that reminds me who I am. What I do. Follow-up questions spring to my lips—about his complicated feelings surrounding fame. Whether it was his difficulty writing and not some rumored diva desire to go solo that catalyzed the end of the band . . .

But Max hasn't even granted me the interview yet—and this really throws a wrench in my plan to ask. How can I expect him to react positively when he's just told me his biggest fear is finding out someone has an unrealistic view of him, or wants something from him?

"That sounds really complicated," I tell the waterfall, trying to regroup. "I'm glad you found somewhere to heal." I try to remind myself that this jerk once offered me the world and yanked it away, devastating me in the process. But this Max seems so unlike that Max that it's hard to even connect the two.

The only thing that's similar is how easy he is to talk to.

"My dad died before I was born," I say before I even realize what I'm doing. My own trick is working on me. I'm lured by the fact that I'm speaking to the falls and not the grown-up version of the boy who broke my heart a decade ago.

I was right. It's much easier to talk this way. Too easy.

"He's from here," I continue. "There's literally a football field named after him. My grandparents abandoned my mom and me when she was a pregnant sixteen-year-old, so I've never met them."

Max doesn't say anything, but I can feel him move subtly closer to me. Goosebumps erupt along my arms that have nothing to do with the chilly mist coming off the waterfall.

"I didn't even think I wanted to meet them, but I'm here, right? So part of me must have been looking for some kind of confrontation. Or closure. Or something."

My brain is screaming at me to stop. That I came here to *extract* information, not volunteer it. But the weight of saying all this out loud to someone who doesn't already have an opinion about my life is somehow liberating. I feel lighter already, so I keep going.

"Last week, my mom told me my grandfather died. A year ago. I think it was some weird attempt on her part to get me not to come back here, but I had no idea he was gone. So, I guess that made me realize you don't always have all the time in the world to reach out. And that maybe I should try to know my grandma before it's too late."

I take a deep breath, blowing it out noisily.

"But now that I'm here it also feels impossibly scary to try to know someone who didn't want to know me. So maybe I should just leave. But also maybe I should stay."

"Stay," Max says, stepping forward to join me at the front rail. His arm brushes mine and he looks down at me, tiny droplets clinging to his eyelashes. "I think you should stay."

I hate to admit it to myself, but *stay* sounds a lot different coming from Max Ryan than it did in the back room of Mystical Moments . . .

"I'm just saying, I wouldn't mind having you around a little longer," Max continues. "And honestly, running from things doesn't fix anything. Take it from me."

Suddenly, the shimmering bubble that's been holding us pops, reality rushing in. Max doesn't know, of course, that *I'm* one of the things he ran from. But somehow that only makes it worse.

He's obviously still in the moment. The one where we're standing too close and confessing too much. But from my point of view, this forest suddenly isn't big enough for both of us.

"We should probably get going," I say, feeling a little vindicated when his face falls.

"Sure," he says, "let me—"

He reaches out to take my arm, and I pull away instinctively. My too-big boots slip on the slick wet wood and I know immediately I'm going down. Not a cute stumble, but a full-blown fall. What I don't expect is for my ankle to twist dramatically under me.

"Shit, Sammy, are you okay?"

Max is kneeling beside me, annoyingly steady on his own feet.

"I'm fine," I say, though I know that's probably not the case. I've sprained my ankle before, and this doesn't feel quite as bad. But I know for a fact I'm not one-and-a-half-miles-down-a-steep-incline fine.

I struggle to my feet anyway, gritting my teeth against the searing pain.

"Let me help you," Max says, and he doesn't wait for an answer, just slides his leanly muscled arm under both of mine and supports my weight as I step gingerly off the bridge.

I try to focus on the pain instead of how good it feels to have his arm around me. How steady he feels, and how capable.

Once I'm settled on a large rock, I lean down to assess the damage. My ankle isn't too swollen, which is good, but it still screams when I put weight on it. I need ice, and elevation, and ideally a helicopter to return me to my car with my dignity intact.

Max hovers awkwardly on the periphery as I try to control my mental tempest. This is a sign from the universe, I tell myself. A sign that getting carried away by Max's chill, charming vibe can lead to nothing but disaster.

"I should be okay in a few minutes," I say, even though we both know that's not true.

"I have a first aid kit," Max says, his eyes a little wary. He's clearly still confused by the atmosphere change on the bridge, and I can't blame him. Not for that, anyway.

"Does it have a bionic ankle and a surgery robot in it?" I ask.

He chuckles, that low, rumbly laugh. "No, but it does have an Ace bandage I think."

Max is rummaging in his backpack before I can decline, and I know I don't really have the option anyway. Willa's truck might as well be a million miles from here in my condition, and there's no cell service in the trees. I tell myself being bandaged by Max Ryan is better than being carried down a literal mountain in his arms.

But that's before I've been bandaged by Max Ryan.

He sits on the rock beside mine, lifting my leg and resting my bare foot in his lap. He winds the weird, rubbery wrap around me so gently that it doesn't even hurt—but once he secures it, I know it's strong enough to support my ankle down the slope.

I reach for the anger I felt on the bridge, but it seems to have been momentarily neutralized by this side of him. Not to mention the euphoria that's flooded me at the sudden reduction in pain the compression brings.

"How's that?" he asks.

"Better," I admit. "Thank you."

"Think you're okay to walk?"

"Only one way to find out."

I let him help me back into my boot—loose enough to accommodate the bandage if I don't lace it. I get up then, testing my weight gingerly and finding that the pressure helps. We take one last look at the falls before heading back into the tree tunnel and down the slope.

"Listen," he says when we're about halfway down. I haven't missed the way he stays close, hands at the ready in case I slip again. "I'm sorry if I overstepped back there. Not sure if you've noticed but I'm pretty out of practice at this kind of thing."

"No," I say. "It's understandable. I laid a lot on you. Has anyone ever told you you're almost irritatingly easy to talk to?"

I'm hoping he'll say I'm easy to talk to, too. Give me an opening to explain that getting people to open up is my job, and wouldn't you know it I'd love to interview him about his new album. But instead he says something much less useful and much more endearing:

"It's okay. It felt nice to be confided in."

I stumble just a little on a protruding root. He catches me by the elbow, steadying me.

We're at the bottom of the slope now, barely ten minutes from the car even at my hobbling pace. I know it's time to confess. Tell him who I am and why I'm here. Let the chips fall where they may.

Best-case scenario, I get my interview. Worst-case, I confirm all his worst fears about humanity and we're even.

"So, listen," he says as the trailhead comes into view. Beating me to the punch. "I know your status here is uncertain for totally legitimate reasons, but if you *do* decide to stay . . . I'd really like to see you again."

I sneak a sideways glance, surprised to find Max's face is flushed along his cheekbones.

"Why?" I ask, interviewer instincts kicking in.

"Honestly, I know I should say something smooth here, but the truth is I just . . . like talking to you. I'd like to do it some more."

It's not at all the answer most of the musicians I've dated would have given. It feels earnest, and it makes me feel guilty and excited all at once.

"What if you find out something you don't like?" I ask.

"That's all part of the fun, right?"

"Like gambling."

"Yeah, it's great until you lose your house."

I laugh again, almost without meaning to. I expected him to have grown up into some smug jerk. The kind of guy that delighted in the adoration of millions of fans. Who felt entitled to it.

I'll see him one more time, I tell myself. *Once more, and I'll come clean, no matter what happens.*

He waits while I ease myself into the front seat of the truck. I start it, forgetting there's music playing and scramble for the volume knob before my pre-hike metal can scare away all the birds.

"Sorry," I say when quiet has been restored. "Forgot that was on."

Max is looking at me in amusement and wonder. "Suddenly realizing there are *so* many topics we didn't get to today."

"Well, if I decide to stick around you'll be the first to know. Can't wait to be grilled about *how* a *female* can *possibly* withstand *blast beats* with her *delicate sensibilities.*"

I expect Max to laugh, or to be defensive, but instead he just looks at me for a long minute.

"You've met a lot of jerks, huh?"

I fake shudder. "You have no idea."

There are clouds rolling in, darkening the little dirt lot. I hand Max my phone, telling myself I'm just buying time. That I need to tell him the truth at just the right moment to have any hope of getting my review. He puts his phone number in, then goes to hand me his.

I don't take it. "I'll text you." If this is going to work, it has to be on my terms. No more surprises.

"Promise?" he asks.

"Sure," I say, just as the first raindrops hit the windshield.

"I really hope you do," he says. "I probably shouldn't admit that, but it's true."

"Bye, Max."

"Bye, Sammy."

I pull out of the parking lot first. I'm pretty sure a second dose of Max Ryan on a motorcycle in a rainstorm is more than my already wobbling resolve can withstand.

11.

Back at Willa and Brook's, the driveway is empty, the house quiet. On the counter, pinned down by a bowl of fresh fruit, is a note on Willa's botanical stationery:

> *Food and wine pairing class tonight,*
> *we got a room in Olympia! Be back tomorrow morning.*
> *Don't do anything I wouldn't do. XO, Will.*

I'm sure they mentioned this last night, or this morning, but I've been understandably distracted so the alone time comes as a welcome surprise. As much as I love my friends, I have a lot to process. I'd rather not have Brook's cheerleading or Willa's well-meaning concern overshadowing my own feelings about what's happening to me.

Just as soon as I figure out what *is* happening to me.

Whenever things are feeling out of control, I've always found solace in being excellent at my job. Ordering my perspective through neat columns of words on a page. A one-sided conversation. No surprises.

To that end, I take out my laptop and settle down across from Willa's usual FaceTime spot at the table. The view is familiar after countless Sundays of seeing it through my phone screen, but it's better in person. The willow tree in the front yard. The sun slanting through the windows. Perfect.

The blank page is waiting for me. A chance to say anything I want. My plan is to write a little background about Max. To look at all this as a journalist instead of as a girl who just had an above-average date.

But ten minutes later, the page is still blank. The cursor blinks accusingly as I utterly fail to come up with one useful sentence about Max Ryan. All I can think about is how green his eyes looked in the trees. The gentle way he bandaged my throbbing ankle. The way I felt when he asked to see me again . . .

It's a cliché for a reason, writers hating the beginning, but I always loved it. I tell myself it's because I've never written about an unwilling subject. That the words will flow easier once I have permission. Have an album to listen to and a definite end goal.

For now, I close the computer, change into my sweatpants and a hoodie, and get down to my second-favorite thinking pastime: cleaning the house to very loud music. I'll be a little slower than normal on account of the tweaked ankle, but I've got nothing but time.

First order of business is to find a playlist. My cleaning go-to is usually pop diva ballads, but they're too sappy for this kind of thinking. I need to *avoid* nostalgia, not lean into it.

But just as I'm looking for the least sappy music I can find, I stumble upon something. A playlist so far down the list I haven't laid eyes on it in years. Haven't listened to it in even longer. The name is a holdover from an old iPod classic I got as a high school graduation gift, transferred from phone to phone:

Seattle Sammy's Summer Faves

It's a playlist I made that first summer in the city. When Willa and I lived in the weird little room with the root beer shag carpet. The summer everything changed.

Most of the songs are by punk and post-hardcore bands I saw live in clubs, X's on my hands in Sharpie, coming apart at the seams in the sweaty crowds while I thrashed until my neck was sore. Grinning at my flushed face in graffitied bathrooms, thinking this was it. The best life had to offer. I painstakingly transferred every song from merch table CDs to Willa's laptop, then onto my iPod, which went absolutely everywhere with me.

The music in my headphones only turned off when the band started up.

I can almost see Seattle as it looked then, from the train window as I went from label to label with my résumé printed in blood-red ink. Dreaming.

I know reminiscing about that time in my life will not be helpful in my current predicament. But there's no one here to judge me, so I push Play before I can think better of it.

Before the vocals even kick in, I'm awash in nostalgia so powerful I can feel all of Adult Sammy's hang-ups shrinking in size.

I should turn the playlist off.

But I don't.

By early evening, I've made my way through it almost twice. The house's baseboards are gleaming. Every picture frame, rock, vase, and the shelves they rest on are dusted to sparkling. The shelves and drawers of the refrigerator have been removed and disinfected, the contents put back in exactly the same places I took them from—I'm not out of it enough to mess with Brook's organization, not even in this emotional state.

The pantry and cupboards have been emptied and dusted and refilled. The shower grout is as good as new. There are no cobwebs, even in the highest corners of the vaulted ceilings.

I am very pleased with myself—though my ankle is definitely hurting again. I feel I've thoroughly earned it when I pour myself a glass of wine around six.

Flopping onto the couch, my cleaning clothes in the washer along with everything else I've worn since I got here, I swirl the pinot grigio, elevate my swollen ankle, and consider my situation with all the mature objectivity I can muster.

Flawed though his delivery might have been, I have to admit, with some distance, that Max was right. Running from things always makes them worse. I think of my reasons for coming to Ridley Falls, what's at stake if I give up too soon.

There's my broken heart, which feels surprisingly lighter upon examination. So that's something. Then there's my job. This part is obviously complicated, but a plan is potentially in progress. That's something, too. The last thing, of course, is my estranged family—altered in my mind for too long by my mother's lies. The mysterious grandmother who leaves white lilies for her dead.

Somehow, this part feels the most intimidating of all. The source of my most formative rejection. The woman who didn't want to know me even before I was born. I run through hazy fantasies of showing up on her doorstep, asking her why I was so easy to abandon even as a zygote. Of asking whether she regrets not giving my mom and me a chance.

But I can't picture what happens next. Maybe that's what scares me the most. There's no predictable verse, chorus, and bridge structure here. No time signature to follow. There's just me, making myself vulnerable to a person who already hurt me, with no idea if anything has changed.

It's becoming a theme, honestly.

It would be easy to just let this one go, I think. Paloma and I are strangers. We could probably pass each other in the grocery store without recognizing each other. I've lived my whole life not knowing her, and while it's hardly been smooth sailing I can't blame that on one estranged grandmother.

Only then I think of Maeve's reading. All my problems coming from a single source. If that can be believed, then to solve one of them will mean solving them all. And she said I'm in the right place to begin . . .

I take out my phone, suddenly determined. I'll type Paloma's name into Google. See if she's listed. And then I'll send a text to Max. Plan a time to meet. I'll tell him what I do and ask for the review and that will be that.

Sure, it's scary to contemplate doing either of these things, let alone both in one week. But if it means righting the wrongs that brought me to Ridley Falls, I'm willing to try.

On the lock screen there are two texts. One from Willa— a photo of the gorgeous vineyard where she and Brook are staying the night, and a selfie of their cute faces smooshed together.

I heart the images one after the other and reply.

> The plants and I have formed a secret society. They're teaching me their ways. Don't send help, I belong to the loam now.

The next text is from my mom. Sorry I missed you earlier, we were only at port for a couple hours and Bob insisted we see the dolphins at sunset. He's a dream, Sammy, you'll love him!

Annoyance flares up immediately, but I temper it. Being angry at my mom won't bring Roberto Espinoza back.

Don't worry about me, I text back. Have fun with Bob. Love you xo

That sorted, I scroll to my newest contact.

So, the fall might have knocked something loose in my brain because I guess I'm sticking around, I type, determined not to overthink it. Any more nature deathtraps you want to drag me to?

I hit Send. I don't stress over the punctuation or the word choice. I don't let myself worry before it's even sent that he won't reply. "I'm totally chill," I say aloud. "Just telling the truth and going with the flow."

The phone buzzes in my hand. I scream and drop it off the side of the couch.

It's ringing. Like, actual out loud phone call ringing. Max's name is much bigger than it was when I sent the text. It's terrifying.

"Who *calls* in response to a text?" I shriek, leaning over precariously to retrieve my phone from the floor.

It's still ringing. I only have seconds to decide what to do.

Go with the flow, I tell myself.

"Calling unannounced," I say without preamble. "Either a bold move—or you learned phone etiquette from an eighty-year-old."

Max chuckles on the other end. It's a warm, comfortable-sounding laugh. I imagine him on his couch, looking up at his glossy guitars and his impeccable art.

"Why not both? The eighty-year-olds I get my advice from are *very* bold."

No doubt about it, he's lying down. I guest-hosted a podcast once and my handler told me people can hear it in your voice when you're horizontal. Ever since, I can't unhear it. It's like a terrible superpower, always knowing if someone is prone.

"Max Ryan, friend to the elderly," I say thoughtfully. "That didn't make the first page of Google search results."

"None of the interesting stuff does," he says.

I resist the urge to ask four rapid-fire follow-ups, remembering he doesn't yet know I'm on the clock. "So what did Ethel and Frank say to do once you got me on the phone?" I ask instead.

"Trick you into going out with me again before you get wise and change your mind," Max answers promptly.

I laugh. "As long as you promise a fracture this time. This ankle strain barely hurts anymore."

"All thanks to my excellent first aid, I assume."

I don't answer right away because I'm trying not to remember how it felt to be close to him. My leg in his lap. His hands wrapping my ankle like it was something precious. I'm not terribly successful. Heat spreads across my face like melted butter on a pancake and I'm suddenly *very* glad this conversation is happening over the phone.

Tell him now, says the Good Sammy on one shoulder. *Rip off the Band-Aid.*

No way, Bad Sammy chimes in. *We agreed to do it next time we saw him. This phone call is a freebie.*

Sometimes I wonder why Good Sammy even bothers showing up. I settle back into the couch with my wine.

"The bandage, I will grudgingly confess, played a part."

"Also the fact that you were walking on air after our hike, admit it." There's a little smirk in his voice now. The rock star who can get any girl peeking through the humble, small-town man facade.

From a stranger it might be charming, but in this moment, it sets off alarm bells. There's still something of the boy who hurt me in the man Max has become. And that part of him is dangerous.

"Too cheesy, huh?" he asks when I'm quiet too long. "I don't blame you if you want to hang up."

"Too rehearsed," I retort. "You have thirty seconds to redeem yourself by saying something uncool."

"Oh man," he says. "So much pressure. Shit . . . I played Danny Zuko in *Grease* in ninth grade. It was my mom's favorite movie so I knew all the songs. That's how I got into performing."

"*Grease*?" I reply, giggling. "Okay that's pretty uncool."

"It's a classic!" he says. I can hear him sitting up. I picture him leaning forward, elbows on knees. "A timeless tale of a twenty-nine-year-old man's struggle to navigate his suburban high school during a fraught period of history."

I'm really laughing now. Wheezing. A snort isn't totally out of the question. That doesn't stop me from grabbing a stack of Willa's Post-it notes and jotting this down. If I get the go-ahead, it's the exact kind of detail that will give my piece depth.

"*Max Ryan* got his start doing musical theater," I say when I'm done. "That didn't make the front page of Google either." *Although hopefully it will by the time I'm through here,* I think to myself.

"I never tell people," Max says. "Apparently it's not edgy enough. But I'll tell you what, there's never been a rush like the one I got opening night in the high school gym. Secretly, I've always thought I might have peaked at fourteen in that faux leather greaser's jacket."

We're both laughing now, and this conversation and the wine and the absence of his overwhelming attractiveness have lulled me, at least slightly. I don't have my guard up as high as normal when he asks: "So, now that I've bared my soul, what made you decide to call?"

"*You* called," I reply. "*I* sent a totally appropriate post-hike text."

He laughs, but doesn't respond. It's my own trick, letting the silence stretch, and it's working.

"It was a playlist," I answer finally. Truthfully. "A really good, really old playlist."

I hear him adjusting on the other end. "First track?" he asks.

"Can't tell you," I reply. "My playlists are a jealously guarded secret, and this one is particularly powerful."

"Fair enough," he says. He's lying down again, and it sounds like the phone is wedged between his shoulder and his ear. Like some nineties rom-com where everyone uses a landline. "Give me the feeling instead."

"First summer in a new city," I say. "That feeling that the world is both bigger and smaller than you knew, and your place in it hasn't been decided yet."

"Endless possibilities," Max says in a sort of dreamy voice. "I love it."

"It made me connect with this younger version of myself, I think. A version of me who didn't avoid things just because she was scared."

Another long pause.

"My mom was like that," I admit. "Taking off anytime something seemed hard. I don't want to end up like that."

"What's she like?" Max asks. "Your mom."

"No way," I reply. "It's your turn for some oversharing. You want to know about my mom? Tell me about yours first."

"Ha, point taken," he answers. I can hear something playing in the background but I can't make it out. It's slow, fingerpicking on a warm-toned guitar. "My mom is great, but I don't know if she was very happy when I was growing up. She was *such* a mom, you know? A wife. School lunches and Sunday deep-cleaning and putting everyone else first. Sometimes I think it must have been lonely to have everyone reduce you to that."

"You said they split up, right?" I ask, sipping. "Your parents?" I don't take notes about this part.

"Yeah," he says. "After I was already gone. It was harder on my sister, she's a lot younger than me so she was still at home. I feel bad for not being there for her more."

I let the silence stretch, thinking of the way this must have informed his life. His mom, unhappy because she wasn't seen as her whole self. Max, uncomfortable with the rock star persona, hiding out in the one place he knows people won't flatten him into a caricature.

"What about your dad?" I ask when it's clear he's lost in thought.

"Oh no you don't," he teases. "I believe we had an equal exchange agreement."

He's right, of course, so I end up telling him more about Dina Rae. At first I plan to keep it light, give him just enough to get him talking again, but before I know it I'm saying things I've never even told Willa. Things I've barely let myself *think,* let alone admit to another human.

"It's hard because I know she did her best," I say, twirling my now empty wineglass, hitching my ankle up higher on the pillow stack where it's resting. "And I know she gave up so much to raise me at that age, with no support, but it's hard not to wish she'd been a little *more* of a mom sometimes."

"That makes a lot of sense," Max says in that gravelly voice. "You deserved to feel like the center of someone's world."

It's utterly humiliating that this makes my eyes sting, my throat feel tight. But no one has ever said that to me before, and it fits into some empty place in me like a puzzle piece.

"Wow," I say when I can trust my voice again. "We are *really* bad at surface-level getting-to-know-you chat aren't we?"

Max laughs. "Can I be honest and say I prefer it this way? I mean, who really wants to know what someone's favorite food is when you can know exactly how their parents fucked them up instead?"

"Touché," I reply. "And on that note, I believe it's your turn."

"My dad, huh?" he asks. He sounds wary.

"Only if you want to," I say. "If I'm allowed to put a moratorium on work you can certainly ixnay your dad."

He's quiet for a long minute.

"No, it's okay. It's just . . . not a very nice story."

"Yeah, because my mom was a walk in the park . . ."

Max chuckles, but it dissolves quickly into a long pause. "He's just . . . a jerk, I guess?" he replies at last. "He was always so sure everyone was trying to disrespect him. Undermine him. Even my mom. No one was allowed to joke with him, or tease, and he blew up about the smallest things."

There's a raw edge to Max's voice now. I realize I haven't heard him angry.

"I can see now that he was probably just really insecure, but it was hard. Every time my mom made a friend, or got a hobby, he'd ruin it because he didn't have his own. Every time I did something well, he had to prove he could do it better. And I was just a kid, you know? I just wanted to make him proud . . ."

The anger makes way for something more complicated, then. Something sad.

"And my little sister, Maya, as soon as she was born he resented her. She took up too much of my mom's attention, and Mom was too scared to stand up to him, so I took care of her as best I could. I like to think she had it easier than I did because of that."

"She was lucky to have you," I say, thinking of my lonely childhood with Dina Rae always in and out. What it would have been like to have someone there who cared.

"She was a good kid," he says. "I felt bad for leaving her when I went with the band. But by then she was in middle school. She had friends. Her own life . . ."

"And you weren't her parent," I say gently. "It wasn't your job to stay for her."

I'm afraid this might upset him, but Max laughs softly. "That's exactly what she told me when I left to record my first album," he says. "Anyway, I told her when I left that I was going to do something so big my dad could never one-up it. Never make it small, or take it from me."

"Sounds like you succeeded," I say a beat too late. I'm thinking about the Max I met during that first Seattle summer, now. So desperate to be discovered. To make something of himself. To justify the sacrifice he made when he left his sister behind.

"In some ways I did." He sounds a little distant, too. "But in a lot of ways I carried that small version of me around the whole time, you know?"

I try not to think about what incredible interview material this would make if Max knew he was being interviewed. It's easier than I expected. Not a good sign.

My stomach growls loudly before I can get too existential about it all and I glance at the clock.

"It's been *two hours*?" I cry, completely shocked. "Did you do witchcraft on me or something? Be honest. There's no way it's been that long."

"Man, I missed *Jeopardy*," Max says without a hint of irony.

"I missed *dinner*," I say. "And I never miss dinner."

He doesn't answer right away, and I know I should wrap this up. Get back to the real world. But I can't stop thinking about Bad Sammy saying this is a freebie. And the fact that the next time I see Max I'm going to have to come clean.

Don't I owe it to the girl I once was to make the most of this strange tear in space and time? How often did she wish she could climb back into that night again?

It's just for tonight, I tell myself. *Then back to reality.*

"Want to stay on while I make a grilled cheese?" I ask, and Good Sammy rolls her eyes spectacularly.

* * *

By the time I've made and eaten a sandwich and drunk another glass of wine, it's nearly ten. Max and I have veered away from family therapy at last and have now discussed our favorite foods, colors, flowers, and seasons.

Despite our shared disdain for the surface level, even these topics feel different with Max. Favorite foods leads to a memory he has from his first tour, when he realized he could literally order anything from room service on the label's dime, so he got one of everything—including lobster mac and cheese, which he swore his forever allegiance to from that day forward.

Favorite flower leads me to rant about Juniper and her pretentious white lily during the onstage breakup. I leave out the stage part, after some consideration. Mentioning I have a history of dating musicians will only get Max's hackles up, I tell myself. I can't afford to do that yet if I want to save my job.

But the truth is, there's more to it than that. In the four hours since my phone rang, I've remembered exactly why Max's disappearance was so devastating. Why a boy I had known for one night managed to break my heart worse than anyone who came after him.

It's because of this. The way we talk. Effortlessly. Going so much deeper than banter and flirting. The way he makes me feel like I can say anything. That he can be trusted with it.

Naively, after our first night together, I thought it was always like that when you really liked someone. But it never has been again. I've been disappointed so much I almost forgot what this feels like. How it's thrilling and terrifying in equal measure. Like standing at the edge of a cliff.

Like a first summer in a brand-new city.

We're just wrapping up a long back-and-forth about our favorite recent movies when Max pauses for longer than normal and I think this is it. He'll say he has to go, and I'll act like I don't mind. Next time we see each other, I'll tell him why I'm here, and no matter which way it goes, this will be over. This playlist between us that we're making together a track at a time.

"Do you mind hanging on for just a second?" he asks instead.

"Sure," I say. "But honestly I know it's late, I'm sure you have something cooler to do at ten-thirty P.M. than hear about how I regret not going to the prom."

"No, no, I have *nothing* going on," Max says, too quickly. Another pause. "I've just . . . honestly had to pee for like an hour, but I didn't want this to be over yet."

I burst out laughing. It's partly that that's a ridiculous thing to admit, but mostly it's sheer relief at the fact that neither of us is ready for this to end.

During the few minutes he's gone, I move myself into the botanical guest room, getting under the covers and turning off the light.

When he returns, some of the pressure is off. We both know the other one isn't going to run off at any moment. Our pauses get longer, our voices lower and sleepier as midnight comes and goes.

"What's your favorite time of day?" I ask at one in the morning. My eyes are closed. I think I might be more asleep than awake.

"This one," he says. "Right now."

"Mine, too."

12.

When I wake up at 7:45 the next morning, my phone is still right next to my head. The battery is at 8 percent. There are two texts on the screen.

One is from Willa, sent at six-thirty:

> Hey! Hitting the road, should be home in two hours if Brook doesn't speed . . . so, probably an hour and a half. Hope you're still sleeping!

I reply quickly, one eye open against the offensively bright screen.

> Begrudgingly awake. Can't wait to hear all about it.

That sorted, I move on to the second message, sent about thirty minutes ago. A text that shouldn't—but definitely does—make butterflies swarm in my stomach.

> MAX: Six-hour phone call and I forgot to tell you I'm picking you up tomorrow at five.

I reply before I can overthink it:

> Sorry, who's this? I had like five six-hour phone calls last night, still trying to get everyone straight.

After I hit Send, I lock my phone and sit up to survey the state of things. I vaguely remember saying a mostly-already-asleep good-night around two this morning, which means I'm running on less than six hours of sleep.

"Doesn't matter," I say aloud, yawning hugely. "The freebie window is closed. Back to business."

> MAX: I'll be the one on the motorcycle if you want to try your luck.

This time, I don't respond. But my pulse definitely does.

"I have thirty-six hours to decide exactly how I'm going to confess," I tell my reflection in the mirrored closet door. "Better start now."

Willa and Brook come home just as I'm taking my first sip of coffee. Blissfully, they're loaded down with takeout from a café in Lacey—which has an impressive seven restaurants to Ridley Falls's three.

My mouth is full of stuffed French toast when Brook bangs a fist on the table and says: "So? How was the date! How did he react when you asked him for the interview? Tell us everything!"

I'm only twenty minutes into my allotted thirty-six hours of planning tomorrow's confession, but I take this as a chance to workshop.

"I . . . uh . . . didn't totally get to the asking for the interview part," I say semi-sheepishly, avoiding Willa's gaze in favor of Brook's more forgiving one. "Or the telling him I'm a journalist part. Due to the fact that he told me the only reason he moved back to Ridley Falls is to avoid feeling like everyone he meets has an agenda."

Brook's eyes are bugging out, but not in a bad way. "So . . . it was *just* a date?"

This time, I do look at Willa. "No, no, definitely not," I protest. "I just realized I might have to show him he can trust me first, then ask him once a sufficient . . . rapport has been established."

Willa raises an eyebrow, but Brook looks convinced enough.

"I'm there, though," I reassure them (and myself) talking around a giant strawberry. "We talked on the phone for like, six hours last night. *And* he's taking me somewhere tomorrow at five, so I'm thinking *that's* the time to let the cat out of the bag."

"Six hours?!" Brook screeches. "And dinner? And no shop talk at all? Sammy, you do realize you're basically *dating* Max Ryan, right?"

"I'm buttering Max Ryan up so I can write a job-saving article," I correct her, willing myself to believe it.

"Yeah, but *he* doesn't know that," Brook says, literally clapping her hands. "This is amazing. I told you Drunk Sammy was a genius."

Brook picks up our empty plates and heads into the kitchen to start on the dishes. Willa, however, stays put. Her eyes are on mine, and I've never been able to avoid her when she has something to say.

"So, six hours," she says. "Seems kind of above and beyond the call of duty."

I do my very best not to be defensive. "I have to show him I'm not just using him for the article," I say, trying not to remember the way it felt to listen to his rough, sleepy voice as I was drifting off last night. "The deadline is in a week. I need to capitalize where I can."

She nods. I can tell she's steeping, and I'm a little afraid whatever it is will be too strong for my current fragile state. I don't know how to tell her that, though. So I just wait.

"I support you," she says after a long moment. "You know that, right?"

"I do," I say without hesitating. "Of course I do."

"Okay, so you know it comes from a place of love when I ask you to make really sure you're doing this for the right reasons?"

"I do," I say again. "I promise. It'll all be settled tomorrow. Either it goes my way and he becomes a subject, or it doesn't and he becomes a . . . pretty angry stranger who's just had his worst fears about humanity validated. Either way the potential for romance is zero."

She smiles, looking relieved as I try to pretend the bleak future I've just outlined for Max and me isn't a little bit of a bummer.

"I should have known you had it all under control."

"This is what I do," I reply breezily. Even though it isn't. Not really. Not like this. "Anyway, if we're done analyzing my total lack of a love life, I need advice about something that actually matters."

"Right!" Willa says, thankfully making the jump with me. "I totally forgot you came in with news after the cemetery. What happened?"

I tell Willa about the Espinozas. Roberto, buried beside his son. My grandmother, still here somewhere, and my plan to talk to her. To try to get some closure while there's still time, even if a relationship isn't in the cards.

"Wow," Willa says softly when I'm finished. "I'm really proud of you, Sammy. This is a big decision. I know how your mom feels about your dad's family, so I'm glad to see you making your own choices about this."

The way she says it irks me a little, but I do my best to hide it. Sure, Dina Rae not telling me about my grandfather's death was the main impetus for this whole thing, but it's not like it's her fault they left her to raise a baby on her own.

"Thanks," I say, giving Willa the benefit of the doubt. "Now all I have to do is figure out where she lives." I don't mention that the reason I haven't done this yet is because I got distracted by a six-hour phone call with Max.

Willa's already pulling out her phone. "Old people are always listed," she says, clacking away at her screen. "Yep, look. Paloma Espinoza. Sixty-four Ponderosa Court."

It seems almost criminal that it's this easy. A lifetime of distance, and just like that I'm less than eight minutes from meeting my grandmother for the first time.

"You okay?" Willa asks.

"Yeah," I say, shaking myself off. "Yeah, totally. Do you mind if I borrow your truck again?"

Willa's eyes widen slightly. "You're going now?"

"I think so," I say, getting to my feet. "Before I lose my nerve."

"Want me to come along?" Willa asks, getting to her feet.

I shake my head. "I know I've been saying this a lot lately, but it feels like something I should do on my own."

"I'm proud of you," Willa says again. "This feels like a big step."

"We'll see." I try not to let the pressure exacerbate my already jangling nerves. I grab the keys from where I left them in the ceramic dish by the door.

Willa stands, still looking a little alarmed by my hasty departure. "Okay, well, call me if you need anything. And don't forget to"—

"Give it some gas when I start it, yeah," I say, grinning sheepishly. "Won't be forgetting that one anytime soon."

Ponderosa Court is in a part of town I've never been to before. Willa's truck protests a little on the steep hills. The houses get bigger as I climb, the trees taller and thicker. An early morning mist hovers between them.

"Volcano" by Tacocat plays through Willa's tinny truck speakers—a song that makes me feel nineteen in a good way. Seeing a girl-fronted punk band and feeling like the whole world was ours. It's an attempt to capture the bravery I felt when I decided to do this in the first place, but the bigger the houses get, the more the feeling of empowerment fades.

I turn off the music when a lady walking a well-groomed poodle scowls at me. The silence that follows only leaves more space for my insecurities to fester.

When I imagined meeting Paloma, I pictured doing it in front of a *normal* house. One like the Cross family's bungalow closer to town. When my mom said the Espinozas had money, I thought she meant the kind that lets you own a home in the first place. Not the kind that puts you in the nosebleeds of town with a view of the bay.

This backdrop has me totally off my game before I even arrive at number sixty-four. I feel out of place, in the spluttering truck and my jeans with a hole in the knee and my expertly applied (but possibly overdramatic) winged eyeliner.

The map says I'm only one minute from my destination. One left turn and the house will be in view. My palms are sweaty on the steering wheel, and I'm feeling definitely queasy from the sugar overload that served as breakfast this morning.

"*Your destination is on the right,*" the cool voice of my phone's GPS lady announces. "*Sixty-four Ponderosa Court.*"

I ease the truck over to the curb on autopilot, killing the engine as I take in the house. Stately, white with dark trim. Bright red door. The house has a steep driveway flanked by two colossal evergreens. It looks like a house they might film a movie in. The kind they pretend is normal but has kids who live in apartments salivating into their boxed mac and cheese.

"I'm going to knock on the door," I tell myself out loud as the mist swirls and parts around the house. "I'm going to tell Paloma who I am, and ask her point-blank why she refused to be a part of my life. If she's awful, I will never have to come back here. If she's not, we'll go from there."

This pep talk, plus a few four-seven-eight breaths, is enough to get me out of the car. I stand straight and tall, walking with purpose across the street. I can do this. Willa said so.

But before I can even make it to the steep driveway, the bright red door of number sixty-four opens wide, and out steps a woman holding a black leather purse and a set of car keys. I freeze in my tracks as Paloma Espinoza comes into view.

She's getting on in years, of course, but she doesn't look frail in the least. She has jet-black hair with a glorious silver stripe in the front, cut into one of those chic old lady bobs. She wears slim black pants and a boxy jacket. She pulls on a pair of driving gloves once the door is closed behind her.

My grandmother still hasn't seen me, but it's only a matter of time. I'm standing in the middle of the street, after all, and I think my mouth is hanging open, though my face is too numb to know for sure.

I thought seeing her would feel like looking at a stranger, but I was wrong. Something is unspooling inside me. Something triggered by the shape of her face—so similar to mine. The set of her shoulders. The way she absolutely rocks a pair of cowboy boots.

This woman might be a stranger to me, but my body knows her. My blood knows her. When I look at her, I see every time someone has spoken Spanish to me, and how embarrassed I felt when I couldn't understand. I see the thick, dark horsetail of my hair and how my mom—with her wispy blond curls—never knew how to cut or style it right.

I see a whole history, a whole *family*, I'd convinced myself I didn't need because it was never an option. Only now a piece of it is right in front of me, and my plan to be upfront and no-nonsense seems ridiculous. Because I am definitely going to cry. Right here in the middle of Ponderosa Court.

Of course, this is the moment she spots me. She shades her eyes with a gloved hand. We're only twenty yards apart at most, but I can't move forward. I can't speak. I can't even turn around and run away.

"Can I help you?" she calls out, and her voice hits me, too. The sharpness. The accent that's unfamiliar and somehow feels like home. My unspooling continues. The tears are welling, and falling. "Excuse me, can I help you?"

I might have stood there forever. Become a monument to myself in the fanciest neighborhood in town. But just then, a car turns the corner, headlights on in the dissipating mist.

The driver lays on the horn, breaking the spell, and I bolt.

Back to Willa's truck. Metal on metal, clanging, securing me inside. It takes a couple tries but the engine guns to life loudly and clunks into gear.

I can feel Paloma's eyes boring through the window as I hit the gas, making for the stop sign and blowing right through it. I don't breathe again until I'm at the bottom of the hill, and then I pull over in the first parking lot I see and burst into tears again.

13.

It's utterly absurd, but the first person I want to call when I catch my breath is Max.

In fact, my phone is already in my hand when I realize what a bad idea it is. Especially because I *know* whatever we're cooking up between us is doomed the moment I confess what I really want from him.

With baggage like his, there's no way he'll trust me even if he does agree, somehow, to share the album and grant me an interview. And, I remind myself forcefully, a personal connection was never the goal. Not after what he did to me the last time I trusted him with my heart.

Even still, it's much harder than it should be to put the phone back into my purse.

When I do, the memory of what just happened at Paloma's house is waiting. My punched-in-the-gut reaction to seeing a living relative of my father's for the first time. I put on a playlist made solely for soothing a bruised heart and slink back to Brook and Willa's with my proverbial tail between my legs. No closure. No catharsis. Just another scar for the collection.

As minor piano chords echo in the truck cab, I feel the mournful yet hope-filled tenor pour into me like honey. I tell myself Paloma was just one piece of the puzzle. I'll shift focus, that's all. If I leave after spending two weeks with my best friends and knowing my job is secure that'll be plenty.

In my head, Maeve is pulling cards again. Telling me I can't run. That I have to stay with my uncomfortable feelings until I break through. That my problems can only be solved together.

But I know I can never go back to that house. I'm filled with panic just thinking about it. So I'll have to do the best I can with the rest.

Willa and Brook are sitting on the porch swing when I pull up to the house.

"Sit with us!" Brook calls. "Will made lemonade!"

"I can't," I say, and I must look bad, because neither of them argue. "I want to get a start on my article."

"Do you want to talk about it?" Willa asks as I reach the door.

I shake my head.

"Anything I can do to help?"

"Not this time, but thank you," I say, smiling so she knows it's not her I'm upset with. "I just need to do something I'm good at for a while."

"Okaaay," Willa says guiltily. "But can you be done by five? My parents invited us over for dinner. I can totally cancel if you need more time though."

"No," I say, surprising myself. If I can't make peace with my own family, at least I can feel accepted by someone's. Maeve and Larry have always been so good at that. "Dinner with your parents actually sounds great."

"Really?" Willa asks, clearly relieved. "Thank you. My mom would have been devastated. She's already cooking."

"It's a date," I say, then head inside.

In the botanical guest room, I take out my laptop and put it on the little white desk. I don't open it though. I feel restless and strange, and I pace back and forth until I realize I'm thinking about my mom. Wishing I could call her.

Of course, I can't. Not about this. Sure, she's the only person who would really understand what happened to me today, but things are still so raw since our fight about Roberto. I didn't even tell her I was officially coming to Ridley Falls, and this seems too close not to open the wounds up again.

I feel a little guilty when I realize what I *really* want is to talk to a regular mom. Not one that brags about us looking like sisters, or would rather talk about her life than mine. A mom that has the maturity and stability to consider how I feel first, before she reacts and I end up taking care of her.

But it's not Dina Rae's fault I don't have a mom like that. In fact, if it's anyone's fault, it's Paloma Espinoza's. The actual adult who could have helped us and chose to walk away instead.

Maybe it's better that I couldn't tell her who I was, I reason. Maybe she doesn't deserve to meet me. Doesn't even deserve a chance to justify her choices.

It's this feeling of vindication that finally allows me to sit down at my computer.

As I consider the blank page for a second time, I try to summon the emotions that little news item about a potential Max Ryan solo album sparked in me. I remember secretly hoping that he had become a narcissistic monster. That his album would be so terrible I'd have no choice but to rip it into tiny little pieces. Simultaneously restoring my readers' trust and getting revenge for the lead singer–shaped hole he left in my heart.

In my wine-soaked breakup spiral, I had blamed Max's rejection for causing my attraction to Juniper (*another* noncommittal lead singer) in the first place. And if that was true, I'd reasoned expertly, that essentially made this whole debacle Max's fault.

It had been compelling enough to turn my Ridley Falls fantasy into reality. But sitting here, after spending time with the real Max, I'm finding the idea of taking him down much less appealing than it was even a few days ago.

It doesn't have to be a bad review, I tell myself. My readers won't care as long as it's honest. I just have to write *something* so I can leave this whole mess in the rearview. And now is as good a time as any to start.

I've written hundreds of profiles, reviews, and interviews over the past decade. I close my eyes, shake off the personal as I always have, and try to think of Max Ryan the public figure—not Max Ryan the man who tenderly bandaged my ankle.

On the surface, the story of Seven Shades of Monday is a familiar one, I begin. *Small-town band makes it big. Gets bigger. Finally, they become too big, resulting in a collapse with all the drama of any dying star.*

I'm getting into the rhythm now, I think, cracking my knuckles. I feel like myself.

But like any supernova, Seven Shades of Monday has remained visible in our collective sky. To their most devoted fans, even the years since the band's mysterious end haven't been enough to dim their shine.

These fans mark the years gone since the last Seven Shades single was released. They puzzle over perceived hints in old interviews or press releases, sure a solo album is on the horizon. They wonder, almost obsessively, what became of the front man who catapulted his group into spectacular stardom, then disappeared just as his legacy seemed assured.

Why hasn't the world moved on from Max Ryan? That's the question I went deep into the boonies of southern Washington—following yet another rumor of a solo album—to answer.

It takes me almost two hours to write this half an introduction. I spend the rest of the time until I have to get ready for dinner staring at the half-page below it, trying to answer my own question.

Why *hasn't* the world moved on from Max Ryan?

And why can't I?

* * *

At six-thirty, I get into the back seat of Brook's Subaru as she drives the four minutes to the home of Larry and Maeve Cross. The former home of Willa Cross. And the once-upon-a-time landing zone of a scared, confused, nine-year-old Sammy Espinoza.

Willa is carrying an armful of flowers and some hand-jarred jam. Brook has two bottles of wine. They're making an event of it because I'm here, but Willa walks the path toward the door with sure steps even in the dusk. She's as comfortable here as if she never left.

"Home sweet home," she says, nudging me.

The Cross house isn't fancy by any means. Nothing like the places I saw on Ponderosa Court today. It's a single story, painted a beer-bottle-brown that was probably all the rage in the '70s. The gutters are crooked and the yard is a little overgrown. But the windows are lit brightly, and I can already see Maeve's plants and Larry's antique gramophone.

As we pause to remove our shoes, I remember the first time I walked up this driveway twenty years ago. My mom was beside me, and I had a little pink duffel bag over my shoulder. Before the door opened to reveal Maeve's smiling face—and nine-year-old Willa peeking out from behind her—my mom told me it would only be a little while. Until she could bring the man of the moment around on the idea of being a stepdad.

In the present, the door is opening again, and Larry is beaming out at us like it's been a year and not a day since we all saw one another.

"Get in here!" he says, hugging Willa and clapping Brook on the back before turning to me. "Must be a trip down memory lane, huh? How long has it been?"

"Too long," I say, my throat a little tight. "But it's good to be back."

"Come on, I've got something to show you," Larry says, and pulls me inside.

The living room hasn't changed in all these years. Still that mustard-yellow velvet sofa, dark wood paneling with family photos crowded all over. A rectangular coffee table covered in magazines and mail.

"Dad, this stuff is from last year," Willa says, affectionately. "You guys ought to throw some of it out."

But *throwing it out* has never been in the elder Crosses' vocabulary. This place is practically a shrine to their family. Pictures of Willa from infancy to last Christmas. Craft projects and artwork. Magazines, both intact and shredded for collages.

I choke up a little when I see—right beside Willa's fourth-grade school photo—a 5" x 7" of yours truly in a frilly dress, grinning so big it looks like my face might split open.

"You loved that dress," Maeve says, coming up behind me and putting an arm around my shoulder. "We found it at the mall in Vancouver, remember?"

"When we went to the aquarium," I confirm. "Black-and-magenta plaid. What a choice."

"You would have worn it every day if we hadn't bribed you back into jeans." She chuckles. "It's good to have you back, sweet pea."

The disappointment from my failure to speak to Paloma today eases a little in this house. I might not share a name with the Crosses, but there's more to family than that. "Good to be back," I say, and it's true. Despite everything that's happened, it feels right.

Maeve, bless her, isn't one to linger on a sentimental moment. She nudges me toward the den, where Larry is frantically beckoning and heads back into the kitchen, where Brook is already loitering.

"You'll appreciate this," Larry says, ushering me down the two steps into the den—a room with orange shag carpeting and a whole long wall lined with Larry's record collection.

The nostalgia here is so powerful I can hardly catch my breath. Yes, this house holds a lot of memories, good and bad. The beginning of the most important friendship in my life. The moment I first realized my mom might not be as perfect as I'd always believed. Maeve's kitchen, Willa's bedroom, they're both key backdrops of a formative year of my life.

But this room. This was where I came when I was lost, or sad, or confused. When I felt like I couldn't talk to anyone about how I was feeling.

This was the room where I learned to love music. To rely on it. To trust that no matter where I was going next or what was waiting for me there, I would always be understood when my headphones were on.

"Check out this baby," Larry says, patting a dark wood console where the TV used to be.

I whistle, walking over to inspect. It's an old cabinet stereo, probably from the '60s or earlier. The speakers are upholstered in a green that clashes horribly with the carpet and it appears to be in mint condition.

"She's a beauty," I say, kneeling down to check out the vintage detail, the buttons and knobs a touchscreen will never be able to match. The gleaming turntable in the center. A promise of what's to come.

"Wait until you hear her."

As Larry cues up a record, I try not to let the wave of sentiment overtake me. The Sam Cooke song that comes to life as needle meets vinyl doesn't help. His voice hooks behind my belly button, tugging me forward into the deep end of my emotions.

"Wow," I say, not able to manage much more. Everything is lighter, lifted by this simple rhythm. My shame over running from Paloma. My fear of botching things with Max tomorrow. Even the butterflies that shouldn't be there at the thought of a date with him.

Nothing disappears, of course. Not really. But with the soundtrack of a perfect song it's all so much easier to bear.

We stand in silence as Sam croons. The sound is so warm. I almost feel embarrassed that I've been subsisting on Spotify playlists and AirPods for this long. When I get back to Seattle, I promise myself, I'll get a real stereo. An old one that sounds like the real thing.

"All right, nerds," Willa says from the doorway. "It's time to eat."

"We don't stop Mr. Cooke mid-song," Larry says, eyes still closed. "Your mother knows that."

Willa smiles, descending the stairs to stand next to me. She bumps her shoulder with mine as the track finishes, replaced by the scratchy quiet preceding the next song. The spell of it remains in the air, though, reminding me I'm not alone.

14.

The hazy memory of dinner is still with me when I wake up the next morning. Maeve made my childhood favorite—whole roast chicken with mashed potatoes and garlicky veggies—and we all talked at the table until almost eleven when Willa fell asleep on her elbow.

Today, I feel like all those lovingly prepared calories have formed a sort of protective cushion around my heart. It's easier to see myself the way Maeve and Larry do: Like someone who deserves happiness. Forgiveness.

I walk out into the living room in search of caffeine. Willa is already at the table, slumped over her own mug. "I swear my parents party harder than I do. I can't remember the last time I wasn't home before ten."

"They're great," I say, sitting down with the warm cup between my hands.

Willa peers at me through her curtain of red hair. "How are you feeling after yesterday?"

Yesterday. A still shot breaks through my cushion: Paloma at the door. Me, standing frozen in the street, about to get run over by a car.

"I might not be ready to get into it yet," I confess. The memory still stings too much to recount, and I feel like Willa might tell me to try again with Paloma—which makes me feel panicky again. "But I promise I'll tell you the minute I am."

"Totally fair," Willa says, though I'm sure she must be dying of curiosity. "I'm sorry, though. I really hoped that would be healing for you."

"Thanks." I smile at her.

She smiles back.

We're quiet until our cups are empty, and by then the heavy moment has thankfully passed.

"So," Willa says. "Ready for your big confession with Max tonight?"

"Absolutely," I say, a little too confidently. "I've got it all worked out. I'll apologize for the mystery. Tell him I didn't want him to think I was only interested in the album. But then I'll say that the more we've gotten to know each other the more I think it would be fun to collaborate while I'm in town, and that he'd totally be saving my ass."

"I like it," Willa says. "It acknowledges the deception without making too big a deal over it."

"Piece of cake," I agree. "Either he rolls with it, gives me the album and an interview, or I know I tried my best and I can search for bartending jobs with my head held high."

Willa chuckles. Beneath the table, I wipe my sweaty palms on my leggings.

The truth is, I'm not feeling half as cavalier about tonight as I pretend to be. Either way, this sparkling bubble Max and I have been living in the past few days has to pop tonight. I know it's for the best, but I can't help the part of me—a suspiciously Teen Sammy–shaped part—that would do anything to stay inside a little longer.

"Speaking of which," I say, getting to my feet. "I only have, like, seven hours to pick out an outfit."

"You should have started sooner," Willa says, slapping her hands to her cheeks in mock horror. "Let me know if you need feedback."

"Roughly every four minutes until he arrives," I promise her, before retreating to dump out my entire suitcase for the fourth time.

By midmorning, I've managed to reject my entire wardrobe, piece by piece.

By lunchtime, I've chosen an outfit that I hope says, "I'm here to facilitate an interesting plot twist in our recent acquaintance-ship," and not "this counts as a third date, right?"

By 4:36 I've stress-edited the half-intro to my article, showered, made a good show of taming my unruly hair, dressed, and have presented myself to Willa and Brook for inspection.

"I didn't know they made sundresses in black, but this one is a winner," Willa says. The sundress in question hits slightly below mid-thigh, has cap sleeves, a T-shirt neckline, and is accented by an oversized blood-red cardigan.

"They make them special for vampires who occasionally have to go out in the daylight," I say, allowing her to gloss my lips and spritz some fruity smelling spray onto my pinned bang-swoop thing for maximum staying power.

"I know romance isn't the goal here," Brook hedges with a wary look at her wife. "But I'm just saying, if there's visible drooling you only have yourself to blame."

The look Willa shoots her makes a response unnecessary, which is good because my mouth is weirdly dry.

"You look beautiful, Sammy," Willa says when Brook has been skewered clean through. "He doesn't deserve it, but definitely store this outfit for future use on someone who does."

"Thanks, you guys," I say. "I feel like I'm going to prom, and you're my too-excited parents taking photos . . . but in a good way."

"If you're back here a *moment* before two, young lady, you're grounded," Brook says, tempting fate.

Willa ignores her this time. "You've got this," she says to me, putting my purse over my shoulder. "And he'd better not be late."

He isn't late. In fact, he's six minutes early. The perfect amount of time to show he's considerate without being inconvenient about it.

Part of me expected him to text today, confirm our plans, but I like that he just showed up. Confidence is sexy—not that that's the point here, I remind myself harshly just before he knocks.

Brook and Willa have retreated to their room for fear that Max will recognize Willa and the whole backstory will unravel. I approach the door feeling excited and nervous in a way even I have to admit is not professional.

It opens to reveal Max—this time in a long-sleeved dove-gray T-shirt and dark-rinsed jeans. His sneakers look expensive. Felted wool, maybe, a slightly darker gray than his shirt. I grudgingly admit they're perfect. Not dorky dad sneakers or try-hard shiny dress shoes. Not clinging-to-my-youth skate shoes, which would be an instant deal-breaker . . .

"Hi," he says interrupting my inner ramble.

"Hi."

For a minute we just size each other up like awkward teenagers. I feel excited, nervous, just like I do before a band I love takes the stage.

"You look great," he says.

"You're not so shabby yourself," I admit, stepping out onto the porch and closing the door behind me. Wondering how long it'll take Willa and Brook to beeline for the front window and spy through the blinds.

"From you, I'll take that as high praise."

You have no idea, I think, following him to his bike, which is parked along the curb.

"So, where are we going, anyway?" I ask as he passes me a helmet and I do mental calculations about what it will do to my hairstyle.

"It must be seen to be believed," Max says, putting on his own. Somehow he looks even more handsome in a helmet—a thing that should definitely be illegal. I feel mine squishing my chipmunk cheeks and flattening my hair as I buckle it.

Pretty soon it won't matter what I looked like, I tell myself. All he'll remember is what I'm going to tell him.

This is almost enough to kill the buzz, but then I slide onto the motorcycle seat behind him.

"You're gonna want to hold on," he says, and I do, wrapping my arms around him in what I hope is a practical, utilitarian way. But the feeling of his lean muscles can't be desexualized, and there's nowhere to put my chin but against his shoulder, and he smells like outside, and citrus, and boy.

The engine roars to life beneath us. I tighten my grip reflexively.

"Ready?" he calls back.

"Ready!" I hope he can't hear the unsteadiness in my voice over the engine.

He eases us out onto the street, not picking up speed until there's straight, empty road ahead of us. I'm a pansexual tattooed music critic who mostly hangs out at show venues; I've ridden on the backs of plenty of motorcycles. But there's something different about this.

About Max and me, leaning together into the turns. The way our muscles tense together, ease together. Action, reaction. A conversation between our bodies, enhanced by the machine beneath us. The intensity of the engine's vibrations between my thighs. His thighs.

Max gets on the highway leading out of town, and I huddle behind him to avoid the wind. The highway is deserted, and ponderosas tower on either side. A sliver of moon is just visible on the horizon, rising early, yellow and low.

I'm almost disappointed when he slows down. I never want to get off this bike. But I know that's a dangerous thought.

We pass a couple farms—one advertising a pumpkin patch—but Max passes this by, winding down the narrow road until we reach a sign lit up from below: HIDDEN HILLS BOTANICAL GARDENS.

Max pulls into the parking lot, which is surprisingly full, and kills the engine. I climb off first, reluctantly, removing the helmet and doing what I can to restore volume to my hair.

As Max digs in his saddlebags, I take a surreptitious look around. Rose bushes line the dirt lot, and a vine-covered arch leads to what looks like a sloping lawn. Above, the stage is set for a truly spectacular sunset, the colors just shifting to lavenders and light blues.

Maybe it's the unexpected intimacy of the motorcycle ride, but I'm suddenly panicking. Watching the sunset together in an out-of-the-way botanical garden feels . . . very romantic. An intense follow-up to a casual hike and possibly the worst backdrop ever for the news I'm supposed to deliver tonight. Have I totally miscalculated this?

Just as the doom spiral is really beginning to pick up steam, I hear a familiar sound that's totally incongruous with our current setting: amplifier feedback.

"Check, check, can you all hear us okay?" A voice drifts toward us as Max turns and grins. "Cool, we'll be getting some music started for you in just a few minutes. Thanks so much for coming out."

Relief floods me, along with surprisingly genuine excitement. A concert on the lawn isn't nearly as much pressure as a solo sunset stroll. Plus I'm so starved for live music in this place I'd probably review a kids' birthday party band favorably right now.

"How'd I do?" Max asks, holding out a blanket and a cooler bag that I devoutly hope is full of snacks.

"Not bad, rock star," I say, bumping his shoulder with mine. "Not bad at all."

15.

The sloping lawn down to the stage is freckled with families, couples, and groups of friends. Blankets and lawn chairs, a few umbrellas just in case. The kids run and shriek and play while the adults chat, greeting friends, sharing food and drinks, making room.

It seems like half of the county is here. For a moment, I panic, scanning the crowd for Larry and Maeve—who would *totally* come to a concert on the lawn. I picture them approaching, giving Max the boyfriend grilling, revealing all the things I haven't gotten around to telling him myself.

Max has been shockingly respectful of my "no work questions" boundary since our first meeting, but even his politeness probably wouldn't hold up in the face of Larry and Maeve's "big-city writer" praise.

Thankfully, Willa's parents don't seem to be in attendance tonight, but I plan to stay on my guard just in case.

We find a spot about halfway down the lawn, right between the two modest stacks of speakers facing the crowd. It's an ideal spot for balanced sound quality in an outdoor venue. I know Max has traveled with true sound engineers, playing some of the most historic venues in the country, but I'm still impressed.

Remember the plan, I admonish myself, sitting down a respectable distance from him on the thick wool blanket and keeping my eyes on the scenery.

Luckily, there's plenty to see. In the distance, the pines tower imposingly over everything, reaching for the sky now displaying streaks of peach and cream. There are more rose bushes here of all different colors, plus a spectacular array of other native plants and flowers. To our left, a sign with a bee painted on the corner announces the POLLINATOR GARDEN, with a little path winding between wildflowers and cozy benches tucked into alcoves.

It's a gorgeous venue. Used to the grimy downstairs clubs and impersonal stadiums of the big city, I can't help but be totally charmed.

"So, who's playing?" I ask. "Let me guess . . . Metallica?"

Max smiles. "Yeah, it's their bluegrass stuff. Totally underrated."

"I like the B sides," I say. "More banjo."

"You can never have too much, that's what I always say."

I realize this is the moment. The one where I should employ whatever graceless transition is necessary to bring up my career, Max's rumored new album, the idea of a review for *Scavenger* . . .

But we only sat down like, two minutes ago, I rationalize, feeling the tense moment deflate with no small amount of relief. It would be totally weird to bring up something so serious so soon.

"So how did you get into black metal, anyway?" Max asks, stretching his legs out in front of him, getting comfortable.

I seize the subject change with enthusiasm. "I go to a lot of shows in Seattle," I say, convincing myself I'm just setting the stage. Easing him into the idea of Sammy the Music Critic. "Most black metal bands put on a hell of a live show—if you can find the ones who aren't white supremacists, anyway."

"Fair point," Max says, his eyes cutting over to me as I stretch out, my skirt riding up my thigh just a little, his gaze tracing from my all-black Vans to its hem.

He swallows hard, and I try not to take it as a victory. That's not what we're here for. But it doesn't feel bad to be admired by him, and I know I should enjoy it for these last few moments . . .

"Uh, so, is that mostly what you're into then?" he asks, looking away, his cheeks flushed. "Metal?"

"I feel like this is such a 'whatever' answer, but I don't really have a favorite genre," I say, a response I've given hundreds of times to music snobs who react like I've just admitted to being a puppy killer.

But Max doesn't gasp, or scoot away from me, or begin a diatribe on why this is the wrong answer and the genre he loves is clearly superior. He just smiles. "I feel exactly the same way," he says. "I love music, but it's not really the genre conventions I'm drawn to. It's the"—

"Emotion," I finish for him, without giving myself permission. "Feeling familiar things through the lens of someone else's experience. The validation and discovery of it . . ."

Max looks at me for a long minute, his expression unreadable.

"Sorry," I say sheepishly, coming back to earth. "You were in the middle of a sentence."

"A sentence you finished more succinctly than I could have after years in the music industry," he says, shaking his head. "Where did you come from, Sammy Espinoza?"

I'd never admit it to Willa, but I want to kiss him so much in that moment that it's become almost impossible to stay seated. "Seattle," I say instead. "I took the bus." I swallow and turn to face the stage where a band is just warming up.

Max and I feign interest in tuning and the friendly laughter of the band members onstage, but there's a tension lingering. One that gives me a heightened awareness of my body, and his, and the easily crossable distance between them.

"Okay, I think we're ready now," says an older guy in a bowler hat I don't think is supposed to be ironic. "Hey, y'all, thanks so much for coming out to hear us play. We're My Aching Back—an all-chiropractor band from just over the hill—and we're thrilled to provide your picnic soundtrack this evening."

I turn to Max, forgetting the tension for a moment, only to be enveloped once again the moment our eyes meet. "All-chiropractor band, huh?" I manage with about half my intended skepticism.

He leans in closer before answering, like he's about to tell me a closely guarded secret. I can feel his breath tickle my ear, and goosebumps chase themselves down my neck as he says, "It takes a bit of adjustment, but they're worth it."

"Seriously?" I groan.

"*Adjustment,* get it?" Max asks, still way too close to me, his mouth stretched into a lazy, self-congratulatory grin. "Because they're chiropractors?"

I thwack him with the back of my hand, and he catches me by the wrist. Our gazes meet. The rough calluses on his fingers against my skin. His eyes darken a little. I lick my lower lip reflexively.

"*One, two, one-two-three-four!*" My Aching Back fires up their first song just in the nick of time. Max drops my hand, and I reluctantly return my eyes to the stage, where the band has thrown themselves heart and soul into a cover of Tom Petty's "American Girl."

"These guys are great!" I say in shock after the first verse, and it's true. The chiropractors are leaving it all on the stage. My body is buzzing in the way it only does when live music is being played well in my vicinity, and I honestly can't believe that feeling— arguably my favorite in the world—has been sparked by some late-middle-aged doctors at a small-town lawn concert.

"Isn't the wholesomeness of it so refreshing?" Max says, reading my thoughts before I have a chance to speak them. "No pretension whatsoever. They're just having a great time because they fucking *love* playing music."

"It's the way all music should be played," I agree, as the lead singer struts around onstage in his bowler hat. "Just because you love it."

"And for the chicks," Max says, leaning in and pointing to the foot of the stage where about twelve wineglass-toting women in their late fifties are clustering to dance.

"Well, that's a given," I say, laughing.

"All right, the million-dollar question," Max says when My

Aching Back has launched into their second cover—"Brown Eyed Girl" by Van Morrison, of course.

"What's that?" I ask, keeping my eyes carefully on the stage.

"Food or dancing?"

"Food," I answer without hesitation. "Always food."

He smiles, opening up the zipper bag. "I remembered that grilled cheese is your favorite, but they don't travel very well so I got as close as I could." He pulls out two massive sandwiches wrapped in brown paper, handing one to me.

It's all I can do to stop my stomach from audibly rumbling as I peek inside the wrapper. This is a legitimately gourmet affair. Thick slices of whole wheat bread, crisp lettuce, slabs of white cheese and tomato . . .

"Is that hummus?" I ask, thinking I might drop down on one knee and propose to this sandwich if it tastes as good as it looks. "When did Ridley Falls get a fancy sandwich place?"

Max chuckles, unwrapping his own sandwich. "When I opened one in my kitchen, I guess."

You'd think someone making a sandwich would be a mediocre revelation. But it's me, and it's Max Ryan, and Van Morrison is happening, so instead of saying "thanks" like a normal person, I find myself thinking of Max's long-fingered hands slicing tomatoes and cheese. Tearing into a crisp head of lettuce. I think of him, thinking of me, and the fact that I mentioned I liked grilled cheese.

Suddenly, it's hard to meet his eyes again. "Impressive."

"I try." He pulls out a bag of salt-and-vinegar chips and two bottles of that fancy natural grapefruit soda in the green bottle. "Don't worry, I didn't make the chips."

"Deep-frying at home can be very dangerous," I say after a missed beat, and Max laughs for a little too long considering how utterly unfunny I am right now.

"Well, bon appétit," he says in an adorably bad French accent, lifting his sandwich as if to cheers mine.

This is good, I think, as the chiropractors pause to thank the crowd and promise more classic rock oldies. We'll focus on eating. I can take a break from the sheer physicality of Max befuddling my senses. There's no way to eat a giant sandwich sexily, right? So this activity will naturally calm things down a little.

But as the band begins their next song, I realize I've never been so wrong in my life.

Max's sandwich quickly becomes the first food item I've ever been jealous of. I keep missing my mouth with my chips because I can't stop watching out of the corner of my eye.

Between the food and the music and the unnecessarily charged atmosphere between us as we eat, there's little conversation to be had. Our gazes keep meeting, resulting in reflexive smiles and slightly flushed cheeks. All in all, this interaction isn't making it any easier to remember the reason I came here tonight—which was *not* to spontaneously combust mid-sandwich.

But I can hardly come clean and negotiate an interview in the middle of dinner, right?

It turns out I can't do it in the middle of grapefruit soda, either. Or after the chiropractors start a spot-on rendition of "I Want You to Want Me," causing both Max and me to shout, then glance at each other in surprise.

"What can I say, it's a great song." I shrug.

"It really is, though," Max says, laughing. "I just didn't expect anyone who was listening to underground black metal at top volume to get excited about Cheap Trick."

"I contain multitudes," I say. I'm flirting. I know it, but that doesn't stop me from looking up through my eyelashes.

"Care to surprise me again?" he asks, getting to his feet, pulling me up with him.

"Depends on what kind of surprise you're talking about." *Is it the kind where I'm secretly a music journalist here in a desperate bid to review your unannounced new album?* I think, trying to rein myself in.

"Well, it usually starts with two people—although it can be done solo or in larger groups depending on your preference," Max says, sending all my warnings out of my head.

"I'm listening."

"It involves semi-coordinated movement at various aerobic levels . . ."

"Okay." We're very close to each other now. He's looking down at me, and his eyes can only be described as *smoldering*.

"And it requires enthusiastic consent from all parties involved . . ."

My heart is beating so loud I'm afraid he can hear it over the second verse of the song. My throat is too dry to answer. He's right there, within kissing distance, within *anything* distance.

"Sammy?" he asks in a low, husky voice.

"Yes?"

"Will you dance with me?"

I smile, taking his arm and allowing him to lead me down to the group of ladies still clustered in front of the stage. But privately, I think I would have said yes to a lot more than dancing. And that thought doesn't worry me nearly as much as it should.

Despite the fact that we're the only people older than seven and younger than fifty-five on the dance floor, it's the most fun I've had in ages.

I'm ashamed to admit that in my advanced age I've become an arm-folding wall-leaner when it comes to live music. I almost forgot how good it can feel to take all the emotion music stirs up and release it—even if you look like a dork in the process.

Max, in another twist, is entirely unselfconscious about dancing in a way I find incredibly sexy. He's not smooth, or practiced, but he clearly feels the rhythm and moves when it moves him.

He also doesn't try to over-romanticize the moment. Instead he lets the crowd enfold us, dancing democratically with me, a pair of old biddies catcalling him from the stage's edge, and a group of little kids who giggle and squeal when he accepts their invite to join in as they spin chaotically around in circles.

I do as much laughing as I do dancing, watching him interact with his community. There's no superiority, no feeling that he thinks he's above them because he played a sold-out Madison Square Garden on two consecutive tours.

He's humble, and fun, and as the sunset streaks the sky behind the stage in a spectacular display, I think maybe this was what I was drawn to eleven years ago. The promise of this exact man inside a beautiful, sleep-deprived boy.

"Ready for a break?" he asks from the center of a group of biddies trying to teach him salsa. They're reluctant to let him go, but he escapes politely and approaches me smiling. He's positively glowing, more beautiful than I've ever seen him. His curls hang in his eyes. His smile is as wide as the magenta swath across the sky.

I know I should say yes to the break. It's time to take him back to the blanket and tell the truth. But I'm swept up in the moment, and there will be time, I tell myself.

"Not yet," I say, stepping boldly forward until we're closer than we've been all night.

His arms move around me reflexively, and like a movie moment, the band switches to a crooner. The kids get bored and run off. The biddies link arms and face the stage. The electric-pink light fades, and twilight makes a cozy bubble of the place where we stand, finding our rhythm.

"This is nice," he murmurs into my hair. "You're a good dancer."

"It's the band," I demure, jerking my chin toward the stage. "I feel like they really have my back."

When Max laughs, I can feel it like I'm the one laughing. His chest rumbling against mine. His shoulders shaking beneath my hands. His stubble rasps against my cheek, and I think I'd like to make him laugh again and again. Like it would be worth becoming the most fascinating, hilarious person in the world just to feel the warmth coming off of him in waves. Just to know I caused it.

"Wow," he says, catching his breath. "Wow."

"I told you," I say, smirking, counting on him to feel it where his cheek is still touching mine.

"Multitudes," he agrees. "I had no idea how right you were."

The tempo slows further. My Aching Back is really reading the room as the evening deepens. Max doesn't let go as they switch songs. If anything his arms tighten around me just a little. I can feel his heartbeat, so I know he can feel mine. My skin is tingling everywhere we're touching.

"Great song," he says quietly, his breath hitching a little so I know I'm not alone in this. The total sensory overwhelm of it.

I don't trust my voice. My body. Max tilts his head slightly, and mine adjusts like our lips are doomed ships heading for the same craggy coast.

"Sammy," he says. His voice is heavy with significance. I know what will happen if I move even a fraction of an inch. What it will mean. Where it will lead.

I take a deep breath, glancing once more over his shoulder, reaching for anything that might ground me as I become totally untethered from my plan. My good sense. I feel the lean lines of his body pressing harder into mine and I think there's nothing that can stop me now.

But as my eyes scan the crowd, they lock on to the only person who might prove me wrong.

It's Paloma Espinoza. And she's staring at me like *she's* the one who's seen a ghost.

16.

"Oh, god," I say. I can feel myself going stiff as a board again, just like I was yesterday morning in the street. "I have to go."

"Whoa," Max says, backing away, taking my shoulders bracingly in his hands. "What's going on? Are you okay?"

"I'm sorry," I say, my voice high and thin, my eyes still locked on Paloma's across the lawn. I can't hear the music over the pounding in my ears. "It's not you, I swear, I just . . . I have to go."

But I don't move. I can't. I feel like Max's warm hands against my arms are the only places I'm still connected to the earth.

"Can I help?" Max asks, his voice barely penetrating. "I can get you out of here."

Paloma takes a step toward us. My nervous system spikes, sending panic electric through my veins. Clenching my teeth, I nod jerkily at Max. "Please." It's not like I have a lot of other options.

Instantly, his arm is strong around my back, steering me away from Paloma and across the lawn toward the Pollinator Garden. We pass under the trellised arch and Max takes a quick left down a winding mulch path, then a quick right, and another left until we're deep in the greenery.

Even if she's an especially sprightly and determined senior citizen, I doubt she could have followed us in here in the near-dark.

Max leads me over to a bench, which I sink onto gratefully. I can't feel my fingers or the tip of my nose. My heart is hammering like a bass drum. The music is still going, but it's fainter in here. A soundtrack instead of a show.

"Take a deep breath if you can," Max says, sitting beside me on the bench. Not close enough that we're touching, but close enough that I know he's there.

I inhale deeply. The evening air is tinged with the smell of lavender. It helps. I do it again. "Thanks," I say when I think my voice has mostly returned. "And, uh, sorry about that."

"Don't sweat it," he replies, waving me off. "I've had my fair share of panic attacks. I can recognize the signs well enough."

"You have?" I ask, looking sideways at him. "You always seem so confident." It's a slipup. The *always*. My nerves are so fried I forgot to lie. Luckily, Max doesn't seem to clock it.

"Years of practice," he says, and his smile has less of a veneer now. "You don't have to tell me what happened. But you can if you want to."

It's more or less the same thing Willa said to me after my fateful trip up Ponderosa Court, and again this morning. But for some reason, here, in this private wildflower garden with a man I was supposed to casually betray tonight, it feels okay. More than that—it feels right.

"Remember when I told you I have family here?" I ask, my heart finally slowing to just above its normal rhythm.

"Estranged family, if I'm not mistaken," Max says. "And a grandma you were possibly planning to meet for the first time."

I nod, grateful for his recall. The less explaining I have to do now the better. "Well, the meeting didn't go quite like I hoped. I was going to ask her why she didn't want to know me when I was a baby. Why she never thought to call since."

"Totally understandable questions to have," Max replies.

"Right. Except when I saw her coming out of her house I just froze. Like tonight. Stood in the middle of the street like a statue until I almost got hit by a car and then literally fled the scene." It feels good to have it off my chest, and I'm aware this isn't the first time I've thought this about a conversation with Max. Not even the second.

"It makes sense," he says, leaning just a little closer. "There's a lot of history there, estranged or not. Anyone could have reacted that way."

It's the same thing Willa would have said, probably. Or Maeve. Or anyone really. But even though it might make me a bad feminist, coming from Max it gets past my defenses. I let myself really believe it.

"I'm guessing the story doesn't end there?" he asks.

"I thought it did." I let myself turn to look at him. "I never thought I'd be able to go back after what happened. It just seemed too . . . impossibly hard. But then you and I were dancing, and there she was. Right over your shoulder. Staring at me like she recognized me."

Max whistles, long and low. Above us, twinkle lights flare to life as the sky deepens to a velvety blue. They reflect in his eyes, softening the edges of my fear, reigniting some of the spark from earlier.

"It was probably an overreaction," I say. "Sorry to drag you into it."

Max scoffs. "If anything, it was an underreaction. I'm surprised you didn't gasp like a soap star, or burst into flames, or vanish into thin air. Freezing up for a few seconds? I do that every time I see a bee."

A giggle escapes my lips. "You're afraid of bees? Are you, like, allergic or something?"

He shakes his head. "Not remotely, they just give me the creeps."

"And you ran us straight into a pollinator garden?"

"I was hoping the cover of darkness would hide my shame?"

I laugh again. The knot in my chest eases. "You're very brave."

He smiles, then covers his hand with mine. "Listen," he says.

"There's a path to the parking lot that doesn't even pass the lawn. You can head for the bike, I'll grab our stuff and meet you there in two minutes. We'll get out of here, and you never have to see her again."

"Or?" I ask, sensing there are more options on offer.

"Or we can march back out there and you can have some moral support while you ask your grandma exactly what you wanted to ask her."

The very idea fills me with panic again, but this night is coming to a close either way, and I think of the feeling I had when my mom told me about Roberto. That there wasn't enough time.

And my promise to myself this morning, too. That I'd tell Max the truth.

I know I have to do both, but if Paloma's here, would honoring one commitment be enough for tonight? Would asking my estranged grandmother why she abandoned me be reason enough to take a little more time with Max?

"What's in it for me if I do it?" I ask.

"I'll buy you ice cream after," he replies without hesitation. "Any flavor you want."

I laugh louder this time. "What am I? An eight-year-old who's afraid to get a shot?"

"Are you telling me you're not tempted?"

I straighten up. I know I shouldn't keep putting this off, but I find I *can't* tell him about the article tonight. About my real reason for coming here. Something has shifted between us, and I don't know what I'm going to do, but I do know I need more time to figure it out. Even if that means breaking a generational curse tonight.

"It just so happens that I love ice cream," I say, getting to my feet. "So let's go."

The music grows louder again as we make our way back to the field. The party is still in full swing. There are twinkle lights here, too, crisscrossing the dance floor area, and for a moment I'm afraid Paloma already left. That the confidence I charged out here with will be wasted . . .

But then I spot her. Eight o'clock. She doesn't even seem aware there's a band playing anymore, she's just looking around the crowd like she lost something important.

"You ready?" Max asks, his warm, solid presence beside me giving me strength.

"No," I reply, but I set off in Paloma's direction anyway, with all the boldness I can muster.

This time, I don't let myself freeze. She clocks me from a few yards away and watches me approach, making no move to meet me. She's wearing black and red again. This time wide-leg pants and a tapestry coat with bright flowers. She looks put together in that moneyed way that has always intimidated me.

I can smell her perfume. Something sharp and bright. Floral, but a little metallic, too.

"You were at my house yesterday morning," she says when I stop in front of her.

"I was," I agree, trying not to let her accent pull at my heart-strings. Not to think of everything I lost when she decided not to know me. "I went there to ask you something, and I lost my nerve. But I want to do it now."

Max is hanging a little ways back, supportive but not stealing the show. His silhouette out of the corner of my eye reminds me why I can't run away. The lesser-of-two-evils decision I made in the garden.

Paloma Espinoza gestures with both her wrinkled hands. Inviting me to go on.

"I'm your granddaughter, Sammy Espinoza," I say in a rush, pleased with my voice for staying steady. "You chose not to be a part of my life after my dad died, and my mom has always hated you for it, but I realized . . . I want to know why." I take a deep breath, determined not to leave anything out. "I want to know why I wasn't worthy of being a part of your family. Why you never once tried to get ahold of me in almost thirty years."

My whole body is shaking as I finish. I can't believe I actually did it. It doesn't even matter we're in a public place, or that Max just saw the whole thing, or that Paloma is still standing there, regarding me like I'm one of the immaculate rosebushes surrounding the lawn.

After a long moment, she finally opens her mouth. Not to answer my question. But to ask her own.

"Would you like to come to my house for dinner?"

"Uh . . . I . . . what?" I stammer.

"Dinner. My house. How's Thursday night at six?"

I feel like a complicated set of gears that's just had a pencil jammed into it. I remember the future vanishing in front of me whenever I tried to predict her reaction, and now there's this. Stranger to dinner guest in one minute flat.

"Okay," I say, before I can talk myself out of it. "But that doesn't mean I forgive you."

"Of course not," she replies simply. "I think we have a lot to talk about. I will see you Thursday. You know where the house is." She glances at Max, who has moved a little closer. "Feel free to bring your gentleman friend. I'm an excellent cook."

Without waiting for my response—which, to be fair, wasn't forthcoming anyway, she turns and picks her way carefully across the grass. She doesn't look back.

"You okay?" Max says, moving to my side once Paloma is out of sight.

I turn around to face him, opening my mouth, then closing it, then opening it again. "I have no idea," I say truthfully. "Whatever I expected, it wasn't that."

Max is quiet. Abruptly, the feeling of vindication is gone, and I realize I just essentially confronted my grandmother about my formative abandonment trauma on a second date.

"Sorry," I say. "A sprained ankle on the first date and grandma drama on the second, I'm really making this a memorable week, aren't I?"

Max chuckles, putting an arm around me. "I told you I don't like the surface level," he says, steering me toward the exit. "I just see this as you rising *magnificently* to the occasion."

It's nice, under his arm. I feel safe. To anyone watching, we must just look like any normal couple—not a former rock god and a music critic in disguise. For a minute, I let myself pretend we are. Erase all the complications.

It feels better than it should, so I lean in as we collect our belongings from the blanket and head toward the gate. He puts his arm around me again, even though he has to carry everything in one hand to do it.

I let the feeling of him next to me blot out my panic about spending an entire evening with Paloma, and my conflicting feelings about my article and everything else. Feeling the delicious way a crush can make everything outside of it unimportant and small.

The electricity of our closeness from the dance floor seeps back in—deepened somehow by the ordeal we've just experienced. The night air does little to break the tension. Clouds are rolling in quick, signaling one of southern Washington's classic storms. The air is damp and sultry. Charged.

There's no one in the parking lot when we reach it—everyone's still back at the concert. We walk slowly, not bothering to stop our limbs from brushing, bumping, overlapping. His jeans grazing my bare thigh. My arm snakes around his waist, pulling him closer.

The motorcycle is just ahead, but I'm not ready to go home yet. To give up this perfect distraction. I slow to a stop beside a little stone garden shed, half-covered in ivy. Max slows with me, looking down like he's going to ask if I'm okay—even though his heavily lidded eyes tell me he's not immune to the energy pulsing between us.

I turn to face him, reaching up to trace the stubble along his jaw. I know I should say something to mark the transition, but for once there are no words in my head. My brain has taken up the rhythmic chant of my body and it's such a relief I don't want to stop.

"Sammy . . ." he whispers, and I can't tell if it's a warning or a plea.

"Max," I say, before I can find out. "I'd really like to kiss you."

For a moment, he looks torn. Almost tortured. He's so close, lips just inches from mine, dark eyes probing mine. For a moment I'm certain he'll put a stop to it. Reject me again. All my poorly healed wounds brace for impact.

"Are you sure?" he asks finally.

I want to say something glib, something to ease this unbearable tension, but all I can manage is *yes.*

Max reacts to this one small word like a starting pistol has been fired. He drops the picnic supplies, then slides his newly free hand down to grab my waist. He presses me against the building, and I can feel the grit of the stone through the fabric of my dress. His heart beats fast and hard against my chest.

When his lips descend they're gentle, exploratory at first. The pounding of my pulse demands more urgency, and I arch my back, pushing into him, deepening the kiss as he hisses into my mouth.

If he's surprised, it's only because he doesn't know we've done this before. But I do. And I've been waiting eleven years for the encore.

He reacts with enthusiasm to my desperation, matching it, urging my mouth open wider. He tastes like the mint he ate after dinner. A hint of grapefruit soda. The pressure of his tongue is relentless. Expert. I try not to think of the way it would feel applied to places with more sensitive nerves . . .

I whimper into his mouth at the thought. A needy sound I don't even recognize, and certainly not one that belongs in a botanical garden parking lot during a chiropractor lawn concert that could let out at any moment.

I'm sure Max will pull away, now that he's realized how out of my head I am. Instead he seems emboldened. His hands find my hips and pull me roughly into him. Against my thigh is all the evidence I need that I'm not the only one getting carried away.

He moves to kiss my neck, and I dig my nails into his hip. He groans into my pulse point. *I'm not going to be able to stop,* I realize, delirious. But fortunately, Max has more willpower than I do. Even still, when he stops I can tell it's costing him something. His eyes are glazed over, his pupils blown.

"I'm sorry," he rasps.

"No, I'm sorry," I say, catching my breath. He hasn't pulled away. His body is still pressing mine to the wall like it hasn't quite caught up. "We definitely shouldn't be doing this here."

He chuckles, easing away, beginning the disentangling. "I think public decency laws are on your side there."

"Maybe . . . a nightcap at your place?" I ask, the thrumming in my body still calling the shots.

His eyes are molten, that desperate war again. Then he steps away. The cool air rushes between our bodies as he turns, and all the feelings I've been trying to push out along with it.

"Actually, it's getting late," he says, not quite meeting my eyes. "I should take you home."

"Oh, sure," I say, but his rejection stings much more than the fall chill.

He holds out a hand perfunctorily to help me out of the ivy, but drops it just after my feet are on solid ground. There are no lingering glances as we put on the motorcycle helmets, and even the ride back feels different. Like he's flipped off a switch and left me in the dark.

It seems to take no time at all to get back to Willa's, and I swing my leg over the seat, thinking I can still salvage this with the perfect good-night kiss.

But when Max kills the engine, he stays astride. I hand him my helmet, then stand awkwardly by as he stows it without dismounting. When he turns back to look at me, it's from the safe shadows of his own helmet.

"Thank you for tonight, Sammy," he says. "I'll see you around."

And then he's kicking the bike back to life, leaving me standing dumbstruck on the sidewalk as the engine groans and his taillights disappear into the night.

17.

I stand on the sidewalk for a long time. Even the numb-
ness Max's departure left is better than what I know is waiting on
the other side of it.

What the hell happened? I wonder. What did I do? Was it the
forwardness of asking to come back to his place? Based on the
way he was behaving during that kiss, I can't imagine him being
too offended by the request. But then, what?

I rack my brain for several long minutes and come up with
exactly nothing.

Nothing but a solid wall of frustration and resentment that I've
just crashed into at top speed.

From here, Willa and Brook's house looks like a cozy oasis in a
scary, fairy-tale forest. I can see the lights blazing inside, hear
music drifting out the open window. I know I should go in, but I
don't know what to tell them. Especially Willa, who warned me
repeatedly not to let Max Ryan get in my head—or my heart.

How can I admit that not only did I not take her very reasonable advice, but I also didn't tell Max about the article. The truth
about who I am. How do I tell her I have no more answers than I
did when I climbed on Max's motorcycle this evening—and about
a thousand more questions?

But then I remember Paloma. Confronting her at last. The dinner invitation I never expected. Anyone would have been flustered by that, right? Who could possibly blame me for not talking

to Max about the article when I was staving off a panic attack in a bee habitat at the time?

Just a little creative timeline rearranging and I can vent to Willa without any judgment.

It's this, and only this, that allows me to turn toward the front door. I'll tell Willa what happened with Paloma, about Max's abrupt departure, leave out any talk of kissing and hopefully by the time I have to give her details I'll have things much better in hand . . .

That is, if Max ever talks to me again.

"Ugh!" I groan aloud, sending several startled birds flapping out of a nearby tree. "Sorry, I'm a mess tonight!" I call to their retreating silhouettes, wondering if this has been it. The last straw. The catalyst that begins my life as a woman who wanders the streets muttering to birds.

To make matters infinitely worse, Brook and Willa are on the couch when I throw the door open dramatically. They're kissing deeply, Willa's hands tangled in Brook's short hair, one leg thrown over her lap. Brook is down to her sports bra, hands around her wife's waist in a way that tells me they're just getting started.

My first impulse is to flee, sleep in the driveway with the birds. But they're already springing apart, their faces both flushed with embarrassment.

"I'm *so* sorry!" Willa shrieks, getting to her feet as Brook throws her shirt on at lightning speed. "We didn't expect you until late, shit, Sammy, I'm really sorry."

"This is your house," I say, walking toward the guest room door, averting my eyes. "I'm the one who should be sorry. Carry on! Someone should be!"

I shut the door before Willa can try to convince me they'd rather hear about my disaster night than have beautiful, connected, married-people sex. She doesn't knock, or text, and a few minutes later I hear the door to their bedroom close across the hall.

It's for the best, I think, lying on my bed in the dress Max couldn't keep his hands off of an hour ago and feeling like the loneliest person in the world.

I have a series of unnerving dreams that night. First, Max peels out on his motorcycle with a JUST MARRIED sign and cans dragging behind him.

Next, I show up for dinner at Paloma's, but it's a squawking bird who answers the door of her fancy house, person-sized, its beak opening up too wide like it wants to swallow me whole.

"You're not my grandma," I say blankly.

And then Max steps forward in all his stubbled former-rock-star glory and kisses the terrifying bird right on the mouth.

When they're done with their interspecies making out, Max turns to me with feathers clinging to his lips and says: *Now, that's an article I'd read.*

When I wake up, I vow to never tell anyone about the dream. Not even my Seattle therapist. Maybe especially not her.

I'm too freaked out to go back to sleep, but also too embarrassed to see Willa and Brook, so I stay in bed for as long as possible—even though the only thing to do is replay the roller coaster of last night over and over in my head.

Standing up to Paloma. The dinner invitation in lieu of answers. The high of feeling wanted by Max and the low of being rejected by him for no reason I can possibly fathom.

I should be thinking about the effect this hiccup will have on my ability to convince him to let me do the article—my deadline is only eight days away—but I'm not. I'm thinking about the kiss, and how good it felt, and how devastating it would be to lose him again.

Rolling over, I groan into my pillow. I knew better than to let myself get caught up in this. Is it too late to walk away? Before last night, I would have said no. But now I'm not so sure.

Eventually, a low headache begins to build behind my eyes and

I have no choice but to venture out in search of caffeine. Unfortunately, I still have zero idea what I'm going to do about anything. And Max hasn't said a word.

When I emerge, Brook is at her laptop in the dining room processing orders. She abandons the keyboard the moment she sees me, eyes widening excitedly behind her giant glasses.

"How did it go?" she asks. "Was he all wounded and betrayed? Or are we writing an epic takedown?"

I sigh heavily, shuffling to the coffeepot and filling the biggest stoneware mug I can find.

"Neither?" I say, not sure if I'm asking or telling.

"Neither because he's thinking it over?" Brook asks with an eyebrow waggle. "Or neither because you chickened out in the face of those chiseled cheekbones?"

"Are you sure you're a lesbian?" I grumble, face half in my mug.

"I'm *also* a connoisseur of fine art," she says, somehow glaring and smirking at the same time. "And don't even bother lying, missy. That hickey you're trying to hide with a barely seasonable scarf is all the answer I need."

My hand flies guiltily to my neck, an admission before I can blame the curling iron.

"You're too observant when you're wearing your nerd glasses." I stick out my tongue at her.

"Willa's in the garden," Brook says through her giggles. "But you better tighten that scarf. You know how she feels about Max."

"I know," I say, and it's all I can do to open the back door, knowing the grilling that's waiting for me.

Willa is on her knees beside a towering tomato plant, considering a fruit that looks just on the verge of ripeness. She smiles when she sees me, patting the grass beside her.

I sit. The storm that was building during my date with Max spent itself overnight. There are raindrops glistening on the leaves and the grass is damp beneath my jeans. A perfect ray of sun shines down on us.

"I wondered when you'd stop hiding," Willa says. "Sorry again about last night."

"You have nothing to apologize for," I assure her. "I'm glad you and Brook haven't succumbed to some boring married-people rut. Just, uh, sock on the doorknob or something next time so I don't kill the vibe with my dramatic entrance."

"Noted," Willa says, her cheeks a little pink. "Speaking of which, do you want to tell me why you stormed in like a not-so-silent film star? Did it not go well when you told Max?"

I remember my plan from last night. The one where I pivot to talking about Paloma to defer any judgment from my extracurricular activities and my total lack of follow-through.

"Actually, Paloma was there."

The plan is off to a good start. Willa claps a hand over her mouth to cover her gasp. "Paloma was on your *date*?" she asks.

"Paloma was at the concert on the lawn Max chose for our date," I clarify.

"Oh god," Willa says. "*Everyone* goes to those things. I'm surprised you didn't see my parents."

"I would have preferred them," I reply drily.

"Obviously," Willa says. "Sorry. Ugh. What happened?"

In order to answer this question, of course, I have to go back to the other morning. The Ponderosa Court near-death freezing. As impossible as this story felt to tell even yesterday, it seems a small price to pay to delay my admission of guilt about Max, so I launch in, sparing no detail.

"Oh, Sammy," Willa says when I finish. "That sounds awful."

"Enough to make me positive I could never speak to her again," I confirm. "I was planning to focus on the article instead so I'd have *something* to show for my time here, but then—"

"You were struck by the small-town curse of seeing the last person you want to see the first place you go," she says sympathetically.

"Exactly."

"So what did you do? Is that why you came home so early?"

I shake my head. "I wish it was that easy. I basically froze again, Max had to half-carry me to a bench out of sight to collect myself, which was humiliating." I grimace. "But we were talking, and I realized I'd regret it if I left town without saying anything. So . . . I did it. I told her who I was and asked her why she let me grow up without half of my family."

"Wow!" Willa says, beaming. "That must have felt great!"

"It did until she scrambled my entire brain by *inviting Max and me to dinner* instead of answering."

This is supposed to be the pièce de résistance. The totally wacky plot twist that gets Willa's attention and sends us down a rabbit hole of figuring out exactly what the invitation meant and what I should prepare for when I go—safely diverting us from any further discussion of Max and me or any totally inappropriate making out we may or may not have done against an ivy-covered shed.

Instead, Willa wrinkles her brow and says, "Wait, Max was with you when you talked to Paloma?"

"Well, yeah," I say, not hearing the trap. "I mean, we were there together, and he kind of convinced me to do it in the first place, so it would have been a little weird to leave him sitting alone."

"So, you talked to Paloma because *Max* convinced you to." The trap is closing, but it's too late now. It was hidden too well in the weeds and I was moving too fast . . .

"No," I say automatically, my hands getting clammy. "Well, kind of. But it doesn't really matter why it happened, does it?"

Willa steeps over this question for a long minute, staring at her tomato instead of meeting my eyes. "I think it's great you talked to Paloma regardless of the reason," she says finally. "But I do wonder why you're opening up to Max so much when this was just supposed to be about work. I mean, what did he say when you told him about the article after all that?"

In this moment, my ironclad excuse that I was too preoccupied with Paloma to mention the article seems about as solid as a wet paper towel.

Willa reads the answer in my long silence. "Guess you didn't get around to that part?"

"Not exactly." I shrug. "It was a pretty weird night with all that family stuff."

Willa sighs. "Sammy, you know I'm not judging you, right?"

"Of course," I answer, even though I'm not sure I really do.

"I know it's been a lot for you. It's just that I was there the first time. When Max swept you away with all these promises and convinced you to change the whole trajectory of your life and then just . . . bailed. Without even a phone call."

"I know," I say, looking at my hands twisted in my lap.

"I was there when you stopped going to shows and applying for internships and barely got out of bed for weeks. And I remember what you said before it all came crashing down, too. About how you guys connected, and he *got* you, and he was so supportive and inspiring . . ."

"Okay," I say, holding up a hand. "I don't need to relive it."

"I think you *do* need to relive it," Willa presses, leaning in closer until I feel absolutely cornered. "Because I'm afraid if you don't you're going to walk right down that same path again, and after everything that just happened with Juniper I don't think that's what you need."

Suddenly, I feel like this conversation is a too-small sweater, shrinking around me even as I struggle to get it over my head. I'm angry at Willa for thinking she knows what I need better than I do, and I'm angry that she might be right, and I can't deal with it. So I get to my feet, tears already stinging the backs of my eyes.

"I hear you," I say, my voice strained and somehow too-casual at once. "Listen, I just remembered there's something I have to do, so I'll see you later, okay?"

Willa sighs again. There's disappointment in every line of her face as she looks up at me. "Eventually you're going to have to stop running from things," she says, and she's probably right.

But it's not going to happen today.

18.

I can't ask to borrow one of Willa and Brook's cars now, and Larry is the only Lyft driver in town, so when I leave the house, I do it on foot.

It turns out Ridley Falls is small enough that you run into everyone you don't want to see at the very worst moment, but large enough that it takes a weirdly long time to walk anywhere that sells sugary coffee drinks.

And then, when I finally reach downtown, the only coffee place is closed for lunch.

"Perfect," I mutter to my reflection in the Cascade Coffee window. Another hour before I can even drown my sorrow in some kind of oat milk mocha that's pretending to be a grown-up beverage.

Downtown is almost eerily quiet, and I feel like a sore thumb loitering around the storefronts in the middle of a workday. Eventually I realize—consciously, though I must have known it all along—that I've been walking toward Mystical Moments.

"Hey, sugar," Maeve says when I enter. "I could get used to you dropping by."

"Hi," I say miserably.

She's labeling some little bottles on the front counter, but when she hears my tone she looks up immediately. "Oh no," she says. "What happened?"

I'm not even sure how to begin explaining Paloma, or Max, so instead I just say, "I think Willa is mad at me?" feeling like a little kid tattling on their sibling in the most pathetic way.

Maeve comes around the counter and wraps me up in one of those no-nonsense hugs that might as well be medicinal. Her arms form a cage around everything that's trying to swallow me whole.

When she pulls away, she gestures at a pair of comfy-looking armchairs beside the metaphysical bookshelf. "That girl of mine," she says when we're settled. "She sure has her opinions, doesn't she?"

Instantly, my defenses are up—even though I know how much Willa's mom loves her.

"She didn't do anything wrong," I say quickly. "She was right about everything."

"Of course she was," Maeve agrees. "Seeing deep down into people is one of her many gifts. But she doesn't always have the gentlest delivery. Or the best timing."

Even though it feels disloyal, I'm forced to agree. Or at least to stay quiet while Maeve continues.

"Do you remember that year you lived with us, when you were sad about your mom extending her trip through Christmas. When Willa told you, no nonsense, that you'd better just get used to living with us?"

I chuckle a little, nodding. "She didn't understand why I was so upset," I say, recalling the scene in the backyard with perfect clarity. "She said I was better off with you guys than Dina Rae, anyway."

Maeve is quiet, letting me reminisce.

"She might have been right that time, too," I say after a long minute.

"So what was she right about this time?" Maeve asks.

There it is again. The wall of obstacles I've managed to build up since I arrived here. Max, Paloma, Ridley Falls itself.

"She says that eventually I'll have to stop running from things," I simplify.

Maeve makes a humming sound in the back of her throat. "We're all running from something," she says. "You stop and face it when you're ready, not when someone else is."

This soothes the burn Willa's words left behind a little. Maybe the fact that I'm not ready now doesn't mean I never will be. Or that I'm doomed to become my mother.

"Paloma Espinoza invited me to her house for dinner," I blurt out before I decide to.

Maeve's eyes widen with shock. "Is that so?"

I nod. "I asked her why she didn't want to know me back then, and instead of answering she just . . . invited me to dinner."

Maeve whistles. "And what did you say?"

"I said I would go," I admit. "But now I don't know. I have no idea what she's planning. And after a lifetime of nothing, an entire dinner sounds like a lot regardless."

"Sometimes it's easier to build a new bridge than repair an old one," Maeve says. "But that doesn't mean the old ones aren't worth fixing."

I try to let this make me feel better, but it doesn't. Not really. "I was hoping maybe the cards could tell me what to do," I say, feeling silly.

Maeve is already shaking her head. "The cards can be a crutch, too. Sometimes you just have to leap, sugar."

For the first time since I met her, I have the feeling there's something Maeve Cross isn't telling me. Something lurking behind her sage advice. Some caution or warning she won't let herself give.

It's not until after we say our goodbyes and I'm sipping on a glorified chocolate milk in a paper cup that I realize with a sinking sensation: I wasn't the only person invited to dinner tomorrow. What am I going to do if Max doesn't call before then?

What am I going to do if he does?

* * *

Willa and I have had enough friend fights over the past two decades that we pretty much have the making-up formula down. A couple hours to cool off. A period of awkward over-politeness. Finally, some kind of unexpected laughing fit that somehow heals it all and puts us back on track.

Dinner that night falls firmly into the second stage. My wineglass is never empty. Willa offers me seconds on everything and I take her plate to the sink without being asked.

Brook watches the show with a sort of amused weariness. This isn't her first time in the audience. She knows as well as anyone that we'll be over it soon.

"So, I won't be here for dinner tomorrow night," I say in my most cheerful tone as we're having a post-dinner decaf.

"Really?" Willa asks with dinner-party curiosity.

"I'm going to have dinner with Paloma."

"Oh!" I can see the strain this puts on Willa's surface-level polish. She's positively *dying* to ask what I'm planning to say. How I'm feeling about it. Whether Max will be joining me. "Well, good for you!"

"Thanks!" I say, beaming unnaturally.

Brook slams her empty coffee cup onto the table with a crash that startles us both. "Would you two knock it off, please? This is giving me a headache."

"What do you mean?" Willa and I ask together innocently.

Brook sighs heavily, then points a rolled-up napkin at her wife. "*You* need to stop trying to control Sammy's life," she says in the no-nonsense voice she learned working a decade-plus in restaurant kitchens. "We both know you mean well, but you can't protect her from everything, so please stop trying before you push her away with your expectations."

I'm feeling guilty, but a little vindicated, until Brook and her napkin round on me.

"And you," she says, narrowing her eyes. "You've gotta figure out what you're doing here, pal. Are you writing an article? Are you dating Max Ryan? None of us"—she cuts a look at Willa—"have any right to choose for you, but ignoring the consequences of stringing him along is gonna end in a big old mess, which is what *she's* trying to save you from."

My feelings of vindication are long gone now. I don't feel defensive anymore, either. Just thoroughly called out.

"I'm sorry, Sammy," Willa says from across the table.

I look up to meet her eyes. "I'm sorry, too," I say. "I know you're trying to protect me, I just do things differently than you and that has to be okay."

"It is," she promises, getting a little teary-eyed. "I promise it is."

We silently emote at each other from a distance for a long few seconds before Brook finally bellows, "HUG IT OUT, ALREADY."

So we do, all three of us, and I go to bed knowing tomorrow will be better, even if I have made a giant mess of absolutely everything.

I also go to bed without having heard a single word from Max all day.

19.

The next morning, I awake with one more plan and zero more texts than I had the night before.

Letting my Max situation and my Paloma situation collide the other night left everything horribly tangled, I can see that now. But now that I know, I vow as I ease reluctantly out of bed, I will separate the threads. Today, I'll deal with Paloma. Tomorrow, I'll deal with Max.

And by "deal with him" I mean say goodbye. Brook was right last night—this whole thing has gotten completely out of control. It's laughable to think I could still be objective about Max's music after everything that's happened between us. And trying to be objective about the music of someone I have romantic feelings for is what got me into this mess in the first place.

This realization is fortunate, because it means I don't ever have to tell Max our meeting was contrived. Maybe now, I think as I finish getting ready for the day, I can be what I always wanted to be to him: a wistful memory of something that could have been.

It's *un*fortunate because it means I'll have to tell Esme I can't write the Max Ryan article, and I'll probably lose my job.

I decide to tackle the conveying-bad-news part of the plan some other time. My deadline is still days away, after all.

Willa and Brook are busy today, looking at some goats two counties over, so I spend the hours before six at loose ends. Mostly I pick at food in a lackluster way and try to ignore my mounting anxiety as dinner with Paloma creeps closer and closer.

I scroll the Seattle job sites. Envision my life as a daytime bartender. At least I leave Juniper's Instagram unstalked. In fact, since I've been here I've barely thought of her.

Probably the rural air, I decide, ignoring the way my heart is still beating Max's stupid name in Morse code.

At five I can't stand the quiet anymore. I call Larry, asking him if he's free to give me a ride up to Ponderosa Court in twenty minutes. He agrees enthusiastically.

While I wait, I dig through Willa's little baskets of scented soaps and jellies for a visitor gift that doesn't make too much of a commitment.

I almost cancel my ride—and this whole ridiculous plan—a total of eight times before the van pulls into the driveway.

"With the article dead, you can leave town whenever you want," I tell myself in the entryway mirror. "If this ends in tears, or fleeing, you never have to see this lady again."

This is the only pep talk capable of getting me out the door and into Larry's Lyft.

"Well now, if it isn't my favorite big-city customer!" he exclaims as I climb into the passenger seat.

We attempt a side-hug over the center console and break apart chuckling.

"Thanks for the ride," I say, immediately comforted by the oldies and the faint scent of patchouli.

"Ponderosa Court, huh?" he asks, pulling away from the house. "Guess you decided to go into the dragon's lair after all." Larry waggles his eyebrows at me.

I nod. I want to ask what he means by "dragon lady" and for any other info he has on Paloma. I always feel better when I walk into an interview with my background complete. But something stops me from interrogating him. The whole reason I came here was to form my own opinions about her, separate from my mom's. I'll just have to wait and see.

A pensive silence settles as we climb higher into the trees. It's still early, but up here the setting sun gilds the trees' silhouettes, sunset not far off.

Larry whistles as we turn onto Ponderosa Court. "Rare air up here," he says. "Bet you can see all the way to the bay from some of these windows."

I want to tell him I wouldn't know, but my throat seems to be stuck shut.

Any minute now, I'm going to have to get out of this van. Walk up the steep driveway just coming into view. Knock on the red door and face all the ghosts that have been waiting for me here.

"Sixty-four," Larry announces, easing to a stop on an incline and turning the wheel away from the curb. "Want me to wait? Be your getaway driver just in case?"

I smile, knowing he really would wait through a whole dinner for me. "It's okay," I say. "Get home to Maeve. I'll call you if I need a ride home."

"Sure thing, kid," he says, patting my shoulder. "Whatever happens in there, you'll always have one family in town."

"Thanks, Larry," I say, blinking hard.

As I cross the street, I think about how blessedly free my life in Seattle is from drama like this. Family and forever-friends and roots a mile deep. It's comforting to know I can stomp the proverbial gas pedal whenever I'm ready. That it'll all stay here, in the rearview mirror.

Thinking about my escape route helps me *not* think about almost being run over in this very spot mere days ago. Or about the fact that for a brief, wild moment I almost thought Max and I would be attending this dinner together.

"You can do this," I mutter to myself as I hike the driveway. "You did it once."

I finally feel ready, but there's a wrench in things by the time I reach the top of the porch stairs.

The front door is wide open.

I check my phone. 5:43. Is it possible she left the door open for me? That she expects me to just walk in like family would?

Off-balance, I knock on the frame.

Nothing.

"Paloma?" I call. "It's Sammy . . . I'm here for dinner?"

Still nothing.

I peer inside just a little, still unable to shake the feeling that I'm being watched. The wood floors are glossy and dark, the furniture a creamy beige leather with pops of color from bright pillows and throws. The hazy sunset light filters through massive windows that—Larry was right—showcase a spectacular view of the bay.

"Um, okay, I'm coming in!" I call out again, thinking maybe Paloma is in the kitchen.

I step inside, holding my little lavender soap in its organza bag, hoping none of the neighbors are watching. But it only takes one more step before all thoughts of the neighbors—and everything else—disappear from my mind entirely.

On the floor behind the love seat, there's an arm extended. The arm of someone who's lying unconscious on the floor.

Without thinking twice, I rush in, my sneakers squeaking on the fancy floors. Sure enough, it's Paloma, stretched out between the coffee table and the sofa. She looks alarmingly pale.

"HELP!" I shout without thinking about the fact that the house is likely empty. I know my father and grandfather are gone, and Paloma has been alone both times I've seen her.

Sure enough, there's no answer.

"Fuck!" I shout, then I reach forward to feel Paloma's pulse. It's quick, but it's there. Relief surges through me. "Paloma? It's me, Sammy. Your . . . uh . . . Sammy from the concert. Can you hear me?"

Silence. It's starting to become horribly clear that she needs to be taken to the hospital.

I pull out my phone and dial 911, then I pause, finger over the call button. I know my dad's family is Catholic, that they're from Mexico, but I don't know anything about their immigration status.

Feeling like a total creep, I find Paloma's purse hanging on a hook by the door, her wallet inside. Front and center is a California state driver's license. One less complication. I ignore the badge that says I've missed two calls and dial 911.

"911, what's your emergency?"

"Hi, um, I need an ambulance. There's a woman unconscious here, I don't know what's wrong with her."

"All right, ma'am, we'll send someone right away. Can you verify your address for me?"

"Sixty-four Ponderosa Court."

"Thank you, ma'am, and can you tell me your phone number?"

"Is this really necessary?" I ask, irritated. "She's, like, on the floor unconscious right now!"

"Please be patient, ma'am, and tell me your phone number, we'll get someone out there as soon as we can."

I relay my phone number, realizing this is the first time I've ever actually called 911. I didn't know it was so complicated to get someone to help an unconscious old woman.

"Now, what is the age of the person experiencing the medical issue?"

"Um, I don't know," I stammer, trying to count up from the birth date on her driver's license. "Seventy . . . something? Seventy-seven? No, seventy-eight." I didn't become a writer because I'm great at math.

"And what is your relationship to the patient?"

I freeze here. I have no idea what Paloma thinks we are to each other. Hasn't she made it abundantly clear over the years that she does not want to be my grandmother?

And what difference will it make anyway?

"I'm a neighbor," I hear myself lie. "I was walking by, saw the door open."

"Okay, thank you. Can you tell me if her heart is beating?"

"She has a pulse," I answer. My fingertips are going numb. "She's breathing."

"Thank you, ma'am, please stay on the line with me until the ambulance arrives."

I can already hear the siren. It's a small town, after all. In five minutes there's flashing light filling the quiet street and paramedics are rushing through Paloma's red front door with a stretcher.

They ask me all the same questions as 911 dispatch. I repeat the lie. That I'm just a neighbor. I tell them she was unconscious with the door open when I found her. I hand an EMT her purse, thinking they'll need it to identify her.

At some point, Larry Cross appears in the driveway, his flyaway hair and tie-dye shirt looking out of place in Paloma's fancy house. "What happened?" he asks, watching them carry her out on the stretcher. "Are you okay?"

"I'm fine," I say, the numbness spreading to my lips now. "She's just . . . she was unconscious. I don't know what happened."

"We'll be taking her to the hospital now," says one of the paramedics. A square-jawed guy that fits every one of the small-town paramedic stereotypes. "Thank you for calling."

"Should I . . . go with her or something?" I ask. I'm starting to feel like this is all happening at a distance, or happening to someone else. "I mean, in the ambulance. Should I ride with her?"

"No need," he says. "We'll get in touch with the emergency contact on file when we get to the hospital. Thanks again."

He's gone before I can argue. Suddenly I feel like the worst person in the world for pretending I didn't know her—even if I was trying to respect her wishes.

"Hey, kiddo?" Larry asks, snapping his fingers in front of my face. "You okay?"

"Not really," I say, half laughing, half sobbing. "Larry, do you think I could get a ride to the hospital?"

20.

The Ridley Falls hospital is a dingy little building on the
edge of town. I managed to avoid it during my year living here,
and obviously I was still in utero when my father was rushed here
on his graduation night.

When Larry pulls up to the ER doors I'm starting to calm down,
the numbness receding from my fingertips and face. But I can't
help thinking this place—which looks like it hasn't been updated,
or even pressure-washed, in my lifetime—doesn't exactly inspire
confidence in their ability to care for sick loved ones.

Or estranged blood relatives, in my case.

"I'll come in with you whenever you're ready," Larry says comfortingly, seeming to understand implicitly why I haven't been
able to open the door of the van yet. "I'm sure she'll be just fine."

I know this is just one of those things parents say. No one could
possibly know this. For a minute, I'm seeing the side-by-side Espinoza graves at the cemetery. I'm sure a lot of people said my father and grandfather would be just fine, too.

My stomach growls loudly in the silence, breaking the tension.
"Sorry," I mutter to Larry. I realize I'm still clutching the little lavender soap I was planning to give Paloma as a gift. "We were supposed to have dinner."

"Here's what I'll do," Larry says, covering my white-knuckled
hand with his and waiting until I meet his eyes. "I'll go get you the
biggest cheeseburger I can find, and I'll meet you back here in
twenty minutes."

"You really don't have to," I say, feeling guilty for how much of his night I've already taken up. His own dinner is probably waiting on the table at home. "I'm sure you have other stuff to do besides deal with my never-ending drama."

"Squirt, I hate that you don't have a lot of experience in this department, but this is what family does. We take you places. We bring you food at the hospital. It's one of those laws of nature."

I'm still for a minute, wondering what it must be like to have this your whole life instead of just one year. What it must feel like to trust it. Rely on it.

"You're gonna sit there and tell me you *don't* want a cheeseburger?" Larry asks when I'm quiet too long.

My stomach growls again, answering for me.

"Scoot on out of here," Larry says with a chuckle and a nudge. "I'll be back faster than you can say extra pickles."

"Thank you," I say quietly. For more than the pickles. For more than tonight.

The hospital's waiting room is even more depressing than its exterior. The floors are shabby tile, the walls a sickly mustard color. The chairs are connected bucket seats like the ones at the bus station. Olive-green to clash with the walls.

On chipped tables sit magazines that look older than I am— tips on how to *Bust That Belly* or trick your kids into eating vegetables.

There's just one person in here, seated behind a counter that says WELCOME like this is a back-to-school night and not a place where people scream, vomit, bleed, and sometimes die.

"Can I help you?" asks the woman when I've crept close enough to be in hearing range. Her name tag reads CLARA and she doesn't look much older than me. Dark, short hair, a round pink face, and scrubs with Care Bears on them.

"Uh, yeah," I say, shaking my head. "I came with a woman who was unconscious? Well, I didn't come *with* her, she came in an ambulance and I . . . followed."

"Okay! Name?"

"Sammy Espinoza."

She clicks through a computer that looks like you could play Oregon Trail on it, then frowns. "Hmm, I don't see a Sammy Espinoza on here. Could she be under another name?"

"Oh, Sammy's *my* name," I say, flustered. "Her name is Paloma."

"Last name?" Clara asks, smiling indulgently. Like this happens all the time.

"Uh, her name is also Espinoza." So much for the sympathetic neighbor bit. Hopefully no one wrote that down on any official paperwork.

"Oh, I'm so sorry," Clara says with real sympathy in her eyes. "Your mom?"

"My . . . my grandma," I reply with some effort.

"Well, I do see a *Paloma* Espinoza. She was admitted about five minutes ago and they're getting her checked out now. You're welcome to wait, someone will come out and update you as soon as we know what's going on."

"Thanks," I say, then retreat to one of the chairs closest to the door, starving, and only 20 percent sure what I'm doing here at all.

I've only been squished into the horrible green chair a few minutes when I remember—like something out of a dream—the missed calls I swiped past on my way to dial for help.

Later, I will summarily deny the storm of butterflies that flutter to life in my stomach when I see the calls are both from Max. One from 5:50 and another from just a few minutes ago.

There are two voicemails, too, and I click the Play button on the first one almost hungrily.

"*Hey, Sammy,*" he says in that raspy too-many-sold-out-shows voice. "*It's me. Max. Uh, Max Ryan. Look, you'll probably think this is ridiculous but I'm . . . outside your house. Or, your friends' house, I guess. I wanted to know if I could give you a ride to your grandma's for dinner."*

He pauses for a long moment, and I can hear him nervously tapping something in the background.

"Call me back, if you want to," he continues. *"Or . . . just come out. I'll stick around for a little while just in case, but I also totally understand if you don't. Okay. Bye, Sammy."*

There's a brief moment before the next voicemail starts to play. I can't even describe how I feel in that little quiet space. Knowing that he came to Willa's looking for me. That he would have gone with me to Paloma's, even after everything.

"Hey, me again," the second voicemail begins. *"Maybe you're already gone, or maybe you just didn't want to see me. Either way I get it. I just wanted to say—in person, but I guess this will have to do—that I'm sorry for the way I took off the other night."*

My heart is racing as he pauses again. I can practically hear him running his hand through his hair the way he does when he's nervous.

"I wish I had some great excuse. I've spent two days trying to come up with one and falling embarrassingly short. The truth is I haven't been close to someone like this in a long time. And taking that next step with you was amazing, but it scared me a little."

He exhales, a self-deprecating half-chuckle.

"Okay, it obviously scared me a lot. There are a lot of boring and probably cliché reasons for that, but absolutely zero of them are your fault. And if you never want to talk to me again that's okay, but I couldn't let you think my leaving was because I don't like you . . . or because I didn't really want to take you home with me that night. Because I did. Want you. So much that it's kind of been torturing me ever since."

If there's one thing I will never forgive Max Ryan for, it's turning me on in a run-down, fluorescently lit hospital waiting room. The vulnerability in his voice. The admission that he wanted me. That he still does . . .

"*Okay, I guess that's all,*" he's saying now. "*I'm going to leave before your friends' neighbors call the cops on the creep with the motorcycle outside. But call me. If you want. Anytime.*"

The line disconnects. In my mind's eye, Max Ryan reluctantly gazes up at the window he guesses is mine. He pulls his helmet on slowly, hoping maybe I'll run out at the last moment. When I don't, he fires up the bike's engine and disappears down the street.

I put my phone back into my bag in slow motion. There's no way I can call him now. Not with the way I'm feeling. Not in a hospital waiting room. In the silence, his words play over and over in my mind. *It's been torturing me ever since . . .*

But layered on top of his confession is Willa's raised eyebrow. Her reminder of how destroyed my first dalliance with this man left me. Even Brook's no-nonsense lecture makes its way in. Her promise that lying to Max about who I really am can only lead to a big old mess.

I know I need to stick to the reasonable plan I made this morning. To deal with this new wrinkle in the Paloma plan. To say goodbye to Max, and my job. To get on with my real life and not whatever small-town mess I've stirred up in Ridley Falls.

The only trouble is, every cell in my body is telling me to do something else.

Something that's the complete opposite of reasonable.

"Cheeseburger delivery!" Larry's voice rouses me temporarily. Well, his voice and the intoxicating smell coming from the bag he's carrying.

"You're a godsend, Larry Cross," I say, tearing into the paper to find not only a double cheeseburger, but an irresponsible amount of fries.

"Maeve's on her way down," he says, sitting beside me and swiping a few. "She was horrified I wouldn't let her bring you *real food.*" He cackles, eating another fry.

"We won't tell her this is the best thing I've eaten in weeks," I say between messy bites. "I appreciate the *artistry* that goes into gourmet stuff, but with the way I was raised? Comfort food will always come from a greasy paper bag."

"Amen," he says.

Larry keeps an eye on things while I refuel, and it's a good thing he got here when he did, because about twenty minutes later— when I'm licking salt off my fingers—Maeve and the doctor enter the waiting room from opposite ends at the same time.

"Sammy!" says Maeve, rushing over.

"Espinoza?" calls the doctor, and I stand up, letting Larry and Maeve sandwich me as she approaches.

The doctor is in her fifties, wearing toothpaste-green scrubs and a cap over her graying auburn hair. She seems reassuringly competent. "Okay," she says, clapping her hands. "Your grandmother is in good shape. She's awake, her vitals are good, we've looked her over for any complications from the fall. We're going to keep her overnight for observation, but you can take her home in the morning."

I can take her home? I think, trying not to show my surprise.

"So, she . . . knows I'm here?" I ask.

"We let her know you were in the waiting room," the doctor says cheerfully, clearly unaware of the long list of preexisting conditions this situation suffers from.

"Does . . . she want to see me?" I ask. "Or . . ."

"You can come on back with me!" she interrupts cheerfully. I feel instantly guilty for wasting her time. She probably has lives to save and here I am about to ask her if my grandma wants to see me like a *grandma* or like a stranger grateful that I called 911.

"Thanks," I say instead, wishing I didn't smell quite so deep-fried.

"We'll wait, honey," Maeve says, touching my arm.

"It's okay," I reply automatically. "I don't know how long I'll be and I've taken up enough of your night."

They're reluctant, but eventually Maeve hands me the keys to her Jeep and tells me I can drop it off at the shop tomorrow. I know I won't talk her into leaving me rideless and alone at a hospital at night, so I accept without a fuss.

They leave then, and the doctor is clearly getting impatient, so I don't have much time to overthink before she leads me at a clip through the swinging door behind the desk. It takes us all of thirty seconds to reach room four, where she stops.

"She's inside," she says briskly. "She's hooked up to an IV but it's just for fluids. She was dehydrated, which is why she fainted."

"Gotcha," I say. "And I can just . . . go in?"

"Yep!" the doctor says, already walking away. "Stay as long as you like. She'll be discharged around eleven tomorrow."

I just nod, even though the idea of coming back here tomorrow at eleven seems completely ridiculous. I was just going to dinner. To get answers to a few awkward questions about the first in a string of abandonments that have characterized my life.

Now here I am, in a hospital, being not-quite mistaken for her real granddaughter.

I take a deep breath at the door, then walk in before I can talk myself out of it.

Paloma's sitting up in bed, an IV in her arm as the doctor warned. There's a nasty bruise on her cheekbone, likely from where she fell, and the olive-green hospital gown makes her wrinkled skin look wan. But her eyes are sharp, and at some point she's found the time to reapply crimson lipstick—if a little unevenly.

"I hope you put the enchiladas in the refrigerator," she says without preamble as I approach the bedside.

My hackles go up immediately. "I was a little preoccupied calling you an ambulance."

Paloma looks at me for a long minute. "Four hours down the drain," she says at last.

I want to say I know the feeling, but I bite my tongue.

"I suppose it's a good thing you showed up for dinner," she carries on, not acknowledging my silence. "Who knows how long I would have laid there with the door open."

"Yeah, well," I say, feeling incredibly awkward. "You're welcome."

"So they told you I get out tomorrow, yes?"

"Eleven," I nod. "They thought I was picking you up, but . . ." I trail off. I've never felt so entirely off-balance in my life.

"But what?" she asks. "You were going to make me walk home?"

I can't help it, I laugh out loud. A humorless bark. "I really don't get you," I say, spreading my hands out. "You reject me as a baby, go thirty years without so much as a birthday card, and now you're acting like I'm a normal granddaughter who knows to refrigerate the enchiladas and is expected to pick you up from the hospital? I just . . ." I chuckle again. "I really don't know what I'm supposed to do here."

"I'll tell you what you do," Paloma says. "You give an old woman a ride home from the hospital tomorrow morning out of the kindness of your heart. You ask me those questions from the concert again when we get there, and then you make your decision about me based on how I answer them like you always meant to."

I'm a little unnerved by this too-accurate assessment of what I was planning. But more than that I find the longing to know where I come from is still there despite the day's events, the deep pull to understand the part of my nature—my *culture*—that my mother could never share with me.

"I'll be here at eleven," I say, pleased to hear my voice is strong and clear. My hands aren't shaking.

"Good," Paloma says, like we've just settled some trivial matter. "Now let me get some rest, Samantha. I have a feeling I'll need my strength tomorrow."

When I walk out the sliding doors, taking my first breath of non-hospital air in over an hour, it's twilight. The evening is warm, like fall stored a few summer hours just for this. I feel light, almost giddy, but strong. I find Maeve's car just where she told me it would be—a slightly newer model of the same beat-up Jeep she drove Willa and me to school in every morning of fourth grade.

In the driver's seat, I take out my phone. Max hasn't called again. It's up to me now, and for the first time since I got here I know exactly what I need to do.

Can I see you? I text.

The response is immediate. Like he's been waiting this whole time. **Yes. My place?**

My heart leaps into my throat and flutters there. The feeling coursing through my body is too intense to qualify as excitement.

See you soon, I text, then start the engine before I can change my mind.

21.

There's a perfect song just starting as I pull into Max
Ryan's driveway for the second time. I think it's called "My Invitation." Sarah Slean, one of the most underrated balladeers of the nineties.

It's heartbreaking and hopeful at once, and it tugs at all my newly revealed heartstrings relentlessly.

Love me for stupid reasons, she croons. *I like those most.*

I can't bring myself to turn it off.

In the driveway, I text Max. Perfect song. Can't turn it off.

Be right there, Max replies.

True to his word, he steps out his front door before the first chorus. I motion for him to get in, and he opens the door to the Jeep, sliding in beside me. His hair is falling into his eyes, which sparkle in the lights from the instrument panel. He closes them as the music washes over him.

"This is a great one."

"You know it?"

"Obviously. It's the Joey and Pacey anti-prom song."

I stifle a giggle. "*Dawson's Creek?* Really?"

Max smiles, that conspiratorial smile I'm really starting to love. "During our second tour I watched every episode."

"No way."

He nods, grimacing. "It started because I lost a bet with our drummer. No matter where we were, what party or backstage VIP event, when the clock struck midnight I had to stand up and loudly announce I was going back to the bus or my hotel room to watch *Dawson's Creek*. And then I actually had to do it. At least one full episode."

I'm laughing so hard I narrowly avoid snorting. "I bet the ladies loved that."

"Less than you would think," Max says. "Anyway, the bet lasted for a week, but by then I was hooked. I started lying, watching it under the covers with headphones in my bunk while everyone else was partying. I just had to know what happened."

Drowsy contemplation, do I let you in? This is my invitation, but how do I begin?

The song is heading into its final crescendo. I kill the engine when it's over, enjoying that post-fade-out limbo for a few delicious seconds. Those moments when the emotion of the song lingers on the air, making a promise.

I know I have to ruin this moment, and I swear I'm about to when Max says:

"Would you like to come inside?"

His eyes are on me, tracing my jaw, the neckline of my dinner dress. "To talk?" I ask, more breathlessly than I meant to. "Because we . . . should probably talk."

"We'll talk," he promises, but there's something in the set of his lips. The intensity in his gaze. Something that makes me positive I'll need all my willpower to get through what I came here to do.

"Okay," I say. "Let's go inside."

"To talk," Max clarifies.

"To talk."

I lock Maeve's car and follow Max to his front door, wishing he'd take my hand. Glad when he doesn't. I know we could keep bantering all night. I could avoid what I came here to say until we're inevitably kissing, making good on the fire that caught in my veins when he said he wanted me.

But that would be running. Setting up dominoes that are doomed to fall. And I can't do that this time.

Inside, Max's house is warmly lit. It smells like sandalwood and something citrusy. The guitars are all hung up this time. Something with a cello plays quietly in the background.

"Can I get you anything?" he asks, drifting back toward the kitchen. "Sorry, the drink situation is pretty bare. I have filtered water or sparkling."

"That's okay," I say, afraid to commit to sitting. Not knowing what will happen when I say what I came here to say. Whether Max will throw me out, or this night will proceed down a different road.

He sits down with his own sparkling water on one end of the burnt-orange sofa. I take the chair across from him, not sure I can withstand the pressure of sharing furniture.

"Look," I begin. My hands are shaking, just barely. There are no words in any language for how much I do not want to do this. "I haven't been entirely honest with you."

Max tenses a little around the eyes. A shadow of the look he gave me through his helmet after the concert.

"And as glad as I am that you called . . . I need to say this before we can take things any further."

There's a definite wariness in Max's tone when he says, "I'm listening."

I take a deep breath. "The other night in the Safeway parking lot wasn't the first time we met." I say this part in a rush, needing to have something out there that I can't take back. "It was about eleven years ago, at a show in Seattle."

There's part of me that hopes this will be all it takes, but of course there's no moment of recognition. No puzzle piece clicking into place. He just waits. So I go on.

"I was living with my best friend, Willa, at the time. She's from Ridley Falls and had heard of your band, so we went to the show. I was applying for label internships, I wanted to work in A&R. Afterward we all hung out at the bar, went to a house party together. You and I stayed up all night drinking and talking and you asked me to tell you the truth about the show. The band's performance."

This is the part where Max's eyes get wide. It's almost like I'm watching the rest of the story play out behind them. "It was you," he says after a long minute. "You were there when I got the call."

I just nod.

"Which means I . . . and then you . . . oh god, Sammy, why didn't you say anything?"

"I was . . . humiliated?" I say, opening my palms. "Here I thought we had this legendary missed connection, and you didn't even remember who I was. All I wanted to do was get as far away from you as possible and nurse my wounds."

Max is obviously reeling. I can see it all over his face that this is the last thing he ever expected me to say. "But we did," he manages finally, shifting forward. "We did have a legendary missed connection. You were the first person who ever told me the truth about my music. I took all your notes. We totally changed the band's sound because of you."

"After you told me you wanted to take me to Chicago with you and I never heard from you again."

Max does not share my blush-less complexion. His face goes ruddy along the cheekbones in half a second. "Look, I'm not gonna pretend I was the most stand-up guy back then," he says. "I woke up the next day . . . I thought we both understood what it was. We were drinking, we didn't even know each other's last names. I had no idea you felt differently."

There's a beat of silence during which I relive it for the hundredth time. The feeling of getting swept away. Building a whole fantasy around the moment we shared. I want to pretend I agree with him. That it would have been silly to expect more.

But I came here to be honest. So I am.

"I was eighteen," I say with a self-deprecating smile. "I had never felt more drawn to anyone. After you asked me, I packed. I subletted the place I was renting. I waited by the phone for days."

Max rubs the back of his neck. "I'm sorry," he says. "I really am. I wish I could say there was a good reason. That it wasn't like me. But it was. I was so . . . single-minded back then. Selfish. I've spent most of my post–Seven Shades life trying to make up for it."

"You do seem different," I confess, as the past closes itself back up like a folded paper box.

"I can't change the choices I made back then," Max says, leaning closer. He's meeting my eyes now, just a little residual flush left over along his cheekbones. "But I can promise you I'd never do that to you now. Not in a million years."

This is it, I think. The moment he'll kiss me if I let him.

But I'm not done confessing, yet.

"It worked out okay in the end," I say quietly. "When I heard that the band had taken my notes I decided to become a music writer. And . . . that's what I've been doing ever since. For work, I mean."

Phase two of the confession. The gauntlet we have to pass through before there can be anything more. I see this next blow register while he's still reeling from the first, and there's no doubt this is worse. He moves back on the couch, curling in as if to protect himself.

"So when you said you didn't want to talk about work . . ."

Every line of his posture says this is a deal-breaker. The exact betrayal he's been hiding from since the moment he walked off-stage at the Staples Center and never graced another. Alarm bells are going off at my very center. Radiating everywhere.

And in those horrible, slow motion seconds, I realize I have a lifeline, and I lunge:

There are only three people in the world who know about the *Scavenger*/Max Ryan article besides me. Willa and Brook would never breathe a word, and Esme is going to fire me anyway.

Max never has to know.

Isn't it enough that I told the truth about the rest? That I'm never planning to write this article—or probably any other—ever again? The panic crashing over me says yes. That I've paid my penance. That everyone has secrets, and mine won't hurt anyone.

"No, I didn't want to talk about work because I got fired," I hear myself say. "About a week before I came back here."

The way he relaxes, even just a fraction, sends a physical flood of relief through my body. "I'm sorry to hear that," he says, but there's no doubt this is good news.

A victimless crime, I reassure myself. A white lie if ever there was one. I move my termination date from tomorrow to two weeks ago and Max and I don't lose our chance.

"I was in a relationship that was circling the drain," I explain, trying to distance myself from the lie. Pad it with enough truth that eventually it loses its sharp edges. "She was a musician, too. Mediocre band. I wrote rave reviews at the end trying to fix things and my readers turned on me. Lost my job, lost the girl, found out my grandfather was dead, and came crawling back to the one place that vaguely resembled home."

"A tale as old as time," Max says. He's thawing. I can feel it.

"It was time for a change, anyway," I say, and in the moment, I really mean it.

"So, when we met . . . ?"

"I was exactly the mess I appeared to be," I promise him. "Crying in a truck, unemployed and recently dumped in a DIY crop top covered in Cheeto crumbs."

Max cracks a half-smile. There's still wariness in his eyes but he hasn't thrown me out yet, and I take that as a small miracle. One I might be able to build on.

"And the first person you run into is the idiot who never called you back eleven years ago," he says. "What are the odds?"

"Rarely in my favor." I grimace, ignoring the guilt attempting to root in my stomach. We'll move past this, I think. It'll fade into the background of our origin story . . .

"I can't believe I didn't recognize you," Max says thoughtfully, some of the lines around his eyes smoothing as his expression turns pensive. "It's been a long time, sure, but I thought about you a lot. The way you gave it to me straight. How easy you were to talk to about things I never said to anyone. What it felt like to kiss you . . ."

These last words catch in my belly, a little flame that burns away the guilt.

"I guess after a couple years you became this kind of mythic, hazy figure in my memory. Dark-haired, great smile. I'd wonder what ever happened to you. I'd wish I still had the phone with your number in it so I could thank you for everything."

There's nothing else in my mind in this moment besides Max's voice, saying the exact words I've always wanted to hear.

"I wondered, you know," he says, his voice a little husky. "Why I was so drawn to you when you came back for your wallet. Why I couldn't let you walk away."

Unconsciously, I shift forward. There's a coffee table between us, but I *have* to be closer to him.

"There must have been some part of me that remembered that night. Recognized you even though I was too self-centered and drunk back then to immortalize your face the way it deserved."

"You didn't have the aid of a life-sized picture of me smirking at you from the wall of every record store for years afterward," I allow. I can be magnanimous now that I know I didn't imagine it. That we meant something to each other. That maybe, after all these years, we still do.

He winces. "Yeah, those things were everywhere, weren't they?"

"I hated them," I admit. "They didn't look like the real you."

"What do you mean?" Max asks.

I grasp for the words to describe the feeling I used to get when I saw them and find they're slow to come.

"The vulnerability wasn't there," I say after a long minute. "That raw emotion that made you so undeniable onstage. You were so afraid of opening up, being seen, but you couldn't help yourself. That war inside you . . ." I trail off, smiling a little. "I just didn't like seeing you airbrushed and vapid like some doll. It wasn't you."

Sometime during this clumsy speech, Max has gotten to his feet. For one delirious moment, I think he might cross the room and take me in his arms. Kiss me like he means it. But what he does is almost better.

He walks to the far wall and reaches for a guitar. "This is *not* what I was expecting to do tonight," he says with a self-deprecating smile. "But . . . would you mind if I played you something?"

The look on his face as he asks me is the exact one that made me fall instantly in love at eighteen. Like he's cracked his chest wide open, exposing the messy viscera beneath, so hopeful that he's found someone who will help him protect it.

A look you would sublet your apartment and move across the country for.

A look that might linger within your own messy insides for a decade, even when all hope was lost . . .

"Yes," I say. Of course I do. "Yes, please."

22.

Max takes down the guitar that was on the couch my first day here. The black Taylor. He returns to his seat on the couch, then hesitates.

"Everything okay?" I ask.

"Yeah, of course," Max replies. He smiles, running his free hand through his hair. "It's just the uh, the acoustics are better over here." He gestures to the couch beside him.

"Wow," I say, getting up and moving to exactly where he's pointing. "Does that line usually work?"

"It's a little rusty," Max admits, and I think back to his voice-mail. *I haven't been close to someone like that in a very long time . . .*

"Well, I'm here, right? So there must be something to it."

He looks at me for a long minute, like he kind of can't believe it's true. That I'm here—not just some girl he met in a parking lot a week ago, but a girl he lost eleven years ago and didn't dare hope to find again.

"You're here," he repeats.

As much as I want to hear the song, I fantasize about taking the guitar out of his arms. The last of the obstacles between us. It's a good thing he starts to play when he does.

It's a quiet melody, but it resonates in the room. His fingering is so precise, so masterful. It's obvious he's come a long way since I told him to ditch the guitar.

He clears his throat, still picking as he speaks. "I haven't told a lot of people this," he says haltingly. "But I've been working on an album here the past couple of years. Nothing like Seven Shades of Monday, but something that feels more like me."

I'm afraid to respond. Afraid to even breathe.

"It's supposed to come out next month," he continues. "A total surprise. But so far the only person I've been able to play it for in person is my manager, James, and he's an old friend. The label is waiting *very* impatiently, and the rollout is all ready but . . ."

Max runs his hand through his hair and sighs, frustrated.

"I know as soon as it releases I'll have to tour. Play it live. I just don't know how to be that guy anymore, and besides James there was no one I trusted enough to take that first step with. So I just kind of . . . haven't."

I know what it means that he's telling me this after my confession. The trust it requires to put this information in my hands, knowing what I could do with it.

"You told me the truth once when I really needed to hear it," he says. "I hope you won't mind doing it one more time."

I nod. I tell the guilt now churning in my stomach that he has all the information he really needs. He believes I'll never betray him, and I won't.

My shoulders relax when Max's do. He closes his eyes.

When he starts to sing, I'm glad they're closed, because tears spring to mine. He's right. This song sounds nothing like the set they played in Seattle that night. Or the Seven Shades singles that played ten times a day on every radio station.

But he's still Max Ryan. The emotion is there. The conduit so clear in the lines of his body and that unbelievable voice filling the space. Filling my chest.

This song has a quiet confidence. A stark loneliness. The lyrics tell the story of a person who's fought hard to become something new, but has lost so much along the way he wonders if it's all been a waste of time.

As he plays, my inner critic goes silent. For the first time in longer than I can remember, I'm not drafting my review in my head, clocking relevant details, making judgments of *inspired* or *derivative* after every verse.

Instead, I'm lost in the feeling. In the pieces of the person *I'm* struggling to become, highlighted so beautifully by his music. I feel like a teenager again, looking for somewhere to hide and finding a home instead.

By the time he finishes the song, I've managed to get rid of the evidence of my tears.

Max looks up at me, his own eyes shining, and for a moment I can see right down into him. Into the place his music comes from.

"That song," I say to the unasked question in his expression. "Was worth the wait."

It must be the right thing to say, because before I know it the guitar between us is gone at last. I'm not sure who crosses the distance, only that we find each other, our lips meeting with the heat of our recent kiss and all the gravity that's been building since our first.

This time there's no phone call to interrupt. No chattering concertgoers. This time there's only us. His long fingers tangling in my hair, mine sliding up his back beneath his soft T-shirt. His mouth urging mine open, the pressure building until it's almost too much to bear.

"Max," I whisper involuntarily, when he moves to my neck.

He pulls me across his lap in response, and I'm surprised by how hard he already is as I straddle him. He drags in a ragged breath, eyes boring into me like he's seeing beyond my clothes. Beyond even my skin.

I grind against his erection instinctively, surrendering to my body and all the urges I've denied these past few days. Max groans into my pulse point and I can feel it through my whole body. My skin is electric. He must feel the hum of want building to a frenzy beneath my skin as he slides his hand into my shirt. His calloused hand cups my breast through my thin cotton bra, the heat of his fingers mapping each touch. Searing it into my skin.

The buzzing in my body begins to condense and focus, increasing in heat and pulse until it collects at my center. I lift my hips, tugging ineffectually at his belt.

"I need you," I hear myself say in a ragged voice.

Max reaches up to grip my chin, to pull my mouth back to his.

"Say it again," he growls against my lips.

"I need you, Max," I practically whimper. "I need you so badly."

He stands up in a fluid motion, arms gripped tightly under my thighs, my legs still wrapped around him. He holds my body flush against his as he staggers down the hallway, not setting me down until we reach the foot of his bed.

My loose dress is over my head in a moment, leaving nothing but a black bralette and matching boy shorts. I undo his belt, struggling with the closure of his jeans while he fumbles with my bra clasp until we trade jobs, laughing softly against each other's skin.

In seconds, he's standing before me in nothing but briefs that leave very little to the imagination. My breasts are exposed, his eyes tracing them, my nipples hardening from just a glance. His voice is hoarse and low when he says:

"I don't want to be presumptuous, but should I . . . is this . . . a condom kind of situation?"

His laugh is adorably self-deprecating, even with its desperate edge.

I want to tease him, but I can't stand the delay it would cause. Instead I reach down and shimmy out of my black boy shorts, standing fully naked before him. I watch his Adam's apple bob with no small amount of satisfaction.

"I'd say so, wouldn't you?" I ask.

For a moment, he doesn't move. Doesn't even seem to breathe. Plenty of people have seen me naked since the night I hoped Max would be the first. But I know none of them have looked at me like this. His eyes on my body are a physical presence, tracing my breasts, my hips. The length of my legs. Coming back to my lips as he licks his own.

"*God,* you're fucking gorgeous," he says. "I spent that whole time trying to think of a better word, but I seem to be having a . . . blood-flow issue at the moment."

Is he *ever.* The shape of him through his briefs stands out in sharp relief, the thin cotton fighting a losing battle.

"Word choice isn't exactly what I'm concerned with right now," I say, stepping closer to him. He swallows, hard. "I think you mentioned a condom?"

"Right, yes. Right." He turns like it's hurting him to tear his eyes away.

While he rummages in a drawer I perch on the end of his bed, watching, feeling the want ripple and pulse through me.

"Okay," he says, crossing the room again. I take a moment to appreciate the lean, subtle muscles dancing beneath his skin. Muscles I've so far only seen plastered with a wet T-shirt in the headlamp of a motorcycle. Somehow this is better.

"Okay," I reply, reaching forward, pulling him to me by the hips. My face is level with his navel. I slide my hands into his waistband and slowly remove the last piece of clothing separating us.

He's so hard it almost looks painful. He gazes down as I take in the sight of him, passing me the condom in its wrapper when I hold out my hand for it. He watches as I unwrap it slowly, unable to hide exactly how agonizing it is to wait.

I put the tip of the condom between my lips and take him in my hand, parting my lips, sliding it on as he enters my mouth.

"Oh my god," he says, his knees buckling.

I don't stop, just roll it all the way to the base, holding him steady by the thighs as I go. Once it's on, I begin. Slowly at first, then faster, encouraged by his gasping breaths, his groans.

Abruptly, his hand is fisted tightly in my hair. "Fuck, *fuck,*" he says. There's a note of panic in his tone as he guides me off him.

"I'm sorry!" I say, peering up. Max's eyes are tightly shut, his whole body rigid. "Did I hurt you?"

He breathes deeply for a few seconds, then opens his eyes to look down at me. There's a kind of tortured smile twisting his lips. "No, you didn't hurt me," he says. "But if you keep that up I'm gonna last about five seconds. I told you . . . it's been a very long time."

"How long are we talking here?" I ask, reaching forward again, pulling him down on top of me. He relaxes, his weight settling on me. He moves his lips back to my neck, the delicious rasp of his stubble raising goosebumps across my skin.

"Seven years, give or take," he says between kisses.

I'm so surprised by this answer that it's an effort not to show it. *Seven years.* I knew he was a recluse, and he said he was out of practice, but I can't imagine *seven years* without *this.*

"Well," I say, running my hands up his back, memorizing every muscle, every rib. "That sounds like long enough."

My legs fall open, making room. He traces his fingers up the inside of my thigh, circling and teasing until I think I might lose my mind. He seems to sense my desperation, because he finds my center then, sliding, testing, acclimating.

I gasp at the sensation. The knobs of his knuckles. Those calloused musician's fingers playing all the right notes.

"God, you're soaked," he says, his voice full of wonder, which certainly doesn't improve my patience.

I nudge his hand aside to make room. I feel him against me, adjusting, searching. His hips between my thighs, finally, hard heat pressing at my entrance. When he slides in I have to brace myself against the feeling of fullness, almost too much to bear.

Once he's inside me he stills, his breathing harsh and ragged against my neck. It's torture, to have him there, solid and ready, denying me the friction I've been craving all this time.

I rock my hips against him, eager, but he stops me again.

"Give me a second," he says. "You feel too good . . . I'm . . ."

"Hey." I reach up to touch his face. His eyes flutter open, finding mine. I pull him down to kiss me and he does so eagerly, his body relaxing as our lips slide over each other's.

When I pull away he smiles. Then, tentatively at first, he begins to move.

The rhythm of his thrusts picks up as we shift and adjust against each other, a complicated dance we're learning as we go. Soon his rhythm begins to match up with some primal beat inside me, and then I'm lost in it. Every sensation heightened by how long we've waited.

I slide my hand between us as the intensity builds, brushing my fingers against the places he doesn't reach. I moan as he increases his speed, a high-pitched thing that has him slowing, tensing again. But I can't let him stop. Not now. I lift my hips up to meet his instead.

"Fuck, Sammy, *fuck*." His whispers are frantic. "If we don't slow down I—"

"I want you to," I gasp. "Max, I'm close. I'm so close. It's okay."

With my permission, his rhythm changes, driving and purposeful now. His breathing is shallow and ragged. "Fuck, fuck, *oh god*."

I feel everything in him seize up as he finally surrenders to the release he's denied himself so long. The intensity of it, along with my fingertips hitting just the right places, sends me right over the edge after him.

Waves of almost punishing pleasure crash over me, matched by the shudders of Max's body on top of mine, one after the other until at last we both fall still.

For a long time, we lay in silence, catching our breath. His arm is draped across my stomach, my fingers trace circles on his scalp. With the urgency ebbing, there's room for so much more to unfold. I wonder lazily, languidly, how I ever thought I could use this man. Ever thought I could protect myself from the hold he had on my heart the moment I first saw him take the stage.

I'm starting to think he's fallen asleep when he rolls onto his side. The look in his eyes is no longer ravenous, but I catch my breath at the intensity of it just the same.

"You okay?" I ask, smoothing the hair off his forehead.

He smiles—face free of the careful tension he normally holds there. "Never better." Max reaches out for me, pulling me into his arms. I rest my head on his chest. His breathing slows and deepens beneath my cheek.

As I drift off I think every one of my fantasies has fallen woefully short . . .

He wakes me in the small hours, hands sliding purposefully over my bare skin. When I reach for him he's already hard again. Hot to the touch.

"Please," he says, his voice heavy with sleep, broken and rough. "Sammy, please . . ."

"Yes," I whisper. "Yes, yes, yes . . ."

This time, he puts the condom on himself, pulling me on top of him. I slide down his length slowly, the heat melting me from inside. I tilt my hips forward, the ridges of him creating a whole new symphony of sensations. At this angle, I'm the one quivering and gasping in minutes.

"Oh god," I gasp. "Max . . . *Max* . . ."

"I'm here," he says, pushing my hair back, looking into my eyes. He thrusts from below me, each stroke long and slow, every inch of him sliding through every inch of me until the heat builds to an unbearable point. "Come for me," he whispers, and I do. I come apart entirely. Boneless and trembling around him, barely able to hold myself up.

Into my quivering core he continues his slow, relentless rhythm from below until suddenly, unexpectedly, his whole body goes taut as a bowstring. When he collapses, released and sated, all I can do is drape my body over his, already drifting back to sleep.

23.

It's rare in life that you're lucky enough to know a moment is important while it's happening. When I wake up beside Max the next morning, I can see it in his halo of sleepy curls. The buttery shaft of light coming in the window. The dust motes floating down, winking and sparkling.

He is already awake, and he's smiling at me.

"Good morning," I say, pulling up the sheet first to make sure no hint of morning breath reaches him.

"Good morning." His voice is low and rough with sleep.

What a privilege, I think, a little deliriously, *to be the person who hears Max Ryan's first words of the morning.* "How did you sleep?" I ask him.

"Perfectly," he says, reaching forward to brush a strand of hair off my face. "And you?"

I just nod. His mattress is probably wildly expensive, it feels like a cloud. But I think I would have slept just as well anywhere, as long as he was beside me. Concrete, gravel, hot coals. It wouldn't have mattered.

"Good," he says. "Do you have an agenda for the day? Or can I make you breakfast?"

"Yes and yes," I say, remembering Maeve's car. Paloma, getting out of the hospital at eleven. The clock on Max's bedside table reads 9:15. Plenty of time.

"Good," he says again, his smile widening. "There's a spare

toothbrush head in the bathroom drawer and towels in the hallway closet, come out when you're ready?"

"Okay," I whisper. The truth is I'm starving, and I definitely
need to shower, but even with all that I don't want him to leave
this bed. Now, or maybe ever.

Of course, that's not the kind of thing you can say to a man you
just slept with for the first time. Instead, I watch him dress from
the safe nest of the blankets. He doesn't hurry. Doesn't appear to
feel bashful about being naked in front of me, even in the full light
of morning. The lines and planes of his body catch the light.

He has a tattoo on his rib cage, I notice—a bird with outstretched wings.

A pair of loose fleece pants go on first, forest-green. Then a
long-sleeved black shirt that looks so soft I want to rub my face in
it. Socks. The ones every boy seems to have. Black with gold toes.

There's a little catch behind my heart once he's decent, making
his way across the room. It occurs to me that I may never stop
waiting with bated breath for Max to disappear.

As if he senses these thoughts, he turns back to me before leaving the room.

"Forgot something," he says, that crooked smile hitching itself
onto his face.

"What's that?" I ask, trying to hide this strange swell of emotion.

He pads across the hardwood floor to my side of the bed, leaning over to take my face in his hands. He kisses me full on the
mouth. A long, sweet, all-lip kiss that acknowledges every second
of what passed between us last night.

My body responds instantly, sore but willing to overlook it, already melting for him. I reach my arms up and around his back,
pulling him closer. The shirt is even softer than I imagined, and
still nothing compared to the skin beneath it.

Max breaks the kiss after a few breathless heartbeats, smiling against my mouth. "If I go one more round without fuel I might never recover . . ."

"We can't have that," I murmur as he recaptures my lips.

"For you it might be worth it."

We kiss for a few more seconds, teetering on the edge of maybe until finally Max's stomach growls and I pull away, laughing.

"Food," I declare,

"Food," Max agrees. "But for the record, this is the most I've ever resented breakfast."

I watch him leave the room, that little tug again, then go about the business of making myself presentable.

There's something about being left in someone's room for the first time, I've always thought so. This contrast between the new closeness that allows you to be there, and all the things that remind you you're still strangers.

I wander naked through Max's tastefully decorated room—dark wood, deep-green bedclothes, a big oak dresser with a vanity mirror over it—and realize he's very neat. Almost militarily so. His shirts are organized by color. His socks are rolled into identical tubes.

The bathroom off his bedroom is more of the same. Meticulously white grout. All the toiletries are the same brand. There's no stray empty bottle of conditioner, no hair in the sink drain, no toothpaste spots on the mirror.

It's a little ironic, I think, stepping into the shower and relishing in the excellent water pressure. I think of the clubs he must have played, the trashed hotel rooms, the tour bus bathroom shared among five band members. Was he always this type-A? Was that why he couldn't stand the lifestyle?

I stop these thoughts in their tracks, recognizing them as journalistic. It'll take some time to tame the impulse. From now on, it's important I let Max reveal things about himself in his own time. I owe him that, to regain the trust he'll never know I broke.

The guilt surges back for a brief moment, but I shove it down relentlessly. Telling him wouldn't have changed anything. It only would have ruined this. And this is *good*.

Showered, teeth brushed, I put yesterday's dinner dress back on—thankful its silhouette works for daytime, too—and follow the sound of drumming into the living room.

It smells heavenly. Max is at the stove with a spatula, looking even better. He smiles at me, unable to speak over the cacophony of sound filling the room. I recognize the album immediately—one of his contemporaries from the Seven Shades days. True screamo in all its angsty, adolescent glory.

It's so much like the music I would have chosen to make breakfast to that I begin to imagine a future blooming in the overlap. Max and me, making a weekend meal together months or years down the line, marveling at how well our lives fit together . . .

"Hope you don't mind!" he calls over the racket. "It helps me with my flip game!"

As he says it, he slides the spatula beneath a truly massive pancake and flips it almost professionally well.

In response, I pull a serving spoon out of a stainless steel holder on the counter and mouth the words to the song, writhing and pretending to scream, raising my arms at the end to an imaginary sold-out crowd.

"Very nice," Max says, laughing as he kills the music. "This album is solid gold. Not a skip on it in my opinion."

"The end of track seven lags," I say, almost without thinking. "They could have cut it after the third chorus and ended on that big cymbal crash."

Max sets the giant pancake and a bowl of fresh fruit on the little table, gesturing for me to sit, looking bemused.

"Also tracks one and three should be switched," I continue, popping a red grape in my mouth as he pours coffee. "Three is the better opener."

Max sits down across from me. He opens his mouth, then closes it, then laughs.

"Feel free to disagree," I bait him with a smirk.

"I . . . don't," he replies, a little helplessly. "I've probably listened to that album a hundred times start to finish and I didn't notice any of it, but you're totally right. Three is the better opener, and seven is a verse too long." He shakes his head, disbelieving. "I had overpaid record execs in the studio that didn't have close to your ear. You don't miss, do you?"

"Not if I can help it." I grin at him a little wickedly, happy to be able to share this side of myself with him. "This looks incredible, by the way."

"Thank you," Max says, looking down at the spread a little dazed. "Forgot I can't live on your incisive music opinions alone."

"Many have died trying," I say somberly.

Max cuts the ridiculously large pancake in half and slides one side onto my plate. I take a sip of my coffee as he dusts everything with powdered sugar. I've done my fair share of first-morning-after breakfasts and found almost all of them intolerably awkward. Like an audition where you're both trying to figure out if the other person is just being polite.

This doesn't feel like that. This feels comfortable. Uncomplicated. *Good.*

"Dig in," Max says, and we do, eating this pancake (which is incredible) while making shifty eye contact and grinning when we're caught. When he's finished, he sips his coffee, resting his hand casually on my upper thigh under the table.

The clock above the stove reads just after ten. Soon, I'll have to pick up Paloma. Return Maeve's car. The real world beckons and I'm not at all ready to greet it.

"So what's on the itinerary today?" Max asks, reading my mind again.

"Actually," I begin, realizing just how much of yesterday I left out. "I'm picking my grandmother up from the hospital." I explain the rest. Showing up for dinner early, finding her unconscious. The casual and imperious way she requested my return at eleven.

"Wow," Max says, his expression searching instead of flirtatious now. "That's a lot. It must have been hard enough to find the courage to go, let alone deal with everything that happened after."

With anyone else, this kind of feelings talk would have me clamming up faster than you can say *intimacy issues*. With Max, as always, it feels effortless. "It was hard," I admit. "But ultimately I decided wanting to know where I come from is bigger than being afraid. If I shut down I'm only hurting myself."

Max nods thoughtfully, like he's processing this deeply. "I always wonder what I'd do if my dad wanted to see me after all these years," he says. "We haven't talked since I left home at seventeen. Not a word. He was such a bastard back then, but part of me thinks I'd feel the way you do. That I'd want answers now that I'm old enough to ask for them."

I squeeze the hand still resting on my thigh. "You deserved better," I say, meaning it. "You still do."

He smiles. Clouds parting. "Thanks," he says. "When you say it, I almost believe it."

I want to stay here for the rest of the day. Forget the world. Talk about everything, then have middle-of-the-day sex on his gorgeous orange couch and start all over again.

"Why don't I follow you to drop off the car," he says, breaking into my fantasy. "I can drive you to the hospital, take your grandma home?"

"On the motorcycle?" I ask with a giggle, trying to picture Paloma in a sidecar with goggles on, urging Max to go faster.

"I do *own* a vehicle," he says. "I just prefer the bike."

"Even in the rain," I tease.

"Helps me meet cool girls in parking lots."

The eye contact lingers. Max flushes along his cheekbones in a way I'm coming to love. "If you don't stop looking at me like that we'll never make it to the hospital on time," I say.

"That would be a disaster," he says, not looking away.

Eventually, I have to forfeit this charged staring contest. I've already had Maeve's car too long, and if I leave Paloma at her most vulnerable moment I'm no better than she is.

But it's with real effort that I tear my eyes away from him. *I'll be back,* I tell myself. *It won't be like last time . . .*

Max's vehicle, it turns out, is a big old truck. A Toyota Tacoma that's almost dazzlingly white.

"It's practical," he says when I gape. "I have to haul the motorcycle around somehow."

"Aren't all you former rock star guys supposed to have, like, a midlife-crisis sports car?" I tease, heading for Maeve's Jeep still parked in the driveway.

"I'm so offended," Max retorts, hopping into the truck and starting the engine. It's weird to see him in here, I think. I'm so used to him on the motorcycle now that it looks all wrong.

"When did you sell it?" I ask.

He sighs. "A few years ago. I sent the money to my sister to help her pay for school."

Of course, I think. *Even his bad sports car story is adorable.*

In the Jeep alone, I let the radio choose. It's some old-timey country crooner, which feels sort of perfect for the moment. Max sticks close behind me as we navigate the streets to Mystical Moments.

When we get there, I hesitate. I'm not sure if it's rude to leave him out here, but I'm equally unsure that I want to bring him inside to meet Maeve. Who might tell Willa. Who reacted to my **Sorry I'm alive I'll tell you everything later** text this morning with *just* a thumbs-up.

"I'll be back in a second," I say, hoping he doesn't take it personally.

"I'll be right here." He's smiling. I know he only means he'll be waiting in two minutes when I exit the store, but with our history the words settle somewhere deeper.

Maeve is just opening up when I walk inside, trying to look normal, not to smile too much. "*You* are glowing," she says without greeting, eagle eyes taking in last night's outfit and clocking the white truck outside.

"I'm not *glowing*," I say with an eye roll I've perfected since she knew me last. "I'm dropping off your keys and going to the hospital."

"With a very handsome escort, it seems."

"Shush," I say, setting the Jeep's keys on the counter. "You're as bad a gossip as Larry."

"No one is that bad," Maeve says, relenting. But she comes around the counter and takes both my hands, doing one of those X-ray stares she passed down to her daughter. "You look happy, sweetheart."

I *feel* happy. But it's still so tenuous that I'm afraid to claim it as more than a fleeting thing. There are still so many questions. Still so much that's undecided. "It's new," I say quietly. "Sort of."

Maeve nods, still holding my hands. Her expression shifts, my eyes are a tarot spread she's reading. "Do you remember what I told you about facing the truth when you first came in here?" she asks.

"You told me to stay." How could I forget.

"I did," Maeve agrees. "I also told you that the different struggles you're having need to be resolved together. And that they'd require *honesty*."

The pit of guilt in my stomach I've been avoiding since last night can't hide from Maeve. It's heavier than ever, threatening to swallow me. I would have lost Max if I'd told the truth. I know that. But what if I lose him anyway?

I pull my hands away reflexively. "I'm sorry," I say when Maeve looks surprised. "It's just . . . I don't really know what this is yet, and I'd rather not make too big a deal about everything right now."

What I'm really trying to say is that I can't handle knowing the future. Even if Maeve knows it. Maybe especially then.

"You got it," she replies with a tired smile. "Just be careful, hm?"

"I will," I promise her. "I gotta go, or I'll be late for Paloma." Right now even the hospital seems like a welcome alternative. "Thank you so much for yesterday, and for loaning me your car. I don't know what I'd do without you guys."

"Of course, sugar," Maeve says. "It's what family does."

But her wary expression follows me out the door, and it stays with me when I climb up into Max's passenger seat.

"Everything all right?" he asks, and I try to figure out how I would even explain Maeve and her readings, let alone the strange feeling that interaction has just left me with. As if there's some kind of a countdown happening, and I don't know how much time is left on the clock.

Instead, I ground myself in the reality of Max beside me. His tousled hair. His beautiful eyes. I look at him like it's been a year since I saw him last and not three minutes. Then I lean across the center console and kiss him, trying not to betray my desperation to cling to this moment. To never let anything change.

"Hey," he says, pulling away. "Are you okay?"

"Yeah," I say. "I'm good. We're gonna be late."

He looks at me for another long second, like he's trying to read the shift in my mood. Finally, he relents, starting the truck and backing out. He puts his arm over the back of my seat when he does, turning so our faces are close.

"You don't have to talk to me about it," he says. "But I'm here if you want to."

"Thanks," I say, but I don't say another word until we get to the hospital.

24.

Even though we're ten minutes early, Paloma is waiting for us when we pull up to the entrance.

"What is she doing?" I mutter, breaking my silence as Max pulls the truck up to the curb. "She's not even supposed to be out until eleven."

She's sitting on the bench outside, fully dressed, lipstick applied and her purse beside her.

I hop out, realizing that my conversation with Maeve and the preoccupation that followed it made me forget to dread this.

"I thought the doctor said eleven," I say as I approach the bench. "Is everything okay?"

"Everything but the smell of death in that place," Paloma retorts, getting to her feet. "I couldn't get away fast enough."

"Okay, but I would have come inside," I insist. "Talked to the doctor. Do you need to pick up any prescriptions or anything? Do you have discharge instructions?"

The glare Paloma levels me with must be genetic, because I know I've used it to shut up a few mouthy bouncers in my life. "I've been managing my health without your help for three quarters of a century, Samantha. I think I'll manage another day."

"Fine," I say, raising my hands in surrender. "I'm just the transportation service, I get it."

"Well," Paloma says as Max comes around the truck. "If all your drivers are as handsome as this one, I'll be calling more often."

"Hello, Mrs. Espinoza," Max says, taking her wrinkled hand

and kissing the back of it. "I'm Max Ryan. Happy to be escorting you home today."

Paloma flutters her eyelashes at Max before allowing him to help her into the passenger seat. I climb into the back, my knees basically a chin rest, trying to remember why I agreed to this in the first place. I'm still thrown off by what Maeve said, but Max asks polite questions and keeps Paloma talking until we turn onto Ponderosa Court.

It's not until he stops the truck that I realize this is goodbye. I'm sure he won't want to spend the day with us—and loath as I am to let him go, this feels like something Paloma and I need to hash out on our own.

But it suddenly seems like an extreme oversight that we didn't lock down future plans before we had an audience.

Max hops out nimbly and assists Paloma down from the truck. By then I'm already out, and my anxiety is spiking, and I'm not at all sure what to say to him.

"I can . . . help you guys inside?" he asks.

"Thanks," I agree, and he takes Paloma's arm.

The three of us make our awkward way up the steep driveway. Paloma digs out her keys and unlocks the red door.

"Thank you for your help today," she says warmly to Max. "Don't forget I owe you an enchilada dinner."

He smiles at her. "You're very nice to invite me back. Feel better soon."

She waves a dismissive hand at him. "I felt better last night. Those doctors just kept me around to liven up the place." With that, she heads inside, leaving the door open behind her.

I turn to Max, heart in my throat, aware that Paloma is probably listening to every word. The last thing I want to do is clue her in to the fact that I went straight from the hospital to spend the night at a newish man's house. "Thanks again," I say, stalling.

"Anytime."

We look at each other for a long moment. He smiles, brushing the hair off my forehead.

Please don't disappear, I want to say. But instead I manage: "Call me sometime?"

He laughs. Strokes my cheek. "Call *me*," he says. "As soon as you're done here."

For a moment, with our eyes locked and his calloused thumb running along my jaw, I forget where we are. Who's inside and everything there is to untangle beyond this door. Maeve and the cards and the future. It's just Max and me, the bubble re-forming around us as we inch closer together.

"Ahem," says Paloma loudly. "I have a lot of food to throw away when you're done with your flirting."

We both laugh silently, the moment evaporating. Max withdraws his hand, then kisses me on the cheek.

"See you soon?" he asks, turning toward the stairs.

"*Soon,*" I emphasize, and then he's gone.

In the house, Paloma is already busy scraping old enchiladas out of the pan. I feel a pang of pity for her when I see the table set with woven placemats, bright colored glasses. The trouble she clearly went to only to have everything end up in the trash.

"I can take care of that," I say. "I'm sorry for not thinking of the food last night."

Paloma waves her hand again. That dismissive, snappy wrist. "You had a lot on your mind. And I haven't said thank-you for calling the ambulance."

She still doesn't, but I decide to let it go. I take a pot of congealed beans off the stove and dislodge them into the garbage disposal. "Seriously, I don't mind," I say. "I'm sure you want to shower, change after the hospital. I can stay a while."

For a moment, it seems like she'll dismiss my offer a second time, but then her shoulders sag just a little. An admission of exhaustion so brief I might have imagined it. "That hospital smells like death," she says again. "Dehydration or not, I'm never going back in there."

"It was pretty depressing," I agree. It feels so strange to be talking to her like this. Like we're family and not something slightly worse than strangers. I know I can't leave here without asking the questions burning in my chest, but I can at least let her shower off the hospital stench first.

When Paloma disappears into her bedroom, I find myself alone in a strange house for the second time today. This time it feels different. This time it's not just Paloma's history on display, but my own, too.

I finish disposing of the food, then rinse the dishes and put them in the fancy dishwasher. I put the glasses and place settings away. I busy myself with menial tasks until there's nothing left to do but look.

One thing at a time, I tell myself, but there's so much in the kitchen alone. So much color. So much life. Knickknacks from far-off places, pictures in frames. Years of stories I can't even begin to guess at. I can picture people laughing around this table. Friends. Family. It's the polar opposite of the places I grew up in. A new beige or white kitchen in every one.

Looking around, it feels like all the history that was missing from my childhood is concentrated in this house. Like Paloma was some Disney movie villain who sucked it all up, trapped it in a shell and left me to my colorless single-serving existence.

The pity gives way, then. It makes room for the anger to return.

I walk back into the living room, noticing everything I didn't when I was busy with Paloma's unconscious form last night. The colorful furniture. The art on the pale green walls. The pillows. The throw blankets. I'm struck suddenly by the realization that my *father* lived in this house. He looked out these big windows just like I'm doing now.

As if the house is egging me on, a row of photos catches my eye from the mantelpiece. An eclectic mix of frames that all somehow fit perfectly together—but I can't be bothered with frames right now. Not when I'm so distracted by what's inside them.

The photo in the middle is clearly a younger version of Paloma, standing beside a man I assume was my grandfather. He's tall, with a bushy mustache and hair pushed back from his forehead. It's thick, his hair, black like mine. I feel a surge of emotion as I recognize more of my features among the neighboring photos.

That's my nose on a stately woman in a wedding gown. My eyebrows on an old man holding a goat. My cheeks on a photo of a smiling baby.

There's more of this baby throughout the years. He grows into a gap-toothed toddler. A tall, lanky preteen. Fills out into the football star he was when he got his scholarship. When he got my mom pregnant. When he died.

"My Johnny," Paloma says, padding into the kitchen in an outfit much more put together than mine. "Such a beautiful boy."

I turn to face her. She looks older, now that I've seen her young, but there's no doubt she's still as sharp as she was back then. And even more intimidating.

Paloma sighs. "I hoped we'd have time for tea before the interrogation, but I suppose we'd better get on with it."

She sits down on the sofa, gesturing for me to sit beside her, but the nascent anger spreading through my body won't let me settle.

"Look," I say, my voice trembling already. "I tried to pretend I could be casual about this, but I can't. And I don't understand how you can be either." I indicate the photos on the mantel, then turn back to face her. "You *stole* all this from me. I grew up without a family, without any sense of belonging around my own name or culture. You know, when people speak Spanish to me, I don't even know enough words to tell them I can't reply?"

I take a deep, trembling breath. Drawing strength from my father's smiling face on the mantel.

"I understand that you're religious," I say, letting my voice crack. Break. Letting the tears well up. "And I'm sure a knocked-up sixteen-year-old from a trailer park wasn't part of your grand plan for your son. But he didn't have a chance to choose us. You did. You could have helped me know who I was, and you turned your back on me instead."

Paloma doesn't nod. She doesn't interrupt. She just watches me with those dark, intense eyes, and waits.

"I want to know why," I say, the tears cresting my lower eyelids at last. Rolling down my cheeks. "I want to know why I was so easy to walk away from. To *stay* away from. I want to know why you didn't want me."

As my shoulders begin to shake, I hear Maeve's words again, echoing in my mind. Telling me all my wounds need to be healed together. Maybe this is what she meant. Could I have opened up this way if Max hadn't encouraged me? If he hadn't made me want to be honest?

Paloma is still sitting stock-still. Her eyes haven't left me, but they went very wide about halfway through my speech. I wonder if she'll tell me to get out. If she'll hug me. If she'll apologize. If she'll reject me again.

What I expect least, of course, are the words she actually says: "She didn't tell you, did she?" Her voice is low, hollow with what sounds like grief. The same kind I felt when I looked at those pictures. The grief of lost time you can never reclaim.

"Who?" I ask, my surprise stopping my tears in their tracks. "Tell me what?"

Another long pause. Paloma seems to be looking inward. Weighing something. "Your mother," she says at last. "She never told you what we offered her."

I laugh, a cruel sound fed by years of my mother's bitterness. "She told me everything. She told me you threatened to cut Johnny off if he stayed with her. That after he died you ignored her in the grocery store. Shunned her until she left town."

Paloma shakes her head, laughing. *Laughing.* How dare she?

"That little minx," she says before I can explode. "I knew she was trouble right from the start."

"Excuse me?" I say, my ears ringing with rage.

"We did tell our Johnny we wouldn't be financially responsible for you," Paloma begins. "We were angry. Shocked. We had worked hard to rise above the stereotypes that followed us through this town. To give him a better life. We felt he had thrown all that back in our faces. All our sacrifices."

I open my mouth furiously, ready to tell her none of this is an excuse for abandoning a half-orphaned baby. But she continues before I can, speaking loudly, as if she expects an interruption.

"The way we spoke to him then is the biggest regret of my life," she says. "If I had the whole thing to live again, it's the first thing I would do differently. The very first."

Paloma pauses for a moment, sniffling. My anger is still there, still burning-hot, but there's something else, too. Something I can't name. This time, I don't interrupt. I want to know what comes next.

"Johnny made it clear he didn't intend to abandon you, nor to pressure your mother into terminating the pregnancy," Paloma continues, dabbing her eyes. "Roberto and I were already discussing the future. We didn't want to lose our son, and deep down we knew we wanted to be part of your life . . ."

"But then he died," I say, unable to stop myself.

Paloma only nods, wiping her eyes again. "But then he died. Horribly. Tragically. And that conversation was the last one we ever had with him."

Waves of shock hit me until I'm physically reeling. The last conversation they ever had with their son was an argument about me.

"After that, despite what we'd said, we knew you were the only piece of him we'd ever have," Paloma says when the tears have stopped. "That's why I reached out to your mother—she was working in that little café, she'd already dropped out of school. I told her we were sorry for the way we'd spoken of her. I asked if we could begin again."

She pauses, the pain harsh in every line of her battered body. I wait, feeling like another wave is rising in front of me. Larger than all the rest. Some part of me knows that when this one crashes, everything will be different.

But I don't stop her. I don't run away. I stand, and I wait for it to crest.

"I asked her to move in with us, here. Told her Roberto and I would help raise you, pay for her to finish her education. It wouldn't be a picnic, mind you. She would be expected to work, to study, to support you with our help until she could do it on her own."

A buzzing sound fills my ears. Then a high-pitched whine. Like amp feedback times a thousand. My face and fingers are instantly numb.

"She refused," Paloma says. There are no tears in her voice now. "She told me she wouldn't live her life on my terms. That she wouldn't be trapped in this little place. That she was already planning to leave, and she wanted nothing to do with us. I called her a few times, left messages, asked her to reconsider. She never returned my calls, and eventually her phone number was disconnected."

The numbness has spread up my arms. I feel dizzy and faint. It can't be true, can it? All those years of moving and worrying and bad boyfriends and evictions. All that time we could have had help. Support. A family.

"I didn't hear from her again until ten years later," Paloma continues. "She called me to explain you would be staying in town for a few weeks. A friend's family. She forbade us to contact you. If I saw you, I was to pretend not to know you or she would take legal action."

It's a miracle these words even make it through, but they do.

The answers I so foolishly asked for. The truth I never wanted to know.

"Of course, I tried anyway. It's a small town, so I found out easily who was hosting you. I reached out to them, they took your mother's side and that was that. I wasn't eager to cause a conflict that might make your life more difficult or confusing. So I had to let you go all over again, Samantha, but not a day has gone by that I haven't thought of you."

She stands, then, makes to come around the table toward me.

Instinctively, I step back. "I need a minute," I say through teeth gritted against the tumult of emotions writhing inside me. "This is just . . . I never . . ."

"I understand," Paloma says, returning to her seat. "I'm a stranger to you, and she's your mother. Call her, if you need to. But please, Samantha. Come back."

The look on her face is so familiar to me. One I've seen in the mirror a thousand times. A look that says nothing you love ever stays, but if just this one thing would, maybe it might all be all right.

"I will," I say. "I'll come back."

She nods in gratitude. There are tears in her eyes again. I pull out my phone with a shaking hand and step out the red door.

25.

For a long time I stand on the porch, feeling as if the Earth is tilting violently under my feet.

When it's still—or as still as it's likely to get—I pull up my mother's contact. Stare at the tiny photo there for a long moment. I wonder if I'm ready to hear her voice. To make this all real.

This photo of Dina Rae and me was taken two years ago. She came to Seattle to see some big life coach speak at the convention center, but she promised to spend the whole rest of the weekend with me.

I spent four days writing from dawn until dusk to make my deadlines early. I cleaned my apartment spotless and bought an air mattress. I made reservations for us at a cool new fusion place downtown. I even splurged on a rental car to go pick her up from the airport.

In the photo, we look like we always do. Like we're having a great time. You can't tell that she called me from the airport bar while I was sitting in the loading zone outside. Told me she'd met a man on the flight, and could you believe it they were headed to the same event. He offered her a ride into town, but she could still meet me for dinner.

You can't tell that I sat at the cool new fusion restaurant by myself until they made me give up the table, worrying that she'd gotten into an accident, or that the man from the plane was a murderer, or a human trafficker. You can't see that I spent all night calling with no answer.

Somewhere in our text history, you probably *can* see the message she sent around noon the next day. A selfie on the balcony of a downtown hotel room. In it, she's wearing a fluffy white robe and smiling. Sorry to miss dinner, but don't you worry, Seattle is treating me just fine! And I'm sure you had better things to do than chaperone your boring old mom around all weekend anyway ;)

She spent the whole weekend with the airplane guy. I typed at least twenty messages telling her how much I'd been looking forward to seeing her, then deleted them unsent. Sure, she was a little old to be falling in and out of love like a teenager, but she'd given up her whole adolescence to raise me. Did she really deserve a guilt trip for trying to have some fun now that I was old enough to take care of myself?

The photo I'm staring at now was taken during the drive to Sea-Tac. The only half hour we spent together during her whole trip. After the airplane guy had confessed to being married and she called me saying it was no big deal, but could I give her a ride to the airport . . . ?

I extended the rental car window to drive her, overdrawing my bank account. We snapped the selfie just before she went through security, at her insistence. I remember she posted it on her Facebook page from the plane—*Nothing like a weekend in Seattle with my little sister* with a tongue-sticking-out emoji.

It took me two days to leave my bed after that. Ever since Dina Rae left me with the Crosses, disappearances have had this effect on me. I just shut down. Sleep twenty hours a day. Cry at the stupidest things.

For the first time, standing outside Paloma's house, I realize my first night with Max hit me the same way. That my desperate attempt to save my relationship with Juniper was only me trying to avoid it at any cost. That ever since Dina Rae taught me abandonment was part of life, I've either bailed too soon or clung too hard to everyone who's ever tried to love me.

I know I have to call my mother, but shutting down isn't the only instinct I learned from her leaving again and again. I learned to make excuses for her, too. Forgive her before she even asked. Fit back into the place she wanted me to belong. Be the parent, or the accessory, it didn't matter as long as I wasn't alone.

Only now, seconds from truly confronting her for the first time in my adult life, I feel the loose stitching that's held us together all these years begin to unravel. All the leaving and coming home. All the forgiveness without the apology. Paloma thinks I'm fact-checking her story, and in a way, I am. But it's not because I don't believe her.

It's because I do.

I start to walk down the block, needing to move my body, not wanting Paloma to overhear. At first I think my mom won't an-swer. That my call will go to voicemail like so many of them do. But halfway through the sixth ring I hear the chatter of a crowd, a cackle away from the mouthpiece that can only belong to her.

"Sammy, baby!" she says after thirty seconds of this. "Your ears must have been burning! I was just telling Bob all about you."

I'm supposed to ask how it's going with Bob. Even though I'm the one who called her, it's what she's expecting. Before she asks if I'm okay. Before she even thinks to wonder why I might be calling her in the middle of what should be a workday.

"I need to talk to you," I say, hearing the tension in my whole body. The way it transforms my voice.

"*So serious!*" she says, away from the receiver again. Bob chuck-les in the background.

"*Hurry back, honey bunny . . .*"

"Sam, I only have a minute, okay? What's going on? Did you and Jennifer break up?"

"Her name was *Juniper,*" I say through clenched teeth. "And I told you we broke up weeks ago."

"Okay, okay, forgive me for caring about my daughter. Now,

what's going on? If it's the money you loaned me, baby, I'm sorry but I'm all tapped out from the cruise. Bob and I are thinking of franchising a Cell City when we get back to dry land, though, isn't that great? We'll be rolling in it before long. I'll pay you back and then some!"

"Did Johnny's parents try to take us in?" I ask before she can breeze away from the topic. Before she can say something that will make it impossible to ask.

There's a beat of silence. "Why would you ask me something ridiculous like that?" I can hear it in her voice already. The defensiveness that means it's all true.

"Because Paloma Espinoza just told me they offered to take us in, Mom. To help raise me. To pay for you to go to college. And that you turned them down and left town. Is that what happened, yes or no?"

Another pause, longer this time.

I wait for her to ask the obvious questions. Where I met Paloma. How we ended up on this topic. But of course, none of that is about her. So she doesn't.

"Oh, Sammy, really? First Roberto dying and now this? It was so *long* ago," she says, but there's an impatient edge to the breeziness now. "And you know those people were sticks-in-the-mud. It wasn't a handout they were offering, okay? They wanted me to work and go to college and raise you according to all these rules. You know that's not me, baby."

I can feel every inch of my skin radiating heat again, this time with a different target. I knew before I called, but there's something about hearing her say it out loud. Hearing her *minimize* it. Like growing up with no family, no idea who I am, was normal.

A small price to pay for her to live without the rules that held normal people accountable.

"And you never thought that maybe *I* would have liked some structure? Some support?" I pause at the entrance to a little dog-walking area. I can hear the heat in my voice. Feel it blistering the satellites carrying it to her. "You didn't think lying to me and making me believe *everyone* had abandoned me might mess me up?"

A scandalized woman gives me a look as she walks her dog toward the park. I didn't even realize I was yelling. My hand is shaking, clenching my phone too hard.

"Sammy, it was thirty years ago," my mom says, exasperated. "Why are you getting so worked up about it now? We did fine! You and me! We didn't need them."

It's so close to what I've always told Willa that I laugh. All this time I thought I had my own opinions about the Espinoza family. About my childhood and the world and my *life*.

But I never got to have my own opinions. I can see that now. My whole life, all I've done is grow into the spaces my mother left empty.

"We were fine?" I ask. "You think we were fine? You left me with another family for *an entire year*! You put me last again and again, and when someone tried to be steady for me you lied and said they'd left me, too."

"I never left you," my mom says, dismissive. Annoyed at me for interrupting her vacation. "I always came back."

"Those aren't the same thing!" I whisper-yell. "I've spent my whole life waiting for people to abandon me because you taught me it was normal. That I should expect it. I forgave you again and again because I thought you made some incredible sacrifice to raise me all alone. That I *owed* you after dad died and his family shut us out. But it turns out that was a fucking lie, too."

"Why won't you ever look at the positive in things, Sammy?" Dina Rae says, as if she hasn't even heard me. "We had good times, too! We had *fun*! We had *experiences*! It builds character, you know. When you're done being mad at me, *again,* you'll see it was so much better than it would have been with them. You'll see I did the right thing protecting you from all that."

There are so many more things I want to say. So much I want to make her understand. Why doesn't she see that all that living she did was at my expense? That I was always the one waiting up, or sitting in the office after school, or living a hundred miles away. Waiting for her to come back. Waiting for her to choose me.

It's so clear to me now that all that *fun* she remembers is just a positive spin she put on leaving me over and over.

But before I can say any of this, she's talking again. Easy breezy. "Listen, Sam, I've gotta go, okay? Bob's ordering another bottle of wine. I think he might really be the one. I hate when we fight, baby. Let's just try to end this on a happy note, huh? There's no need to dwell on something that happened so long ago."

This string of words is so far removed from my reality that I don't even know how to respond. To tell her it can't have been a long time ago, because for me it never ended. For me all her leaving, all her lying, has shaped every moment of my life. Including this one.

There's no happy way to end a conversation like that.

So instead, for the first time ever, I hang up on my mother. Without asking when she'll call again, without extending a lifeline to make sure she won't disappear.

I'm ashamed to admit I wait for a whole minute to see if she'll call back. To insist we make up. To apologize. To say anything that would make this earth-shattering fracture that's just split the ground between us a little easier to bridge.

But she doesn't. It's back to Bob and wine and fun and life.

And I'm on my own, walking up the block to a stranger's house that could have been home, tears sliding down my cheeks.

I walk back into Paloma's house after what feels like a long time of standing on the porch. I was trying to process, but nothing makes any more sense than it did when I hung up the phone.

Paloma is still sitting there, right where she was when I left. Her eyes snap up to meet mine.

"Well, you were right," I say in a hollow voice. The kind of post-crying hollow that says there are plenty more tears where those came from. "She lied. She lied about all of it."

Paloma gestures to the sofa beside her. I don't have the energy to fight, so I sit. I look at her, this stranger who could have made my life different if there'd been anyone there to choose what was good for me.

"Don't be too hard on her," Paloma says after a long silence. "She was so young. That's why we were against it, you know. Children have no business raising children. It's not time for them to make sacrifices yet. We wanted better for you."

I laugh in that same, empty tone. "Pretty big of you to defend her after what she did."

"I was thirty-one when my Johnny was born," Paloma says. "We thought we'd never be blessed with a child. We tried for ten years. We'd given up. But then . . ." She smiles, like there's sunlight touching her face despite the thick layer of clouds outside. "A miracle. He was my miracle. By then I knew what it meant to love something more than myself. And even with all that I made my mistakes."

The injustice of this feels more extreme through the newly opened wound in my chest. How is it fair that Paloma wanted a child so much, wanted to give him everything, and he was taken away from her before he could even grow up?

Whereas Dina Rae, who'd toted me around like a purse when it was convenient, setting me down when it wasn't, still got to be a mother.

I have no idea what to say to the woman sitting in front of me. I've spent my whole life putting all the resentment my mother deserved on Paloma's shoulders, and even though I know that was wrong, I can't make the new reality fit into the space where the old one has been for so long.

"Look," I say. "I don't mean to be awful, but this is all a lot to process so would it be okay if we just . . . did something normal? Like, didn't talk about this at all for at least an hour?"

Paloma smiles. "I have a fantastic idea," she says. "Let's make enchiladas."

26.

I've eaten enchiladas before—or at least, I thought I had—but it turns out the process of making them to Paloma's standards is much more involved and time-consuming than I ever would have thought.

In short, it's a perfect activity for two people who have no idea what to say to each other.

For the first thirty minutes I really know my grandmother, I'm in an apron taking orders. We boil a whole chopped chicken in salted water with bay leaves. In a pot beside it we put tomatillos, onions, garlic, and jalapeños. Steam fills the kitchen. The apron I'm wearing over last night's dress is bright yellow, embroidered with flowers and wings.

Paloma's is white with a giant pair of red lips. A gift, she tells me when I stare too long, from her husband. My grandfather.

"Tell me about him," I say in a lull, while we wait for the chicken to turn white and the onions to become translucent. The oven is preheating.

There are photos of Roberto Espinoza in every room of the house. Paloma wipes her hands, retrieving one from a little shelf beside the sink.

"He left me last year for paradise," she says, turning the photo so we can look together. "This was taken the day he asked me to be his wife." She sniffs, unashamed of the emotion in her voice.

We're supposed to be avoiding the subject, but my anger at my mother bubbles back up, hotter than the salted water on the stove.

I will never know my grandfather because of her selfishness. We can never get that time back.

"I'm sorry I didn't get to meet him," I say around the lump in my throat.

Paloma smiles at me. "He would have loved you. He *did* love you."

I thank her, but my eyes don't leave him. This handsome square-jawed man that my father so resembled. "What was he like?"

She laughs, and in that sound I swear I can hear sixty anniversary toasts. The joy of a father finding out he's having a son. Vacations and Christmases and fights and whispers. "He was the whole world wrapped up in a man," she says. "The most perfect creature God ever made. And he was *mine*."

My heart swells as she tells me he was a wood-carver. A whiskey drinker. A lover of boats and rivers and lakes. Of sleeping beneath the stars. That he was a wonderful father, an even better husband. That they met when she was nineteen. He had just opened his first stateside golf resort. Paloma was a guest, on a trip with another man, lounging on a chair by the pool.

He swept her off her feet that weekend. They never looked back. In fact, they fell asleep holding hands every night until his heart stopped beating.

As she speaks, I imagine my life if things had been different. Growing up in this house, the names of the people in the photos as familiar to me as my own. Roberto would have been like a father to me, teaching me to ride a bike. To fish. To camp.

I'm spiraling when Paloma glances at the stove and it's time to leap into action again.

We hack the chicken off the bones, which Paloma saves for stock. It's almost comical to watch someone so tiny wield a giant cleaver, but she uses it expertly. Once the job is done she gives me two forks and lets me shred the chicken.

Next we blend the sauce, which is green and velvety and looks much better than anything I've ever ordered at a restaurant. Paloma adds a little to the rice, after we toast it and before the broth goes in. Her secret ingredient.

"The beans have to soak overnight," she says. "So we'll have to make do without."

"Who taught you how to cook like this?" I ask as we roll the spiced chicken into corn tortillas just off the griddle. We place the little tubes in a deep-blue ceramic dish, working in tandem. Next time, she promises, we'll make the tortillas from scratch.

The words *next time* tug at my heartstrings. This is a commitment I don't have to chase.

"I learned to cook from my mother," Paloma says, a little wistfully. "She's been gone twenty years now, but I still feel her in this kitchen with me every time I make one of her recipes."

I feel like one of those people they find on desert islands after months, starving and dehydrated, yet only able to consume tiny sips and bites at a time. I've been starving for history, for context, my whole life. There's so much I want to know, but everything I learn threatens to overwhelm me . . .

And then, between the cooking and the stories, there's my father. Filling in every space between. Daring me to know him at last.

By the time we've made and eaten our enchiladas, it's late afternoon.

I have just spent the day cooking with my grandmother, I think, testing out the words in my mind. They make me feel warm. Safe.

"I'd better get going," I say once I've loaded the dishwasher and started its cycle. "I'm sure you want to rest."

Paloma looks like she might argue, but she doesn't in the end. She does look tired, and who could blame her? A fainting spell, the hospital, all that would have been enough without today's emotional revelations and an all-day cooking project.

"How long will you be staying in town?" she asks, and the rest of the world threatens to barge right in. Between last night with Max and today with her, I've barely thought about my impending firing. The empty Seattle apartment that I can definitely no longer afford. What's next . . . in almost any capacity.

"I'm not sure yet," I say. It's not time to share any of this with Paloma. I don't want her to feel obligated to help me, to fix anything, when all I want to do is get to know her. "It's complicated."

"Mhm," she says, smirking at me. "I saw *Complicated* this morning. He looks great in a pair of jeans."

I'm so shocked I start laughing, hard. She joins in, and it feels like reclaiming some of what was stolen from us.

"Well, if you'll be around another few days I could use a little help," Paloma says when we've caught our breath. "The doctor says I shouldn't drive for the rest of the week after my fall, so it would just be a few errands here and there, groceries and things."

There's so much of this too-casual posture, this feigned indifference that I recognize. We're two people who have lost so much we're afraid to reach for each other. But I won't let my mother take that from us, too.

"I'd love to help," I say sincerely. "The only thing is I don't have a car with me, but I can always use Lyft or walk, it's no big deal."

Paloma holds up a finger, then retrieves her purse from the back of a chair and fishes through it, pulling out a set of keys with a fancy fob. "You can use mine," she says. "It's no use to me sitting in the garage anyway. As long as you don't mind a few errands, you can do what you like with it the rest of the time."

I reach out for the keys. They feel expensive. "I don't want to impose," I say, even though I really, really do.

"Nonsense," she says, waving that snappy wrist again. "It's not an imposition when you're family."

It's the same thing Larry, Maeve, and Willa have been saying to me for years. But it feels different, somehow, coming from someone whose DNA you share. I can feel my eyes prickling and I blink them fast.

"Thank you," I say.

"It's nothing," she says, but her expression says she knows it isn't. "Now get going, let me live vicariously through your *complicated* youth while I rest my old bones."

"I'll see you in the morning," I promise her.

She nods, walking me to the door. There's an awkward moment where I realize I don't know how to say goodbye to her. Handshake? Wave? Before I can overthink it, I let my lonely inner child take over. We step forward together and I hug her tightly around her frail shoulders. She smells like peppers and lime and a hint of that bold perfume.

Paloma stiffens in surprise, but in the space of a heartbeat she relaxes, wrapping her arms around me in return. We stand there for a long minute. She lets me be the one to let go.

I've done a decent job of keeping my anger and all my various neuroses at bay during my afternoon with Paloma, but the moment I'm alone they come back full force.

There's my job, which still expects me to turn in an article about Max Ryan, former rock star, in six days. Then there's Max himself, who was much too hard to walk away from this morning. There's Dina Rae and the blast crater our earlier conversation left in our relationship and my life.

On top of all that, there's Willa, who has yet to say anything beyond the thumbs-up react she sent this morning. A sure sign that whatever ceasefire we reached due to Brook's intervention the other night is on shaky ground.

In short, it's a lot, and part of me wishes I could just run away. Escape from everything.

But I've learned the very hard way today what escaping does to the people you run from. And I have never wanted less to be like my mother than I do right now.

Thoughts in an utter tangle, I walk down the steps. Paloma said she'd open the garage from the inside, and as I round the corner I realize I did not think to ask what kind of car she drove . . .

My jaw almost drops when I reach the driveway. The garage door is open as promised, and on the all-weather carpeting is parked a glossy, nearly new Mercedes SUV.

I'm not sure what I was expecting. A Buick or something? But I should have known that someone who can afford that view of the bay wouldn't drive a *cheap* car.

I let myself in with the key fob, feeling like a thief. Like the police will be after me the second I start the engine. I've never even *sat* in a car this nice before, let alone driven one. It starts with the push of a button on the dash. The noise it makes as it purrs to life is downright luxurious.

Before me is a screen that looks like something from a space-ship. It's asking me if I want to connect my phone to hands-free Bluetooth—which I *obviously* do.

"One new message," says the pleasant voice of my robot driver's assistant. I realize I've been avoiding my phone since I hung up on Dina Rae, and I'm instantly worried it's from her. There's no way she'd apologize, right?

"Open message?" I say out loud, and there it is on the screen. Only it's not from Dina Rae. It's from Max, sent just after noon.

Hey, it reads. I left a little something in your bag for later. Hope you can forgive the sleight of hand. Is it weird that I'm impatient to see you again already? Don't answer that. Or maybe do.

The butterflies have set up a colony that takes up my entire torso. I don't bother shooing them away this time. I know it's hopeless. I dive for my bag amid the swarm, rifling through it until I find a USB flash drive in a Ziploc bag with a note in Max's untidy scrawl:

> S— You've always told me the truth, and I hope you
> will again. Maybe a little gently this time, though.
> XO, M

I know what it is before I plug it in (of course this ridiculous car has a built-in USB port) and I'm not disappointed. I haven't even backed out of the garage when Max's voice fills the car, velvety through the surround-sound speakers.

My plan was to go back to Willa's. Change my clothes. Suss out whether the thumbs-up was busy or annoyed. But instead I turn the other direction on Main Street, heading for the open roads Max and I took on his motorcycle and leaving everything else behind.

I drive without a destination, letting the music wash over me. I'm visited by the same feeling I had when Max played for me, eleven years ago and yesterday. The same one I've been chasing since I was a nine-year-old falling in love with Crosby, Stills & Nash in Larry Cross's den.

The feeling that no matter what's happening in the world, in my heart, in my tangled mess of thoughts, I'm not alone. That feelings like mine aren't only allowed, they're *necessary* to make the art I love most in the world.

When the album ends, I turn back toward Ridley Falls and start it again. The ponderosas welcome me back. A hawk flies overhead. And I have a plan.

27.

It's so strange that I left Willa and Brook's for dinner with Paloma less than twenty-four hours ago. It feels like it's been a year.

Brook's Subaru is missing when I pull up in Paloma's fancy Mercedes, and I feel immeasurably guilty for hoping they're both gone. That I'll be able to sneak in for a judgment-free costume change before hopefully meeting Max.

But there are lights on inside, and I know eco-conscious Willa would never waste energy, which means she's home and Brook isn't. I can't decide if that will make this easier or harder.

To stall, I turn off the car and pick up my phone, opening my text thread with Max.

Listened to the album, I type, lips curling into a grin when I think of seeing him again. **I think I can help. Are you free tonight?**

The reply comes immediately this time, too. The butterflies are pleased.

Yes. What do you have in mind?

My foolproof plan is too good to deliver over text, so I say simply: **I'll be at your house in an hour. We're going out. Don't dress up.**

Counting down the minutes, he replies.

It takes me five of them just to tame my goofy expression for long enough to walk through the front door. If I'm going to sell

Willa on the idea of Max and me, I can't look like a crushed-out teenager.

Even though that's exactly what I feel like right now.

Inside, Willa is curled up in the big chair under the window reading a book. She smiles when I come in, setting it spine-up on the arm.

"Hey, stranger," she says. She looks tired, and I suddenly worry that she stayed up waiting for me last night.

"Hi," I say, perching on the ottoman. "Sorry I didn't come home."

She laughs. "You're my best friend, not my wayward sixteen-year-old daughter. My parents told me Paloma was in the hospital, is everything okay?"

"It was a weird one," I say. "She was just dehydrated, I guess, but they kept her overnight for observation."

"And you stayed?" Willa asks. "That was awfully nice of you, all things considered."

There's a moment where I know I could lie to Willa. Tell her I spent all night dutifully sitting at Paloma's sleeping side. But I don't want any more distance between us than there already is, even if I have to hear all the reasons I'm being reckless.

"I didn't stay at the hospital," I say. "I was with Max."

In Willa's long pause, I can hear her replaying Brook's lecture. Tamping down the urge to tell me exactly why I'm wrong.

"I guess you probably weren't conducting an overnight interview for *Scavenger*."

I shake my head. "I'm not doing the piece," I say. "I can't. I'm gonna tell Esme I couldn't get ahold of him and she'll fire me and that will be that. Maybe it's for the best."

Another interminable pause. "Are you sure that's what you want?"

I nod. "There's no way I could use him, Willa. Not now. I think there's something real between us."

This time, she doesn't pause. "Real enough to give up your whole life for?"

"I'm not giving up my whole life," I say, hearing the impatience creep into my voice. "I didn't even want to be a critic, remember? I wanted my own little label. To build artists up and help them succeed."

"I remember you were lower than I've ever seen you because of him," Willa says. "And you fought your way through it to find something you were great at, and now you're about to give all that up even though you already know how this ends."

"God, Willa, I'm allowed to make my own decisions," I say. "I'm allowed to take risks! I don't regret meeting Max that night, I never did, even when I felt the absolute worst I ever felt. And if this crashes and burns—which it won't, because we've both changed—I won't regret it this time either."

Willa is standing now, too. Her eyes are flashing. "And I suppose you were totally honest with him, right? He knows who you are and why you came here and miraculously this *real thing* between you survived it all?"

"It's none of your business!" I say, feeling the stab of guilt in the pit of my stomach, unwilling to take it back. "I don't expect you to present every single detail about your marriage to me for judgment."

In this moment, Willa looks exactly like she did in fourth grade when I wouldn't admit Princess Twilight was a better pony than Rainbow Dash. She puts her nose in the air a little, holding up her hands and physically backing away from me. Like my terrible life choices might be contagious.

"If that's how you really feel, fine," she says. "You're right. None of it is my business so I'll just . . . stay out of your life."

"Great," I say, as she flounces off toward her bedroom.

"Wonderful!" she says over her shoulder.

"Fantastic!" I shout as she slams her door.

I throw myself down into the chair Willa just vacated, burying my face in my hands, so mad I want to punch something. So sad I want to cry.

For a minute, I can feel it all threatening to break through. My fight with Dina Rae. Everything I learned about Paloma and the family I never knew. Max and the last remaining secret between us. Willa. The way she can never just be on my side when I need her to be.

Before I can totally lose myself in the spiral, my phone buzzes. I lunge for my purse, hoping it's her. Telling me she's sorry for overreacting. Promising to have my back from now on . . .

But it's Max. A photo of Max, to be more specific. He's clearly not a practiced selfie-taker, because this is not his best angle. Luckily for him it seems to be impossible to take a bad picture of him.

He's wearing relaxed-fit jeans with a hole in the knee, a fitted black T-shirt and a flannel. His hair, as always, curls into his eyes. He's almost smiling.

Don't think I've ever taken a selfie before, reads the accompanying text. **But this seems important, so I had to get outfit approval.**

The best thing about this plan I've concocted to help Max with his return to the spotlight is that it suits my purposes too. It's not running to take a brief hiatus from your unsolvable problems, right? I'm pretty sure the internet just calls that self-care.

Nailed it, I reply. **See you in half an hour.**

He hearts the message, and the ticking clock is enough to get me out of the chair and into my wardrobe without any more self-pity.

Willa stays behind her closed door the whole time. I hesitate before heading out, my hand on the front doorknob. I know leaving here without even attempting to repair things is a choice, but I have no idea how to make it right without taking back everything I said.

In the end, I just go, telling myself that time will smooth the edges of things and we'll talk when we're ready. But I can't shake the feeling that it might not be soon.

When I pull Paloma's ridiculous car into Max's driveway five minutes early, he's already waiting outside.

"I could hear the angst from down the block," he says, leaning in the open window. "You okay? Or should I take a hint from the fact that this song is literally called 'I'm Not Okay'?"

He's half joking, but I can see in his eyes that he would listen if I wanted to tell him. All about my day with Paloma and my fight with Willa and my horrible mom and my uncertain future.

But I don't want to talk. Not tonight. Not even to Max.

"This outing is not about me or my complex interpersonal conflicts," I say, killing the engine and climbing out to Max's apparent surprise. "It's about getting you back in shape."

It's such a ridiculous thing to say that I laugh, thinking of some sports montage where Max lifts weights and runs up and down stadium stairs like he isn't already all lean muscle and chiseled angles.

He raises an eyebrow, and I like that he doesn't pretend to be modest about it.

"Not that kind of shape," I clarify, closing the door behind me. It doesn't clunk, of course. Not at this price point.

I'm about to elaborate, but Max steps into the space in front of me, pinning me against the champagne-colored exterior of Paloma's car.

"I *missed* you," he says, with a rough, almost disbelieving chuckle. "I didn't get anything done all day." When he kisses me, his mouth is warm and soft. I feel my body melt into him, all the issues of the day lost in the rising tide of breathless want that leaves no room for them. For anything.

But just as we're getting some real high-school-parking-lot make-out traction, Willa's words echo up from somewhere deep in my mind. *You already know how this ends.*

I pull away from Max reluctantly. "There's a whole plan, you know."

His eyes glint a little in the exterior light on his garage. "Plans keep."

"Not these ones." I take a step back, letting the cool air and the absence of full-body contact bring me back to my senses a little. "Some things are more important than the pleasures of the flesh."

Max's eyes are still heavily lidded, his thumb tracing circles on the inch of exposed skin between my jeans and my self-cropped shirt. "Having a hard time thinking of even one, right now . . ."

"Your album," I manage with some effort. "It's good, Max. It's really good."

His demeanor changes. I can feel the walls go up, protecting him from what's coming.

"But you're going to have to perform it," I continue. "And when you do, you can't sound like you're not sure you deserve to be singing your own songs. You can't sound like you need people to like them."

"I *want* people to like them," he says, spreading his hands out at his sides. "Is that a crime?"

"No," I say. "But it's not what you need to be focused on. You need to believe in your music. You need to not care if some people hate it, because you know the right people are going to love it."

"Easier said than done," Max says, turning away from me at last, looking up at the sky as if it has all the answers.

"Tell me something," I say, leaning against the car beside him, looking up to see what he's seeing. The silhouettes of treetops reaching for the first glimmering stars. "When you were writing music for Seven Shades, did you ever think about those songs this way? Like you weren't sure?"

Max laughs. "I was focused on . . . other things back then."

"*Exactly,*" I say, turning to look at him. "You were performing, and partying, and dating teen drama stars, and gallivanting around the world having an absolute debaucherous blast."

There's a moment of hesitation, then Max relents. "I mean, an oversimplification, but correct in essence."

"So that's what we need to tap back into," I say, picking up steam. "That unshakable twenty-two-year-old rock star confidence."

Max's expression is no longer amused, just perplexed. "You're saying you want me to do cocaine with radio DJs and date four underwear models in a month on a dare because . . . it'll make my music better?"

The underwear models are a tough pill to swallow, but I do, pushing forward to make my point. "In theory, yes," I say. "In practice, this is Ridley Falls, so we're gonna do the best we can."

"Which is?" Max asks, still looking wary.

"The most rock star night we can possibly have in a town that shuts down before eleven," I say, with as much enthusiasm as I can muster. "Whiskey shots and karaoke."

For a minute, Max looks genuinely horrified, and I wonder if I've underestimated the extent of his anxiety around performing live. If it's been seven years since he was on stage, maybe I've overstepped here, and he'll hate me for even suggesting it, or else he'll totally shut down . . .

"And you?" Max asks finally.

"I'll be there. The whole time. For sure," I promise. "Look, your album is beautiful. And when people listen to it they're going to be amazed. But you're going to have to perform these songs live. This is just to shake the dust off. To remind you what a badass you've always been."

"And you think cheap whiskey and karaoke is the only way to do that?"

"It's the quickest, easiest way to start," I say. "Plus it'll be *fun*. Remember fun?"

"Vaguely." His expression says he still hasn't committed. That inner war he's been fighting since the moment I met him is on full display.

For a minute he looks so tortured that I want to tell him to forget the whole thing. Pull him back into his comfort zone. Go inside and curl up on his soft orange couch and talk until there's nothing left to be afraid of.

But I don't, because I think he needs this. And after today, so do I.

"You know what?" Max says finally. "Fuck it. Let's do it."

"Really?"

That dangerous glint is more pronounced now. "If you're sure. It's been a long time since I was a rock star," he says. "Who knows what might happen?"

A little shiver of anticipation goes up my spine. "I'll take my chances."

28.

Given that the plan involves straight liquor, Max and I decide to walk to Ridley Falls's one actual no-minors bar. There are a few restaurants *with* bars, but Joyce's—on the outskirts of town so no one is bothered by the Harley engines revving and the loud off-key renditions of various country ballads—is the real deal.

It only takes us fifteen minutes to get there, and as we walk there's a sort of lightness to Max that I haven't seen before. Like he's let go of a very heavy burden. Just left it on the side of the highway as we wind our way toward the neon sign with its pink-and-green arrow.

The door creaks as Max pushes it open. The glass is covered by layers and layers of paper flyers. Concerts. Landscapers. Lost dog signs. He holds the door open for me, then smacks my ass as I walk through.

I whirl around, not sure I'll find the same man behind me who color-codes his socks, but there he is. Smirking. Beautiful.

"Remind me to take you out more often," I say, letting him sling his arm over my shoulders as we make our way up to the bar.

It's a little early on a Friday for much of a crowd, but there are a few weathered regulars at the sticky bar, a pool table with an abandoned game. It smells like cigarettes and spilled beer. A crooning country song plays on the jukebox.

"Don't worry," I say as Max takes it in. "The Yelp reviews say it really gets going once the karaoke starts."

"You can say that again," says the woman behind the bar, approaching us with a nod.

She's gruff, and cool in a way that makes me wonder what she's doing in a place like this. She wouldn't be out of place in Seattle in her dark jeans and black tank top, tattoos snaking up her arms.

"You guys here to perform?" she asks. "Competition's pretty fierce but the best number gets a spot on the wall of fame." She gestures behind her to a wall of blurry, overexposed Polaroids. Drunk, beaming Joyce's patrons posing for their victory shot.

"Oh, it's in the bag," I say, turning to Max.

He looks a little pale, like maybe he's regretting this whole thing.

"Anyway, it kicks off at seven so you have a little time before the crowd shows up. Get you two a drink?"

I'm about to order when Max snaps out of it. "Two shots of Jim Beam," he says, like he's done it a thousand times. "And something for the lady, too."

I raise an eyebrow. "Damn, really getting in character, are we?"

Max shrugs, smirking, the lightness back.

"I'll have the same," I say, slapping the bar top—which doesn't seem to want to let go of my hand right away. It's the kind of sticky that feels permanent. Part of the architecture. In my experience, this general griminess is the mark of a good dive.

The shots show up, and Max takes one in each hand. I follow suit, turning to face him. "To getting your mojo back," I say, doing a double clink before downing my first.

"To you," Max says with a slow smile that heats me all the way to my toes. He downs his one after the other like a pro.

"Okay," I say, taking my second to sip while Max orders a beer. "We have an hour. What would you do if you were on tour?"

"Pretend I was bad at pool and make a hundred dollars," he answers promptly.

I laugh, the whiskey giving it bass. "You're saying you think you can take me?"

His eyes narrow, but his smile remains. Feline. "Only one way to find out."

The truth is my sad bank account doesn't even have a three-digit balance at the moment, but I accept the bet anyway. That's how sure I am that I won't have to pay up. And Max is a gracious loser, anyway, more impressed with my skills than annoyed at his rustiness. I beat him three times before the karaoke crowd begins to trickle in.

By then I've finished sipping my second shot and am having a requisite between-drinks water. Max is nursing his beer, but his limbs hang looser, his shoulders slouch in a way I've associated with coolness since I was twelve.

He loops an arm over my shoulder. He smells the way whiskey always smells on boys. Like a dare.

"So, what are the odds you'll just let me build my confidence by watching quietly from the corner?"

"Zero," I say flatly. "Performing for a low-stakes crowd is a key element of the Sammy Espinoza Rock Star Confidence Recovery Protocol. Plus, if you think I'm gonna miss the chance to watch a two-time AP Music Awards nominee do backwoods karaoke, you're dreaming."

"*Watch?*" Max asks, leaning close, his forehead almost pressing against mine. "You think you're gonna get away with *watching* after you dragged me down here? No way, missy, I hope you have a duet picked out because *that's* where this protocol begins."

I blanch. In no universe was I prepared to actually *sing* karaoke tonight. There's a reason I've always been behind the scenes, and it's not because I hate attention.

It's in that moment that I realize there's truly nothing I wouldn't do for him. Even make a total fool of myself at Joyce's Bar in Ridley Falls.

"Fine," I say, laughing, shaking my head so my cheek rubs back and forth against the arm of his soft flannel. "But I'm picking the song."

Despite the fact that I made it to the sign-up sheet before it even officially opened, we're sixth on the list. Max begs me to tell him what we're singing, but I know better. I keep my mouth shut, minimizing the flight risk.

"What if I don't know it?" he cajoles as we take two new drinks and a basket of fries to a back table to watch the show.

"You know it."

Luckily, the first act is up before he can put too much pressure on my paper-thin resolve. A woman who's easily Dina Rae's age, wearing cutoff shorts and an American flag crop top. Her hair is bottle blond and looks like it might snap off if you touched it. Seattle Sammy would mock, but I feel softer around the edges after being here a few days.

When the music starts she closes her eyes, her face transforms, and she proceeds to deliver a rendition of Patsy Cline's "Crazy" that might make the artist herself weep. I know I'm certainly emotional when she finishes, and I stand up with the rest of the crowd to send her off, clapping until my hands sting.

"Wow," I say when I sit back down. "I didn't think I could be more surprised than I was by My Aching Back, but I stand corrected. She was incredible."

"You *stand corrected*?" Max asks, his eyebrow arched. "As one might after a chiropractic adjustment?"

"That one wasn't even intentional!" I insist, dissolving into giggles as Max snorts into his beer.

The next act completely makes up for the first one. It's two white guys who barely look old enough to be in here singing the karaoke classic—"Baby Got Back." One of them has a wallet chain hanging from his too-big jeans. The other is wearing a backward baseball cap.

They're so absurdly awful that I can barely catch my breath when they're through, but they leave to raucous applause from the regulars, beaming.

"So, I've changed my mind," I say to Max when they're gone. "I don't think music is for me."

"It's funny, I was just thinking the same thing."

There's a group of tipsy girls that screech together through "Ironic" by Alanis Morissette, a nervous-looking first-timer in a sundress who sings Kacey Musgraves so quietly and sweetly I want to hug her, and then the cutest little old man I've ever seen doing a warbling "Walk the Line" that brings the house down.

I'm having so much fun I almost forget we're up next.

"I can't believe you're making me do this," I mutter as Max and I make our way to the front. "I'm not the one who needs rock-star-confidence classes, and I can't even sing!"

"Don't worry," Max says, with a cheeky grin that sends an electric shock through my whole body. "I can."

For some reason, this doesn't make me feel any better.

I've seen countless musical acts in the past ten years. Thousands, probably, at skill levels ranging from humiliating to masterful. But until this moment, being dragged against my better judgment, I have never taken any sort of stage myself.

You're doing this for Max, I tell myself as we reach the monitor. It keeps me walking forward even if it doesn't fix my shaking hands or my very dry mouth.

I glance at him to reassure myself I'm doing the right thing. He's staring out at the crowd, expression unreadable.

"Hey," I say, bumping my shoulder into his.

Max looks at me like he's surfacing from very deep water. His eyes are wide, his face a little pale. "I don't know if I can do this."

"You can," I say, away from the mic the tattooed bartender

hands me. I grab his hand, surprised to feel it's cold and clammy. The gesture seems to give him strength. He smiles. A wan, queasy smile but a smile nonetheless.

"You guys ready?" the woman asks. She seems bored. This happens once a week for her. A man has taken her place behind the bar—one almost as absurdly handsome as the one I came here with. I wonder if there's something in the Ridley Falls water before looking back at Max, waiting for him to respond. He looks longingly back at the beer he left on our table, but eventually he gives a terse nod.

Somewhere, a button is pushed. The monitor lights up. The opening notes fill the room, and I laugh. In all the drama of this moment I almost forgot which song I picked.

"Are you serious?" Max asks, as the intro to "You're the One That I Want" fills the bar. "*Grease?*"

"It's a classic," I say with a smirk, and then Max is laughing, and the words are crawling up the screen, and when the first one turns from blue to yellow he's gone. Transformed into a hip-thrusting, gyrating John Travolta as good as any I've ever seen.

It's been a long time since he played Danny Zuko, but Max hits every note. He's confident and swaggering, and everyone in the room—even the people who talked through the other performances, even the people waiting for a drink at the crowded bar—stop what they're doing to watch.

I'm not immune to his sparkle, either. Halfway through the song I find myself wagging my finger and jutting my hip to the side like I'm at an audition, desperate to land the role of Sandy.

When we finish, I sneak a look at Max beside me. He's breathing heavily. His face is completely consumed by his smile. He looks right at home in a way that's so incredibly sexy I almost leap into his arms right then and there.

Before I can, the next group is being called up—three wine moms who make eyes at Max as we squeeze past them. I want to bare my teeth at them like some kind of animal, but I haven't had quite enough whiskey to justify it.

I'm about to head back to our table, flush with victory, when I notice Max hanging back.

"You okay?" I ask him.

He smiles a little sheepishly. "Yeah, just . . . do you mind if I sign up for another?"

I've felt a lot of feelings for Max Ryan over the years. Lust. Heartbreak. Anger. Envy. The stirrings of love, even. But the pride I feel in this moment eclipses them all. I can feel it rising in my chest like the sun.

"I could listen to you all night," I say, and he steps forward to kiss me, a beat too long for a public place, but somehow not nearly long enough.

It takes another hour for Max's name to be called again. By then we've had another drink, watched the talent wax and wane.

When Max makes his way up to the stage, alone this time, he doesn't look nervous at all.

It's later now, people are chattier, and sloppier. Most of them—besides the die-hard karaoke contingent crowded behind the monitor—don't even glance up as Max takes the mic, perches on the tall stool behind him.

"Anyway," he says with a crooked smile as the intro begins. "Here's 'Wonderwall.'"

There are a few scattered chuckles throughout the room, including mine, but when Max starts to sing the laughter stops immediately.

This isn't comical hip movements and smirking. It isn't a joke, despite the way he introduced the song. The grimy walls of Joyce's disappear, and I picture him alone on the stage at The Paramount. Lit by a single blue spotlight. The crowd silent, reverent, holding up their phones like glowing flames.

The crowd here tonight probably doesn't know it, but I do. *This* is the official return of Max Ryan to the stage. A return that's been whispered about, and rumored, and prayed for by fans across the world for years.

It's not karaoke, when Max sings. It's a cover. A respectful interpretation of one artist's work by another. Max, with his longing and his hope electric in every word, makes it his own.

He looks right at me when he sings the first chorus, a faint smile on his lips. *Maybe you're gonna be the one that saves me.*

But I'm still dwelling on the line that came before: *There are many things that I would like to say to you, but I don't know how . . .*

Before he's done, there are tears in my eyes. I don't wipe them away. I want him to see them. To know that he still has it. The thing that made millions of fans fall in love with him back then. The thing that made *me* fall in love with him first.

When the song is over, the applause is overwhelming. Every single person in the bar is on their feet, clapping and whistling. Even the jaded bartender. Even me.

It takes Max a long time to get back to our table. People keep approaching him. One or two of them—the younger crowd—must recognize him, because a few selfies are snapped. He signs a bar napkin.

I watch him make his slow way over, that melancholy still heavy in my chest though the song is over. This is what I wanted, I remind myself. The whole point of tonight. But the humble, small-town man who packs incredible picnics and alphabetizes his spice rack is already disappearing before my eyes. Soon he'll be *Max Ryan* again, and what will that mean for me?

I down the rest of the drink I left on the table. Max is surrounded now. I can just see his mop of curls over the tops of his adoring (and mostly feminine-presenting) public. In the back of my mind, some long-held instinct tells me I should leave. Slip out the back. Abandon him before he can abandon me.

But before I can fully process the impulse he's beside me, and he's alone, and he's bending down to whisper in my ear.

"Let's get out of here," he says, and the relief that floods me is too intense.

I can't even speak. I don't have the words to tell him how good he was or how happy I am that he came back to me. I just take his hand and let him lead me out the very door I was considering as an escape route moments ago.

29.

We walk away from Joyce's without deciding on a destination. We hold hands, our fingers interlocked.

"If we'd stayed, you'd be getting your picture taken for the wall," I say. I left most of my melancholy back at the bar. Being alone with Max makes the future feel further away.

"We'll have to go back next week," he replies, squeezing my hand. "Claim our crown." He says it like children say they'll fly to the moon someday. Like he's dreaming.

"I don't think it's me they want."

"Then they're idiots," he says, spinning me like we're dancing, kissing me on the lips on the side of the highway. "I want you enough for all of them combined."

We're only a fifteen-minute walk from Max's house, but he leads me past the street that would take us there.

"Where are you taking me?" I ask, squeezing his hand, huddling close for warmth as the night turns chilly.

He wraps an arm around my shoulder, letting me lean into him. "I don't think I'm the only one who needs a little debauchery tonight," he says cryptically.

I don't ask any follow-up questions. The truth is, I don't even care where we're going. I just want to prolong this night, this feeling of Max and me alone in the world, for as long as I possibly can.

Because I'm so focused on his presence beside me, I don't notice where we are until it's too late to protest. The lights are blazing even at this hour, the gate open in that small-town trusting way you'd never experience in Seattle.

The sign out front is brand-new. White paint, dark blue letters to go with the school's colors. I didn't realize until this moment that I've been avoiding it since I got back. Driving the long way around.

Espinoza Memorial Field. My dad's only legacy.

"You helped me overcome one of my biggest fears tonight," Max says as I stare at it, trying to manage my unruly emotions. "I thought maybe I could help you with one of yours."

Max reaches into his pants pocket and pulls out a ballpoint pen. It's black and has the Joyce's Bar logo on the side. I take it even though I'm not sure what he wants me to do with it. I'm still too overwhelmed by this place. By all the feelings I've been trying to keep at bay.

I've shifted so much of the blame for not knowing the Espinozas onto my mom today—and for good reason. But this hurt isn't so easy to push off on someone else. Because the truth is my dad would have been taken from me either way.

Max is quiet as I hold the pen, making my way through the tangled web of feelings I've never let myself feel about Johnny. About how unfair it is that I never got to know him. About how hard it is to grieve someone you never knew, and how lonely.

I've avoided Ridley Falls for twenty years—because my mom couldn't cope with her grief over him. Because she never taught me how to cope with my own. I feel like I've carried a piece of this town with me everywhere, this albatross I couldn't get rid of but couldn't get used to, either.

Since I arrived here at the beginning of the week, the burden has grown lighter and lighter. I've faced things I never thought I'd have the courage to face and found myself equal to them. Strong enough.

Suddenly, standing there in front of this field, I realize something. This field, this *town,* isn't my dad's only legacy. I'm here, too. And in that moment, I know exactly what Max meant for me to do with this pen.

I kneel down in front of the sign, pressing the tip of the pen to the new white paint at the bottom corner. It takes a few passes to make my words visible, and when I'm done my knees are grass-stained, but I stand up feeling like I've healed, just a little.

"'Sammy Espinoza Was Here,'" Max reads out when I've pock-eted the pen. "It's perfect."

I feel so light as I look at it—not overly large or showy, only visible if you're really looking—and the buzz of my realization has me giddy, so when Max asks what I want to do next I don't suggest we go back to his house. I just start running.

"Race you to the end zone!" I call over my shoulder.

I hear him laugh behind me, his footsteps catching up. By mid-field we're neck and neck, and I just barely manage to touch the goalpost before he does.

Whooping with victory and no small amount of smugness, I spin myself around the pole, watching him catch his breath.

"Not sure whiskey, beer, and fries was the right precursor to vigorous exercise," he pants. "You're clearly the superior athlete."

"Don't forget it," I say as he staggers a few steps away from the pole and collapses into the grass with a groan.

I lay beside him, both of us on our backs, heads almost touch-ing. The lights in the field are bright, but there are a few stars vis-ible. For a while we watch the clouds move across them, hiding them, revealing them again. I'm aware of his body beside me, but the awareness has mellowed. I feel comfortable. Safe.

"What are you thinking about?" I ask, after we've been quiet a long time.

"The last time I was onstage," Max answers after a beat. "Be-sides tonight, I mean."

"Staples Center, right?" I ask, hoping he won't think it's creepy that I know.

"Mhm," he says. "No one knew I'd never play again. Not even me."

"Why did you really quit?" I ask. While I wait for him to answer I think of the message boards and social media accounts, all the fans that have been asking this same question into a void for seven years.

"It felt like . . ." Max begins finally, pausing again just a few words in. "It felt like I started running the first day I got that record deal. And for a while it was fun. A race, or a game, maybe. But somewhere along the line I realized I was running *from* something. And that whole third tour it was getting closer and closer, until I finally saw it behind me. This huge, awful monster. And I just knew if I kept running it was going to catch up to me, and that would be it."

"Is it still there?" I ask.

"Of course," he says, and there's a hint of bitterness in his tone. "Monsters are hard to get rid of."

I feel a little helpless in that moment. I want to know the shape of his monster. I want to know its name. I want to tell him that whatever it is, he doesn't have to fight it alone. That this thing between us, whatever it is, is bigger than just a couple of weeks on vacation in a small town. That I want him to count on me.

The speech I want to make swells up in me until it's undeniable. Until I know I have to say it. Until I'm *ready* to say it.

"Max," I say, a little breathless.

He turns to look at me, and his eyes are so beautiful that my heart stops for just a second, and I feel like it's raining big cold drops and . . .

Max shouts, rolling away, and I realize the giant water drops are not a hallucination brought on by his beauty and the feeling of falling for him, but are instead coming from the massive sprinklers that have just come on in the field.

I shriek as the world crashes back in, getting to my feet in a primal attempt to escape the freezing cold droplets from at least twenty water *cannons* now soaking everything in range. Which absolutely includes Max and me.

I've seen this scene in movies a thousand times. The sprinklers come on, misting everyone, leading to some adorable coming-of-age scene where they run playfully off the field holding hands.

This moment is nothing like that. This is a military-level water assault. The sprinklers move in punishing arcs from all directions, hitting our skin with the force of golf balls. It takes us at least ten seconds to get our bearings, to orient ourselves toward a place that isn't under fire. By then we're stinging and soaked, screaming and shouting in a decidedly not adorable way as we run as fast as we can out of the action.

30.

"Well, *that* was unexpected," Max says when we reach the sidewalk, shaking his hair out like a dog as I wring water from mine.

"I guess that's one way to sober up," I reply, my teeth already chattering. The crisp September night is a little less novel when you're wearing soaking wet clothes, as it turns out.

Max is quiet for a moment, but before I can think anything of it, he's holding out his flannel—which is slightly less sopping than the rest of our clothes. "Your lips are turning blue," he says.

"I've been told blue is a good color on me." The breeze slices through me like a knife, undercutting my would-be-casual tone. I shrug on Max's shirt, and it smells like him, that sharp citrus. The lingering whiskey and smoke from the bar.

I've always loved swapping clothes with a lover. A permanent and tangible display that leaves no doubt . . .

We don't talk much as we walk back toward Max's place. I try to recapture the things I wanted to say to him in that moment before the water came on, but the urgency has passed. I tell myself there will be more time for proclamations.

By the time we reach Max's driveway the whiskey has worn off. I feel a little unmoored, like we're on a different planet than we were an hour ago. For a moment I hesitate by Paloma's car, wondering if he'll invite me in, relieved when he continues to the door without stopping.

"You coming?" he asks, with a smile that looks a little tired.

He lets us in with his keys, turning on lights as he moves through the front room. I'm almost afraid of how good it feels to be back here for a second night. To feel that sense of belonging.

"I turned up the heat," Max says, coming in from the kitchen. "But I can grab you something else to wear."

I'm shivering again. "That would be nice."

There's an odd sort of formality between us, like all the courage we've claimed tonight was doused by the sprinkler attack. Last night we were acting on days, years, of pent-up feelings and fantasies, but tonight is different. Even with the drinking and the cavorting through the streets we're in our right minds. If anything happens, we'll be choosing, not surrendering.

Max disappears into the hallway, presumably to his bedroom, but he doesn't ask me to join him. There's little left of the guy he was in the bar, drenched in whiskey and ego and sex appeal. He's more the man I've been getting to know this week now. Reserved, a little careful. Fascinating and beautiful.

He returns with a stack of clothes. Sweats, a T-shirt, another flannel.

"Hopefully some combination of these will work," he says, pushing his hair back with his free hand. The nervous tic is back.

"I'm sure they'll be good, thanks." I take the pile from his hands, our fingers brushing in the transfer. I feel suddenly shy about undressing in front of him even though we were naked together just this morning. "I'll just . . ."

"Oh, yeah, the bathroom is down the hall." He points.

I nod.

Behind the closed door of this large, totally clean and tasteful bathroom, I look at myself in the mirror. I'm paler than normal, though my cheeks are flushed. My bangs are plastered to my head from the water and the rest of my hair is already starting to frizz.

I start by peeling my wet clothes from my goosebumped skin. Then I think about his hands on said skin, and I decide that between the clamminess and the hair a quick shower might not be the worst idea. . . .

The hot water revives me. This shower is just as nice as the one in his bathroom, and just as organized.

When I'm done I towel off, looking at myself in the mirror. Trying to see myself the way he'll be seeing me if this night goes the way I hope it will. I've washed off all my makeup, but my ass gets at least an R rating.

Unfortunately, the ass in question presents an obstacle during the next phase. There's just no way it's fitting into Max's narrow-hipped men's sweatpants—even with the elastic waistband.

For a moment, Teen Sammy's insecurities surge back with a vengeance. It was one thing undressing in the dark of his bedroom, knowing what was coming next, but walking out into the well-lit living room will be different.

I try not to picture the girls he must have been with in the past. Little waifs who would drown adorably in these pants. Girls like Juniper, who wear clothing like hangers would, making everything look like fashion.

I've never been one of those girls (though I have been *with* a few of them) and most of the time I don't even want to be. But here, surrounded by Max's turquoise mid-century bathroom accents, aware that he's waiting for me to emerge, I almost do. If only just to have that perfect moment. The one they all probably take for granted.

Instead, I think of Max's hungry gaze on my body last night. All the ways he showed me how much he wanted me. This is the moment this *thing* between us officially becomes a two-night stand. I won't let that be ruined when I've waited so long . . .

I finger-comb my hair until it's loose and waving over my shoulders. Then I put on the oversized flannel, only buttoning the two middle buttons. From my purse, I pull tinted lip balm, dabbing a little on my lips and rubbing a little into my cheeks. I've never been put-together enough for purse makeup, so it'll have to do.

I emerge after just eleven minutes—transformed from a shivering drowned rat into what I hope is closer to a lumberjack goddess. My one nod to practicality is the wool socks he put on top of the pile. My feet are freezing.

Quietly, I pad down the hallway. Max has his back to me, sitting in a chair with his head leaned back. There's music on, I realize. Something sweeping and big at a low volume. I don't recognize the song but it's good. I can feel my pulse changing to match the beat.

We all have a hunger, I make out as the chorus kicks in. *We all have a hunger.*

"Hi," I say as I walk into view.

Max's eyes are closed, but he opens them when he hears me, and they widen when he takes me in. Bare legs, flannel slipping off my shoulder.

He swallows, hard. "Come here," he says, and they're the sweetest words I've ever heard. As soon as I'm within range he reaches for me, pulling me into his lap.

"You're beautiful," Max says, his hands moving warm and rough across my skin. "You're so fucking beautiful."

I run my hands through his hair. The damp curls. Thick and glossy, heavy in my hands. I don't dare open my mouth. I don't know what might come out if I do.

"We don't have to do this," he says as his palms rub up and down my thigh. "I know we've been drinking, and I . . ."

"Max," I interrupt. "I want to. I *really* want to."

"Thank god," he says, and claims my mouth with his.

Max kisses me like he's trying to burn himself into my skin. The world melts away, all the melancholy and the secrets and the uncertain future. There's nothing but now. Tangled heartbeats and breath catching and nails digging into skin.

Max pulls his flannel open across my chest, the buttons clattering onto the floor. He lifts me easily, pivoting so I'm in the chair and he's kneeling before me, kissing my bare thighs, sliding my

panties down and discarding them before returning to his reverent exploration.

There's a vicarious joy welling up in me as he tastes and teases.
I know the joy of discovering someone this way for the first time.
The triumph of mapping the sensitive places, the pleasure of feel-
ing their body respond to your touch, your tongue . . .

It's without shame that I let my thighs fall open.

"Oh god, you're sexy," Max moans from between them, returning to my inner thighs, his stubble tickling deliciously.

I'm the one moaning then, feeling entirely combustible. This
entire night has been foreplay, maybe the entire week. I remember
feeling the pressure of his mouth on mine when we kissed in the
garden, the fantasy of what *this* would feel like.

"Please," I say as he traces his finger lightly along the most sensitive part of me, his mouth still busy worshipping my thighs.

"They say patience is a virtue," he says, peering up at me with
a taunting expression.

To hell with patience, I want to say, but I know that will only
delay things further. He's clearly enjoying torturing me, but two
can play that game.

I wriggle out of the flannel completely, using my hands to
stroke and squeeze my breasts.

"*Fuck,*" Max whispers.

I run my hands down over my curves, ignoring him, moaning.
It's not a performance—or at least it's an honest one. I was ready
the moment the buttons hit the floor. "I *need* you," I say, remembering how he responded to these words last night.

He kisses up my body then, his mouth hard and demanding on
mine, his fingers finding just the right strings to pluck down
below. He kisses me like he's drawing out my soul a bit at a time,
and I'm so gone I would give it to him just so this never had to
stop.

I'm teetering on the edge, and he must be able to tell, because
he withdraws his hand, making me cry out in frustration. I don't

have to wait long before his head is between my knees again, and this time there's no teasing. His mouth is tender, as precise as his fingers, his enthusiasm clear as he groans against my most sensitive skin.

The vibration this causes has me panting again, reaching down to fist my hands in his hair, pushing him against me, needing more, *more* . . .

Before long I'm unraveling, arching my back against the soft upholstery of the chair.

"Don't stop," I cry, ragged. Close.

He growls in response to this, lips and tongue and teeth and stubble all creating a textural symphony until I'm climbing, peaking, then free-falling, my body weightless as ripples of pleasure pulse through me.

Max rides the wave with me, surfacing only when I'm boneless, breathless. Sliding back up my body once more to kiss me softly on the mouth.

"I've been thinking about doing that all night," he says softly in my ear, nipping its lobe, sending a smaller, weaker pulse through my fried pleasure sensors.

"It showed," I manage. "That was . . . I . . . wow."

Max allows himself a smirk.

"Give me a second to catch my breath and . . ."

He puts a finger to my lips. "It's okay," he says. "I'm okay. I just wanted to make you feel good."

"Mission accomplished."

Honestly, I'm relieved. This endless, emotional day is starting to catch up with me. I feel tired all the way to my bones. Plus, I tell myself it's a good sign. That he must be planning for an eventual next time if he's so willing to forgo his own pleasure.

I'm aware this background abandonment calculus is constantly running, conscious or not, and it makes me even more exhausted. I wrap the buttonless flannel around myself, and Max—still clothed—helps me to my feet. Together we walk to his bedroom and slide beneath the covers.

I don't want to fall asleep. I don't want to miss a moment with him. But the second I'm horizontal, a losing battle with my eyelids begins.

Max moves close to me beneath the blankets, pulling me onto his chest. He's warm and solid. I can hear his heartbeat, reassuringly steady.

"Good night, Sammy," he says softly, turning to kiss me on the forehead.

"Good night," I murmur, already drifting away.

31.

When I wake, it's morning. Yellow sunlight pours in through Max's bedroom windows. And I'm alone.

I sit up, stretching like a cat, listening for the shower. A voice. The sound of Max's breakfast-making playlist. I don't hear anything.

"Max?" I call sleepily.

No answer.

I yawn widely. The clock on the bedside table says 8:45. I still have an hour or so before I should head to Paloma's. Maybe if I'm lucky I can convince him to continue where we left off last night . . .

"Max?" I try again, standing up. I'm still wearing his buttonless flannel, and I wrap it around myself more tightly before padding on bare feet into the hallway. The hardwood floors are chilly. Out the windows, the sky is overcast and gray.

The doors to the bathrooms are both open, and in the one off the hallway the wet clothes I left last night are folded neatly on the counter. I smile, passing the door, thinking I'll find Max in the kitchen, making coffee or tea. Or maybe in the living room strumming his guitar again. Writing something new.

But the living room and kitchen are both empty too. The guitar is on its hook. Even the chair looks innocuous. There's no sign of the misdeeds we got up to in it just hours ago.

There's a door off the kitchen I haven't been through, and I feel strange opening it, but I'm running out of places to look. I'm expecting a garage, but it's been converted into a home studio. A cozy room with soundproofing on the walls. A mixing board. A booth with a sliding glass door.

It almost looks like the one I imagined during Maeve's ritual-in-a-bag. The one where Max and I were in love, and Paloma was proud of me. I smile at the memory. I need to remember to tell Maeve how powerful she is.

But unlike the fantasy version, this studio is empty. None of the equipment is on, and Max's headphones are sitting on the seat of his chair.

I close the door and wander back through the house, double-checking places I've already looked. My heart is starting to speed up, and my thoughts along with it.

Settle down, I tell myself as I gather my clothes. *Your abandonment issues are showing.*

I dress in my jeans from last night, which are a little stiff, but dry. I borrow a sweater from Max's impeccably organized closet—a soft, olive-green one that smells like him.

The whole time, I tell myself I'll hear the door open. Any minute. But the house stays silent as I run through my hair with a brush I find in his medicine cabinet—wrestling with the tangles last night's adventures left. I use the same toothbrush head as I did yesterday morning.

Still, when I'm as presentable as I'm going to get, when the clock reads 9:15, there's no sign of him.

I open the front door. The driveway is empty. The motorcycle gone.

Doing my best not to buy a ticket to the worst-case-scenario fest beginning in my mind, I retreat inside to comb through the place once more, looking for a note. Any clue as to where he might have disappeared to.

Nothing.

I sit down on the couch, spot my phone on the coffee table. It's dead, of course, and relief surges through me. Here I was searching for *handwritten notes* when Max probably sent a text like any normal human being would.

Heart lighter than it's been since I got out of bed, I hurry back to the bedroom, find a charger, scramble to connect. *Any second,* I think as I wait for the phone to power up, I'll see the message that explains it all. An unmissable appointment he forgot to mention last night. A promise of takeout for breakfast.

But when my phone finally connects, there's only one text. A photo from my mom. The first contact since our blowup yesterday. My thumb hovers over it, but I can't commit. Not right now, when everything feels so uncertain.

Not now, when there's nothing from Max at all. And nothing from Willa, either.

I open the thread between Max and me the same way I walked through the house the second time. Like maybe I missed something, even though I know I didn't.

Sure enough, the most recent message from him is the one from last night. The selfie he sent for outfit approval. I stare at it for a beat too long, then type **Heyyy**, only to delete it immediately.

Missed you this morning . . . I try again, but that isn't right either.

Wish you were here! Nope.

This bed is lonely without you . . .

I throw the phone against the pillows, then retrieve it again. I wanted to be at Paloma's by ten. But I'm so afraid to leave this place. Like if I do I'll never be able to come back.

I wait until the last possible moment before walking out the front door. When I close it behind me, I tell myself it's silly to worry. Max didn't know I was planning to go back to Paloma's this morning. He doesn't even know what I discovered about my family history yesterday. About my mom's deception. He'll probably be surprised when he comes home and finds me gone.

This idea cheers me up so much that I pull my phone out again, tripping over his welcome mat in my haste to click on his name. Typing before I can talk myself out of it:

> Morning! I never got around to telling you about
> yesterday, but long story short I'm hanging with
> Paloma again. Taking off from your place now, but
> come by later? I'm sure she'd be happy to feed you.

I hit Send, satisfied. He'll reply. The mystery will be solved. I'll reward him for his vulnerability last night by regaling him with the whole saga of Paloma and Dina Rae tonight . . .

When I turn onto Ponderosa Court I'm feeling almost normal again. The feeling only improves when Paloma opens the door without waiting for my knock.

"Good," she says with a familiar smirk. "I was beginning to think you'd made off with my Mercedes."

"It would have been a pretty bad trade," I say, and her smirk becomes a genuine smile.

"Come in," she says. "I made fruit salad and I have some boxes to take to the women's shelter. Later this afternoon I'll teach you how to make my famous arroz con pollo."

"Sounds good," I say, hanging my purse on the hook. Considering Max still hasn't replied, and Willa probably isn't speaking to me, the distraction will be good.

Paloma ducks into the first door off the hallway, and I follow.

"Would you mind if we had a guest for lunch?" I ask, suddenly inspired to be optimistic. If I don't actively court disaster maybe it'll leave me alone for once.

"Not if it's a handsome one," she says with a little wiggle of her hips.

I laugh, feeling better already. The room we're in is a guest room, bright blue walls, a white duvet. Against one wall are a few boxes, a few garment bags. Nothing I can't take to the car on my own.

"Cleaning out closets?" I ask, peering into one of them.

"It was supposed to be the whole house," she says, shrugging. "But I ran out of steam."

"I can help you," I say before I can really think about what it means. "I mean, if you want to keep going. Clean. Donate. I'm great at organizing, provided it isn't my life."

Paloma looks at me for a beat, like she's not sure whether she can trust the offer, but eventually she says, "Thank you, Samantha, that would be kind of you." And that's that.

As I load the first boxes into the Mercedes to make room, I sneak a glance at my phone.

Nothing new.

Paloma makes tea, and we spend the rest of the morning going through the blue bedroom.

There are four bedrooms in the house, she tells me as I make folded boxes three-dimensional. Three bathrooms and a family room downstairs. An attic, too. Full of memories. For the sheer amount of *stuff* she's accumulated, it's all remarkably clean. Dusted, vacuumed, organized. All we need to do is sort.

She perches like royalty on the end of the bed, declaring *keep, toss,* or *donate* as I hold up objects one by one. Each of them has a story. There's a vase that was owned by a great-aunt back in Mexico. Paloma is sure it carries a curse, so we put it in the toss pile. It's beautiful, but I don't dare ask to keep it. I'm cursed enough as it is—my silent phone is proof.

There's a real fur coat she received as a gift from one of Roberto's business partners—he owned other golf courses besides the one where he swept Paloma off her feet. A family business he began in Mexico, then brought to the States along with his brother when they were younger men.

I ask about the brother, but he's gone, too. Twelve years ago, Paloma says wistfully.

The coat goes in the donate pile. Paloma doesn't believe in real fur, but she also thinks those PETA people are taking it a little too far.

Near the back of the closet is a box of model cars, lovingly painted. These, we keep. They were my dad's. He built them as a little boy with *his* dad, who had built them with his. Paloma is quiet for a long moment after I put this box carefully back on the shelf. I'm not sure what to say. In some ways, I know we're bonded by losing him, but I don't have any idea how to talk to her about it.

She must feel the same way, because she claps her hands then and declares it's time for lunch.

My stomach drops. It can't be lunchtime already, can it?

But it's nearly twelve, and Max still hasn't texted. Hasn't called. I'm forced to admit that disappearing before I woke was a choice. Not texting is a choice. I just wish I knew what any of it meant.

Luckily, Paloma's recipe is so involved I barely have a second to obsess.

In my world, lunch is a sandwich. A salad. Maybe takeout if you're feeling fancy or leftovers if you aren't. To Paloma, lunch is a counter full of raw ingredients and a whole lot of marching orders for yours truly.

I combine lime juice and spices to marinate the chicken thighs in. We sear them after, two at a time on the cast-iron skillet. I follow Paloma's (mostly) patient instructions until—despite my complete lack of culinary talents—an actual meal is bubbling away on the stove.

"While it cooks, why don't you tell me what's bothering you," Paloma suggests, sitting on a tall stool at the counter and looking at me through her glasses.

"What do you mean?" I ask quickly. "I'm completely focused on arroz con pollo."

"Except when you're looking at your phone like it's a spider about to bite you."

I slump defeated onto a neighboring stool. I'm doing my best not to give voice to my mounting anxiety even in my mind. Confessing it out loud would make it too real.

"It's the handsome driver, hm?"

I nod. Nodding is fine. Nodding doesn't change anything.

"And he hasn't called?"

"It's not even a big deal," I say, the words ringing false even to my own ears. "I'm sure he'll call. I'm sure I'm just psyching myself out for nothing. We don't have to talk about it."

"Samantha," Paloma says sternly. "The world is a hard enough place without pretending you're alone in it."

I let out a noisy sigh. "Things have been going really well," I say. "I thought . . . I mean, it doesn't matter what I thought. He took off this morning before I woke up and he hasn't answered my texts. I'm sure there's an explanation but it just . . . feels like crap. Pardon my language."

Paloma purses her lips. "If a man is making you guess, he isn't the right man," she says after a long moment of silent judgment. "The right one will make sure you know how he feels. The right one will fall down at your feet and worship. Anything less is a waste of everyone's time."

My initial instinct is to defend Max. To explain that he would never normally do something like this. That something must be wrong, or he wouldn't have left me wondering.

But instead I think back to last night. Max Ryan, onstage at Joyce's. The praise. The autograph. The melancholy that stole through me at the thought of what would happen to us once he was back where he belonged.

"I'm sure he'll call," I tell Paloma and myself. "It hasn't been long enough to worry. Not really."

She purses her lips again, but it's time to take the food off the stove.

We talk about other things while we eat. The house—when it was built, Roberto putting a new roof on it just before he died to make sure Paloma was taken care of. The golf courses—the business sold when he was gone because there was no one to take over.

This is the closest we get to talking about my father's death, and like the model cars it happens only by accident. The tragedy of his loss is the strongest link between Paloma and me, but we circle it like scared dogs around an outstretched hand, afraid to approach directly.

I tell myself there will be time. When we're ready it'll feel right. But every time I sit in a chair, look out a window, or walk past a door in this house I imagine he's been right where I am. I wonder what this all looked like through his eyes.

We return to the sorting after lunch. There are boxes on top of the closet and storage containers under the bed. We don't finish until nearly six, but the donation pile is high and the room feels better. Lighter.

"You were a big help today, mija," Paloma says as we make our way into the living room.

"What does that mean?" I ask, curious. "Mija."

Paloma looks momentarily surprised, like maybe the Espinoza DNA would have been enough to grant me full fluency in a language I've never spoken. "Technically it means *my daughter*," she says. "But it's used as a general term of endearment."

My throat feels a little tight when I say, "I like it."

"By your age, you should have heard it a million times." She looks tired. A little sad. We stand in silence for a long moment and I can tell we're both thinking about how much time was stolen from us.

"Tomorrow," I say decisively. "I'll come back early. We can take the donations into town and work on whatever room you want to do next."

She smiles, reaching out to pat me on the cheek. "You're a good girl," she says. "I'll look forward to it."

"Me, too."

32.

Back in the Mercedes, I sit still for a few minutes, letting the day wash over me. I feel almost as weary as Paloma looked.

When I finally turn the key, my phone connects to the car's Bluetooth automatically.

"*One new message,*" says the cool and pleasant robot, and my heart leaps into my throat like it was launched from a cannon.

A new message? I've had my phone volume up all day. I've checked a humiliating number of times. Could I have missed a message from Max somehow? Maybe it's from hours ago, explaining everything, and this whole day of worrying and stomach-churning obsession has been for nothing . . .

"Open the new message," I say.

"*Opening your message,*" comes the reply, and my heart returns quickly and painfully to the pit of my stomach.

It's not a new message at all. It's the one from my mom this morning. The photo I didn't want to see is now four times larger than it would have been on my phone screen and I have no idea how to get rid of it.

Dina Rae smiles with an ocean sunset behind her. It's so pretty it looks fake. Like one of those backdrops at the mall portrait studio. She's standing beside a man in a cheesy straw tourist hat—presumably the one she cut our conversation short to drink wine with.

Bob.

I'm prepared for all of this. It's what I imagined when I chose not to look this morning. This is business as usual. Total denial about the foundation-shaking truths I've learned in Ridley Falls, and about the way our conversation ended the day before.

It would be irritating, but not devastating, if it weren't for the hand she's holding out to the camera. The ring on its fourth finger.

Below the image, her message is too large to avoid on the Mercedes's spaceship screen.

> I said YES! Say hello to the future Mr. and Mrs. Newmann!!

No mention of our conversation, or even my name. It looks like a mass text, going out to everyone on her contacts list at once. I laugh until I realize I'm crying.

About the fact that my mother has committed a lifetime to a man she met a week ago, and Max has officially gone a whole day without contacting me. The fact that Willa was probably right about Max but isn't even speaking to me, and now I have to go back to her house anyway because I have absolutely nowhere else to go.

I listen to "When You're Gone" on repeat on the way home. Only The Cranberries understand my pain. With a herculean show of effort, I avoid driving by Max's house to see if he's home. To see if he's entertaining someone else tonight.

There's nothing simple when I'm not around you . . .

It shouldn't matter, on top of everything else I'm going through. But it does. Of course it does.

Brook is sitting alone on the porch when I pull up, and I hate myself for being relieved.

If things were going great with Max, I might be able to be magnanimous. Forgive Willa for being so wrong about him. About us. But her words have returned to me more than once during this long, silent day, and I know she'd misunderstand what's happening here. Take it as proof that she was right about me making terrible choices.

"Hey," Brook says when I reach the stairs. "Didn't know if we'd be seeing you tonight."

I instantly bristle. What has Willa been saying about me? That I'm spending too much time at Max's? That this whole thing is doomed to fail?

"Settle down," Brook says a little wearily, clearly reading my posture. "I don't have the energy to take sides tonight."

It's a nice thing to say, even if we both know it's not true. Marriage—at least the way Willa and Brook do it—means always being on each other's side. But I take comfort in the fact that Brook doesn't seem to be pushing any anti-Max agenda tonight.

I lean against the post at the top of the stairs, not quite ready to commit to sitting. "How is she?" I ask.

Brook exhales, half-breath half-chuckle. "You guys are both nightmares when you're fighting. I'm giving her some space."

I'm not sure what to say, so for a while I don't say anything. If Brook wasn't Willa's wife I could tell her about Max's silence. The persistent rhythm of my abandonment fears growing louder in the background. My recent realization that those fears predate my first brush with this boy by a lifetime.

But it wouldn't be fair to ask Brook not to relay what I divulge to Willa. And even though we're fighting it feels disloyal to tell anyone else first.

"Willa loves you," Brook says now, cutting into my horrible loyalty math. "That's where this all comes from. Just try to remember that."

"I love her, too," I say without hesitation, because it's true. "But I can't live my whole life being afraid of her judgment. I have to be able to be myself."

"She just worries about you," Brook says, closing her eyes, tipping her head back. "And I know she comes on strong sometimes, but it's hard. Knowing someone that well and not being able to stop them from getting hurt."

I nod. I wish there were an easy answer. I can't let Willa run my life, and she can't let me suffer, so where does that leave us?

"Just . . . try to go easy on her, okay?" Brook says when I don't respond. "She's got more stuff going on than just this."

I want to ask what stuff Willa is going through, but I know Brook won't tell me. And she isn't the one I want to hear it from anyway. In that moment I realize how infantile this whole thing is. I'll go inside. Clear the air. Willa and I will talk and everything will be okay.

"I'll do my best," I say to Brook, and let myself quietly into the house.

Willa must have heard me coming, because her bedroom door is closed, a strip of light visible beneath it. I reach for the knob—we've never been much for knocking—but I hesitate before I turn it. My silent phone is too loud in my pocket and I can hear Willa's voice again, condemning Max and me like everything was already decided. Like there was no hope.

You already know how this ends . . .

I stay for another few seconds, divided, then I withdraw my hand and head for the guest room, closing the door quietly behind me.

Despite my early turn-in, I'm up for hours. I listen for signs of life outside—not many, besides Brook entering their bedroom and closing the door again. I stare at the photo of my mom and Bob until it's burned into my retinas.

I write a text to Max, then delete it, then write another, then delete that.

My last thought before I drift off to sleep is that Paloma was wrong. Besides her, I am alone in the world.

* * *

After a fitful night of sleep, I wake up with a heavy feeling in my chest. A glance at my phone only increases the weight. There's nothing from Max. Officially twenty-four hours of nothing.

My first instinct is to stumble out and whine to Willa and Brook, but then I remember. Willa's prediction. Her judgment. How even when I'm dying for some validation, or commiseration, I can't admit she was right about this without also admitting it to myself.

Max could still call, I think. *It's only been one day.* I can almost see him in my mind's eye, pinning me against Paloma's car, telling me he missed me after less time than this. There's no way he changed his mind in one night, right?

But there's no one to ask.

I think about Brook last night, hiding out on the porch. Willa shut up in her room for the second night in a row. The tense atmosphere invading their little paradise. As upset as I am with Willa right now, I can't make her feel awkward in her own home. If I can't apologize, can't tell the truth, there's only one thing I can do.

Fighting back tears, I pack my stuff. I can't stay with Larry and Maeve without making everything even worse. It's *way* too soon to ask Paloma if I can take over one of her many guest rooms. I check the balance on my credit card and find I can afford two nights in a hotel before it starts getting declined.

And for what? I ask myself, flopping back onto the guest bed. I came here to do a job I'll probably never do again. I haven't even told Esme I can't write the article. I'm in complete denial about what's waiting for me outside this rapidly shrinking bubble.

I should go back to Seattle sooner than planned. Find a new job. Schedule an immediate meeting with my therapist about everything that happened while I was here. But I can't make myself leave. Not just because I want to spend time with Paloma, but because this is the place my improbable, magical second chance with Max Ryan happened. And I know when I leave it will be over.

If it isn't already.

When I finally make my way out of the guest room, I've managed to get a handle on my panic. I'm braced for an awkward scene. A chilly Willa drinking coffee at the table, Brook hiding behind her laptop in the back.

I'll tell them I don't want to be a burden, I decide. I won't be petty.

But nobody's home. There's no note.

If they're not here to talk this is clearly what they want. I tell myself it'll be easier to leave this way, no awkward goodbye . . .

But it's not. It's harder.

33.

"There's absolutely no way I'm letting my granddaugh-ter sleep in a *motel*," Paloma says when I ask her for recommendations later that morning.

"I really don't mind," I assure her, setting down the extra boxes I picked up from outside Safeway before plopping down in the nearest chair. "I've been on tour with bands, so I've slept in worse places than a Ridley Falls roadside motel, I promise you."

"Samantha," she says, joining me in the living room. Her stern voice is becoming familiar. Even my mom never called me Samantha. "I'm not offering because I feel obligated. I *want* you here. I always have."

The words stun me for a moment, and I realize it's true. When my mom was pregnant with me, again when I was nine . . . Paloma has been trying to make Ponderosa Court my home for longer than I've even been alive.

Something warms in my chest at the idea that someone wants me. Really wants me. It feels a little like healing, even considering all the open wounds I'm nursing at the moment.

"Okay," I say, slowly. "For a few days, that's all right?"

"This is the Espinoza family home," Paloma says with emphasis. "That means you. You stay as long as you like." She's smiling, dabbing at her eyes until I find myself doing the same.

"Thank you," I say. "Things are a little weird at the moment so having somewhere to call home is . . . really nice."

"Good," Paloma says, clapping her hands as if to mark the transition out of sappiness. "Now let's get to work, hm? We're gonna continue with our cooking lessons, so you'll need to get some things from the store."

"Yes, ma'am," I say, thinking this must be why people like having parents. When your day is entirely structured by someone else, there's a lot less time to wallow in your own misery.

We clean out the room I'll be staying in next. It's the largest bedroom aside from the master—which I've never seen. Paloma keeps the door at the end of the hall closed, which is fine by me. Even an old woman needs her privacy.

There's not much in this room, it turns out. Some under-bed storage containers full of sweaters, a few more family photos, table linens in the dresser drawers that Paloma doesn't seem to remember the origin of.

We donate these, and most of the sweaters besides a knee-length black one with leather pockets that I beg to keep for myself.

"I bought it on sale," she says dismissively. "Too big."

But it fits me perfectly. And it'll be nice, I think as I hang it in the closet. To have something of hers when I go back to Seattle.

As we work, Paloma tells stories like she knows I'm starving for history. She talks about life in Mexico as a little girl, immigrating to California in first grade before she knew any English.

"I learned quickly," she says. "Faster than my sister or brother. When my parents needed things translated, they came to me."

She sounds so proud, so I don't tell her it sounds like a lot of responsibility for a child. Instead, I think some more about what it would have been like to grow up with Paloma and Roberto. They would have taught me Spanish, of course. Maybe we would have visited Mexico, to see where they grew up. My differences, instead of causing confusion, could have been a source of pride like they clearly are for Paloma.

"Did you teach my dad to speak Spanish?" I ask, forgetting we've hardly broached the subject of Johnny. I freeze, seconds from taking it back, and Paloma waits a long minute before she speaks.

"We did," she says. The words come slowly, then. Like she's fighting through a physical wall of grief. "We taught him from when he was a baby. He was fluent, you know. We didn't want him to feel ashamed of who he was even though it wasn't always easy fitting in in a place like this."

"Did people discriminate?" I ask, feeling selfish for pushing her, but wanting—*needing* to know more about him. About this family I thought I'd never get to be a part of.

"It's ignorance, here, more than hate," Paloma says. "People learn the stereotypes young and they don't know anything else. Roberto and I took pride in showing them we were different. Our own little small-town diplomats."

This, too, sounds exhausting, though I keep that thought to myself along with the others. I want to tell Paloma she shouldn't have had to prove anything. That she should have been able to live her life without being a model representative of her maligned culture.

That even if she had fit into one of those harmful boxes, she still would have been deserving.

But this idea cuts too close to the reason she and my grandfather rejected my existence at first. The responsibility they'd put on their son to be a model Mexican American. To play football and get a scholarship and not contribute to the ignorant stereotypes held by his community.

Luckily, now that the seal is broken, Paloma seems happy to move on to more stories about her beloved son. I let the more complicated thoughts go, focusing on my father, who has never been more real to me than he is today. Paloma tells me about Johnny's first school dance, when he got so nervous he threw up red punch and called for a ride home after an hour.

A camping trip they took as a family to the Olympic National Forest, where they saw a bear, and how he decided if he wasn't going to be a pro football player he wanted to work with animals.

She stops when the room is finished and I want to beg her to go on. To keep telling me about him until I've memorized every moment. Until I can see him and hear him and smell him.

"Another room?" I ask instead, hoping to prolong the moment, but Paloma shakes her head.

"Lunch," she declares. "And after that, there's a shopping list on the fridge. You go, and get whatever you like to eat, Samantha. I won't have you going hungry under my roof."

Paloma whips up chilaquiles for lunch with the leftover tortillas from the enchiladas.

"These are traditionally eaten for breakfast," she explains as she chops the tortillas into strips and instructs me to whisk together four eggs. "But Roberto and I liked to rebel sometimes when we had a busy day."

It's so adorable, the idea of rebelling by eating eggs in the afternoon. I try to picture them smiling guiltily at each other the first time they did it. Thrilled and terrified by how scandalized their mothers would be.

The dish comes together in no time, elevated dramatically by the homemade pico de gallo Paloma pulls out of the fridge, and she dismisses my praise with a wave of her hand.

"Save it for tomorrow," she says in an ominous tone. "You're learning to make tortillas by hand."

Between the grocery shopping, a linen closet in the hallway, and the first trip to drop off donations at the Ridley Falls Women's Shelter, the day passes quickly. It's a mercy, because Max's silence has not been broken.

Nor has Willa apparently noticed that all my stuff is gone.

In an effort not to let Paloma in on how little I'm capable of behaving like an adult, I don't buy Swiss Rolls and hot chips with the debit card she hands me along with the shopping list. I stock up on boxed mac and cheese and cereal, though; I'm only human.

"Preservatives!" she declares, as I fill one of the empty cupboards. "How do you expect your skin to look as good as mine when you're seventy-eight if you insist on eating that junk!"

"Oh, please," I say. "My skin doesn't look as good as yours *now*. It's all downhill from here. Let me destroy my collagen in peace."

She looks torn between pride at the compliment and a desire to continue lecturing me. In the end she leaves me to stash my junk food without further comment.

Not long after, she claims she's too old to stay up past eight and heads toward her room. Before she disappears around the corner she looks me over. "Why don't you go out tonight?" she says. "A beautiful young woman shouldn't keep an old lady's schedule."

"I was already planning on it," I lie through my teeth, ashamed to admit I have nowhere to go and no one to go there with.

"Good," she says. "You're only young once, Samantha, don't waste it pining away. No boy is handsome enough to deserve a martyr."

"Noted."

Unfortunately, there's nothing to do after that but actually get dressed and leave the house. I'm sorting through my clothes (which Paloma insisted I hang up in the closet) when I see Max's olive-green sweater sleeve peeking out from between my jackets.

It wasn't even forty-eight hours ago, but I almost can't remember the feeling of optimism that allowed me to put it on in the first place. The belief that I'd be back that very night, curling up in his arms.

With everything that's gone on today, I've almost let myself pretend nothing has changed. But alone in this room, in this giant, silent house, I'm forced to admit things aren't looking good. My imagination takes this opportunity to run wild.

I imagine him back at Joyce's, hitting it off with the girl who asked for his autograph. But of course I'm thinking too small. Maybe he was emboldened by his karaoke success, took the first red-eye to the last place he met up with a model.

My phone is in my hand like some horrible, self-loathing demon is at the controls. I'm typing Max Ryan into Google. I'm adding "dating history" because the demon is insatiable . . .

The first two rows of results are just photos. All of them are at least seven years old, but Max doesn't look much different. It's easy to imagine this one—where he has his arm casually looped around the shoulders of a woman who looks like a living, breathing Barbie doll—was taken just this afternoon.

That the all-legs brunette with perfect teeth in the next one is laughing at a café table because he just impersonated me trying to sing Olivia Newton-John.

I only let myself look at that first page before I close the tab. When that doesn't feel like enough, I power the phone down completely.

Heart pounding, mouth dry, I hold his sweater to my chest. I think of the six-hour phone call. That first kiss against the garden shed. How beautiful he was when he finally took off his last piece of clothing. The urgent heat of him when he woke me in the middle of the night. The guttural sounds of him worshipping at the temple of my thighs.

I missed you, I remember him saying in my ear. *I didn't get anything done all day.*

That all happened, I tell myself. Days ago. I'm getting completely carried away because this is what I do. I overinvest so the other person can't leave me, or I sabotage by giving up first.

But what if I picked a third thing tonight? A path of honesty and directness . . .

I fold his sweater neatly, changing into an outfit more appropriate for showing Max what he's been missing. When I'm satisfied, I walk out of Paloma's house with purpose. Put the sweater next to me on the seat of her fancy car.

It's a cliché for a reason, returning lost property. I'll take it back to him. Say I was in the neighborhood. It's the kind of risky maneuver that could immediately and horribly blow up in my face if he's not alone, of course, or if he really was trying to unsubtly drop me. But right now, I'd rather the clean pain of rejection than the absolute agony of wondering.

I turn onto Max's street feeling brave. Powerful. But when I pull into the driveway—killing the engine along with my Bad Bitch playlist—the windows are dark. The motorcycle isn't here. He's not home.

That's when I notice the doormat—the one I tripped on as I was leaving the other morning. It's still crooked. The man who lives here, who organizes his socks by color and doesn't have a single hair in his shower drain, wouldn't have been able to walk by without straightening it, would he?

Is it possible Max hasn't been home *since I left*? Or am I reading too much into this?

Sitting there in the dark, I feel myself deflating. The confidence flees, leaving room for my worst-case scenarios to flood back in. Maybe he did leave town without telling me. And so what if he did? It's not like he owed me anything. We spent a few days together. We didn't make any promises. Only I thought there had been something growing roots between us . . .

I'm back at Paloma's before even twenty minutes have passed, glad she's in bed already and can't see me slinking inside, embarrassed to have been thwarted so quickly.

But in bed, the lack of closure haunts me. I went there expecting a clear yes or no. This limbo is going to be the death of me.

I turn my phone back on, typing into the message field before I can talk myself out of it. I tell myself double texting isn't more embarrassing than showing up at his house.

Hey, I text. Just wanted to make sure a feral karaoke fan didn't kidnap you after the other night. I'd have no choice but to feel responsible.

I read it over six times before admitting I have absolutely no idea what's appropriate here. Probably I shouldn't be texting him at all. My last message sits there like a dud in a box of fireworks. If he'd wanted to talk to me, he could have.

But doing nothing feels even worse than continuing to dig this hole, so I send it anyway.

By the time I'm tired enough to attempt sleep, he still hasn't replied. I read back over the message, suddenly hating every word of it. The forced casual tone. The inside joke that betrays my insecurity. It's so obvious. What was I thinking?

I fall asleep vowing I'll never double text again. I'll remember this moment. But ten minutes later I'm pulling my phone back out, thinking I'll explain. I'll say something reasonable that will make up for the cringe-fest that was my previous text . . .

Before I can type anything, three dots appear on the screen. I nearly scream before realizing there's an old woman sleeping down the hall. I grip my phone tightly, staring as they disappear. Reappear for a tenth of a second. Disappear again.

Twenty minutes later, they haven't come back. There's no message. And I think being dragged off to Karaoke Kelly's basement myself would be better than feeling like this.

34.

The next two days are even busier than the one before.
Even still, Paloma's endless to-do lists barely distract me at all. I
think about those three dots the whole time, until Paloma chas-
tises me on the second day for burning the tortilla I'm making
from scratch.

It's the second day in a row of this. I'm not improving.

"You know, my mother used to give her children five balls of
masa when they turned twelve. If they couldn't make a good tortilla out of one of them, they never made another. She said that
was enough to tell if you had the gift."

"Okay, you're telling me not *one* of these is good?" I open the
top of the tortilla warmer beside me. The pile inside is pretty pathetic, I have to admit. And I've made way more than five.

"All I'm going to say is that you're lucky I'm more forgiving
than my mother."

"Why don't you show me how it's done then?" I challenge her,
stepping aside now that the offending tortilla is off the stove.

She waves a hand. "This is about you learning, Samantha, not
me showing off. I won't always be around to show you how it's
done."

A slightly awkward silence follows this pronouncement. I still
haven't been able to bring myself to tell her I need to go back to
Seattle. That I'm one email or three days away from being unemployed.

I'm about to broach the subject, let Paloma know there's a ticking clock on this whole bonding situation, but then she says the one thing I couldn't interrupt if I wanted to:

"Today I think we'll go through your father's room."

My confessions and plans retreat into the corner they like best. An out-of-sight one populated mostly by cobwebs. I've been wondering about Johnny's room since the first day I came here—whether Paloma had left it alone or turned it into a home gym or something. I'm relieved to know there's something of him left here. Something tactile I can experience.

After we eat—very misshapen chicken tacos with cilantro and onion—I follow Paloma down the hallway to the closed door opposite hers.

"There isn't much," she says when we stop. She looks at the doorknob like it's a poisonous snake baring its fangs at her. "We donated most of his clothes. Shoes. Let his friends take mementos. But . . . it was his room."

"Do you want me to . . . ?" I ask, gesturing at the door.

She nods, blinking hard. I wonder how long it's been since she set foot in here. How long this tightly closed door has been haunting her.

With a trembling hand, I reach out, swing the door open like he must have a hundred times. For most of my life my dad has just been a story, poorly and infrequently told by a mother who only wanted to leave her grief behind.

But after a week of knowing Paloma, my father's memory has never felt more alive.

There's a full-sized bed under the window. A deep-blue comforter in a sealed bag at the foot of it. The dresser is the same dark wood as the furniture in the rest of the rooms. The closet doors are closed. There's a mirror hanging on the wall behind the door. Full-length.

I suck in a breath when I realize there are things stuck into the frame. Photos. Notes. Decals on the glass.

"When he was alive, I was always telling him to clean it up,"

Paloma says in a strained voice behind me. "Put it in a scrapbook. Stop cluttering up the mirror." She steps forward, brushing her fingertips along the edges of the photos. "When he was gone, I felt so stupid. Who cared about a mirror? Roberto tried to take them down, box them up, but I wouldn't let him. I scratched his arm when he got too close."

It's not hard to picture Paloma, half-gone with grief, protecting the one window she had left into her son's heart.

"Take a look," she says sadly, stepping away. "I already have it memorized."

There's something surreal about standing in a mirror, framed by photos of the boy who made you and never held you even once. There are the obvious things, of course. A team photo of the Ridley Falls Rangers suited up on the field. Football cards. Concert tickets.

My first shock doesn't come until the prom photo. Johnny and a sixteen-year-old version of Dina Rae. She's wearing a slinky velvet formal dress. Dark purple with lipstick to match. Her hair is *crimped*, but her smile is wide. She holds his arm proudly.

His smile is the goofy teen boy version of mine, mostly front teeth—though he doesn't look ashamed of them like I am of mine. He's so handsome, with his hair hanging in his eyes, his tux fitted close, like his parents didn't mind the expense.

"Can I . . . ?" I ask Paloma, reaching out to take the photo.

"Don't worry," she assures me. "My arm-scratching days are over."

I take the picture, pull it carefully free of the thirty-year-old Scotch tape sticking it to the glass. I just want to see it up close. This evidence of where I came from. I wonder if Dina Rae knew already, that I was on the way. If she'd told anyone.

But as the photo comes loose, something else flutters to the ground. Lands on the floor in front of me.

"Sorry," I say, bending down to pick it up.

I never make it back to my feet. I just slump there on the

ground in front of the mirror, holding what is unmistakably an ultrasound image. It's black-and-white, just a roundish shape with a little gummy bear nestled along one edge.

"What is it?" Paloma asks, coming up behind me. "I've never seen that before."

I'm not quite ready to give it up yet, so I stand on shaking legs. Hold it out so she can see. "I think it's . . . me?" I squeak, and then I'm crying. Big, horrible, ugly sobs that feel like they're being forced up from the deepest part of me. A place I've never had access to until this moment.

"Oh, mijita." Paloma reaches her arms out to me, and I collapse against her tiny, frail old-lady frame.

"He wanted me," I say, sniffling. "I never knew if he wanted me."

"He would have loved you," Paloma said. "You're so much like him. I'm sorry, mija. I'm so sorry."

It takes a long time for the tears to stop. When they do, I feel like my insides have been pressure-washed. Like this burden I've been carrying my whole life has grown a little lighter.

"Come on," she says. "Enough cleaning. Enough cooking lessons. We need red meat and a stiff drink."

"Now you're speaking my language," I say, laughing around one last hiccupping sob.

When we get back from Badger's—the upscale burger place downtown that replaced my favorite ice cream shop—it's nearly eight. Paloma is tipsy, and I feel lighter than I have in days. We're laughing as we walk through the door. She wobbles a little in her impractical boots and I steady her.

I know even now that I'll remember this night for the rest of my life. There's a photo in my phone, one the cute bartender took of Paloma and me leaning toward each other on our barstools, clinking our shot glasses together.

I'll remember when she ordered a double hamburger with extra pickles, and when she insisted on a second drink. When she got up to dance in front of the little stage even though there was no band playing and I joined her, not caring who was watching.

It felt good. Like a window into a future where I visit her here and we get up to no good. For the first time, we really felt like a family. Even a little one.

"I'm going to bed," Paloma declares once her shoes are stowed and her purse is on its hook. She looks me right in the eyes before she does, placing a hand on either side of my face. "I love you, Samantha."

In this moment, my heart feels like the Grinch's, swelling beyond its frame. The fears that have made it impossible for me to trust splintering, giving way.

"I love you, too."

When she's closed up in the master bedroom, I pour myself a glass of wine from a bottle I find on the counter. The house is so big when you're alone in it. So quiet. I think about the day I've had. The beauty of it. The sadness. I wish I had someone to share it with.

But when I pull out my phone, it all comes rushing back. Willa and Brook, our fight. My mom and Bob "Cell City" Newmann. Max.

Max.

In the end, I pad back into Johnny's room. Snap a photo of the prom picture we left on the dresser when we fled. I'm so angry at my mother, but even as the villain of this story she's on every page.

I hope you'll be happy, Mom, I type. **I'm just not ready to talk.**

Below, I attach the photo. The crimped hair. The awful lipstick that makes her look like a vampire. My handsome, beaming dad, frozen in time with no idea what's coming for him. For all of us.

I press Send, and then I open the thread with Max's name on the top.

There's nothing new, of course. Four days and nothing at all. Even my imagination—so talented at spinning reasons for people to leave me behind—has run out of worst-case scenarios. The mystery of Max's silence stings in all the places my heart is so newly vulnerable.

Bold from mezcal and dancing with my fearless grandmother, I call him without overthinking it. What do I have to lose now, anyway? If he answers, I'll ask every question I need the answer to. I won't hold back.

His voicemail picks up after just two rings. "This is Max," it says, his voice low and resonant. "Sorry I missed your call. Leave me a message."

I tell myself I'll hang up before the beep, but I don't. I think of the voicemail he left me after our first real date. The one where he admitted he was scared. The one where he told me he wanted me.

"Hi, Max," I say. "It's Sammy. I guess . . . I guess I just want to know if you're okay. If I pushed too hard, or if you just got over it, or if it's something else that has nothing to do with me."

I take a deep breath. My hands are shaking a little as I go on.

"I just need you to know it wasn't a casual thing to me. That I really felt something with you. And if there's any chance you still feel it, or if you ever did, can you just let me know? It's the not knowing that's really getting to me. Again."

Already regretting my honesty, I hang up without saying good-bye. It's been eleven years since I last waited by the phone for Max Ryan, and it turns out time has done nothing to dull the pain. It's a humbling realization.

I think about the other times I've been left. The times I've left other people, and what it felt like, and why. None of it answers my question. There are maybe only two people in the world who can do that, and one of them sent me to voicemail after two rings.

So I call the other one.

"Sammy, my love! What are you doing? It's already tomorrow in Barcelona!"

"Hi, June," I say, knowing she hates the nickname. "How's the future?"

"*Drenched* in sunshine," says Juniper Street without hesitation. "I'll never do autumn in the States again, it's magical here! Are you busy? You should come out!"

She's not alone, but when is she ever? I can hear the clinking of expensive glasses, the chatter of beautiful people. None of it bothers me at all. In fact, it seems empty and vapid instead of glamorous now, so I guess that's something.

"Why did you break up with me?" I ask without replying to her ridiculous offer.

"Oh no, not one of *these*," she says, with the long-suffering tone of someone who's had to do hundreds of dumping post-mortems in her life. "Sammy! You always seemed too cool!"

"Too cool to date?" I ask, laughing. Glad I can laugh.

"Too cool to call me in the sad hours and ask for a justification," she says, and she's laughing, too, and I'm suddenly grateful for time. "Hold on."

I wait as she swishes and makes excuses and the background noise dies down.

"Listen, Sammy, I don't know what to tell you," she says, her voice a little less faux-breezy now that she's alone. "You were like two different people! When I met you, you were this fortress. So armored and strong and self-sufficient."

Hearing her describe me like that might have hurt a week ago, but now I can look at it from a distance. To see what she must have seen. A facade, intended to prevent me from ever getting hurt.

"And I flipped for that, you know, you were so sexy. So intimidating. But then . . ." She trails off, and I know she must be thinking, because she'd never worry about hurting my feelings. "It was like you changed. You got all gooey. You needed me so much."

I want to deny it, but I can't. Not even to maintain some form of dignity. Seeing it the way she sees it, it makes all the sense in the world.

"You felt like I tricked you into loving me," I say. Because I did.

Because I was taught—intentionally or not—that it was the only way anyone ever would.

"Oh, come on," Juniper says, laughing again. I can almost see her batting her eyelashes. "This is just what I mean. You got so serious. I wanted the *fun* back! Remember fun? Remember sixty-nining in the back of a limousine?"

I feel my face flush at the memory. She'd sweet-talked the guy at the rental place into a free hour. Showed up outside my apartment with a bottle of champagne. It was a fantasy, but all I remember now is that she dropped me off at home afterward. Didn't want to spend the night.

"I guess I wanted more," I say. "I wanted something real."

"What's more real than dining-and-dashing lobster and nine screaming orgasms in someone else's penthouse?" she asks, and I remember those things, too. The things I told myself I'd do until I earned something stable with her. Movies and pumpkin patches and couples therapy and boring shit I never would have admitted I wanted.

"We had fun," I say, realizing this is all I'm going to get from Juniper. The flirtatious retconning of a beautiful, insecure woman who's still running.

"We did," she agrees. "But next time, be honest about what you want. Otherwise you'll keep pulling in people who don't want the same thing."

It might be the most honest she's ever been with me. The closest I've ever gotten to the real Juniper, even after over a year of an allegedly monogamous relationship.

We hang up after a few minutes of fake promises. That I'll call again. That we'll catch up next time she's in town. But I lie awake and think about what she said until the early hours of morning, wishing I'd understood it all before it was too late for Max and me.

35.

The next morning dawns. Day five without a word.
By the time I'm dressed, I'm almost looking forward to Paloma's daily list of chores. At least it'll take my mind off Max. But when she comes out—later than normal, I'm already drinking tea—it's only to say she's not feeling well. That we'll have to resume tomorrow, and I should enjoy a day off.

"Take my card," she says. "What do the kids say? *Knock yourself out*? Maybe get a few new clothes, hm?"

"You sure you'll be okay?" I ask. She looks a little pale. Her hair is sticking up at the back—it was perfectly coiffed even in the hospital. "I can stick around. Put on a movie or something."

The truth is I'm not being entirely selfless. I can't think of a single thing to do in Ridley Falls for an entire day. Especially considering the horrors of my current social landscape.

"I'm fine, Samantha, I'm fine," she says. "I haven't had mezcal in twenty years . . . that kind of thing hits you hard when you're my age. I need a day of rest. And *you* need an outfit that doesn't look like you dug it out of a weekend bag for the third time."

"Harsh, but fair," I say, trying not to giggle at how adorable a grandma hangover is. "Promise you'll call if you need anything, though?"

"Yes, yes," she says, already heading back to her room. "Try to have fun."

"Yeah, right," I say when the door to her room closes behind her. "Fun is my middle name."

I get in the car, but I've never felt less like shopping. I'm planning to drive around until I have an epiphany of some kind, or at least until I've spent enough time out of the house that Paloma won't worry I'm becoming an agoraphobe.

I drive out of town on the highway, headed for that long, straight stretch of road crowded by ponderosas. When I try to start a playlist I fumble the fancy screen, almost laughing when it connects to the USB flash drive that's still plugged in and Max's voice fills my ears.

It's typical, but I don't turn it off. Instead, I try to listen to it impersonally. It sounds different from the other side. Like the goodbye I'll probably never get.

I'm farther than I've been from Ridley Falls since I arrived when the song he played me in person comes on. A closing track. A heartbreaker.

Tears fill my eyes as I remember that night. My confession. Max saying all the things I always wanted to hear. So much happened later that it's all almost a blur, but hearing this song brings back his words as if he's sitting right beside me:

I can't change the choices I made back then. But I can promise you I'd never do that to you now. Not in a million years.

"Only you did," I whisper as the song ends. And all of a sudden I'm angry.

All this time I've been telling myself Max and I didn't make promises. That he didn't owe me anything. But I was wrong. He lied to me, smoothing over the pain of the past to move us into the future.

I could have forgiven him for lying. I did the same thing, after all. But *I* didn't break my promise.

Not yet, anyway.

* * *

I drive back to Paloma's without a soundtrack. She's still in her room when I get inside. I've been gone a little over an hour, but right now I don't care if she thinks I have no social life.

For the first time in days, in weeks maybe, I have a purpose.

I tiptoe into my room so as not to wake her. I need to keep the feeling I got out on the road if I'm going to do what needs to be done.

I dig out my laptop for the third time during this trip, plugging in the flash drive, fitting my fancy noise-canceling headphones over my ears and beginning track one again.

My deadline is tomorrow. In all the tumult of the past few days, I never managed to officially pull the article. If Maeve's view of the world is correct, if there are no coincidences, this was by design. I latch on to that belief as I open the file I haven't looked at since before Max and I kissed.

The first thing I do is delete it all, leaving the page blank and full of promise. Before my second date with Max, I was terrified of this view. Too consumed with my growing feelings for him to do what I do best.

This time, when I start writing I don't stop. It feels like it did before Juniper. Before I felt like my skills were leverage, and I could use them to hold on to the people I loved. I don't use anything Max told me in confidence. This will be a review, and only a review. The way it was when I first started out—before I could get bands to let me interview them.

Music only. No complications.

If he can use our meeting to fuel something bigger than us, why can't I do the same?

The compliments I give Max's album are genuine. The depth of his lyrics. The maturity he's gained as a storyteller after seven years of isolation. But the criticisms are there, too. The bud of brilliance stunted by his own insecurity. His hesitation. His fear of how he'll be received. I don't think about how he'll feel when he reads it. Instead, I think of Esme, who will never have to know how close I got to giving up.

It's nearly dinnertime when I write the last paragraph of the draft. I feel like I always do when I finish a piece that's important to me. A little empty. Like I've put everything inside me into it and now *I'm* the blank page.

As I crack my knuckles and stretch out my neck, I think of how I felt when I first started writing—trying so hard to make my experience with Max into something life-altering and good.

Back then, I hoped telling the truth would work like it had on that porch in Capitol Hill in the early hours of the morning. That my insights would help bands make their music better. But the longer I wrote, the more I realized my reviews were often the end of a conversation, not the beginning.

It doesn't matter, I tell myself as I close the laptop, feeling the blood rush as I stand up for the first time in hours. *This conversation is over. Max and me are over. Whether I write about him or not.*

I still have sixteen hours before my deadline. I'll check on Paloma, make us some dinner, do my final edit and sleep better than I have all week. Sometimes the world doesn't give you closure. Sometimes you have to make it yourself.

Only when I come out, Paloma's door is still closed. I tap on it gently.

"Paloma?" I say. "Are you all right?"

For a long time, there's no answer. I'm just thinking I'll peek inside, make sure she hasn't succumbed to her mezcal injuries, when she opens it.

"Didn't I tell you to entertain yourself today?" she asks, but there's no venom in her voice.

She's dressed in black pants and a cheetah-print sweater with boxy shoulders. Her hair is behaving again. Her face is a little wan, her mouth pinched, eyes shadowed, but otherwise she doesn't look much worse for wear.

"I promise I'll never peer-pressure you into drinking liquor again," I say, putting my arm around her.

Her shoulders feel so tiny under my arm. Her bones light as a bird's.

"As if a whippersnapper like you could pressure me," she says grumpily. "I was drinking mezcal before you were a twinkle in your mother's eye. Dancing salsa until the sun came up with my choice of suitors."

"You'll have to tell me all about that," I say, trying to cheer her up.

"Another time," she says with a tired smile.

I make us a pot of Kraft macaroni and cheese—the extent of my cooking abilities before this week. Paloma sits in a winged chair with a crocheted blanket covering her legs.

"This isn't even food," she complains when I hand her the bowl.

"It tastes better with hot sauce," I say around a mouthful.

She grimaces, but she takes the hot sauce.

"Eighteen years and my Johnny never ate a meal from a box," she says when she finally sets it aside—half-finished.

My own food is gone. I feel a little less empty. "He was lucky to have you," I say.

Paloma nods, but doesn't reply. I'm so used to her driving our conversations with pointed questions and endless stories that I'm not quite sure what to do with this tired, introspective version of her.

"Want to watch a movie?" I ask.

"It depends," she says wryly.

"Trust me," I say.

There's no TV in the living room, so I bring my laptop out, closing my article after I make triple sure it's saved. I put on *The Fast and the Furious*, because I want to get a rise out of her—and because it's one of the best films of our time.

She surprises me by loving it.

"I love a bad boy with a heart of gold," she says of Vin Diesel's character. Of Michelle Rodriguez's Letty: "That's a smart girl. Don't let your man boss you around, and learn how to fix a car, because you never know."

My favorite by far, however, is her take on Paul Walker's undercover officer: "Never trust the police, that's what I always say. They should have been able to smell it on him."

When the end credits roll, it's nearly nine, and Paloma looks to be in much higher spirits.

"I could have done with a little less swearing and engine noise," she says, getting to her feet. "But the story had a good heart, Samantha, thank you for showing it to me."

"Anytime," I say, steadying her arm when she stumbles. "I can't tell you how many hangovers this movie and a box of mac 'n' cheese have gotten me through." I wink at her.

She swats me again, but then she pulls me in for a hug. "You're a good girl, Samantha," she says into my hair. "I'm proud of you."

Suddenly, the macaroni and the emotions of the day are forming a bowling ball in my stomach. "I would be better if I knew you sooner," I say.

Paloma pats my back, then pulls away. "God is always on time," she says. "You remember that."

She goes to bed, then, and I wash the dishes and fold her blanket. I feel less alone in the house than I used to. More like I belong.

My phone buzzes in my pocket, and my heart leaps into my throat like I've trained it to these past few days. What if it's Max, proving me wrong just in time?

But it isn't. It's Dina Rae again. Ignoring my last text about not wanting to talk. Ignoring even the photo of her and my dad at the prom.

Wedding's in two weeks! says the message, below another picture of her and Bob on what looks like a Florida beach. **Nothing splashy—at our age there's no time to waste! We'll have you out to Boca soon! XO, Mom.**

My anger is all used up today, so I skip right to sad. The feeling crawls up inside me with claws. I think of being held in Max's arms the night after I found out about my mom's lies. How good I felt. How safe.

But you weren't, I remind myself. It was all just a trick we were playing on each other.

With this thought in mind, I perch the laptop on the kitchen counter. I read through the story one more time. It doesn't feel like a first draft. It needs very little editing. A word swap here and there. A few sentences that can be condensed or split up. As much as I told myself I wasn't going to do it, I think I've been writing it in my head all week.

When it's done, it's after ten. I know it's better than anything I wrote about Juniper. Maybe better than anything I've written period.

I open a new email and address it to Esme. It's exactly what she wanted, and I dig deep for the part of me that lived to please her before wondering if that was just more of Dina Rae's conditioning. It doesn't matter. With the piece turned in I'll get paid at last. I can decide what to do when the dust settles.

Hey Esme, I type, feeling so far away from the person I was the last time I wrote to her. **Sorry this is under the wire. Hope it will be worth the wait. Let me know a good time to chat about what's next. Best, Sammy.**

I attach the piece feeling hazy, like this is all happening in a dream. But it isn't. I'm about to do something I can't take back. Even still, I know I can't make Max care enough to keep his promises. I have to take care of myself for once, even if it means breaking one of mine.

After I push Send, I feel like I might cry, but I don't. I tell myself it's progress before going to bed alone.

36.

With morning comes more clarity and acceptance than I've felt in a long time. I don't check for a text from Max. I don't even check to see if Esme has confirmed receipt of the piece.

Instead, I get dressed in my black sundress and cardigan and get ready to go out.

I know the place in my heart reserved for Max will ache for a while, but I understand now that him leaving then didn't start me down this path, it only kept me on the track Dina Rae so selfishly laid when I was born. It was easier to blame him than my mother— but I know a thing or two about misplaced blame now. And I have an apology to make.

Paloma still isn't up when I make my way out to the kitchen, but it's early. And maybe when you're almost eighty a hangover can last more than a day. I scribble a note telling her to call me if she needs anything and head out to the car, determined to make at least one thing right today—even if that's all I can do.

The morning is freezing, the wind cutting like a knife, making me wish I'd worn something warmer than a sweater. Fall always turns on a dime like this in the Northwest. One day it's the beautiful, temperate autumn of your dreams. The next it's stinging eyes and goosebumps and chattering teeth.

I press on. I didn't bring a coat, and what I have to do this morning is far too important to delay. Also the Mercedes has incredible temperature control and heated seats, so I make my way down the hill in luxurious comfort despite the iron-gray skies.

I have two stops to make this morning. I came here for more than one reason, after all.

"Oh, Sammy," Maeve says when I push open the door to Mystical Moments. "I'm so sorry. I'm so, so sorry."

She rushes me before I can even begin to comprehend what's happening, hugging me tightly, sniffling into my hair. My initial reaction is panic. Does she know something I don't? Did someone die? Are Willa and Brook okay?

Before I can help it my thoughts stray to Max. His long silence. His empty house. Did she see something in the news? Recognize his face from the time I brought him here?

"We knew it wasn't the right thing to do," Maeve is saying now, pulling away from me, teary-eyed. "But your mom was so adamant, and she said she had her reasons, and we didn't think it was our place to get involved but we should have, Sammy. For you."

My vision of Max's tragic death being announced on the news poofs out of existence as she speaks quickly, the tears falling now. Willa is fine, I tell my jack-rabbit heart. Brook is fine.

This isn't about them. It's about me. Me and Dina Rae and Paloma.

"It wasn't your fault," I tell Maeve, my eyes teary, too, as I pull away from her.

"We were worried that if we went against your mom's wishes we'd never get to see you again," Maeve says, sniffling. "She was so sure, but we should have found a way. You should have known you had a family."

"I had you guys," I remind her. "You did everything you could, but it wasn't your responsibility. It was hers."

"Well, our worst fears happened anyway, of course. We wanted to keep you with us, you know," Maeve tells me, bustling behind the counter for tissues and leading me back to the cozy library corner. "When your mom told me she was coming back for you after all that time, I said you'd be better off staying. The same school, the same house. We'd take care of you until she got on her feet, help her get settled in town."

I wonder dimly how many more awful surprises I can take.

"She didn't like that idea much," Maeve chuckles tearfully. "I always wondered if I did the wrong thing offering. She was furious, told me I had no business judging her parenting. Never spoke to me again, never brought you to visit. Two decades of friendship down the drain."

All because seeing someone else love me made it too hard to avoid looking at all the ways she was doing it wrong, I think, almost numb at this point.

"I'm trying not to hate her," I admit to Maeve, who's settled into a chair across from me, looking calmer. "But it's hard not to. My grandfather *died.* I never even got to know him. I've spent my whole life feeling like no one wanted me, like I had to trick people into loving me. Like everyone would always leave. And it's all because she thought of me like some toddler's toy. She didn't want me, but she couldn't let anyone else have me, either."

I think Maeve might jump in here. Tell me Dina Rae is my mom, and she's had her own struggles, and I should forgive her.

But she doesn't. She just lets the silence stretch. Lets me feel safe in the tempest of my anger until it calms.

"You deserve love, Sammy," she says after a long moment. "Dina Rae may have set you on this path, but now that you know the truth? You can choose to take another fork whenever you're ready."

There are so many things this could mean, but right now there's only one that comes to mind. "Remember when I was here with that guy in the truck?" I ask, before I can stop myself. "And I wasn't ready to know what was coming?"

"Something tells me you've changed your mind," Maeve says, her keen eyes on me.

"I guess I already knew what was coming," I say. "And what I chose to do. But there's one question I still want an answer to."

I think about what this might mean—learning the truth that had Maeve acting so solemn when I was in here last. But I've taken a new fork. And in order to leave the old one behind, I need to understand.

"What's that, sugar?"

"*Why?*" I ask, not for the first time this trip. "I want to know why it ended this way."

Maeve looks hesitant, but after a couple of seconds she stands. "Let's go."

The back room of Mystical Moments is extra quiet today. No tea kettle, no rain outside. I sit down in the dim light feeling like I'm standing at the edge of an abyss, not sure what I'll see in the depths.

"All right darlin'," Maeve says, sitting down across from me, starting to shuffle the cards. "If it's the truth you're after, this is the right deck. But it doesn't coddle, you understand?"

"I understand," I say, meaning it. "I just have to know."

Maeve nods, continuing to shuffle. "Why don't you tell me exactly what you want to know?"

I take a deep breath, letting the montage of images wash over me. Max bandaging my ankle. Dancing at the concert on the lawn. Kissing against the garden shed. The song he played me and the way we entangled our limbs afterward . . .

Waking up alone, then. The building of tension. The slow-motion heartbreak of it all.

"I just want to know if it was ever real," I say, hearing the tears in my voice. "And if it was . . . when it changed. I want to know why he promised not to leave when he didn't mean it."

"Okay, sweetheart," Maeve says, setting the cards before me. "Cut the deck in three."

I do as I'm told, letting Maeve scoop the cards back up into a single pile and begin laying them out on the table between us. The only one I recognize is right in the center. A hairy red devil with two people dangling like puppets from the strings he's holding.

"This is a complicated situation," Maeve says after a few minutes. Her tone is always different when she reads, like someone else is speaking through her.

"Yeah," I breathe. "That much I knew."

"First off, it was real. The feelings were reciprocated, and there was power in them."

Past tense, I note, my heart sinking.

"But meeting you activated something in him," Maeve says. "A wound from his past. You each had options, but your paths have already been chosen. His path has taken him back to an old place. Whatever emotional wound he's responding to is taking precedence over what you two were building."

An old wound, I think, remembering his skittishness around fame. How resistant he was to stepping back into the spotlight. Meeting me activated something in him, and he's regressed. Forgotten all about me. Just like I thought.

"In terms of *you,*" Maeve says, returning to the cards. "There's a regression, here, too. Progress interrupted. But not lost. In fact, this interruption has been a necessary step for you. This cycle is about much more than a romantic relationship. It's about coming to terms. Taking stock. Deciding who you want to be when the dust settles."

I know I should be focused on this new version of me she's describing. The post-dust-settling Sammy who will know who she wants to be. But instead I let myself ask the burning question. The one I might never have a chance to ask again.

"Will I ever see him again?" I choke out.

"That's entirely up to you," Maeve says, and I know the reading is done.

"Thank you," I say, getting to my feet, suddenly realizing I need to be alone. To process everything I've just heard. "Not just for this, but for . . . well, being my family."

"Always will be, sugar," she says. "You can count on that."

My second stop is only a few minutes away, and I spend the whole time thinking about what Maeve said. That Max *did* share my feelings, but something else was more important.

Of course, my first instinct is to feel guilt for writing the piece now that I know he didn't set out to betray me. But didn't we make the same choice? The difference is, I never would have betrayed him while there was still a chance. I take some comfort in that.

I think of him now. The wound of fame that kept him from the stage for seven years. The activation of meeting me. The plan to rebuild his confidence that worked too well—sending him off to a future that doesn't have room for me. And not for the first time.

I think of that younger version of me. The way I believed making myself indispensable to the people I loved would keep them with me. I tried to parent my mother even though it only drained me. I put my career on the line to get Juniper good press, pretended to be someone else just to please her. I hid myself from Max because I was afraid he couldn't handle my truth. Tried to heal his trauma around fame rather than just admitting I wanted him to stay . . .

And now my mother is engaged, supposedly happier than she's ever been. Juniper is on tour in Barcelona surrounded by models. Max moved on to something bigger. Something more important.

Willa is suffering because she was the only person safe enough to blame for all this. Suffering when she least deserves it . . .

I don't let myself think about the last part of the reading. The part where seeing him again isn't off the table. Because it's up to me, isn't it? And how could I choose that after everything he put me through?

The Subaru and Willa's truck are both in the driveway when I pull up to the yellow house, and I try to let go of the things I can't change. To turn toward the thing I might still be able to. My stomach is in knots.

What if Willa doesn't forgive me? What if I finally pushed too far?

But I'll never know unless I go inside. So I do.

"Anybody home?" I call, feeling weird about walking in without knocking. "It's me!"

No answer. The house is quiet, the bedroom door is closed, but the back door to the garden is slightly ajar, and I know that's where I'll find her.

Sure enough, Willa is kneeling in her overalls, pulling up potatoes from the chilly ground. She's got dirt on her hands and her knees, not seeming to mind the cold. I love her so much in this moment I just want to erase everything. Tell her how much I missed her.

"Hey," I say instead, trying not to startle her.

She looks up like I've just pulled her out of a dream. "Hey."

I move closer as she wipes her hands off, then stands up to face me.

"Hey."

We look at each other for a long time, and I can almost see all the years we've been friends right on her face. Little nine-year-old Willa who got me through the hardest year of my life. Eighteen-year-old Willa who held me together as everything fell apart. And this Willa. My best friend in the world.

"So, I've been a total monster," I say, just as she says, "I'm so sorry, Sammy."

We laugh, and she gestures for me to go first.

"I've been going through a lot lately," I say, feeling myself tear up already. "I've found out all this stuff about my family, and my mom, and then this whole Max thing happened, and I was so scared but you were the last person in the world I should have blamed. I love you, Willa. I'm sorry."

I step forward to hug her, but she holds out a hand.

"Wait," she says. "Me next. Because I haven't been a very good friend to you. I've been controlling and bossy and judgmental, and I should have just been supportive of you. I should have asked what you needed, and listened when you told me. I'm going through stuff, too, and I just let it get me all twisted around and I'm sorry, Sammy. I love you, too."

We do hug then. The kind of hug you only get after a fight. One that feels like the bridge of a perfect song, telling you the best part is yet to come.

"Oh my god, you're freezing!" Willa says, pulling away. In the midst of our reunion I've almost forgotten my total lack of appropriate outerwear. "Come here!" She leads me through the rows of plants to a little greenhouse. It's toasty inside, all her favorite year-round flowers blooming. In the back corner there's a table and two chairs, twinkle lights hanging in strands.

Every bit of me relaxes, like sinking into a warm bath. This is such a Willa place. Magic in all the ways she is. I feel so honored to be let back in that all I want to do is hear everything that's happened since we last spoke. Erase this rift between us so it doesn't even leave a scar.

"Okay, so what stuff are you going through?" I ask before we can even sit down, remembering guiltily that Brook said something similar the other night. "I'm so sick of my own problems I could puke."

"Oh, that," Willa says, her cheeks turning bright pink. "Um, I'm . . . pregnant? And I'm sorry I didn't tell you sooner but I—"

I interrupt her with a completely undignified shriek, my whole body suddenly feeling like a shaken soda can about to explode. "You're *pregnant*? Like actually *pregnant* with a human baby?!"

She nods, tears falling down her face. "It's still early and the doctor says we shouldn't tell people until the second trimester, but it felt so weird not to tell you. But also you were going through so much I didn't want you to worry about me on top of it all."

The joy of this moment feels almost foreign in the lonely, uncertain landscape of my own life. But in the best way. Like it's bringing the sunshine back. "Oh my god, I can't believe we're having a baby!" I say after a long pause, absolutely sure I'm going to cry, too.

Willa laughs through her own tears. "Yep," she says, gesturing for me to sit down. "So I've been a hormonal nightmare, and on top of that . . ." She hesitates, looking at me like she's afraid I'll be mad.

"This is an air-clearing moment," I say, waving my hands magnanimously from Willa's adorable garden chair. "Give me your worst."

"I just . . . this is so stupid, but I just wanted to get you settled and make sure you were okay before I was distracted by the new baby. Like I needed you to be okay so much that I tried to dictate the terms of your life instead of just supporting you, and that really wasn't right."

"It's not your job to take care of me," I say, wiping my eyes again. "You're my friend, not my mom."

"I know," Willa says. "But your mom is objectively bad at being a mom. And your dad is gone, and you always pick these asinine egomaniacs to date and someone has to take care of you."

I laugh, wondering how I ever could have felt alone when I always had Willa. "I think I'm supposed to learn how to take care of myself," I tell her.

"Are you?" she asks, wiping her eyes and X-raying me in that way of hers.

"I'm trying," I say. "You were right about Max, he's gone again. And you were right about Dina Rae, too. She lied about Paloma rejecting us. She lied about your parents offering to take me in. It's been . . . a lot."

I can see Willa exercising herculean effort not to show her vindication in this moment. "I can't even imagine how that must feel," she says finally. "I'm so sorry, Sammy."

"Thanks," I say. "I'm doing my best to get through it all. I wrote the article for *Scavenger,* and I'm staying with Paloma, helping her organize her house, trying to make up for lost time. But honestly, I'm just going through the motions. I have *no idea* what I'm gonna do with . . . any part of my life."

"I didn't want to be right about any of that stuff," Willa says in a small voice. "It's just hard to watch you let people treat you badly. You deserve so much better, Sammy."

I nod, knowing that even a week ago I would have dismissed this sentiment as a cliché. "I think I'm starting to understand that," I say.

"Good. Now tell me everything. Dina Rae, Max, all of it. I promise I will act surprised by how awful it all is and there will be zero judgment whatsoever."

I take a deep breath and dive in, hoping Willa doesn't notice that I go for Dina Rae first, protecting Max's and my story until the last possible moment. I get through Paloma's revelation, Dina Rae's total dismissal during our phone call. The engagement. The prom photo, and my conversation with Maeve.

I'm crying a little as I recount my recent revelations. That Dina Rae didn't know how to love me right, and out of her own fears of inadequacy made sure no one else would ever have a chance to do a better job.

"Sammy," Willa says after half an hour or more. "I know I've never been Dina Rae's biggest fan, but this is . . . next-level. I can't believe it. I'm so sorry."

I nod, squashing the urge to defend my mother. That instinct borne of my fear that she'd disappear if things got too difficult. If I wasn't always pleasant, and easy.

"And she's getting married," Willa says, shaking her head. "I never thought I'd see the day."

I'm about to tell her I *won't* see the day. That I wasn't even invited to the blessed event. But at that moment, Brook sticks her head into the greenhouse with a very odd expression on her face.

"Um, Sammy?" she says.

I wave. "Hi, don't worry, we've called a ceasefire!"

"And as happy as that makes me . . . there's someone at the door for you."

My mind goes blank. I can't think of a single person who would come here looking for me. I check my phone, no calls from Paloma—who doesn't even know where this house is.

"It's . . . a *Max Ryan*–shaped someone," Brook stage-whispers, and my heart stops beating.

Willa's eyes are open extremely wide when I look at her for confirmation that this is really happening. "It's been almost a week," I say, like I'm hearing myself from far away. "I gave up."

"Do you want to see him?" she asks. "Be honest."

I think of Maeve's reading. It's up to me. I just didn't think I'd have to decide so soon.

"Yes," I say after a long moment, not entirely sure if I mean it. I think about the article. All my realizations. The distance I was just starting to feel okay about.

"Then go," Willa says. "We'll be waiting for you after, no matter what happens."

And they really will, I think. The family I chose. With them waiting for me, I can do this. I can do anything.

37.

Every one of the careful boundaries I built around my feelings for Max comes tumbling down the moment I lay eyes on him.

I see him before he sees me, giving me time to school my features. To remind myself of everything that's changed since I fell asleep in his arms with no idea what the morning would bring.

He's standing between my car and his motorcycle like he hasn't quite decided whether to run. I look my fill before I move closer. The long, angular lines of his body. The hair falling into his eyes.

When there's no more avoiding it, I pick my way across the front lawn toward the street, shivering again in the cardigan, too aware that this is the same outfit I was wearing when he pushed me up against a garden shed.

He sees me at last when I'm about thirty feet away. His face transforms. That vulnerability that's always gotten past every single one of my defenses. I hoped by the time I reached him I would know what to say.

"Hi," he says softly when I'm within range.

"Hi."

I fold my arms. Inadequate armor against the cold or the feelings welling up inside me.

"You have every reason to be furious with me." He pushes his hair off his face in that heartbreakingly familiar way.

"I'm not," I say automatically, before I realize there's no reason to hold back. Not anymore. "I *was* angry. And confused, and very sad. But I understand now."

"I'm sure it's been awful," Max says, and for the first time I notice he's not looking so good. His eyes are bloodshot, dark circles under them like he hasn't slept in days. His shoulders—usually so broad and straight—are curled slightly forward. Like he's trying to protect himself, too.

"It *was* awful," I say, putting him firmly in the past tense. "Of course it was. You promised me you'd never do what you did to me back then. I believed you. That's on me. And it seems you got what you needed from me, so I'm not sure what's left to say."

He winces like this statement physically hurts him. There's a very small part of me that's moved by it. How vulnerable he seems. I want to take care of him, build him back up, be pleasant and easy and make him need me.

But I can't do that anymore. Not now that I finally know better.

"It isn't like that, Sammy. I promise you it isn't. And if you'll just give me a chance to explain . . ."

"Look, Max," I say, trying not to shiver in my too-thin dress. "It's not exactly new territory. You got your mojo back. You went out to spread your rock star wings. Or you went all fear-of-intimacy and disappeared for a week. Either way it hurt. Part of that is because of our history, part of it is because of issues I already had, but you can't think there's anything to save here."

He steps closer to me like it's involuntary. Like he's drawn forward by the gravity of us.

"It isn't like that," he repeats. "Please, believe me."

What no one really tells you about the stages of grief is that they're not linear. For instance, this morning—even four minutes ago—I believed I had reached acceptance. But now I'm right back to anger.

"Fine, Max," I snap, wrapping my sweater more tightly around myself. "You clearly have some justification you want to make, so go ahead. Just don't expect it to change things, because I've already made up my mind."

Again, he appears stung, but not surprised. He steps as close as he dares, then clears his throat, like he's getting ready to read a prepared statement.

"When I walked onstage at the Staples Center that last night, I had drunk a fifth of whiskey by myself. Probably also taken a few painkillers. And I remember thinking it wasn't enough."

My irritation flares. Why would I want to hear about Max's old party lifestyle? What does this have to do with anything? But I sense that the quickest way through this is just to let him talk, so I do, glaring at the ground between us.

"That was a normal day, for me," he continues. "I used to start drinking before I even got out of bed. It made me feel normal. Like I could be the version of myself everyone paid good money to see. But that night, onstage, something went wrong. I thought I was having a heart attack. I walked off because I was positive I was going to die, and I didn't want to do it in front of twenty thousand people."

He scrubs his face with his palms, taking a deep breath before continuing.

"Someone took me to the ER discreetly to avoid the publicity. I don't even remember who. When I was coherent again the doctor told me it was a panic attack, but that it was lucky I had come in when I did. My liver was at ten percent function. He told me if I didn't quit drinking, quit everything, I would die. Soon."

Through the clouds of this seemingly random story, a tiny ray of illumination begins to shine. I move my eyes from the ground to Max's face.

"I'm not gonna pretend it was an easy decision," he says, looking right at me. "During those first days in the hospital I fantasized about breaking out. About finding the first liquor store I could.

About choosing to die rather than face the damage I'd done to myself."

"But you didn't," I say, caught up in the story, forgetting my anger for a moment.

Max shakes his head. "They took me through medical detox. Five days of absolute hell. After that I went to a rehab facility where I stayed for six months. My publicists kept it out of the media somehow, but in my therapy sessions, I realized the source of my addiction was always fear. That I wasn't good enough. That I couldn't be the person my band needed, that my fans wanted. That I was always disappointing someone."

I uncross my arms. I'm barely breathing. This is it. The real story of Max Ryan's departure from the music scene—endlessly speculated on by fans and journalists and industry insiders alike. And he's telling it to me. Finally.

"When I got out, the band wanted me back on the road right away. We were losing momentum. We needed to record another album. But I was frozen. I didn't know how to be *Max Ryan* without opening myself back up to all that fear."

He pauses, taking a long, shaky breath.

"I might have gone anyway if it hadn't been for James."

"Your manager?" I ask, unable to help myself.

Max nods, pushing his hair back. "He'd been sober ten years by then, and he was the lone voice of reason. He told me I needed to choose what was right for me. Even if it meant walking away from everything.

"So I walked. Dumped most of my money into fines for breach of contract. The guys were livid. None of them ever talked to me again. I bought a little cabin about fifty miles east of here and stayed there for two years. Like a halfway house. I didn't see anyone but James, who became my sponsor. He stayed with me for a while before moving back to Seattle, and by then I was good at being alone. I liked it. It was safe."

"Max," I say, moving toward him, starting to understand at last.

He puts up a hand and I stop. Every line of his body is tense with pain, shame. All the wounds our meeting awakened in him. Just like Maeve said.

"By the time I moved back into town, started making music again, I had just accepted that I was better alone. That no one who didn't know about my past would get me, and that no one who did would ever see me separately from that curated image. I told myself I was happier this way. And then I met you, and the way I felt about you was *it*. The thing I had convinced myself could never exist. And I liked you, and I *wanted* you, and you got me, and I felt myself waking up . . ."

"But then I told you you'd have to take whiskey shots to get your confidence back," I say, going numb with horror.

"No," he says emphatically. "No. That wasn't your fault. It was my choice. I could have told you everything right from the start. I could have said it then. I'm responsible for my own actions, not you."

"Why didn't you tell me?" I ask, all the venom gone from my voice.

"I just didn't want to be this guy with all this baggage," he says helplessly. "I didn't want to scare you off. I figured I'd tell you eventually if things got more serious, but then you put so much thought into your plan that night and I just . . ." He exhales noisily. "I wanted to be the kind of guy who could let loose. I thought after seven years of sobriety I'd earned it. That there was no way I could lose everything I'd built in one night . . ."

I try to picture how it must have felt to let those walls fall down after that many years of holding steady. I can't even get close. I dreamed up a hundred nightmare scenarios for why Max had disappeared, and none of them held a candle to this.

"You fell asleep that night and I was just . . . falling apart. I was so panicked and ashamed. All that fear I'd been keeping at bay for seven years was back like it had never left. I kept telling myself I was a failure. That I didn't deserve you. That I didn't deserve anything good. More than that, I wanted another drink. I got on my bike at five in the morning and rode to the cabin. I've been there this whole time, talking to James. My therapist. Trying to get my head right."

Our bodies are as close as they've been yet. Close enough that I could reach out and touch him.

"I wanted to call you so many times, Sammy," Max says, his eyes haunted. "It killed me to leave you in the dark, but I was such a mess. It wasn't your job to help me through that, and I had to figure out how to even look at myself in the mirror before I could *begin* to explain . . ."

I nod. Even though understanding is the last thing I expected to do in this conversation, I find I can't help it. That I can see it so clearly. The fear he felt of letting people down from the very beginning. The monster it grew into. It was bigger than me. Bigger than us . . .

"But you came back," I manage.

"I came back," Max says. He looks up and meets my eyes. "Because the one thing I knew the whole time was that I wanted to be with you. So I had to hope you could forgive me. That you might still want me even if I'm not the guy you met eleven years ago, and I never can be again."

His eyes—even bloodshot and ringed with exhaustion—are smoldering. Telling me this is the moment. To let him kiss me until the past week is washed away and there's nothing but a shining, blank page ready to be filled with our story.

I step forward, letting him encircle me in his arms—a blessed reprieve from the chilly wind I've almost forgotten again. We're forehead to forehead, and he's smiling, transforming his gaunt, haggard face, and our lips are centimeters apart . . .

"Wait," I whisper, tears already filling my eyes. I don't move out of his embrace. I don't even look at him. Instead I speak to the buttons on his flannel. "I have to tell you something, too."

He's quiet. Waiting. But the smile is gone.

"I thought you'd abandoned me again. I can't explain how that felt. I was angry. I was heartbroken. And I . . . I wrote about you." I whisper this last part. "About the album, I mean. I sent the story to my editor last night."

His body goes rigid. Slowly, carefully, he untangles himself from me and steps back.

Max doesn't say anything, and I ramble into the silence, knowing that after everything I've discovered these past weeks, I can't build something this important on a foundation of lies.

"It's the reason I came here," I say, looking at him now even though it's painful. He deserves that much. Even a small one. "I saw some blog post about how you were recording in your hometown. I thought I could come and use the fact that you broke my teenage heart to convince you to let me review it early."

His face is carved from stone. For once, it gives absolutely nothing away.

"But then you didn't remember me, and I was humiliated. I froze. I was going to just give up, focus on healing, get to know Paloma. But you asked me on a date as a stranger, and I told myself I could work up to telling you. That I could still save my job. But all I did instead was fall in love with you."

It's one of my most frustrating qualities, that I can't get through moments like these without crying. My voice breaks and the tears spill over, but I can't stop. I know it's my last chance.

"When I told you I was a journalist that night I planned to tell you this, too, but I could see it on your face that we wouldn't survive it. So I told myself I'd pull out of the article. Quit writing altogether if it meant I didn't have to lose you."

"But you didn't." Max's tone is colder than the wind.

"Because you left!" I say. "You disappeared, just like last time, even though you promised me you wouldn't. I thought you'd lied to me. Left me again after I broke your dry spell and helped you get your confidence back. I told myself it was only fair I got something out of it, too."

It sounds so petty, even to me. Some cruel and childish tit for tat.

"You have to understand what it did to me to think you'd abandoned me," I say again, pleading now. "After everything I thought we were starting to mean to each other. I wasn't myself. I never would have gone through with it if I was."

"I have to *understand*?" Max says, like he's fact-checking a quote. "I have to understand that the first time I disappointed you, you decided it was okay to use me. To take something I showed you in deep confidence and . . ." His voice breaks, and I feel it in the center of my chest.

"I'll withdraw the article," I promise. "Right now. I don't care what they do to me. Max, please. I didn't know. I couldn't have known."

He takes a moment to collect himself, and I scramble to find *anything* to say that won't result in him walking away.

But there's nothing. Nothing to save me. Nothing to stop him.

"There are people who would never do something like that," Max says. His eyes are sparkling with unshed tears, his shoulders hunched forward again. "No matter how hurt they were. There are people who would never even think of it."

"You're right," I say. There are tears streaming down my face now. I don't bother to wipe them away.

He looks at me for a long minute. So long I can almost see every moment that's ever passed between us reflected in his glassy gaze. Every one of them a nail in our coffin.

"I'm so sorry, Max," I say, feeling how woefully inadequate those words are. Not knowing any better ones.

"I'm sorry, too," he says at last. "Goodbye, Sammy."

When he turns away, I want to cling to his sleeve. To follow him sobbing across the street to his bike. To beg.

But I don't. Because on some level I knew. That this was the way it was always going to end. That Willa was right, and Brook was right, and Maeve was right. That my lies have finally sunk this thing for good.

He rides off down the street without looking back. I stand in Willa and Brook's freezing yard and cry until I'm afraid I'll turn myself inside out. Loud, ugly, snotty crying that feels like it's about so much more than just this moment.

Crying that might be about my whole life and every terrible thing I've ever done to try to protect myself from feeling like I do right now.

I cry for a long time. Maybe ten minutes, maybe three hours. I totally lose track.

When I can trust my voice, I call a totally flabbergasted Esme at the office to tell her I'm withdrawing the article. When she protests, I tell her calmly that it was all a lie. That I never heard the album. That we could be sued for even publishing it.

She's deadly silent for a long moment, and when she speaks again there's none of that mentor warmth in her tone. "You know what this means, don't you?" she asks.

"I do," I reply.

"This will get around town," she says, as if I don't understand. "Even if I wanted to stop it, I couldn't. No one will hire you, Sammy. This will be it for you."

I think about how I felt when I finished this review. The wish I've always harbored that my criticism could be the beginning of a conversation instead of the end. I know in this moment that I won't regret my choice. That even if Max never speaks to me again, it will have been the right one for me.

"I know," I tell Esme. "Thank you for everything you've done, but my heart isn't in it anymore."

Another long silence. "Okay then," Esme says, like the sharp snap of a book closing. Then she hangs up without a goodbye, and ten years of my life is gone.

Might as well burn it all down at once, I tell myself. I'm sure it will hit me soon, the enormity of what I've done. But for now I let myself feel the first thing that surfaces: relief. It's enough to get me up off the ground and back through the door, into the warm living room where my friends are waiting for me.

38.

When I'm securely ensconced in my favorite corner of Willa's couch with a blanket and a cup of tea, I know I can ignore their expectant faces no longer.

"It's over," I say, and the tears are back again. "Officially and totally over."

"What happened?" Willa asks, her eyes wide with sympathy. Totally free of judgment.

"I'm warning you, it's a long story," I say with a sniff and a self-deprecating chuckle.

"We know what we're signing up for," Brook says with an affectionate ruffling of my hair. "Start at the beginning."

So I do. I tell them all the things I've been avoiding talking about for two weeks. I tell them about my growing feelings for Max, and the night I decided never to tell him about the article. The promise he made me. I tell them about karaoke and waking up alone. The endless six days of no contact.

I tell them about my decision to write the article. Max's appearance here today. His confession, and finally mine.

"So he's gone," I say when I've been talking for half an hour straight. "And he'll never speak to me again, which honestly makes sense. And I withdrew the article, told Esme I made it all up, which means I'm not only unemployed, I'm now actually unhireable in my field."

I force a chuckle, wiping my eyes, draining my tea and setting down the mug.

"It's just ironic that all this time I thought it was a choice between the boy and the job and now I don't have either."

There's a long pause, during which I remember Maeve's first prediction. That my problems would be solved together or not at all. I can see out of the corner of my puffy eyes that Willa and Brook are having one of their silent wifely eye conversations. Brook gets up after a minute of this and excuses herself to make lunch. Willa turns to me.

"Look, I won't sugarcoat it," she says. "I do understand why Max is hurt. But . . . I also understand why you did it."

"You don't have to say that," I mumble.

"No, I do," she insists, moving closer to me on the couch. "When you're scared of everyone abandoning you, that also means you're expecting it. You see everything through that lens. When Max disappeared, you told yourself you had to act like he was gone forever. So you did."

"Funny," I say, even though it isn't. "I thought I was making progress by letting him go."

Willa gives me a sympathetic hand squeeze. "It might take a little longer to untangle it all."

"Noted," I say, sniffling again.

Brook comes back with lunch, and I force them to change the subject. Talk about the baby. Get a hit of vicarious joy along with my tomato soup and grilled cheese. They rise to the occasion spectacularly, talking about plans for a nursery, pulling up a list of gender-neutral names, endlessly speculating about what it might be like to really be parents . . .

After we've exhausted the subject, I excuse myself to check on Paloma—who hasn't called. But it goes to voicemail.

"Just checking in," I say. "I'm hanging out with some friends, but I don't want to leave you stranded. Call if you need anything."

I hesitate. I'm still not used to this whole having-a-grandmother business, but if today has taught me anything it's that I have to hold on tight to the things that don't change.

"Also," I say into her answering machine. "I just want you to know how happy I am that we finally get to know each other. I love you."

I'm hoping we can get right back to baby stuff when I'm finished, but it's clear Brook and Willa have been talking in my absence, because when I sit down it feels like they're about to start an intervention.

"So, we've been thinking," Willa says when I sit down.

"Why does that terrify me?" I ask.

"Well, we know things are a little up in the air for you right now," Willa continues.

"Understatement of the century," I mutter as she presses on undaunted.

"So we were wondering if maybe you'd want to stay with us on a little more long-term basis." She's speaking quickly now, like she wants to get it all out before I can say no. "You could spend more time with Paloma, do some freelance stuff while you figure out what your next move is. My parents would be thrilled to have you around, and Brook would have someone else to help field all my cravings and hormonal outbursts."

"Please," Brook interjects. "I can only make so many midnight pigs in blankets before all my culinary training straight up evaporates."

I laugh at this, and of course I'm crying again. It's such a generous offer. And it would feel so good to have an anchor. To be part of something that felt good and real . . .

But it's not long before Max's silhouette creeps into my rose-tinted fantasy. I don't know if I can handle running into him at the grocery store, and the coffee shop. Seeing his motorcycle at a stop sign and knowing he's right there but still out of reach.

"You guys are the best friends—the best *family*," I correct myself, "anyone could ever have. And there's nothing I want more than to play Three Queers and a Baby with you. It's just . . . things have changed a lot in the past few hours. I might need some time to think about it."

"Of course," Willa says, smiling. "We're not going anywhere."

I stay with them for hours. Until I almost forget there's a world outside these walls. We talk about big things and small things and generally revel in the return of our camaraderie.

Despite the consequences, I can't believe how good it feels to have everything out in the open. Not to have to keep track of lies or temper my words. The only time I'm not free with the truth is when Brook asks me what I might want to do next, career-wise, and it's not because the truth is damning, but more because it's embarrassing.

I say I don't know, but the truth is there's been a kernel of an idea slowly and shyly growing in the back of my mind since I first stepped into Max's house. Since I imagined the future in Maeve's ritual . . .

The truth is I've been thinking about my very first dream. Working for a music label. Helping to discover and nurture young artists. The conversation my writing could never start.

I don't say it out loud because it's ridiculous. What am I going to do, be a thirty-year-old label intern? It's laughable, and impractical, and it doesn't pay—but I go back to it again and again anyway.

When it's nearly dinnertime, I get up at last. Paloma is obviously glad to have the house to herself, but I want to make sure her hangover is fully gone. Maybe convince her to watch *Point Break* since she liked *The Fast and the Furious* so much.

Willa, Brook, and I have a massive group hug before I leave, with promises to think about their offer, and to come back tomorrow. When I climb back into the Mercedes, the quiet is almost too much, the panic starts to creep back in. The cracks in my heart exposing themselves. It will take time, of course, I tell myself, but I won't be alone.

I know something is wrong as soon as I pull into Paloma's driveway. I can't explain how. Everything looks normal. But my heart is pounding when I open the door.

The quiet is too quiet. A hush has settled over the rooms that were filled with the sounds of engine revving and laughter and timeless Vin Diesel platitudes just last night.

At first, I think the note I left Paloma this morning is still sitting on the counter. But then I realize it's an envelope. An envelope with my name scrawled across the front.

I don't pick it up. I can't. I feel my fingers going numb. My lips after them.

"Paloma?" I call out, but I know she won't answer. I just know.

The door to her room is open just a crack. The only light comes from the sunset through the floor-to-ceiling windows overlooking the bay. In that rosy light, her cheeks look pink where she lays too still on her pillow.

In movies, people always think dead people are just sleeping. They shake them. Speak to them like they'll answer. But in this moment I know death can't be mistaken for life. I know before I even get close enough to confirm that her chest has ceased to rise and fall. I know.

I sleepwalk over to Paloma, reaching down to check her pulse. Confirming.

She's gone. She looks exactly like she did in life, but there's nothing of her spirit. Nothing of what made her the unique, incredible person I barely got to know.

This is just a body. A thing. The woman I knew, the woman I *loved,* is gone.

I've been crying all day. My eyes are swollen and my throat is raw but right now the tears don't come. Right now, I need to be her next of kin. Her *last* of kin. I need to do the job she's been training me to do all this time.

Calmly, I take out my phone. I call 911. But there's no urgency this time. Not like when I first came here and found her, when I was tripping over my words and wishing I knew more. I can answer all the questions now, and I do.

Her name is Paloma Espinoza.

She's seventy-eight years old.

She's not breathing, nor does she have a pulse.

She's my grandmother.

She *was* my grandmother.

When I hang up with dispatch, my hands are still numb, but I'm coherent enough to make another call. In the past, I might have thought I could handle this all myself. But I know better now.

Samantha, I can almost hear her say, *this world is hard enough without pretending you're alone in it.*

When Willa answers, I tell her what happened. Ask her to come. To help.

"We're already on our way," she says.

The next few hours are a blur. Paramedics. Police. A long wait for the coroner who has to come from the next town over.

Through it all, Willa's hand is in mine. Brook makes tea and talks to all the official people, only asking me questions when she needs to. I feel hollow. I can't warm up no matter how hard I try.

"Sammy?" Brook asks when the police have gone to wait outside. "They wanted me to show you this." She hands me a thick stack of paperwork.

It's Ridley Falls Hospital paperwork I've never seen before. Diagnoses. Medication lists. Instructions for continuing care. The top few sheets are dated barely a week ago. The hospitalization for dehydration. She must have made the doctor promise not to tell me the rest.

It takes me three flip-throughs to realize I'm not capable of taking in more than the date. That I still don't know what happened to her. What it all means.

"Can you . . . ?" I ask, passing the packet to Willa.

"Of course."

A few minutes later she sets it on the counter. Squeezes my hand again. "Do you want to know?"

I nod.

"She had congestive heart failure. Diagnosed a few years ago. She was on medication but the prognosis wasn't good."

Congestive heart failure.

I think of yesterday. Her low energy. Her pale complexion. I thought she had a *hangover,* and she was dying. She was dying the whole time.

"Oh," I finally manage.

I think this might be it. That I'll cry. That it'll all feel real.

A knock on the door sends those feelings back into their shell, and the carousel starts again. The coroner rules her death "natural" in about thirty seconds. The assembled medical and emergency and death professionals make arrangements to have her transported to the local funeral home.

"Do you know what her wishes were?" asks one of the men with pity in their eyes.

One more night with her husband, I want to say. *Mezcal and salsa and dancing into the wee hours. A granddaughter who could make a passable tortilla.*

"I . . . I don't . . ." I begin, but suddenly I realize I do. "She'll want to be buried," I say with confidence. "Beside my dad and grandfather at the Ridley Falls Cemetery."

The man nods. "You can make the arrangements at the funeral home tomorrow," he says, tearing a piece of paper off his clipboard and handing it to me. I don't even read it. "They open at nine. I'm so sorry for your loss."

My loss, I think. I can't even thank him. What does he know about it? What does anyone know? This isn't the way people are supposed to lose their grandparents. After knowing them a week. We should have had my whole life. I should be surrounded by family, sharing stories, grieving together.

But everyone else is gone. And I'm not losing just a grandmother I barely knew. I'm losing a whole life I could have had, again. A past, and a future.

I start crying at last as they take her body out of the house. The home she shared with her family for almost thirty years. The place she was a mother. A grandmother. A place she'll never come back to, because she's gone. She's really, really gone.

Willa bundles me onto the couch, wraps me in the crocheted blanket Paloma had over her legs just last night. When she sat in that chair. When she was alive.

When I'm able to speak, I say, "You guys can go home now, if you want. Thank you so much for being here . . . I just . . . I couldn't face all that alone."

"Don't be stupid," Brook says, punching me on the shoulder. "We're staying. I already ordered a pizza. We're not leaving you alone."

I nod, my heart overflowing and empty at the same time.

"Have some water, okay?" Willa says. "And don't feel like you have to entertain us. We're here for you. Whatever you need."

"Thanks," I croak, walking into the kitchen.

After I've replenished some of the water I've lost, my eyes fall again on the envelope. My name scrawled across the front. In movies, people are always carrying missives from the dead around for weeks, letting them get orange-juice-stained and edge-worn, unable to read the last words their loved ones will ever say to them.

But I didn't get enough of Paloma while she was alive. Not

nearly enough. I take the envelope immediately, relieved that it's heavy. "She left me this," I say. "Like she knew . . ."

"They say some people do," Willa offers gently. "Do you want us to sit with you while you read it?"

I shake my head. "I think I need to be alone, if that's okay."

"Of course," she says. "Take your time."

Letter in hand, I walk back through the hallway. I feel like a part of the house, not a person moving through it. This place is all I have left of her. Of any of them. I want to distill it down into a little bottle and wear it like perfume.

I think about the things she was teaching me. The cooking. The Spanish words here and there. What does it all mean now that I'm alone with it? Is any of it real without her?

In the hallway, I hesitate. I can't go into her room. Not so soon. But mine feels too impersonal.

The door to Johnny's opens easily. I feel the rightness of it the moment I enter. I've never been a big believer in any afterlife, but it comforts me to think of them together.

On my dad's mirror is a wallet-sized photo of the family I hadn't noticed before. One of those Sears Portrait Studio–type things against the cheesy dark blue backdrop that looks like a bruise. Johnny can't be older than eight or nine. His hair hangs down to the collar of his little gray suit.

Paloma's in red, of course. A blazer and skirt with heels and pearls, her early '80s hair defying gravity. Beside her is Roberto. Square-jawed and handsome. Smiling contentedly. There's a twinkle in his eye I didn't notice in any of the other photos. Like he has a little mischief in him, too.

He would have had to, I think. To keep up with her.

I set the picture on the bed beside me and open the envelope. There's some official-looking documents inside, but what I'm looking for is beneath them. A handwritten letter in her half-cursive scrawl.

Samantha, it begins, and I'm already crying. Reading the rest through tear-blurred eyes as she must have known I would. *By now you know, and I won't apologize for not telling you sooner. If you'd thought of me as dying, it would have gotten in the way.*

> *It must feel overwhelming, being the last of our family. I wish I could have had more time to tell you what it means to me—being an Espinoza. An immigrant. A Mexican woman. But maybe that's just my ego talking. This way you can find out for yourself. Make the name, your connection to our culture, whatever you want it to be.*
>
> *At my age, you make a choice about regrets, Samantha. To cast them off or let them swallow you. Mostly I'd chosen the first, but knowing you, even for a short while, it's hard not to feel angry there wasn't more time. We never have long enough with the people we love. Remember that, too. A week, eighteen years, fifty-five . . . When you truly love someone, an ending is a tragedy whenever it comes.*
>
> *I've left you the house. The bank account. The car. All of it. It would have been yours whether we'd met or not. But I believe God brought you to me for this last time, Samantha. To help me remember what it means to love. To live.*
>
> *I only want one thing in return, and I won't take no for an answer. Promise me you'll be brave. That you'll tell the truth to the people you love, even if it scares you. That you'll live every moment with them as fully as you can—whether it's fighting and screaming or laughing or making love. Don't waste your moments on lies or half-truths. I've seen you holding yourself back, afraid to be left behind. Life's too short for all of that.*
>
> *Jump in, with my blessing and my love, and know that I'll be with you, always.*
>
> *All my love, from the glorious world beyond.*

I read it three times, absolutely stunned. The house, the bank account . . . I rifle through the official papers below, which I assume probably prove this, but I can't make any sense of them right now. I can't imagine deserving this. Can't even fathom what it might mean.

The rest I read more carefully, more tenderly. She could hardly have given me a more difficult assignment. Create my own connection to my name. To our culture. Tell the truth to the people I love.

I think of my mom, first. The perpetual blank slate, never sticking around long enough to reckon with her choices.

I think of Max, sitting somewhere right now believing the worst. About me, about hope and love and opening up. What truth can I tell him about me that he doesn't already know?

But then I think of Larry and Maeve. What they risked in the hope of helping me back then. How they've never let go of me since, no matter the distance between us.

And Willa and Brook. The way we embody our fights and our makeups. Every meal, every movie night, every backyard ritual. The offer they made to me just this afternoon. If there's any evidence in my life that honesty and vulnerability can work, it's in this house with me right now.

To that end, as much as my instincts tell me to stay in this room alone, I stand up and head for the door. Maybe I don't have a bunch of Espinozas to celebrate with, to mourn with, but I have a family of my own. I always have, ever since Dina Rae dropped me on the Crosses' doorstep twenty years ago.

Willa and Brook are sitting on Paloma's couch. Brook is rubbing Willa's feet while her hands cradle her not-yet-visible belly. They smile at each other. For the first time, I can see what this house was to Paloma. To my father. Not an empty monument to family gone too soon, but a living one to the people who are still here.

"You okay?" Willa asks, sitting up, letting her lime-green socks hit the floor.

I shake my head, but I smile, too. "Not at all," I say with a laugh. "But it's easier with you guys here."

They scoot over to make room for me on the couch. The pizza arrives, and I surprise myself by eating the slice Brook plates up for me. They ask me questions about Paloma. I tell all my favorite stories, laughing and crying, wishing there had been time to learn more.

"Do you want to get some rest?" Willa asks when the pizza is gone and the clock is inching toward midnight.

I shake my head. "Too much going on in here," I say, pointing to my head. "But you guys definitely should. Take my room, I'll sleep in my dad's."

They don't argue, sensing, maybe, that I'm ready to be alone again. Once I have them all tucked in, I make my way back out to the kitchen with Paloma's letter in hand. I'm planning to look at the documents. To try to understand the enormity of the gift she's given me.

But before I can get into it, I see the comal on the stove, and I smile.

It's two o'clock in the morning before I'm satisfied. The counters are covered in masa harina and little bits of dough. There are misshapen, imperfect circles all over the kitchen. But in my hands, I'm holding the holy grail. A perfectly round tortilla that puffed up as I cooked it and settled right down afterward.

And sure, maybe it took me more than five tries. But I'm proud of it. And I know Paloma is, too.

39.

The next morning, I'm up early. The sadness is enor-mous, but there's peace, too. Peace that I know what Paloma wanted—for herself, and for me.

When Willa and Brook wake up, I make us chilaquiles from all of last night's failed tortillas, remembering the way Paloma stood at the stove when she was teaching me. The way she cut the tortillas. The consistency of the eggs when she scooped and flipped them. I use the last of the pico de gallo in the fridge, and another wave of sadness hits me.

"Damn, Sammy!" Brook says, inhaling hers. "This is amazing! I didn't know you could cook!"

I'm about to make a self-deprecating remark, but instead I stand up a little straighter. "Thanks," I say. "Paloma taught me."

When we're done, I send them home. Last night I needed support. Comfort. Family. Today, I need to prove to myself that I'm capable of handling what's next.

"We're on call," Willa says as she hugs me goodbye. "Whatever you need, okay?"

"I know," I say. "And you, too. Take care of that baby, I'm pretty fond of them already."

"Hear that?" Willa looks down at her stomach. Brook joins her. "Your godmother's already fond of you."

My overworked tear glands are up and running again immediately. "Godmother?" I ask in a whisper.

"There's no one else we'd trust them with," Willa says, and then we're all crying, and hugging, and I think this is what Paloma meant. Living in each moment fully. Loving the people you love with your whole heart.

My best friends rise to that challenge every day, I think as Brook helps Willa down the stairs so tenderly, and Willa kisses Brook's cheek before she gets into the driver's seat. Even though I have the best chosen family a girl could ever have . . . my heart aches in a familiar way to watch them.

The most perfect creature God ever made. And he was mine, Paloma had said of my grandfather, and I think of Max. Handing me his flannel as I shivered. Max, waking me in the middle of the night. Brief glimpses of something bigger than both of us.

But we can never go back there. Not after everything I've done.

I'll just have to hope fate has a great love in store for me—though how I'll be able to look at them all mixed up in memories of him, I have no idea.

I've never been inside a funeral home before, but I'm surprised to find it much less creepy than I imagined. It's a homey place, with worn, cozy furniture.

The elderly woman who answers the door introduces herself as Eden Rose, the funeral director. Her husband offers me tea, which I gratefully accept.

"So," she says when he's gone. "You're Paloma Espinoza's girl."

I nod, proud of the epithet, which feels so hard-won.

"I remember when she and your grandfather came in about your dad," she says kindly. "You look like him, you know."

"Thank you," I say, wondering when the tears will stop surprising me. "No one has ever told me that before."

"Well, it's the truth." She hands me a box of tissues, but I don't need them. The tears dry up as soon as they arrive. There's just a warm feeling in their place.

"So, I know she would want to be buried beside my dad and

grandpa," I say. "The issue is . . . I'm not sure what that costs. She left me an inheritance, but I haven't really figured it all out, and I don't have a ton of money, but I—"

"Sweetheart," Eden interrupts. "The arrangements have all been made. There's nothing for you to take care of but hosting the wake."

I want to be surprised, but of course I'm not. She wouldn't have left this to chance. Not with how fiercely she loved them both.

"Of course," I say. "There's no family left besides me. We can do it soon. Tomorrow, even."

"Tomorrow it is," Eden says. Her husband brings tea.

We chat for a while as if we're not surrounded by evidence of our inevitable demise. She tells me stories, as all small-town proprietors seem to, about celebrity sightings in town, her children and the places they've moved on to. She gives me the name of Paloma's estate lawyer, who she says can help me make sense of the house, the car title, the bank accounts.

I want to ask Eden about my dad's funeral. What it was like. But then I think of Paloma's letter and realize the (admittedly kind) stranger at the funeral home isn't who I want to be asking.

Armed with a business card for the estate attorney and the details of tomorrow's service, I get back in the Mercedes and take a few deep breaths.

Be brave, I can hear Paloma telling me. *Tell the truth to the people you love.*

I feel like I can't claim this inheritance before I've done what she asked—or made an honest start at least.

My mom's phone rings three times before she picks up, sounding breathless. "Sammy?" she says. "You have some timing! I'm trying on my wedding dress, can you believe it?"

I feel myself wanting to get sucked back into the old script. The one where I tell her I'm happy for her. Where I forgive her before she's asked for it just to make things easy. But I'm supposed to be brave, for Paloma. So I don't.

"Mom," I say. "I'm really angry at you."

There's a long pause. A rustling. A whisper away from the mouthpiece. Then she's back.

"I know you are, Sammy," she says.

"Do you really, though?" I ask her. My hands are shaking. "Because I wonder if you've ever thought about me, Mom. If you ever did back then, if you ever do now. If you spent a second wondering what kind of life I wanted, or what would be best for me."

The words are pouring out of me—into the right ear for once—and I can feel myself growing lighter with every truth that clears my lips.

"I wonder if you ever thought about coming to my school play instead of going go-karting with some guy named Randy, or reading any of the articles I sent you, or making an appearance at my high school graduation even if it was during a girls' trip to Reno."

"You always said you didn't care if I was there or not," Dina Rae says in a small voice.

"Of course I said that!" I say. "I was a child, and I felt guilty for taking away your adolescence, and I felt responsible for all your feelings. I said whatever you wanted me to say, I always have."

"I never asked you to do that." I can hear her choking up.

"You *did*," I argue. "Maybe not in words. But think about it. You were always so quick to leave me behind when things were difficult. When I didn't fit. You dropped me on a stranger's doorstep because your new boyfriend didn't like kids. You promised you'd be back in two weeks and didn't come back for a year. You taught me that if I didn't make myself fit, make myself useful, I'd be left all alone."

Dina Rae is quiet for a record amount of time. At least thirty seconds. "There was no one to teach me how to be a mother, Sammy. I was practically a kid myself. I did the best I could."

"You never had trouble learning something when you wanted

to," I tell her, flashing back to years of reinventions. "Rock climbing for Todd or golf for Big Jerry. Watercolor painting, cross-country skiing. Parenting is a skill. I just wasn't important enough to learn it for."

"It was just so long ago, Sammy," she says, flustered. "Don't I deserve a little forgiveness?"

"And what about what I deserve?" I ask. "I deserved a mother! A family! I deserved to know that the right people stay—not because it's convenient for them, but because I *do* deserve it. Because I'm worthy of love. Now I have to start learning that lesson on my own, and I shouldn't have to. *You* should have taught it to me."

She sniffles, and I picture her. Forty-six, bottle-blond hair. Skin wrinkled from tanning beds. Too-long nails in some garish shade. She's sitting in the dressing room of a mall formal dress shop in a wedding gown designed for someone twenty years younger.

"I love you, Mom," I say, because it's true. Despite everything. "But I can't keep going like we have been. If you're going to be in my life, I need you to understand what you did to me. How it's affected the way I see myself. My relationships. Everything." I pause, taking a deep, shaky breath. "Until you can really understand that, I don't think I can talk to you. But I hope you try this time, Mom. I really do."

"Oh, Sammy," she says. "Can't it just be normal like it is for other people? Why do we have to drag all this up? I'm getting *married* for god's sake."

"I know," I say. "Congratulations, Mom."

And I hang up the phone.

I stare at it for a long time, like it's a live snake I just found out isn't poisonous.

Out the window, the sun is shining brightly. A rarity for Ridley Falls.

I'd planned to head straight to the estate lawyer's office, but sitting there, thinking of her, I realize I need to be brave one more time.

* * *

Back at Ponderosa Court, I text Willa and Brook, let them know I'm all right and resting. That we'll be celebrating Paloma's life tomorrow at noon at the cemetery and I can't imagine doing it without them. I ask Willa to invite Larry and Maeve. Everyone confirms within minutes.

That settled, I get my laptop out and get comfortable on the couch. The early afternoon sun through the floor-to-ceiling windows is beautiful. The bay is a bright blue that reflects the sky, surrounded by the towering evergreens this place is famous for.

I think about growing up in a house like this. What it must have been like for Johnny. The certainty of a home. Of people who love you. Who stay, no matter what. I think about how safe he had to feel to stand up to Paloma and Roberto when I was conceived. How certain that they would choose him in the end.

In the past, this kind of thinking might have made me bitter with envy. But through this new lens, I see it as what it is. An opportunity. Maybe I didn't have parents who could create those circumstances for me, but there's nothing stopping me from doing it for myself.

When the computer wakes up, I open a new Word document. I title it simply:

"Sammy Espinoza's Last Review."

40.

I write until the sky turns the blue-green of twilight over the forest. I don't look back to edit. I don't second-guess. When I'm finished, I know I was wrong before—*this* is the best piece I've ever written. The beginning of a conversation I hope to be having with myself for a long time.

In it, I explore the life of a woman track by track. In the opener, she's a child, twisting herself into pretzels to be loved, trying to find the faulty thing inside that makes everyone want to walk away. Vulnerable, I call this one. Honest, but sad. Music to cry in your car to.

Next, the girl finds herself somewhere new, gets a glimpse at the kind of life she might feel safe in. Feel loved. In the end, though, the ghosts of her past come back, pulling her into chaos.

When the girl finally breaks free, there's an upbeat one. I call it a song that feels like summer in a new city. Like anything is possible. This track ends with the collision of boy and girl. A fork in destiny's road . . .

Of course, it's followed by another heartbreaker. A breakup song, pure and simple. The kind that makes you glad you never have to be eighteen again.

A girl-boss anthem that barely hints at the loneliness of the narrator comes next. Moving up in the world, making a name for yourself.

The official closing track is my least favorite on the album, I warn. In it, the girl (a woman, now) finds the boy again, and this time it's right. The first real thing she's ever been close to grasping. But in a twist ending I call *predictable and unnecessary,* she betrays this love in the worst way possible. Pushing him away out of fear that he'll leave her again.

At the very end, I mention a bonus track. One the listener could not be blamed for skipping. In it, the girl confronts the wounds of her past and begins to glimpse a life beyond the pain of them. A life where she stops bracing herself for betrayal.

The wrap-up is a mixed bag. Overambitious, but with moments of genuine potential. Not enough to redeem it, but there's a glimmer of promise that might make the next volume worth a listen. Though this, I caution, is a decision the listener will have to make for themselves.

I print the piece on the ancient machine I find in Paloma's home office—shocked that the ink isn't desiccated. An act of God, Paloma would have called it.

Folding the article into thirds, I dig an envelope out of a drawer and pull a blank piece of paper from the printer, sitting down to write.

Max, I begin. *I know it's probably too late, but this will be my last review. The one I wrote about you will never run. I promise. I'm done bracing for the end of everything. I'm interested in beginnings now. If there's any chance you'd want to begin again with me, I'll be here. Yours, Sammy.*

I stuff the note in along with the review, grab the olive-green sweater from the guest room closet, and get in the car before my nerves can get the best of me.

The windows are lit up at Max's house. His motorcycle is in front of the garage. I park on the street and take a deep breath before darting into the driveway, praying he doesn't have a motion light.

Thankfully, nothing inside the house or out of it reacts to my presence. I set the sweater with the envelope on top outside the door. I can hear him playing guitar through the door. Starting, stopping, starting again. Like he's beginning something, too.

I run back to the car, grateful that didn't turn out a hundred times more awkward. *Be brave,* Paloma had said, but she probably would have drawn the line at stalking.

On the way back to Paloma's—the way back *home,* I correct myself—the radio serves up a song I've never heard before. It's a sunny pop song about every day being a new start. The kind of generic song I've always disdained. But I don't change the station. Instead, I try to believe the words.

By the time I get home, I realize I'm not a fan. I don't buy into the genre hierarchy, but I still have standards, okay? Even still, I'm glad it's possible to feel that way, and I hope—I hope *so* much— that I will someday, too. Even if I'm listening to different music when I do.

41.

All in all, Paloma's funeral isn't particularly well at-tended. I asked Maeve to spread the word around town so none of Paloma's friends would feel left out, even though I didn't have time to get to know them.

A few of them show up, mostly other older women. One or two I think I recognize from the concert on the lawn, but the rest are strangers. We offer one another generic condolences and it feels nice.

Mostly I stick to the group of people I do know. Brook and Willa, Larry and Maeve.

The funeral director called the closest Catholic priest, which was part of Paloma's instructions. She decided a full funeral mass was "too fussy," but the priest was a necessity.

We huddle around the graveside, all dressed in black, listening to the priest intone in Latin. He does his best to describe the life of a woman he never met. A woman who's lying here in a coffin she selected for herself, getting ready to enter the Kingdom of Heaven if the man before us can be believed.

I try to listen as Willa and Brook sandwich me protectively, and not to giggle at the most somber outfit Larry Cross could scare up. The black pants seem to have been cut into shorts, and his jacket is a little tight. But at least there's no tie-dye. Maeve stands beside him, sniffling, patting his arm.

Thirty minutes later, the sky is threatening rain, the rites have been performed, and my grandmother is lowered into the ground.

I recognize the enormity of the moment, even though it doesn't feel quite personal. Not the way it did in Paloma's home. Not the way it will when it's finally time to go through her things, clean out her room.

Maybe a lifetime of telling myself I don't get sad at cemeteries will be hard to break, but this all feels like a performance to me. The real moments of missing her will be smaller. They'll come more unexpectedly. I should know.

Still, I feel a sense of wholeness as I look at them beside one another. Paloma's headstone isn't here yet, but her grave is on one side of my father's, and Roberto's is on the other.

The ladies behind me mutter about the storm clouds. The priest approaches then, offers some words of comfort. I turn away from my family, interred here in a place I never thought I'd return to.

"You're more than welcome to join us at the house for the wake," I tell them all once I've thanked the priest. "I'm afraid I don't know all the protocols, but there will definitely be food."

"I'd be delighted," says the priest, and several of the ladies agree, as well.

I tell them all the address, tell him we'll be heading there soon.

"She was an incredible woman," Maeve is saying when I return to the group. She's sniffing into what looks like a black fishnet handkerchief. "I'm so honored to be here today, Sammy, thank you for having us."

"She would have loved you both," I say to her and Larry. "Please come up to the house after, we'll have food and"—I lower my voice—"I honestly don't know what to say to the priest or the ladies, so I need backup."

Everyone laughs. Willa squeezes my hand.

"We'll be there, sugar," Maeve says. "And it's your house, now, isn't it? Does that mean you'll be staying in Ridley Falls?"

The question snags. I still haven't given Willa and Brook an answer. After meeting with the estate lawyer, I know I don't have to worry about finding a new job immediately. That I can take my time deciding which of my nebulous paths forward is the right one to follow.

In the past, I might have tried to pretend there wasn't a reason for my indecision. Especially not a *Max Ryan–shaped reason,* as Brook would call it. But I'm trying to be more honest these days.

Max didn't text after last night's delivery. Didn't call. I know I have to confront the fact that he may not. And if he doesn't, I don't think I can stay.

I realize Maeve is still waiting for an answer. "It's a big question," I manage. "And—"

"And I suspect," Willa interrupts, looking over my shoulder, "that part of the answer just arrived."

"*What?*" I mouth to her, my heart leaping into my throat.

"Behind you," she whispers, and then, to everyone else: "Why don't we make our way over to the cars, everyone! We don't want to keep the priest waiting, and it's bound to start raining any minute."

"Is that him?" Larry asks in a very not-subtle whisper as Willa ushers him away.

My best friend winks at me as she shepherds the small crowd toward the parking lot. I can't believe how much better it all feels with her support. How much less scary, even as my heart hammers against my ribs.

I'm afraid to believe it until I turn and really see him. Max Ryan, walking toward me in a black suit with a crisp white shirt and a skinny black tie. His hair is as orderly as I've ever seen it, pushed back off his face. He looks rested. More like himself.

As I walk toward him, I feel like I'm sleepwalking. This moment already feels like nostalgia. A memory that will haunt me if he's not here to say what I really, *really* hope he's here to say.

"Hi," he says when we reach each other.

"Hi," I breathe.

"I'm sorry about your grandma," he says.

"Thanks. How'd you know about the service?"

He shrugs. "Small town. Not too many Espinozas."

"Right. Well, thank you for coming."

"I would have been here earlier," he says, "but I didn't want to interrupt. I didn't really know her, and I thought it might be . . ." He cuts himself off, flashing that self-deprecating smile, running his hand through his hair until some of it hangs in his eyes again. "I'm rambling."

"It's okay," I say. I want to tell him I love it when he rambles. That I'd happily listen to him ramble for the rest of my life if he'd let me. But I still don't know what he's here in a suit to say, so I wait.

"I got your letter," he says after an agonizing minute. "Your review."

There's no hint on his face of which way this is going to go. The waiting is torture. I'm too aware of the audience by the cemetery gate, many of them invested in their own way. It feels like the whole place is holding its breath.

"I'm not going to lie, Sammy, what you did hurt me in a way I didn't know I could be hurt anymore. And I *want* to say it's okay, and that I'm over it, and that we can start again, but . . ."

The old Sammy would have interrupted here. Rejected him before he could reject her. But I can feel Paloma in the wind passing through the alder trees, telling me to be brave.

"I can't forget how it felt to find out you were using me. I don't know how to erase that. To start over with you."

This is it, I think clinically. He's going to say he's sorry, but it's done. He's going to walk away. And I know, seeing him standing here, looking like that, that I really won't be able to stay in Ridley Falls if he does. That my heart will never stop breaking every time I see him. Or anything that reminds me of him. Which at this point is everything.

"Okay," I say in my smallest voice. "I understand. And I deserve it. Thanks for coming down here to tell me in person, I—"

"You didn't let me finish," he says, and he's looking down at me through his lashes, and there's something in his eyes that looks so much like hope I can't help but grab on. "I don't know how to start again. But I'm not ready to give up, either."

He steps a little closer. My heart is beating so hard I'm afraid he can hear it.

"When I read what you wrote, I realized we're both hurting in the same way. Both looking for people to disappoint us. I'm waiting for them to use me, you're waiting for people to leave. And we did exactly that. To each other. You weren't the only one."

"I'm sorry, Max," I say. "I'm so sorry. You can't possibly know—".

"But I do know," he says. "I knew how you felt after the last time I left. I knew what I promised you. I could have written a note. Could have texted or called. Anything but disappearing. And I know it doesn't make the rest right . . . but I think . . ." He chuckles. Rubs the back of his neck. "I think there was enough promise in that bonus track that I want to hear the next album. Maybe even collaborate, if you're still willing."

"Are you sure?" I ask, my voice wobbling dangerously. "Because I have a lot to figure out, Max, and I can't promise I won't mess up again."

"I can't either," he says. "Maybe we will. But if we do, I won't run, okay? If you promise not to push me away or, like, enact revenge."

"I think I can agree to those terms," I say, not sure whether I want to laugh or cry.

"Does this mean we can kiss?" he asks, those eyes boring into mine, heating every inch of my skin. "Because the last seven days, twelve hours, and six minutes without kissing you have been the absolute worst."

I step closer, a smile tugging at my lips involuntarily. The look in his eyes is the same one I fell for more than a decade ago. The one that says there's so much more beneath the surface.

Our lips are a fraction of an inch apart, every part of me straining toward him, when suddenly the sky opens up, emptying buckets full of rain over us.

"We should run!" I shriek over the tossing trees, the deluge falling all around us.

"This is Ridley Falls," Max says, holding me tight. "If we stopped everything when it rained, we'd never get anything done."

And there, with the sky opening above us, Max's lips meet mine. This time it's not desperate. Not frantic. It's the kind of kiss that says you're planning to do it again and again and again.

The kind of kiss that says this is only the beginning.

From the cemetery gate, Willa, Brook, Maeve, and Larry, and even the priest start whooping and cheering. I smile against Max's lips, knowing my makeup is running. That my hair is ruined. I've never cared less.

He kisses me until I can't even feel the rain. Can't feel anything but the start of what we're just beginning to build between us.

After an endless, heart-stopping moment, we pull apart.

"Okay," he says, taking off his jacket and draping it over my shoulders. "*Now* we run!"

Hand in hand, we tear up the hill to where my friends are waiting to usher us into the car. To head back to Paloma's. To celebrate the life of the woman who made all this possible. Who made me realize I didn't have to be alone. That there have always been people who wanted me.

Before I duck into the Mercedes beside Max, I glance back at the cemetery just in time to see a rainbow appear over the evergreens. I've never been much of a believer in things like this, but somewhere deep inside I can feel it. Paloma, telling me she's proud.

"I love you," I say to her, around the tears in my throat. "Thank you."

Max is out of the car again, standing beside me, letting me lean on him. His white dress shirt is soaked through, plastered to every one of those lean muscles. My insides go wobbly like Jell-O at the sight, and I hope they always do. "You ready?" he asks after a moment.

I nod, taking his hand and squeezing. "Let's go home."

Eighteen Months Later

Paloma's house is a mess. But it's the nice kind of mess.
On nights like this I can feel them here. Paloma, Roberto, my dad.
I think they would have loved it.

The remnants of an epic meal are still strewn around the table.
Larry and Maeve have taken baby Zephyr to the living room to
bang a wooden spoon on the coffee table. I've already told Willa I
want dibs on recording their first album when the time comes.

Brook is clearing plates, smiling at Willa who's leaning back in
one of the chairs, looking tired and happy.

There's only one piece of this perfect puzzle missing, and I
check the clock over the stove with increasing excitement. Any
minute now . . .

Before I can even finish the thought, I hear the door. Zephyr
screeches in delight, and Larry and Maeve laugh along, waving at
the new arrival.

Max Ryan steps through the door with a duffel bag. He's wearing those jeans I love, a long-sleeved T-shirt, and a beanie. His
smile is tired from hours of travel, but he's here. I don't relinquish
my place against the counter, letting him come to me, making his
greetings along the way.

By the time he's standing in front of me, anticipation is humming through my body. His smile shifts, not the goofy wide one
he reserves for Zephyr, or the polite respectful one he insists on
using with Larry and Maeve. Not the brotherly grin Willa and
Brook get as he passes them.

This one is softer. A little awestruck. And it's all mine.

"Hi," Max says softly, setting his bag down on a chair.

"Hi," I breathe, and then I'm in his arms, and everything is complete.

"Two weeks is too long," he says into my hair, in that gravelly voice that almost makes me wish we were already alone.

"Way too long," I agree. "But you can't disappoint your adoring fans."

"And you can't let down your new band." He releases me briefly, reaching into his pocket for a long, skinny box. "Speaking of which . . ."

"A present?" I ask, feigning surprise. "For *me*?" He's brought me a gift from every leg of the tour, ranging from truly goofy to genuinely thoughtful. But this looks like jewelry, and my interest is piqued.

"A present for you," he agrees, opening the box to reveal a gold necklace. One of those nameplate ones I always coveted as a teenager. But instead of my name, it reads *Verdad,* and my eyes mist over immediately.

"It's perfect," I say, sniffling, and it is.

Verdad. It means *truth* in Spanish. It's also the name of my brand-new record label. The one I opened with Paloma's inheritance. I like to think it's an evolution from the pen name Max inspired all those years ago. The one I retired with my last review.

"In honor of signing your first artist," Max says, unclasping it and settling it between my collarbones. Fastening it behind my neck. The feeling of his fingers against my skin makes me shiver.

"Second artist," I murmur, admiring it. "You'll always be my first."

"Contracts should be final any day now," Max says with a little smirk. "If it was up to me, we'd cave. But you know James is a tough negotiator."

I think back to the day I told Max about my plan, sleep-deprived, half-feral after all the time I'd spent putting together my business plan, scouting locations, researching start-up costs and profitability . . .

I'd expected him to tell me I'd lost my marbles, but instead he insisted on being my first act, no matter how many contracts he had to break.

In the end, we settled with James. As long as Max released his album, *Dinner for One,* and toured as agreed, James would get him out clean. Max would be free to sign at Verdad—and James would become our business manager. A family affair.

"I'm so proud of you," Max says, looking down at me, stroking my jawline with his thumb.

"I'm proud of you, too," I say. "Another successful run?"

He nods. "The breathwork helps. Five shows, zero panic attacks."

"Impressive," I say, feeling myself settle against him, getting used to the feeling of having him here in the flesh again. "I missed you, you know?"

His eyes darken a little. His arms tighten around my waist.

"Get a room!" Brook heckles just as he opens his mouth to reply.

Max laughs instead, kissing me lightly before releasing me, with a gaze that promises more, and soon. We head into the living room, joining in with the laughter of our family. Max lifts Zephyr into the air. I settle in beside Maeve, who smiles at me as I watch him, dreaming of what's to come.

It's amazing, I think, how much has changed since that night in the Safeway parking lot. Him, isolated out of fear, extending a helping hand. Me, braced for the worst, but secretly hopeful.

Both of us were alone, hiding from ourselves and the world. But now we have each other. We have our passions. We have our family.

And as perfect as it all seems, I remind myself, this is just the beginning.

ACKNOWLEDGMENTS

My most sincere and heartfelt thanks go out to

Shauna Summers, Mae Martinez, and the rest of the amazing folks at Ballantine Bantam Dell. This book would be a shell of itself without your insightful questions and the many invitations to dig deeper. Sammy's story and I are both better for having you in our corner.

My indefatigable agent, Jim McCarthy, who handles my nerves with grace, enhances my celebratory moments with limitless fuel, and keeps the many plates of my career spinning with a deftness that astonishes me daily.

The most inspiring, talented bunch of writer friends and colleagues anyone has ever had the pleasure of knowing: Lily Anderson, Michelle Ruíz Keil, and Nina Moreno—who kindled this spark of an idea into a roaring blaze with enthusiasm alone—Emily Henry, Becca Podos, Roshani Chokshi, Emily Prado, Stephanie Adams-Santos, and so many more.

My nonpublishing friends and community, who keep me grounded when this business becomes overwhelming (shoutout to the Bite Squad and the Soup Council).

My families—chosen, of origin, and the rare folks who transcend those distinctions.

Alex, mi vida, I never wrote a true love story until you.

And Ave, of course, forever and always.

ABOUT THE AUTHOR

Tehlor Kay Mejia is the author of the critically acclaimed young adult fantasy duology *We Set the Dark on Fire* and *We Unleash the Merciless Storm*. Their debut middle-grade series, *Paola Santiago and the River of Tears,* is currently in development at Disney as a television series to be produced by Eva Longoria. Tehlor lives with their kiddo, partner, and two small dogs in Oregon, where they grow heirloom corn and continue the quest to perfect the vegan tamale. *Sammy Espinoza's Last Review* is their debut adult novel.

tehlorkaymejia.com
@tehlorkay